Eternal Life Inc.

D0029446

WITHDRAWN

Eternal Life Inc.

James Burkard

COSMIC
EGG
BOOKS

Winchester, UK
Washington, USA

First published by Cosmic Egg Books, 2015
Cosmic Egg Books is an imprint of John Hunt Publishing Ltd., Laurel House, Station Approach, Alresford, Hants, SO24 9JH, UK
office1@jhpbooks.net
www.johnhuntpublishing.com

For distributor details and how to order please visit the 'Ordering' section on our website.

Text copyright: James Burkard 2014

ISBN: 978 1 78279 570 4

All rights reserved. Except for brief quotations in critical articles or reviews, no part of this book may be reproduced in any manner without prior written permission from the publishers.

The rights of James Burkard as author have been asserted in accordance with the Copyright, Designs and Patents Act 1988.

A CIP catalogue record for this book is available from the British Library.

Design: Stuart Davies

Printed in the USA by Edwards Brothers Malloy

We operate a distinctive and ethical publishing philosophy in all areas of our business, from our global network of authors to production and worldwide distribution.

To my wife, Herdis
Through thick and thin with all my love
and
To William Hathaway
Whose encouragement, advice, and inspiration always picked
me up when I was down

"Tyger! Tyger! Burning bright
In the forest of the night,
What immortal hand or eye
Could frame thy fearful symmetry?"
The Tyger – William Blake

Book One of the King of the Dead Trilogy

Prologue

2387 A.D.

Rielly huddled close to the fire. The smoke reeked of burning plastic and rotten wood. He could feel the cold seeping out of the moldy, concrete wall at his back. Outside, the wind whipped through the overgrown ruins of the city, howling down weed-choked canyons of broken concrete. A vagrant breeze blew through the rubble, dusting the floor with snow. Rielly watched it slowly melt.

His backside was numb with cold. He shifted uncomfortably and a white-hot spike of pain drove up his left leg. The leg was splayed at a broken angle just below the knee and a bone splinter pushed through the blood-soaked layers of dirty rags.

He threw a last shred of plastic into the flames. When it was gone... He shook his head. What did it matter? He'd wanted to die almost from the moment he was born. He looked at the pale spray of star-like scars on the back of his hand. Even if his voice and hair didn't give him away, those stars would. They covered his twisted body with the sign of the Norma-gene and in the Quarantine, where mutants were the norm, none were more hated and feared than the Norma-gene. It's because we're special, his mother had told him as she pulled open a door of light in the air and drew out super-strings of power.

It's because she was special she's dead, he thought. He was with her when it happened. They'd climbed up from the sewers in search of herbs when they stumbled on a hunting party of mutants, scarred by their own brand of genetic judgment. As soon as she saw them, his mother pushed him into a breach beneath a concrete slab and drew the mutants after her instead.

After they killed her, they came looking for him and he ran. What else could he do? He was only ten years old. He fled through the ruins of the once mighty city where now only the highest, broken spires poked through the forest canopy. He soon got lost in the bramble-filled labyrinth of rotting concrete and rusting steel that was slowly disappearing beneath the green weight of centuries. He kept running until long after his pursuers had given up, until he could never find his way back to the secret entrance and the Norma-genes living beneath the Chicago Quarantine.

His father was dead, and his mother was all he had. After she died, there was no one who cared enough to risk leaving the sewers to look for him. For five years he struggled to survive and find his way back. Now, it was over.

He'd been out checking his traps. He'd been lucky, two rabbits and a large sewer rat. He'd eat well, but on the way back he got careless climbing over a fallen wall of ice slick concrete. He might have been okay when he slipped, but the rotting concrete splintered beneath his foot, trapping his leg in the hole; and when he pitched forward, the bone snapped.

If his mother was alive, she could have healed it. She was a Norma-gene witch and one of the weirding. She would have opened a hole in the air and pulled out bright strands of superstring power. After she wrapped them around the broken bones, they would have pulled back and knitted together beneath fresh skin. He'd asked her once to heal his crippled Norma-gene body, but she shook her head and told him about the Genetic Wars that ended almost four hundred years ago, leaving countless broken coils of DNA heartbreak that were beyond her power to change.

He stared into the flames, sputtering fitfully across a piece of rotted wood. He was half-delirious with fever and weak from starvation and loss of blood. Maybe that was why when he looked up, he thought he saw his mother sitting across from him. Maybe she really was there. After all, she was a Norma-gene witch. Maybe she could reach back through the walls of death as she reached through the walls of life.

She smiled and raised her hands, weaving them back and forth like when she opened a hole in the world and worked her magic. No hole appeared this time, but she continued weaving her hands through the complex patterns until at last Rielly lifted his hands and repeated the movements.

After a few seconds, a hole appeared in the air above his fingertips. It was as big as his fist and filled with twisting filaments of light. He stared at it in wonder. He shouldn't be able to do this. No man should be able to do this. It was woman's magic. He looked up at his mother for an answer but she was gone. When he looked back, the hole had grown more than a foot across; and super-string filaments of light danced and twisted inside.

He was lost in wonder at the sight and did not hear the faint click of claws on concrete, or the low, guttural growl of the large, grey timber wolf that stepped out of the shadows with its mate beside it and its pack crowding behind. They'd picked up his blood spoor outside and followed it in.

As Rielly reached up to grab the superstrings, they were suddenly swept aside by a glaring demon that grabbed his hands instead. At that moment, the pack leader stepped forward, bearing its fangs with a low growl. The demon's attention shifted past Rielly, who turned to follow its gaze and saw the wolf, crouched, ready to spring. Its mate stood beside it and snarled. Behind her, the shadows swirled with matted, gray pelts and bared fangs.

Rielly felt a sharp, painful tug in his navel, and the demon let go of his hands and became a long swirl of black smoke that shot out of the hole. It brushed past Rielly's face with a touch like silken ice and hit the pack leader between the eyes and disappeared inside.

The great, gray wolf froze into electrified rigidity. Then, it sank onto its haunches, lifted it head, and howled in a frenzy of fear. Its body began twisting in on itself and bulging out again.

The wolf rolled on the ground kicking, clawing, and nipping at itself as if fighting some invisible enemy.

Its mate stood her ground, alternately growling at Rielly and snarling at her mate. The rest of the pack cringed back, mewling with fear. The she-wolf decided this was all Rielly's fault and sprang. Once again, he felt a tug at his navel, and another black form shot out from the hole in the world that he had opened and caught the she-wolf in mid-leap.

That last tug of manifestation left Rielly feeling as if a plug had been pulled from his navel, and his life was spilling out like water down a drain. His mind began shutting down. Darkness rushed in from all sides, crushing reality into a pinprick of light. Then there was nothing.

Prelude

2412 A.D.

Isis broke open the slave pens before she fled. It had nothing to do with humanity or compassion. She knew she was condemning them to death in the jungle, but she needed a diversion to cover her escape. The invasion was coming just as her father predicted, and she had to get the warning out.

She lay flat against the outstretched neck of her mount. She could feel the silken softness of its mane against the side of her face as she raced towards the border of the Nevada Quarantine. Behind her, in the distance, the howls of the wolf pack mingled with the screams of dying slaves. Soon the wolves would pick up her trail. Then, they would shape-shift into their real bodies and the God Hunt could begin.

By now, they knew she was gone and that she stole a Pathfinder. Why did it have to come to this? Why did it have to be Rielly who opened the door and let them in? Why did she have to fall in love with the son of a bitch?

With a slight, telepathic nudge, she spurred her mount on. Its muscles uncoiled like spring-loaded steel, driving its hooves pounding down the dirt road. Its muzzle was foamed with exhaustion, but it would keep running as fast as it could until its heart exploded. That was the way they made them.

You knew they were going to infect me, didn't you Rielly? You knew and you just stood by and let them. "YOU LET THEM INFECT ME!" she screamed into the night, hot tears blowing across her cheeks.

"I beat them though!" She laughed. "I beat their dirty, little, mind parasite! It didn't get possession, not a hundred percent anyway, not even close!" She could hear her laughter walking the ragged edge of hysteria. Gotta get hold of yourself, she thought

5

and clamped her jaws tight, biting off the laughter. She had to get out before she lost it completely. That thing was still down there. She could feel it floating in a cesspool of madness at the bottom of her mind.

She thought she could hear its snarling, mewling cries calling the pack to come and tear her apart and take back what she had stolen. She reached down and touched the shaft of the Pathfinder, making sure it was still securely shoved beneath her belt. She had to get it to Diana. She'd know what to do with it.

The thing inside her must have felt her touch the Pathfinder, or maybe her thoughts leaked through, because, suddenly, the cesspool heaved up, smashing against the concrete cap of resolve she'd poured across her mind to keep it down. The cap held for a second and then shattered, and a predatory, howling insanity broke lose, overflowing her mind with visions of rotting blood and body parts and filling her with an insatiable desire to enslave, torture, mutilate, and kill!

By the time she drove it back down and got the cap back in place, she was drenched in cold sweat, gasping for air, and limp with exhaustion. She didn't know how long she could keep this up. If she let her guard down or was too exhausted to stay awake, it would try again and she might not be able to stop it.

She had to get out before that happened and before they phase-shifted the whole Nevada Quarantine out of her universe. Then, there would be no escape and when they caught her, there would be no mercy.

1

A Shooting Star

"Afraid of dying? You should talk to Harry Neuman. He's got a contract to die. You name it, he's tried it. He's been shot, stabbed, drowned, infected, and poisoned and they bring him back every time. Hey, they have to, don't they? He's insured. Besides, he's a movie star hero and the best advertisement Eternal Life has got. When people see Harry walking around, they know they're going to get value for their money. As long as they keep paying their insurance premium, Eternal Life will keep bringing them back just like Harry.

As policyholder number 001, he's got free resurrection forever. Even if he wanted to die, he couldn't. You see, the company always keeps a fresh clone waiting for him. Whenever and wherever Harry decides to cash in, the company always knows. They've got a monitor on his ghost ka, his soul. If it leaves his body, Eternal Life just pulls it in before it can go to wherever kas go when people die for keeps. Once that ka gets close enough to Harry's clone, there's no stopping it from resurrecting.

Now, you'd think Harry would be the happiest guy in the world. He's got guaranteed immortality. What more do you want? But I heard that Harry's not happy. I heard that he's not going to renew his contract with Eternal Life. I heard other things, things that have no business happening, like people not coming back from resurrection or coming back insane or something worse, things Eternal Life is trying to cover up. Maybe Harry heard them too."

– Chad Graham, New Hollywood talk show host

Harry Neuman stood on the fluted edge of the marble balustrade. Spotlights outlined him against the night sky. He was a tall, ruggedly handsome man who wore his black tuxedo with casual grace. A vagrant breeze ruffled his thick, black hair. Beneath his feet, New Hollywood spread out, sparkling in the night. On the horizon a thousand spotlights illuminated the Emperor's palace, a fairytale confection that even the great Disney would have envied.

Harry looked down and saw the layers of worm-like air traffic come to a halt twenty floors below. That would be the police blocking off the streets and airways. Wouldn't want any uninsured citizens accidentally killed by falling objects. Eternal Life didn't need any more lawsuits.

He looked past the spotlights at the guests, sitting at their tables, waiting breathlessly. The band began playing "Auld Langsyne". A nice touch, he thought. It conjured up images of faded elegance, of brave men standing on the stern of a sinking Titanic. It was show time.

He squared his shoulders and raised his champagne glass in a silent toast to the guests and to the grav-corders, floating just outside the spot-lit circle. He sipped his drink perfunctorily. Then he set the glass down, reached into an inside pocket, and took out a pack of cigarettes and a lighter.

"Ladies and gentlemen," he said as he shook out a cigarette. "As you know, my contract with Eternal Life ends this evening. To celebrate this ending and the new beginning that Eternal Life has given us all, I thought it would be appropriate to go out in a blaze of glory."

He put the cigarette to his lips and nonchalantly flicked the lighter. Instantly, his body burst into white-hot phosphorous flames. For a second, he stood there with a slight smile on his burning face. Then, he raised a flaming hand in salute and turned and stepped off the edge of the balcony.

He became a shooting star, arcing down into the glittering chasm of the street. The fire burned furiously in the slipstream of his fall, drawing a long tail of flame behind him. He held his breath to prevent sucking fire into his lungs. It was no use suffering any more than necessary. He'd been through it all before. By his own count he had died fifty-one times, although never quite like this. The combination of burning and falling created an odd dramatic twist. The public relations boys at Eternal Life already had tomorrow's headlines prepared, FALLING STAR GOES OUT IN A BLAZE OF GLORY.

The flames were eating away at his face and his thick black hair was a fiery halo. Vaguely, he could feel the terrible searing pain on the other side of the mind block he had set up. As the lights of the surrounding buildings streaked by, he calmly composed himself to die. He would not wait for the inevitable, crushing, traumatic impact. He had suffered the agony of dying too many times for that.

Death had been a harsh teacher, but it had taught him how to block the pain and how to die. With an odd shrug and twist, he stepped out of his body like a man stepping out of a suit of old clothes. His heart stopped in mid beat. The neurons in his brain sputtered on for a few moments and then quit.

Everything that was Harry Newman now floated ghost-like and invisible beside the lifeless husk of his tumbling body. He watched impersonally as it burned its way through the darkness. He didn't even flinch when it hit the ground in a bursting shower of sparks because that wasn't Harry anymore… maybe it never had been.

Harry was this luminous energy being, this ghost ka that now rushed down a long, ribbed tunnel towards a beckoning, distant light. It drew him on with its promise of unending peace, love, and happiness. Sometimes, he caught a glimpse of a beautiful woman, a Madonna incarnation of the Goddess, beckoning to him from within the light and he longed to go there.

He tried to steel himself for what was coming, but no matter how many times he had been through it, it always came as a shock more profound than death itself. One moment he was falling peacefully into the light, his ka opening to embrace the warm, loving brilliance, and the next, he was jerked violently aside, his ka dragged around in a wide arc away from the light and towards the distant whine of the spin-generators at Eternal Life.

With a devastating sense of loss, he watched the light slide away beneath and behind him, and soon he was rushing through a dense, gray fog with only the rising whine of the spin-generators to guide him. In this gray nothingness time and space lost all meaning and so he was unable to say when he first became aware that he was not alone. Black shapes were pacing him on either side, sliding in and out of the fog. They looked like tumbling, fluttering, black rags, without any distinctive shape, but full of dark menace.

He wondered about them. They first appeared two deaths ago. At first, one or two hung on the periphery of his awareness so that he wasn't even sure they were there. But last time, they had gathered in a pack, following him at a distance. Now, they paced him on either side. He could make out six, maybe seven. Slowly, they closed in. The sense of dark menace grew. In front of him, he saw the fog begin to glow with the sputtering, blue fire surrounding the spin-generators at Eternal Life. By now, their distant whine had risen to a high-frequency shriek. If he could just make it there, he would be safe.

Suddenly, one of the black forms put on a burst of speed and broke from the pack. As it drew closer, it lost its fluttering, ragbag appearance and grew sharp teeth that snapped at him out of a feral, pointed face. Yellow claws slashed and tore inches away. Harry's ka flared with energy as he pushed his awareness towards the spin-generator, letting it pull him in faster and faster. It loomed beneath him like a massive black hole surrounded by an event horizon of crawling blue flames.

The pack snapped and snarled at his heels. As they closed in, they took on the forms of huge black wolves, their eyes burning with a terrible, inhuman intelligence. Harry fell through the event horizon of cold, blue fire. He was almost home-free when the lead wolf leapt at him. Its claws raked a trail of darkness through the flaring back of his ka. Harry screamed in agony and tried to shake it off. He could feel it trying to claw its way in, trying to become him.

The impact of the attack started his ka tumbling. In desperation, he exaggerated the motion, whirling faster and faster like a top. He felt the claws tear free one by one until finally the thing lost its grip and centrifugal force hurled it away, shrieking with frustration. Moments later, he dropped through the black hole of the spin-generator positioned over his cloned body. Automatically, the machinery shut down, and Harry sank into and became once again flesh.

His first sense was always a feeling of suffocating heaviness, of being trapped inside thick meat. It was never a pleasant feeling; but this time, he was grateful for the secure solidity of flesh. It was like slamming a solid oak door in the face of a ravening wolf pack. He could almost feel them snuffling and scratching at the edges of his ka. He let it sink deeper into flesh; felt the slow push of blood through arteries, the heavy rise and fall of lungs as they sucked in air. He began feeling all the minor aches and pains that usually hide just under the threshold of consciousness.

Suddenly, he felt a terrible, searing pain rake across his back as if a memory ghost of the attack finally caught up with him and ripped its mark in his flesh. His eyes bulged open; his body convulsed, and he screamed in fear and pain. Foamy amniotic fluid sloshed over the edges of the glass cloning tank he floated in. He tried to force himself up and away, ripping through the maze of plastic life-support tubes and electrode monitor wires. His only thought was to escape the nameless terror that had set its claws in him. Firm hands tried to hold him down as he struggled to clamber out of the tank.

"Harry! Harry, now take it easy!" He heard someone say, but he couldn't see who it was. He blinked his eyes trying to clear them of amniotic fluid. His breath was coming in harsh gasps.

"Harry, it's me, Doc Jericho. You know me, Harry. Now just take it easy."

The familiar voice of the old man cut through the clawing panic. Harry blinked his eyes again. The concerned, bespectacled face of his old friend swam into view. Jericho made a point of being on hand whenever Harry resurrected. He was always a reassuring sight, and Harry felt himself calming down. He looked around wonderingly at the clean, softly lit room. He was safe in the birthing chambers beneath Eternal Life. Here, everything was orderly and familiar. The black wolves had no place among the white-clad technicians, blinking electronic displays, and gurgling pumps.

"Harry, are you all right?" Jericho asked, watching him closely.

Harry looked down at his naked body, dripping with milky amniotic fluid. He could still feel the pain, tearing across his back; but he was safe now, safe in his new body.

In the background he heard a familiar recorded chant, recited over and over again: "You live again, you revive always, you have become young again and forever." It was the motto of Eternal Life Inc. stolen directly from the Egyptian Book of the Dead, along with the idea of the ka. It was chanted at every resurrection. Even though Harry knew it was just a publicity gimmick, he found it comforting by its very familiarity.

"Come on, Harry," Jericho said soothingly. "Lie down and take it easy."

Harry smiled sheepishly and began to slide back down into the warm, fluid-filled tank.

"Jesus Christ, Doc! What's going on?" Roger Morely, Eternal Life's CEO, shouted as he burst through the double doors of the birthing chamber. He was still dressed in his black tuxedo and must have hurried down right after Harry's performance. His fat, florid face was layered with concern as he leaned over the cloning tank and smiled.

Harry looked up into Morely's pale blue eyes, and something black seemed to flutter across his vision. Harry heard himself whimper in fear as Morely's pug nose elongated into a feral snout. His curly, ginger hair straightened into a coarse, black pelt; his smile turned into a fanged growl.

Harry felt his fear suddenly turn into a wild, unreasoning rage. This was his world! They had no right to be here. He would not run again. He levered himself up and grabbed a fist full of Roger's tuxedo. With an inarticulate roar of triumph, he brought his other fist around in a flat, hard arc that snapped Roger's head back. The black demon face disappeared and Harry was confronted with the surprised, bruised face of Roger Morely. The man was dazed from the blow and tried feebly to pull away.

Just then, Harry felt a sharp prick in his arm. He let go of Roger and swung around, ripping the hypodermic out of Jericho's hand, but the anesthetic was already taking effect. Harry felt consciousness spiraling down into soft blackness. He could have transferred his awareness to his ka and remained awake but didn't dare. Instead he let the darkness take him, welcoming its healing oblivion. Slowly, he slid down into the tank of amniotic fluid, floating there gently with the hypodermic still stuck in his biceps.

2

Sanctuary is a dangerous Place

Her grav-car crossed the first defense perimeter five miles out from the island. The rain was coming down hard by then. Her sensors picked up the first ping of incoming targeting radar. She felt the tell-tale tingle of a graviton detector beam wash over her body. Then, every alarm in the car began to scream a warning. She ignored their squawk of protest as she shut them off and continued on her course heading.

Isis lay slumped against her in the front seat, her head lolling, feverish, her skin slick with cold sweat. Every once in a while she'd mutter something incoherent and then drop back into her inner battle with the demon that was trying to take possession.

Diana had used the grav-car's safety harness to restrain her after the battle turned particularly nasty and she woke up screaming and snarling, punching the air, tearing at her clothes, and raking her own skin. After that, the fight internalized into this cursing mutter of choked off screams interspersed with low animal growls and hisses. Sometimes, it sounded almost like language before dissolving into a guttural rage of gibberish again.

Suddenly, she felt the dull thump of a lamprey mine fastening to the body of the car. A moment later the car's holo-screen lit up with a zombie slave program of a square-jawed, military construct. "You are entering restricted air space! Please stop and identify yourself!" Its voice, laced with threatening subsonics, boomed from the speakers.

Diana looked over at her sister. The muttering, hissing growls had gotten louder as she tossed her head from side to side and occasionally banged it against the head rest in a fit of violent frustration. Blood began to drip from her nose and ooze out of her ears. Diana decided to ignore the robot defense warnings and pushed on through the inner defense perimeter.

The grav-car's sensors recorded weapons systems locking on, and the military construct raised his voice. "You have entered restricted airspace! This is private property. According to Jurisdiction Law 58j6, paragraph 5, we can use all necessary force to stop you. Please be advised, you are putting your life at risk if you continue."

Once again, Diana ignored the warning and pushed on. By now, alarm bells should be going off all over the island. That should fire up his processors and make the old fart sit up and take notice, she thought.

"This is your last chance!" the construct screamed. "Weapons system are activated and locked on!"

Diana slowed fractionally and shouted, "Jericho it's me, Diana Lloyd! I need your help!"

The military construct's threatening protests cut off in mid screech, and the holo-image dissolved into distortion pixels and went blank for a few seconds.

When it cleared, Jericho appeared pulling on a ratty, old, velvet robe that had once been the color of vintage burgundy. His thatch of gray hair stood out in disheveled spikes. He blinked sleepily as he fumbled on an ancient pair of wire rim spectacles. When he set them on his nose, the lenses dissolved into a glowing pixel fog. A second later, they cleared again as the spectacles connected to the data sphere. The old man stared through them directly at her. "Diana?" he said.

"You should know," she said and glanced over at her sensor array. The number of weapons locking on to her had gone way beyond overkill. "Now call off your dogs!" she shouted.

Jericho said nothing. His china blue eyes studied her carefully as if she was some kind of rare butterfly he was considering for his collection. At last, he turned and shuffled over to a leather, wing backed chair and sat down. He steepled his fingers and tapped them thoughtfully against his chin and waited.

"Nano Trees… Jake Lloyd… Anubis invasion!" Diana shouted in exasperation. "God Damnit, it's started! My father was right!"

"Ah, why didn't you say so?" Jericho smiled and, with a wave of his hand, all targeting systems cut off. He shook his head. "One can't be too careful, you know."

3

Playacting

Harry rode the long, slow waves of consciousness up out of darkness. He did not try to force the process but instead lay quietly monitoring his body and letting his senses expand, rippling outward, testing the world around him. He was in bed. He could feel the rasp of fresh linen against his newly cloned, naked body. Usually when he woke up in a new body, there was a feeling of vigorous health and well-being. This time he felt a sense of physical depletion coupled with a dull, throbbing pain in his back. He felt the pull of bandages and the cooling touch of medicaments against pain. He was almost tempted to regress to his Ka and explore the source of his discomfort but decided not to risk it. They would be watching him closely. Better wait until later.

He heard the soft hum of the monitors and felt the cool, metallic touch of the pickups attached to his skin. He was careful to control the output of information the pickups received, a man resting peacefully, just coming into the first stages of awakening from deep sedation. There would be no sign on the monitors of the wide-awake mind that hid behind his sleeping features.

He could almost taste the sharp, antiseptic tang of the negative ions in the air, almost hear the feel-good subsonics behind the piped in "natural" sounds of bird song and burbling brooks that came from the hologram screen. He knew that if he opened his eyes the lighting would be soft and indirect; the walls done in gentle pastels. Everything designed to soothe the newly reborn in the recovery rooms above the birthing chambers at Eternal Life.

It was all so familiar... except the restraints. He felt them almost immediately upon awakening. They were something new. Imperceptibly, he tensed individual muscle groups, testing the extent of his imprisonment. Thick nylon bands were snugged down tightly over his ankles, thighs, hips, chest, and arms. There was even a band across his forehead holding him totally immobile. He smiled to himself. He must have scared them badly. If the stories he had heard were true, they had reason to be scared.

Someone came quietly into the room and Harry began feeding new data to the monitors; a man about to wake up. There was a faint rustle of movement beside his bed and someone took his wrist. He felt the familiar cool, dry touch of Jericho's long, sensitive fingers. He was relieved that they had let the old man stay after what happened. They could have just isolated Harry and refused to let anyone near him. Jericho was Harry's best friend and knew more about resurrection technology than any man alive. He should, he invented it, although he didn't have much say around Eternal Life anymore.

Harry pushed the thought aside. It was curtain time. He saw to it that his pulse quickened and breath rate went up. The monitors dutifully recorded a change in his brain wave pattern towards full wakefulness. A moment later, he let his eyes flutter open and gave a low, theatrical moan.

"Take it easy, Harry," Jericho said gently.

Harry blinked, let his eyes go in and out of focus, and feigned a look of disorientation. His performance was not aimed at Jericho, but at the grav-corders hovering above his bed, and at the men behind the two-way mirrors set in the opposite wall. He could easily imagine them bent over banks of computer monitors and TV-screens, eagerly studying diagnostic printouts and watching his every move.

Right from the beginning, Harry had used his acting skills to conceal the strange powers he began acquiring from his ka. He told no one at Eternal Life about them except Jericho. Even now, he wasn't quite sure why he had been so secretive. In the beginning, maybe it was just to spite Roger or maybe to salvage a little bit of dignity and self-respect at a time when the rest of his life was sliding into the sewer. Later, when he began to realize the potential of what he was dealing with, he decided that it was simply too dangerous to put such knowledge in the hands of someone like Roger Morely and his greedy shareholders.

And so the charade went on, he thought, and let his eyes swim into focus and at last looked up at Jericho's kindly, old face. The old man studied him carefully. He looked uncertain and worried. "Welcome back to the land of the living... Harry," he said with a forced smile and hesitancy in his voice that almost turned the greeting into a question. It was as if he wasn't completely sure of who or what he might be dealing with. Harry's violent reaction in the birthing chamber must have scared him too. He'd probably heard the wild stories and whispered rumors going around about Eternal Life.

"How are you feeling?" Jericho asked with forced casualness as he took out a large, antique pocket watch and made a show of taking Harry's pulse. The old man looked tired. His body was stiff with tension, and he never even looked at the watch. His eyes never left Harry's face.

Harry grinned lopsidedly and said in his best Bugs Bunny cartoon voice, "Na-a-e-e-h, what's up Doc?" It was the way he always greeted Jericho after a resurrection, a sure sign that everything was okay.

A look of tremendous relief passed over the old man's face. "Boy, you don't know how glad I am to see you back!" he said as if he couldn't believe his luck.

Harry tried to push himself up, but the restraints still held him tightly. He let a look of surprise settle over his face as if he had just become aware of the restraints. "Jesus Doc, am I that dangerous?"

"Some people seem to think so," Jericho grinned.

Harry smiled ruefully for the cameras. "How's Roger?"

Jericho let go of Harry's wrist and put away his watch. "Don't worry, he'll live," he said. "He's been asking for that for years. But what got into you?"

Harry made a show of trying to move again. "Look Doc, how about taking these off? I'm not going to bite anyone."

Jericho cocked his head with a mischievous grin. "Maybe you should tell that to Roger," he said as he stepped away from the bed and straightened up. He was over six feet tall, stoop-shouldered, and rail thin. The rumpled, black suit that he habitually wore hung on his scarecrow frame like a potato sack. His white linen shirt was yellow with age, open at the throat and frayed on the collar. With his unruly shock of silver-gray hair, bushy eyebrows and sharp hawk-like features, he looked like a cross between an Old Testament prophet and a funeral parlor director gone to seed. "Okay let's see if you've got it all together," he said and held up his hand. "How many fingers am I holding up?"

"Five."

"Good, and now?"

"Two."

"And now?"

"Three."

"What's my middle name?"

"Randolph. For Christ's sake, Doc! What's this supposed to prove! Your name is Jeremiah Randolph Arnold Jericho. Age?" Harry shrugged. "Who knows? You're presently unmarried, and the man who made all this possible." Harry rolled his eyes to encompass not only the room but all of Eternal Life. "Is that enough or would you like a thumbnail sketch of my wasted life too?"

"That won't be necessary," Jericho grinned, obviously enjoying Harry's performance. "You know, you really had us worried," he said as he began undoing the restraints.

"I had myself worried," Harry said as he started to push himself up on the pillows and winced with pain. It felt as if his back had been torn open with red-hot tongs. For a moment, he was tempted to put a mind block on the pain but was afraid the monitors might pick up the anomaly. So instead, he just gritted his teeth and tried to move as slowly and carefully as possible.

"Hurts, doesn't it?" Doc asked, cocking his head like a bird eyeing a particularly tasty worm. Light flashed off his round wire-rimmed spectacles.

Harry grimaced. "What is it?" he asked, although he was pretty certain he knew the answer.

"There are blistering welts like claw marks all up and down your back," Jericho said. "I've never seen anything quite like them before. Would you mind telling me who you were out with last night?" He grinned. "She must have been some lover."

"Doc, you don't know the half of it!" Harry was about to continue but something in Jericho's eyes stopped him. "... and I wish I knew the other half," he finished lamely.

"Why don't you be quiet a minute and lift up your shirt," Jericho interrupted in a no nonsense tone of voice and took out his stethoscope and listened to Harry's heart.

"Doc, is this really necessary?" Harry protested when Jericho finished. "I feel great."

"Who's the Doctor here, you or me?" Jericho barked as he put away the stethoscope. "Now open your mouth," he said and took out a tongue depressor. Jericho made a big production out of scanning Harry's throat and then checking his eyes.

Finally, he leaned back and beamed. "Congratulations, son!" he said and grabbed Harry's hand and began shaking it. "You're healthy as a horse. Now, close your mouth and tell me what happened." His bantering good humor was belied by a strange tension in the air and by the folded piece of paper he had slipped into Harry's hand when he shook it.

Harry let a look of confused disorientation slide across his face. "Something happened in transition..." he said hesitantly and glanced at one of the grav-corders hovering just over

Jericho's shoulder."... But I can't remember what. There's only a vague feeling of fear. I guess I was pretty hysterical, wasn't I?"

"Harry, this could be important. Can't you remember anything?" Doc asked.

Harry made a show of trying to concentrate and then shrugged. "I'm sorry, Doc. There's nothing."

Jericho patted his shoulder. "Take it easy for now. We can try regression therapy in a day or two when you've got more of a grip on yourself."

At that moment, Roger pushed through the door of Harry's room. He had changed his clothes and now wore conservative banker's pinstripes with a powder blue silk tie. His thinning ginger hair was disheveled and even his good ol' boy, Chamber of Commerce smile could not hide the look of worry on his face. Harry noted with satisfaction that the bruise under Roger's eye was well on its way to becoming his most prominent feature.

"Okay Doc, thanks for your help," Roger said officiously as he took Jericho by the elbow and began frog marching him to the door. "We appreciate your concern, but I have some important things to discuss with Harry. He'll be getting a complete physical later. Don't worry, he's in good hands. So, you can go now. Take care of yourself, champ, and thanks again." He slapped Jericho on the back and then pushed him unceremoniously out the door. Just before the door closed behind him, Doc looked back over his shoulder and winked at Harry.

4

Roger Morely, In Your Face

"The old fool," Roger muttered, closing the door and brushing an imaginary piece of lint from his suit. "He insisted on staying right beside you ever since you came back, "monitoring your condition personally", he calls it. He doesn't trust the diagnostics, doesn't even trust the computers. Everything's got to be hands on, the old tried and true stethoscope and pulse reading. He thinks he's living in some old twentieth century, Doctor Kildare movie. I think he's getting senile." He walked over to the bed. "I only keep him around for your sake," he said looking down at Harry. "Otherwise I'd have gotten rid of him a long time ago."

"Yeah, probably right after you stole his resurrection technology and turned it into the Eternal Life money machine," Harry replied caustically.

Roger leaned over the bed and pushed his fat, florid face into Harry's. "That's bullshit and you know it!" he snapped. "If it wasn't for me, his invention never would have gotten off the ground, and the scientific community would still be laughing at him."

Roger thumped Harry on the chest with his forefinger for emphasis. "Didn't I put together the backing that made it possible for him to develop it? Didn't I believe in him when nobody else did? Hell, I gave him the best deal he could get. I even offered him a full partnership. Can I help it if he threw it all away?"

Roger straightened up and began pacing back and forth. "Hell, he wasn't even going to take out a patent. If it wasn't for me, he would have been robbed blind. Now, he's got more money than he knows what to do with and could resurrect in a younger body any time he wants. Instead, he walks around looking like an old, skid row bum.

"Come on, Harry! What more do you want me to do?" Roger threw his hands up in a theatrical display of despair. "He can come and go here as long as he wants. He's even got complete access to all our research facilities. They're the best in the world, and he never uses them. Instead, he prefers to sit out in his Long Island mansion and tinker around in his basement workshop." Roger turned his back on Harry and walked over to the holo screen that covered the far wall. "I just don't understand," he muttered as he took out a gold cigarette case and snapped it open.

There was a lot Roger didn't understand and didn't even know he didn't understand, Harry thought. For example, Jericho's "basement workshop" where he just "tinkered around" was, in reality, one of the most advanced research and development centers in the Empire, but Jericho liked to keep a low profile and few people suspected its existence. Even fewer knew that he developed the Eternal Life technology, an oversight Roger was happy to promote. To the outside world, Jericho was just an eccentric old recluse whose one claim to fame was that he was friends with Harry Neuman.

Harry sighed resignedly and looked at Roger, standing with his back to him, staring at the holo screen that covered the far wall. The screen resembled a big picture window, looking out on a quiet forest glade. Two deer were drinking from a brook that bubbled in the foreground while the wind rippled through the trees. The image was as clear and sharp as digital technology and computer enhancement could make it. It was almost too real, the colors too bright, the contours too sharp, the details too clear. Once again, Harry felt the soothing subsonics beneath the sounds of bird song and burbling brooks.

Suddenly, he was sick of the whole manipulative setting, from the soft pastel colors and indirect lighting to the optimistic

and stubbed it out in the saucer that covered a glass of water on Harry's night table. "She was wondering why we don't see you anymore." He squinted at Harry from the corner of his eye. "Why is that, Harry?"

"You son of a bitch," Harry snarled. It surprised him every time how easily the old wounds could be torn open.

5

Losing It

Even after seven years, the nightmare memories still ripped apart his sleep and left him screaming in the dark, covered in a cold sweat. Seven years ago, he had everything a man could want. He was at the top of his career, the brightest star in the New Hollywood galaxy, rich, famous, and head over heels in love. Susan wasn't even part of the New Hollywood dream machine. Instead, she was a law school graduate, intelligent, beautiful, and witty, and on top of that, she loved him. They were living a beautiful dream that they thought would last forever, but it took only one night to blow it all away. He didn't want to think about it but once he started he couldn't stop.

They went to a party at an exclusive country club. The producers of his latest film wanted to celebrate its success. As usual, he drank too much. None of these new, sophisticated designer drugs or electronic pleasure implants for Harry Neumann. No, he preferred his poison traditional, straight up, and out of a bottle. He quickly reached the stage in his drinking that gave him a loud-mouthed, belligerent belief in his own infallibility and superhuman prowess. He was ready to take on any man in the place and more than willing to let them know it.

Unfortunately, someone took him up on his challenge and suggested a cannonball run down through the Sinks, the sunken heart of old Los Angeles. It was the newest sport among the jaded New Hollywood elite, and its aura of old-time outlaw daring and macho bravado would have appealed to Harry even if he had not been drunk.

Strictly speaking, the races were illegal but the police never interfered. In fact, they tried to keep out of the coastal channels altogether. For the most part, the Sinks were a lawless, half-sunken ruin inhabited by a witch's brew of pirates, Slavers, Seraphim religious fanatics, and renegade Tongs. A high-speed grav-car race through the twisted, rubble-strewn waterways, even in daylight, was close to suicidal folly, and no one had ever tried it at night.

Susan begged him not to do it. He was in no condition to drive, she said. If he didn't get killed in a crash, he'd get killed in an ambush.

But he was blind, pigheaded drunk and wouldn't listen. Hadn't he been a professional racing driver before going into films, he challenged, waving his whiskey glass. And didn't he have one of the newest, fastest, best armed grav-cars on the market? Hell, he'd whip any man in the place. Racing through the Los Angeles Sinks was a piece of cake.

6

The Crash

In some ways the Sinks epitomized all the tragedies of the previous centuries. The new millennium had not been kind to humanity. The ecological destruction of the last half of the twentieth century came back to haunt the earth with a vengeance as monster storms, floods, and droughts swept across the planet.

Even the earth itself seemed to rebel as massive quakes and volcanic eruptions shook the world. The quakes had been gathering momentum for years as a brown dwarf star that had been hiding in the far reaches of the solar system swept in unannounced beneath the plane of the ecliptic and crossed the orbits of the inner planets. They called her Nibiru, and as she approached, her enormous gravitational drag raked across the earth, setting off volcanos and worldwide earthquakes that killed millions and changed ancient geographies overnight.

Panic-stricken nations went to war, fighting over dwindling resources, and millions more died in the aftermath of radiation poisoning and man-made genetic plagues that swept across the world. Civil society broke down as individuals gathered in gangs and tribes, fighting over the ruins of their once great cities.

It was as if the apocalypse predicted for the start of the new millennium had finally arrived. People looked to their bibles to give a name to their sufferings, and they found it in the "Tribulations" of the latter days. But as disaster piled on disaster, even Tribulations couldn't cover it and, at last, it became known simply as the Crash.

In California the long awaited "big one" hit early on in the beginning of the Tribulations, and the state shattered like a dropped jigsaw puzzle. The quakes hit in a haphazard, almost capricious fashion. In some places the land rose, while in others huge sections of the state sank into the sea. Some places were even left relatively unscathed.

When the quakes finally abated, San Francisco was gone, along with a big chunk of the northern coast that collapsed back almost into the middle of the state where the sea now pounded against the Sacramento Palisades, a line of high, jagged, cliffs guarding a shattered interior.

A long chain of volcanic islands started in what had been San Francisco bay and hooked southeast into a deep sea trench that had once been the San Joaquin Valley. The Trench extended all the way east to the foothills of the Sierra Nevadas that had been pushed up thousands of feet and now had foothills of their own. Cold, deep sea currents flowed up the Trench from the Mexican Break all the way past the Sacramento Palisades.

South of San Francisco, the coastal range sank into a long chain of tropical archipelagos that extended almost all the way down to what had once been Santa Barbara. From there they spread out into a tight, jumbled labyrinth of rubble choked channels, junkyard reefs, and tens of thousands of small, overgrown islands that became known collectively as the Skeleton Keys. The Keys flowed southward and gradually merged into the sunken ruins of Los Angeles.

The city had been luckier than most of the rest of the state. The same capricious forces that pulled San Francisco and the northern coast into the ocean pushed the Los Angeles Basin more than fifteen hundred feet into the air. It was almost as if a compassionate Gaia had lifted it up out of the way of the enormous tsunamis that swept in from across the Pacific with the collapse of the Japanese islands and the Indonesian Archipelago.

As the earth changes gradually subsided over the next fifty years, the city slowly sank back into the ocean. It did not happen all at once or in one piece, but different sections broke off and settled at different rates, leaving a cracked, haphazard jumble that rested in a shallow sea.

Parts of the Los Angeles Sinks still remained above water with whole city blocks almost untouched. In some places long spans of freeway could be seen, arching across the sky in pristine splendor only to break off abruptly where the sea washed against the concrete rubble below. In a grotesque twist of fate, much of Hollywood's mammoth production facilities around Burbank survived almost intact on a broken stem of islands stretching to the northeast.

At the end of this stem hung an enormous kidney shaped island that became known as the Hollywood Burst. It bent east and south in a long, sweeping arc that included most of the Mohave Desert all the way down past the Salton Sea, almost to the Mexican Break. From there it swept back north in a ragged concave curve that gave the island its roughly kidney-like shape.

The same tectonic forces that lifted the Los Angeles basin also pushed the eastern back of the Burst up over a thousand feet, breaking it off from the continental landmass and tipping the whole island westward into the Pacific. The old Southern California coast down past San Diego slid into the sea, and a new coastline of long, sandy beaches and shallow coves formed the western shores of the Hollywood Burst, while hundreds of small islands that had once been coastal mountains were scattered up and down the coast, gradually fading into the Sinks to the northwest.

In contrast to its western seaboard, the eastern back of the Burst broke off into a sweeping palisade of sheer cliffs, rising almost a thousand feet and separated from the continental mainland by a fifty-mile chasm that plate tectonic had unzipped and turned into a treacherous sea that became known as the Dire Straits.

The Straits stretched all the way north into what was once Death Valley and south into the Mexican Break, where a large chunk of Baja California broke off from the subsiding Mexican landmass and rose into a towering island plateau surrounded by rocky cliffs and broken fjords.

As the earth changes stabilized and the climate gradually rebalanced, the survivors began picking up the pieces. The weather was no longer southern California arid but lush monsoon tropical, and on the thousands of scattered islands that had once been California, geography and luck combined to kick-start the rapid development of a new civilization centered on the two great island landmasses in the south, the Hollywood Burst and the Baja Plateau.

In the first one hundred chaotic years after the Crash, pirates, Slavers, and outlaws of every kind ruled the southern seas, fighting over the ragbag remnants of a once great civilization. Out of this grew the first Slaver Empire, centered on the southwest coast of the Hollywood Burst with its lush tropical forests, deep water bays, and close proximity to the junkyard wealth of old Los Angeles. The first cities of the new era sprang up in those deep water bays around the huge shipyards that serviced the expanding Slaver Empire.

The Empire lasted almost a hundred years before it was brought down by two very different forces. As it expanded northward along the coastal archipelago, the Slaver Empire ran into a loose federation of pirates called the Tong Syndicates. They came from north of the Seattle Firewall and were led by a brilliant Chinese commander.

In the first engagement he wiped out most of the Slaver fleet. Then, he started island–hopping southward towards the Hollywood Burst and the heart of the Empire. At the same time, the Slavers were facing rebellion at home led by a charismatic leader with a belief in old-time democracy and a burning hatred of the repressive regime.

Together the Tong Syndicates and the democratic rebellion smashed the First Slaver Empire. Afterwards, they somehow managed to settle their differences and set up the Tong Relegate, a kind of constitutional monarchy, with a Tong Emperor sharing power with a weak, democratically elected parliament.

There followed fifty years of relative peace, prosperity, and consolidation. Then, within another forty years everything changed. First, a time vault was found deep in the central highlands of the Hollywood Burst in what had once been the Mohave Desert but was now tropical jungle. The vault contained the basic tools and instructions for kick-starting an industrial revolution. It seemed that some secret government agency of the old USA had had the foresight, or more likely foreknowledge, of what was coming and tried to save what could be saved to get the survivors started again.

There were hints of more vaults buried all over the former USA, but few people ventured across the Dire Straits between the Burst and the Continental Quarantine where plague wars and radiation burn were still producing a deadly harvest of genetic damage. In a grotesque twist of fate, the early quakes that shattered California left nothing for the rest of the world to fight over, and so spared its survivors from the long term damage that resulted from the plague wars and tactical nukes that so devastated the mainland.

Within ten years of the discovery of the time vaults, scavengers digging in the ruins of the old film studios on one of the tail-end islands of the Hollywood Burst unearthed another kind of time vault. This one was not put down by secret government agencies but was Hollywood's own contribution to the future and contained a vast film library covering the whole history of movies and all the production and projection equipment from celluloid projectors to quantum DVDs. It was probably meant to be a kind of time vault, museum, or theme park in praise of the film industry but, by a quirk of fate, the quakes buried it almost intact, although water damage and scavengers destroyed or stole most of the films from the late seventies onward.

This library was a treasure-trove beyond imagining for a

people starving for a vision of a better world, a golden age before plague wars, earth displacements, and radiation burns. Within ten years, the first spring-loaded projectors were unreeling film classics from Chaplin's "Modern Times" to Bogart's "Casablanca". Portable wind-up projectors soon began to find their way into even the most remote and backward communities where they filled an insatiable hunger for the old, time-honored Hollywood formulas of love conquers all, good winning over evil, and courage triumphant against all odds.

For isolated communities digging out of the ruins of the Crash, these old movies became the touchstones for a shared, almost mythological past, a Golden Age that promised a new and better future, a shared dream of hope and faith that might once again be theirs. It was not long before New Hollywood picked up these themes and began producing movies of its own.

Forty years later, these wind-up projectors were spreading their flickering light dreams through the northern ruins of Sacramento where William Danzig was putting together the first anti-gravity engine. Like most great inventions, it was an amazingly simple, efficient device that happened almost by accident. Danzig wasn't trying to produce an anti-gravity engine. He was just tinkering around with copper coils, old car generators, bar magnets, flywheels and an eclectic assortment of junked pre-Crash technology, scavenged from deep in the city ruins.

When he finally realized what he had, he built a larger engine, attached it to the chassis of an ancient Ford pickup that had somehow survived beneath the ruins of an old dealership parking garage, and headed south. He had been brought up on the flickering light dreams of those spring-loaded projectors. They fired his vision with a can-do optimism that produced the first anti-gravity engine, and now, he was going to return the favor and carry it down to the fabled city of New Hollywood.

When he arrived, floating across the deep water bay of New

Hollywood in his old Ford pickup, he set off an explosive techno-logical revolution such as the world had never seen. His anti-gravity engine was the zero-point energy, perpetual-motion Holy Grail of pre-Crash energy research, producing clean, free, unlimited energy.

With Danzig spin-generators at its disposal, the twin islands of the Hollywood Burst and the Baja Plateau exploded into dynamic centers of reconstruction and development for a whole new era. The cities of New Hollywood and Baja grew and expanded upwards with shiny new skyscrapers shooting into the sky almost overnight.

But behind all the boomtown reconstruction, New Hollywood kept doing what it did best. The New Hollywood dream machine rolled on, entertaining, inspiring, giving hope, and spreading the egalitarian values of self-reliance and democracy, "with life, liberty, and the pursuit of happiness" for all.

More than anything else, it was the New Hollywood dream machine coupled with the Danzig spin-generator that midwifed the birth of a new civilization. From the Mexican Break to the borders of the Oregon Quarantine, they knitted together isolated communities into one nation. These same twin forces operating a hundred years later would defeat the Seraphim Jihad and turn New Hollywood into a continent spanning empire.

Even after the city of New Hollywood became the center of culture, wealth, and power for a continental empire, its most important business still remained the Hollywood dream machine. Its actors, producers, and directors became the new nobility. They were rich, famous, powerful, and politically connected and, like all elites, they were pampered, jaded, bored, and always on the lookout for the next thrill. The cannonball runs through the LA Sinks were only the latest in a long series of fads to fill this craving.

7

A Core Sample of the Dark Side

Over a dozen grav-cars were lined up in the parking lot beside the country club that night. The club was built in the cup of a shallow bay. Its white, sandy beach extended all the way up to the end of the lot where the cars floated a couple of inches off the ground with their grav-coils whining in anticipation and their drivers tense with excitement, waiting for the start signal.

Harry let his gaze slide over the newest models, the low sleek sports cars, the coupes and cabriolets with their clean aerodynamic lines that had about as much character as the computers that designed them.

This being New Hollywood though, there was also an eclectic collection of cars modeled on the behemoths of the Golden Age. There was a cream colored nineteen fifty-nine Cadillac Eldorado convertible, mounting dual, chrome plated, .50-caliber Gatling guns like an ostentatious hood ornament. Another Cadillac parked beside it was a pink, Elvis knockoff driven by three giggling young starlets, posing for the grav-cams and dressed mostly in undress. A heavily armored Godfather, Crown Chia limousine pulled up behind them. It was as black as Darth Vader with dark tinted windows and oversized grav-coils that thrummed intimidation.

Harry shook his head and wondered how they expected to maneuver those dinosaurs through the narrow, twisting waterways of collapsing, overgrown debris that defined the Sinks. They'd either get jammed up or have to pull up and quit early.

A beautiful copy of the original James Bond, Aston Martin DB5 slotted in beside him. He recognized the driver, a young, upcoming, action star. Harry eyed the car and nodded appreciatively at the subtle way weapons systems and grav-drives had been integrated without spoiling the classic lines of the car. He gave it a thumbs-up, and the young star grinned as if he'd just received a Christmas present.

A balding New Hollywood director, dressed in an immaculate white tuxedo, strode drunkenly up to the starting line, waving a woman's red, silk panties. He raised them and paused dramatically as the grav-cars revved their engines. The whine of the grav-coils rose to a tearing screech, and the vehicles bounced impatiently up and down on their grav-fields.

Unlike the others, Harry ran his grav-coils up slowly; and his sleek, midnight blue convertible seemed to hunch down like a lion getting ready to spring. The car was modeled on a classic Steve McQueen, nineteen sixty-seven Ford Mustang but had been heavily customized to accommodate powerful grav drives and state-of-the-art weapons systems.

The old wheel wells were covered front and back with sleek teardrop-shaped weapons blisters, each housing a pair of miniguns that could be rotated three hundred and sixty degrees while spitting out a constant stream of .45-caliber explosive slugs.

In the front fenders beneath the headlights, he'd mounted a pair of high-impact rail-guns. If push came to shove in the Sinks, the magnetic coils lining their barrels would kick a half inch ball bearing up towards light speed in nanoseconds. At those speeds a half-inch of steel massed enough destructive power to bring down a battlewagon or blow a man-sized hole through a half a block of concrete walls. If you were looking to make a fashion statement with overkill status, R-guns couldn't be beat.

For close encounters he kept a pulse rifle clamped to the inside of the driver's door and an original, antique, snub-nosed .38 Police Special in a shoulder holster beneath his tuxedo. The Police Special was worth a small fortune and was more a status symbol than a serious weapon, although at close quarters it could still kill.

There was nothing exceptional about this arsenal. Personal weapons were de rigueur for all citizens of the Empire. They strapped them on as casually as slipping on a pair of shoes. A citizen's limitless right to bear arms was a cornerstone of New Hollywood's constitution, backed up by history, tradition, and sheer necessity.

The Slaver Empire was never really defeated. Instead, it retreated into the ruins of the Los Angeles Sinks and the vast labyrinth of islands and mangrove swamps that made up the Skeleton Keys. From there it carried on low-level guerrilla warfare that lasted more than a hundred years as it gradually devolved into squabbling gangs of thieves, pirates, and murderers, that still carried the old Slaver banner when they rode out, attacking any target of opportunity from long-haul merchantmen to solitary travelers, or isolated island communities.

Even after the advent of the Danzig spin-generators, New Hollywood never had the resources to police over a hundred thousand islands scattered from the Sacramento Palisades down past the Mexican Break, and most of its citizens were left to fight off Slaver attacks on their own. It forged a kind of survivor mentality, an individualistic, Wild West self-reliance where each person was responsible, not only for his own defense, but ultimately for his own life, for the decisions he made, the actions he took, and the consequences that resulted. There was no court of appeal for, "I didn't know what I was doing", "I didn't mean to do it", or "I was forced to do it". You punched the ticket, it was yours and you paid the penalty, which was often swift and deadly.

For over a hundred and fifty years, this loose federation of individuals that grandly called itself, The New Hollywood Empire, went about its business expanding, consolidating, growing richer, and every once in a while fighting off Slavers.

Then about eighty years ago The Tong Relegate, which had

ruled New Hollywood from the beginning, was ripped apart by rebellion. In a way, it was inevitable. The old fault lines that ran through the Relegate between the Tong Emperor and the growing democratic demands of parliament finally split wide open. The Tongs themselves were split, one side favored the absolute power of the Emperor, the other a parliamentary democracy. When the dust settled, the rebellion was crushed, the Emperor became a figurehead, and his Tong renegades fled into the Sinks and drove the Slavers north into the Skeleton Keys. Once they gained control of the Sinks, the renegades established The Second Tong Relegate, which was nothing but an excuse to join in pillaging the wealth of New Hollywood, which they proceeded to do with bloodthirsty gusto. And once again individual citizens had to take up the slack and fight off yet another enemy.

As New Hollywood grew in wealth and power, it began expanding eastward over the Dire Straits and across the southern coast of the continent where radiation scars and genetic plagues were gradually burning themselves out. At first, its traders and caravans brought back only distant rumors of troubles in the East, but as the Empire continued to expand, it began running into swarms of panic-stricken, plague-scarred mutants, fleeing the outriders of something called the Seraphim Jihad. These holy warriors of the Caliphate of the Blessed spread a witch's brew of old time religion, racial purity, and holocaust cleansing, all mixed up in the end-of-days revelations of their mad Caliph.

The Seraphim were disciplined fanatics, spreading their brand of hell with guns and fire all along the underbelly of the continent. You were either with them or against them; there was no middle ground. You either converted or died. You were either pure-blood human or died.

All across the Caliphate from the shattered eastern seaboard and across the shores of the Mexican Break, the ovens burned, consuming all those with unclean, plague-scarred genes or infidel beliefs. The Seraphim called them all, "Muties", non-human abominations in the eyes of their god, who called upon his righteous to cleanse the earth of them.

When the two empires met, war was inevitable. The Caliphate War was short, brutal, and a foregone conclusion. New Hollywood had the Danzig Spin-generator, the Caliphate Empire didn't. It was as simple as that. The Caliphate was a steam-powered behemoth, condemned to crawl across the ground and the surface of the sea and be cut to pieces from the air by New Hollywood gunboats.

In a final desperate attempt to salvage victory from defeat, the greatest war fleet of the Caliphate Empire made an end-run through the treacherous waters of the Mexican Break to attack New Hollywood from the rear. They might have succeeded if it hadn't been for a monster storm blowing out of the Pacific that smashed their proud war fleet against the ruins, reefs, and shoals of the Sinks.

Out of over twenty thousand holy warriors, only a thousand survived the wreck of the Seraphim fleet and were stranded in the Sinks. Within a year these disciplined, well trained fanatics quickly took over the ruined city, driving the disorganized bands of Tongs and Slavers into the ruined northern suburbs and the mango groves of the Skelton Keys. With the end of the Caliphate War, New Hollywood inherited a continent spanning empire, and an enemy host camped in its own backyard.

Although the Seraphim were now the titular rulers of the Sinks, the situation remained fluid. Borders were nonexistent and turf wars a constant. Pockets of Slavers and Tongs could be found throughout the Sinks while Seraphim holy warriors made deep incursions into the Keys and southwards into the Slaver islands of the Mexican Break. There was also a steady trickle of disaffected, New Hollywood outcasts and fortune hunters, forming small infected pockets throughout the Sinks.

The only thing they had in common was a hatred of New Hollywood and a desire to plunder its wealth. They rode out of the Sinks and Keys on patchwork fleets of stolen grav-cars, Banshee grav-bikes, and armored gunboats, cobbled together from scrap metal and stolen grav-units, while the citizens of New Hollywood fortified homes, armored grav-cars, and fought back with everything from heavy Gatling guns to the latest plasma cannons.

After nearly three hundred years, the Sinks and Keys had become a kind of core sample of the dark side of New Hollywood's history, and it was into this dark side that Harry and his cronies were riding with drugs, alcohol, machismo, and the arrogance of money fueling an illusion of invulnerability.

8

Cannonball Run

Susan had no illusions about what they were riding into, but she loved Harry too much to let him go alone. At the last moment, she jumped into the open convertible with him. If she couldn't stop him, she could at least be there if he needed her.

Harry looked over at her and winked owlishly. "Through thick and thin, right, Sue?"

"Yes, Harry." She smiled tiredly. "Through thick and thin." At that moment, the director swung the panties down with a theatrical flourish, and Susan was thrown back in her seat as the car reared up and leapt into the night with grav-coils screaming.

Harry took the lead as they shot off across the bay and out into the oily blackness of the sea. Even though the grav-car floated effortlessly over the earth it was still essentially a ground effect vehicle, incapable of climbing higher than three hundred and fifty feet. Speed and altitude were in an inverse relationship. The closer you stayed to the earth, the more speed you could get out of the coils, and Harry kept the car skimming the waves, inches above the sea.

He'd also chopped his spin-dampers, filing them down to a razor thin safety margin. The dampers were there to prevent a runaway coil explosion. In case of a major systems failure, they instantly shut down the coils. They also prevented the coils from exceeding their spin safety parameters.

Old racing drivers like Harry knew these parameters had a safety margin of their own and routinely filed their dampers down to a hair trigger, pushing the coils deep into the red, balancing on the edge, and getting the last fraction of speed out of their engines. A few, with a death wish and an addiction to winning, even removed the dampers altogether.

With his dampers chopped, Harry was already pushing his engines to the limit. At that speed and altitude there was no margin for error. Any sudden obstacle in their path could rip out the bottom of the car and send them pin wheeling to their death, but Harry was determined to secure his lead before they got into the twisted maze of the sunken city. Besides, he had the latest navigation radar, grav-wave detectors, and infrared sensors to help him and could even keep the car on autopilot and let it steer itself, but he knew from experience that the built-in safety parameters would never allow him the kind of speed and maneuverability he needed to win the race. Instead, he disengaged the autopilot and took control himself. Even though he had raced grav-cars professionally, he had to admit that racing through the LA Sinks at night was in a league all by itself.

The lights of New Hollywood quickly faded to a misty glow behind them. The night was still and the sky sparkled with stars as they sped effortlessly across the shimmering surface. Harry drove the sports convertible with the top down and the slipstream gently ruffling his hair. He breathed deeply of the night air and felt intensely alive, filled with a wild exhilaration that embraced the universe and laughed at death.

He glanced over at Susan sitting beside him. She gave him a concerned, loving smile, and Harry threw back his head and laughed with pure joy. What more could a man ask for than to have the woman he loved beside him, speeding through the night in a two million dollar car, with the whole world at their feet. "God, I love you," he said and reached over and squeezed her hand. "And I love our life together."

By the time they entered the twisted, broken outskirts of old LA, the moon was up. It was fat and creamy and almost full and lay on the horizon like a big, slightly deflated beach ball. It cast long, jagged shadows through the overgrown ruins like haunted memories of past madness. The headlights on Harry's car picked out collapsed walls of rotting concrete sticking out of the scummy water. The navigation computer had plotted their course through the center of the city. It wasn't necessarily the safest way but it was by far the fastest. Random pulsed, snapshot radar-sonar, infrared, and gravity detectors cast their ghostly computer-enhanced montage of the city on screens mounted on the dashboard.

Outside, the ruined city closed in around them, and they rode through saw grass and reed choked chasms, lined with collapsed buildings, draped in a mad profusion of tropical growth. Lianas crawled up the sides of broken walls that were covered with a ragged skin of fat, glistening leaves and extravagant night blossoms as big as dinner plates and as pale as death. Palm trees burst like raggedy umbrellas through caved-in roofs and tattered drapes of Spanish moss hung from blind windows. In places the vegetation took over completely, burying whole city blocks in thick mounds of rampant, jungle growth.

They were in no-man's-land now, a place even the imperial police hesitated to enter. So far, Harry had managed to maintain his lead through a combination of alcohol daring, blind luck, and professional skill. Now, even he was forced to slow down and keep a wary eye on the detector screens as he wove through the wreckage of a collapsed building and veered around a rusted steel girder sticking out of the middle of the channel. In the rear view mirror he could see the headlights of the other cars strung out behind him.

Suddenly, one of the pursuing cars broke from the pack and began accelerating just when everyone else, like Harry, was slowing down. The driver came on like a maniac, tearing around blind corners and scrapping over piles of rubble, his undercarriage trailing a screaming plume of sparks. He seemed totally oblivious to danger as he bore down on Harry's taillights with the suicidal determination of a Kamikaze pilot.

Harry watched the headlights grow in his rear-view mirror and smiled. Who the hell did this joker think he was playing with? Maybe it was time Harry showed him. And once again he pushed the accelerator into the floorboards, pushing himself and his machine further and further out onto a razor's edge of control, where the odds grew slimmer by the moment. A part of him knew what he was doing was crazy, irresponsible, suicidal stupidity, but he couldn't stop. He was in the grip of an ecstatic madness, riding an alcohol induced, adrenaline-fired rush that filled him with a godlike sense of power and an absolute certainty that he would win this race and that nothing could stop him.

Susan, on the other hand, was terrified. "Harry, please slow down!" she cried and put a hand on his knee. "Do you hear me, Harry!" She leaned over and shouted in his ear, "Let him pass! It's not worth it!"

Harry remained hunched over the steering wheel, his eyes jumping from the windshield to the dash screens, his hands flicking the wheel gently, his foot steady on the accelerator. "Harry, listen to me," Susan shouted, her voice hysterical with fear. "Harry!" she screamed again, and when he did not respond, panic took hold, and she grabbed his arm to get his attention. Irritably, he tried to shake her off and for a fraction of a second lost control.

At the speed they were going, there was absolutely no margin for error. The car veered wildly, careening against the wall of a building in a screeching crash of sparks and torn strips of carbon fiber. The driver's side rose with almost majestic slowness as the car started to tip over. The grav-coils screamed as Harry fought desperately to pull the car back down. They were inches away from flipping over and going into an uncontrollable anti-gravity driven spin that no one ever walked away from. For an eternal moment, they balanced between life and death. Harry sat perfectly still. He knew there was nothing more he could do. Finally, the car started to settle back down and with a sigh of relief, Harry retook control.

"Harry, please!" Susan screamed and this time he heard her, heard the pain and terror and pleading in her voice. He glanced over and saw her face, bruised with fear, the look of a hunted, wounded animal in her eyes. "Please, Harry, slow down!" she begged. "It's not worth it."

Sanity came crashing back. The ecstatic madness, the trance-like tunnel vision of speed and danger collapsed, and all that was left was he and Susan alone at night in a speeding car with an abyss of pain and terror between them. "You're right," he said, "It's not worth it. Nothing is worth this."

Suddenly, he was stone sober. His foot eased up on the accelerator. How could he have put Susan through this? He had risked her life, their love, everything, and for what? Just to prove that he was a better man than anyone else, that he was king of the hill? What kind of an egotistical asshole did something like that?

The "BLAT! BLAT!" of a trucker's powerful Dumbo air horn slapped the night as the pursuing car flicked up its high beams, pinning Harry and Susan in their blue-white halogen glare. The channel had widened here and the driver blatted his air horn again as he swung out to pass. Up ahead a large section of concrete wall had collapsed into the channel, leaving only a narrow gap that was hardly wide enough for one car, let alone two. Harry picked it up on his radar screen and immediately pulled over to let the other car pass.

As it swept up beside him, Harry glanced over at the low, cream colored, Cadillac convertible with its decorative pair of chrome Gatling guns mounted on the hood. A busty, blonde starlet sat in the passenger seat. Beside her sat a well-known, silver-haired producer hunched over the steering wheel. As they started to pull ahead, he turned and looked at Harry.

The producer's eyes were large and bulging, the pupils dilated to pinpricks of wired lightning, his face flushed and glistening with sweat. His whole body was jittering to sharp amphetamine rhythms that were pushing him faster and faster.

Suddenly, he threw back his head and laughed, howling like a madman. Then he jerked his steering wheel and deliberately rammed Harry's car forcing it in towards the ruined wall of a building.

Harry fought the wheel and stepped on the brakes reversing the polarity of the grav-coils and sending the car into a steep climb. As the other car shot past, the silver haired producer yelled, "Pussy!" and gave Harry the finger. The blond starlet laughed stridently, her lips a red smear in the night. Then they were past, their taillights accelerating towards the narrow gap between the collapsed wall and a relatively intact, overgrown, five-story building on the other side.

Harry's car was still braking, climbing at a steep angle away from the wall on his right with his headlights slashing across the distant building bordering the gap. Just then, he caught a glimpse of movement on the roof. He tried to keep the headlights steady on the building as something was pushed over the edge and started to fall. For a second he couldn't believe his eyes. It looked like an ancient freezer that had been chained shut.

He watched in helpless horror as the calculus of death unfolded before his eyes. Whoever pushed the freezer over the edge had calculated perfectly. The trajectories of the speeding car and the falling freezer intersected just as the Cadillac entered the gap. The freezer crashed right through the front seat, and the car folded up around it. The goddamned freezer must have been filled with concrete, Harry thought.

He felt a wave of pity for the man and his passenger. They never knew what hit them. A moment later, the crumpled up car flared into white hot incandescence, and he realized the asshole producer had chopped out the spin-dampers on his engines and the containment fields were collapsing as the coils spun up uncontrollably. Steam boiled up around the slowly settling wreck. Then, the munitions stores blew. Extreme G-forces from the madly spinning coils drove the explosion away from the core housing, accelerating the initial blast exponentially.

Harry had been braking before the attack and so was some distance back and slightly above the explosion. Instinctively, he drove the brakes into the floorboards and fed power to the forward grav-units tipping the car up on its tail and letting the heavily armored undercarriage take the brunt of the blast. The car bucked and rocked and Susan screamed as a raging front of carbon-fiber and metal shrapnel tore into the undercarriage.

A second later the coils on the other car went critical and the grav-field, expanding at trans-light speed, tore a nano-second hole through space-time, releasing a near-infinite burst of Planck energy. It ripped apart what was left of the wrecked car, stripping it right down to its sub atomic components in a plasma shock wave that instantly blew away the front of the five story building and torched the rest.

The shock wave hit the battered undercarriage of Harry's car like the burning fist of God. It flicked the car up and over its tail as easily as you'd flick a crumb off the sleeve of your coat. Harry managed to cut his grav-units before the crash harnesses came down and immobilized him. A moment later, the on-board computers registered an imminent stage-three disaster, and Harry was engulfed in a foam crash-cocoon.

The car was knocked, pin-wheeling sideways, back across the channel at well over two hundred miles an hour when the passenger side hit a concrete wall and collapsed like an old aluminum beer can. Years later, Harry would wake up at night bathed in a cold sweat with the memory of that crash still fresh in his mind. He would hear the tortured, screeching scream of the car as it ground its way up the concrete wall, sloughing off clouds of broken glass, strips of carbon fiber, splinters of titanium alloy, and chunks of crash-cushion foam.

After that, he must have blacked out, because the next thing he remembered was cold, black water filling the car as it slowly settled into the channel. The foam crash-cocoon had dissolved minutes after doing its job and the padded restraints sprang away as soon as he began moving.

Miraculously, he came through the crash without a scratch, but Susan remained motionless beside him, slumped over in her padded restraints. When he managed to release her, she fell limply into his arms. Blood ran out of her eyes and nose, and the right side of her head looked as if a giant sculptor had stuck his thumb into the wet clay of her head, leaving a deep, bloody depression.

Harry's memory of what happened after that was like a broken mirror, full of cracked, sharp-edged, cutting pieces, with big black holes of nothing in between. He remembered crying and screaming in panic as he fought to get Susan loose from the sinking car; then later, supporting her dead weight in the black water, kissing her lifeless face, crying her name, begging her to be all right.

The moon was still low in the sky casting long, smashed shadows across the channel. Then, he saw the headlights of the other grav-cars led by the black Crown Vic, nosing carefully up the channel. They hadn't abandoned him, he thought and tears of gratitude ran down his cheeks.

Without warning, an ancient .50-caliber machine gun began hammering at the on-coming cars from a shadowy pile of overgrown rubble in the middle of the channel. In the coughing back-light of the muzzle flash, Harry could just make out the silhouette of an old military grav-car and the figure of a man hunched over the machine gun mounted on its hood.

When the shooting finally stopped, Harry could hear the distant screams and shouts of his friends down the channel. He was afraid that they would turn tail and leave, and he wouldn't have blamed them if they did.

A few had, but most of the others just backed off except for the James Bond, Aston Martin and the Crown Vic. The Aston Martin was hugging the far side of the channel and easing slowly down towards Harry. The Crown Vic hadn't moved. The .50-caliber slugs had knocked out one headlight, starred its diamond glass windshield, and scratched the paint on its armor plating but aside from that had done no real damage.

Now, as he watched, the front end of the Crown Vic's hood split open and a squat, snub-nosed canon rose into sight. It rested on a gimbaled gun carriage and had what looked like a tightly wound stainless steel spring wrapped around a stubby barrel that ended in a funnel-shaped, blunderbuss muzzle. The butt end of the barrel fit into a brass drum at least eighteen inches across and a foot thick. Two large copper nodes stuck out of the top of the drum with thick electrical cables and glass insulators attached. The cables snaked back into the grav-core.

Suddenly, a pencil thin beam lanced out from the barrel, and Harry recognized the distinctive mewling hiss of a gigawatt plasma canon as the beam grew as thick across as his own wrist. The crazy son of a bitch had come loaded for bear, he thought, his hopes rising as the bright, neon-purple particle beam walked up the channel towards the machine gun nest, leaving exploding geysers of superheated steam and torn atoms in its wake.

The machine gun began firing blindly into the curtain of steam in a panic-stricken attempt to knock out the plasma canon before it zeroed in.

Then, down the channel behind the Crown Vic, Harry saw the flare of a rocket launch. It burned down from the top of a huge, jungle covered mountain of debris that might have once been a minor skyscraper. The rocket cut a flat arc through the night sky and zeroed in on the limousine. There was the sharp slap of an explosion and a gigantic flashbulb seemed to go off behind the curtain of steam that the plasma canon had kicked up. The particle beam instantly cut off as if someone just pulled its plug. The machine gun kept up its mad chatter for a while longer and finally coughed into silence.

The veil of steam blew apart into long misty tendrils, and

Harry saw what was left of the limousine settling nose first into the water. Slowly, its rear end lifted straight up like the sinking of the Titanic. The car slid down, hit the shallow bottom of the channel, and stopped with a sudden jolt. Only its rear end still stuck out of the water like a surreal black tombstone. Ghostly white clumps of crash-foam floated on the oil slick water.

Mother of Gods! Harry thought. That had to be a Seraphim Stinger to do that much damage! He'd heard of them but had never seen one in action. There weren't many weapons that were against the law, but a Stinger brought down an automatic death penalty.

The Seraphim didn't care. Like the freezer, the Stinger was a low-tech weapon of opportunity, cheap and easy to build. It was basically just a miniature grav-coil, no bigger than a small stack of old DVDs, wired to a rocket and a cell phone running a simple targeting program. The coil had only a rudimentary containment field and was spun into the red when the rocket fired. When it hit its target, the impact breached the containment field, the coil went critical, blew a hole in the fabric of space time, and released a nanosecond blast of pure Planck energy. Simple coil physics and "Presto!" No more car problems! Harry thought.

He noticed that the Aston Martin that had been sneaking towards him had turned around. It was badly battered by the shock wave from the blast, and its containment field must have been breached because it was leaking gravity waves and weaving and hopscotching drunkenly back up the channel, chasing the dwindling taillights of the other cars.

Harry watched in despair as they fled. "No! Don't leave us!" he sobbed. "Please don't leave us!"

As the taillights dwindled to pinpricks in the distance, Harry heard shouts and cheers from the ruined buildings. A searchlight punched down from a roof across the channel. It probed the wreckage of Harry's car that was half-submerged, resting on a concrete slab under the water. Frantically, he pulled Susan behind a broken section of overgrown wall.

He could feel his strength ebbing as the adrenaline rush that had sustained him for so long gradually burned itself out. Even the effort of trying to keep both their heads above water was becoming too much. He tried to find a handhold in the darkness, but the back of the wall was slick with a jelly-like scum that gave no purchase. He clawed blindly at the concrete until, at last, his desperate fingers found a rusting reinforcing rod sticking out of the wall and he grabbed it and held them both above water.

The searchlight played back and forth across the channel. In its flickering backlight, Harry could see his own hand, pale and claw-like, grasping the twisted steel rod. He noticed that he was still wearing his wrist phone. He had forgotten all about it. With a surge of hope, he hit the emergency-call button. Nothing happened. The phone was dead. The intense electro-magnetic pulse from the grav-core blast had fried its circuits. With a sob of despair, he ripped it off his wrist and threw it away.

Time lost all meaning after that. He vaguely remembered holding Susan close, brushing wet strands of hair away from her face, and whispering in her ear, telling her that it was going to be all right, everything was going to be all right, just wait and see, help was on the way, he lied.

Later, he heard the whine of a grav-car slowly coming towards them and his heart leapt with hope. He pulled himself up and looked over the edge of the wall. He was about to scream "Here! Here we are! Save us!" when he saw the armed men standing in the grav-car, silhouetted against the glare of the searchlight from across the channel. One of them wore a hooded robe. When he shifted position, the searchlights picked out a large, silver medallion that hung from a rawhide thong around his neck. Harry recognized the medallion instantly. It was the Seraphim, scimitar crucifix with the gun-sight circle centered where the swords crossed.

This wasn't help, this was who ambushed them! He noticed

the rocket tubes welded into the front fenders of the car and a small plasma canon mounted on the hood. Then the hooded Seraphim flicked on a handheld spotlight. The light swept back and forth across the water and Harry ducked back behind the wall as the car glided towards him.

Maybe they were just scavenging, he thought hopefully. Even wrecked, his car would be worth a fortune. All they had to do was put a couple grav-units on it and pull it out. On the other hand, they could be looking for him and Susan. In that case they might both be better off dead.

The stories of psychopathic cruelty and cold-blooded slaughter that came out of the Sinks were legendary. Hollywood had turned more than a few into blood-dripping B-movie classics. Hell, Harry had even played in in a couple, but nothing had prepared him for the sheer, helpless terror he felt cringing behind that wall, holding Susan's lifeless body and hearing the grav-car closing in. The spotlight played over the concrete block they were hiding behind, etching its shadow sharply against the water.

With Susan unconscious, her breathing shallow, he could not even risk diving underwater for fear that she would drown. Any moment now, the grav-car would sweep around the corner and the spot light would pin them like insects against the concrete. Harry held Susan close and steeled himself for what was coming.

Instinctively, he reached into his jacket and felt the butt end of the ancient thirty-eight, snug in its shoulder holster. If this had been one of his heroic blockbusters, he would have taken out the little thirty-eight, killed the four Seraphim in the oncoming car and then, with Susan slung over his shoulder, he would have jumped aboard and manned the plasma canon, blowing away the oncoming Seraphim gunboats and shooting his way out of the Sinks in a blaze of glory. Reality was a whole other ball of wax, he thought, as he took out the little thirty-eight and prepared to die.

Then, in the distance, he heard the howl of police sirens.

Someone had managed to call in an emergency. As the sirens drew nearer, the spotlights flicked off, and Harry heard the grav-car turn and speed away.

After that, the night was filled with the flashing blue lights of heavily armored police cruisers and then the rocketing, screaming ride in the back of an ambulance, hanging over Susan, refusing to leave her side, begging the doctors to do something, to please make her better and later, the looks of sorrow and pity, the shake of the head, the words of regret and compassion. Susan was not dead but she might as well be. She had sustained massive brain damage and would never regain consciousness.

Only the life supports were keeping her alive. It would probably be a mercy to her to shut them off, the doctor suggested months later, when he thought Harry might be able to make such a decision. But Harry refused. How could he kill her again? She was alive, and he refused to believe that she would never wake up. Every day he went up to that sunlit room where he made sure there were always fresh flowers and he sat with her and waited.

Then one day, he didn't go. He was too drunk; too drunk to even remember. It happened again the next day and the next and the next... And Susan lay alone in the hospital as Harry descended deeper into his own private hell of guilt and pain.

His career went on the skids, but he didn't care. The only thing he wanted was the oblivion that hid in the bottom of a whiskey bottle. It was the same old story from Shakespeare to Hollywood; overweening pride followed by the fall from greatness and the precipitous descent into the depths. It was almost mythic in its sheer banality.

9

The Stuff that Dreams Are Made of

"Harry!" Roger yelled and shook his shoulder. "Are you listening, Harry? Don't go nodding off on me."

Harry opened his eyes. For a moment, old memories floated across his vision, like crash-foam floating on scummy water in the night.

"Look Harry, I'm sorry. Why don't we just let bygones be bygones?" Roger ran his thick fingers through his thinning, ginger hair. "I mean, it all happened a long time ago. It's water under the bridge."

"It's been five years," Harry said. "And two since you stole my wife."

"Roger leaned over and pushed his face right up into Harry's. "I'm sick and tired of this bullshit, you hear! I didn't steal anything!" His breath smelled of expensive cigars, aged whiskey and a hint of rotting meat. His bloodshot eyes stared straight at Harry. "I just picked up what you threw away with your drinking and womanizing."

He straightened up, his face red and blotchy with anger. "Maybe you're forgetting that it was me who brought her back to life. If it wasn't for me, she'd still be a vegetable with plastic tubes running in and out of her and machines keeping her alive." He jabbed a thick finger into Harry's chest. "Remember, asshole, it wasn't me who put her there in the first place!"

"I know what I did," Harry said quietly. "And I know what you did. So spare me the noble Sir Galahad act. A suit of shiny armor and a white horse was never your style. All Susan was to you was a hot business prospect, a means to an end, a way of getting to me."

"Don't flatter yourself!" Roger said contemptuously.

"Alcoholic has-beens like you are a dime a dozen. You were just lucky I happened to choose you."

"Luck had nothing to do with it. You chose me because I was just what you needed, the perfect tool, and you knew I couldn't say no. So let's cut the crap! You didn't give a shit about Susan, but hey, if she could put that perfect tool in your hands, you'd be willing to play Santa Claus for a day."

Roger clucked his tongue and shook his head. "So much cynicism in one so young."

"Come on, Roger, let's talk straight for once. Five years ago, you were just another Hollywood hustler, a wheeler-dealer with a knack for bringing money, talent and know-how together to produce second-rate box office successes. Then, you ran into Doc... I have to give you credit, you recognized a winner when no one else did. You saw that this could put you into the big leagues. The only problem was they played hardball up there. I don't think you realized just how hard."

Roger looked down at him with a smile like a razor slash. "I was raised playing hardball," he growled. "I don't think you or they realized just how hard the game can be played."

For an instant, Harry seemed to look straight through Roger's sagging, dissipated features to a younger, harder Roger, all sharp angles and harsh planes. There was the smell of spilled blood and sudden violence in the air, and Roger's tired, bloodshot eyes were cold and clear and without mercy. Roger chuckled and shook his head. "Babes in the woods, Harry, you're all nothing but babes in the woods." And once again he was the overweight, self-indulgent CEO of Eternal Life.

Harry felt as if he'd just stepped off the end of the continental shelf into very deep water. Stuff like this was happening to him more and more frequently lately. Reality was becoming a very tenuous affair. He remembered Roger's face turning into the snout of one of those things that had chased him down the resurrection trail. How real was that? How real was any of that? He shifted uncomfortably in the bed and felt the welts on his back rasp painfully against the sheets. At any rate, those were real enough. So where did that leave him?

Roger took out his gold cigarette case and lighter. He slid out a cigarette, lit it, and took a deep drag. He tilted his head and blew a couple of perfect smoke rings at the ceiling. "When Jericho came to me with his invention, I knew he had something so revolutionary that it was going to shake the social structure to its foundations," he said. "I also knew that a lot of very rich, powerful people had a very big stake in maintaining the status quo that kept them rich and powerful. They didn't want anyone rocking the boat. They weren't necessarily against the technology; they just wanted to control it themselves. They saw me and my company as upstarts, loose cannons and they wanted us out of the picture. Only, I wasn't about to leave. This was my ticket to ride, and I intended to ride it all the way to the top."

Roger began pacing back and forth as he talked and smoked. "I knew I had a war on my hands, not the shooting kind, but it could have come to that. If it did, I knew they had me outgunned. So instead, I turned it into my kind of war, a media war, a public opinion war, a war for hearts and minds. And I won it!" he said and slammed his fist into the palm of his hand.

"I used every trick in the book, every New Hollywood connection. I twisted arms, bribed, blackmailed, and called in every marker I had. I knew I could sell Eternal Life to the public. Hell, hadn't I sold them some of the biggest turkeys New Hollywood ever made? I'd sell Eternal Life the same way!"

"But no matter how good you were, you couldn't have done it without me," Harry said with undisguised self-contempt. "The perfect poster-boy front man, someone with New Hollywood star quality to lead the campaign, someone people would recognize and trust, someone they could identify with, someone who would reassure them, and someone who would be willing to die for them again and again, just to show them that, yes, this worked, there's nothing to be afraid of, just trust me and we'll all have ETERNAL LIFE! You needed someone like good ol' Harry Neuman, that honest, clean-cut hero of a dozen blockbusters."

Harry shook his head wearily. "But most of all, you wanted me because you knew that I couldn't say no, that I'd even jump at the chance, because you could give me the one thing I wanted most. You could bring back Susan. You could wipe away all the pain and guilt and bring back the dream.

"All I had to do was sign a five-year contract with Eternal Life, and I'd get Susan back and everything would be like it was before, and we'd live happily ever after. Only it didn't work out that way, did it? There were a couple of things you neglected to tell me."

In the beginning, though, it really was like a dream come true, Harry thought. A clone was prepared for Susan, and she was taken off life support. A short time later, she died, only to be resurrected again in the amino acid vats of Eternal Life; Susan, alive and whole, with all her memories and love intact.

The media boys spun it into the love story of the century. It was irresistible, a living fairytale. Sleeping Beauty revived by her Prince Charming, a love that transcended death. Their faces were on the front pages of every newspaper, magazine, and holo screen in the country. They became icons of the new age, as familiar as the first pictures of the earth taken from space.

And when Roger's media circus had milked that story for all it was worth, there came the final revelation, the price Harry had been willing to pay to bring back his love. Of course, no one was so crass as to talk about five-year legal contracts. No, this was the noble lover, who only wanted to pay his debt of gratitude to Eternal Life by allowing himself to be killed and resurrected again and again, so that everyone could see the wonderful benefits and dependability of this new technology.

The reality was far from the glitzy, media hype. The first year of Harry's contract was sheer hell. He died twenty times that year, in car crashes, fires, muggings, even a malignant brain tumor. In every case the pain was excruciating, the death trauma worse, and rebirth a nightmare without end.

Somehow, Roger had forgotten to mention these little details when they were signing the contract. Harry would wake up in the amino acid vats in the cellars beneath Eternal Life begging Jericho to let him die for real. But the old man just shook his head, his eyes full of pity because there was nothing he could do, he said, because he didn't make the decisions anymore.

Later, Harry learned that Jericho had gone to Roger, demanding that he release Harry from his contract or, at the very least, that he not be made to die so often. It was in no one's interest, he argued, if Harry went insane.

But Roger dismissed Jericho's concerns. Eternal Life was fighting for its life, he insisted, and Harry was all they had. Major political, financial, and religious interests all over the empire felt threatened by this new technology. Why save or invest for your old age, when you knew there wasn't going to be an old age? Why insure yourself against accidents, disability, or death when you knew you could just jump out of this old, broken body and into a new, healthy one? Savings banks, pension funds, insurance, medical, and drug companies all saw their profit margins collapse, and they fought back trying to discredit Eternal life, break its monopoly on resurrection technology, and get a piece of the action for themselves.

In the halls of the imperial parliament they used their political influence to lobby and buy votes while in the news media and the talk shows they thundered against the socially destabilizing effect of this new technology in the hands of one company, controlled by one individual.

But the churches were the worst, the most ruthless and vicious of all. Those old snake oil salesmen had been selling their particular brands of eternal life for centuries. Now suddenly, they were being put out of business, and they didn't like it. Religious communities all over the Empire put aside their differences and closed ranks. They thundered against Eternal Life from the pulpits of thousands of churches and temples. People who came back from the dead were soulless monsters, they screamed; they were possessed by the devil and the whole thing was a demonic conspiracy to destroy humanity. Then, they called for a new crusade, a just war, a jihad, to crush this satanic abomination.

The only religious order that did not hop on the bandwagon was The Church of She. The Church was born in the Crash and worshipped the Goddess in all her guises as ruler of this earth. If New Hollywood had had a state religion, the Church of She would have been it. Its cathedral dominated the city's skyline and a large proportion of the population favored it over all the other splinters of old-time ersatz Christianity, Buddhism, Islam, etc.

In the conflict with Eternal Life, the Church of She maintained a neutral wait-and-see attitude, pointing out that the technology, far from being at odds with religious teaching, in fact supported one of its basic tenets, the existence of life after death in the form of a soul or ka. For this reason alone, the Church favored caution over condemnation, but its message was drowned out by the fear-mongering, demonizing scream pouring like raw sewage from an unholy alliance of business, politics, and religion.

In the end, only Harry Neuman and the might of Roger's New Hollywood media campaign stood between Eternal Life and destruction. When Harry died the first time, Roger's media machine went into high gear, whipping up interest to a fever pitch.

When Harry emerged from the rebirthing chamber with his boyish grin and thumbs up expression, Roger made sure the image was plastered all over the empire. And it worked! People went wild with enthusiasm. Not since Charles Lindbergh, in another age, flew alone across the Atlantic, had one man so captured the public imagination and transformed the spirit of the times. And Roger milked the story for all it was worth. Harry became the symbol of hope and courage for a new age.

But it didn't stop there. It couldn't stop there. The pressure on Eternal Life was too great. Harry had to die again and again, and each time he walked out of the rebirthing chamber, joking and grinning with that irresistible, "aw shucks twern't nothin," Gary Cooper strength and humility, the world went wild and Eternal Life's stock soared. The people loved him, loved his quiet courage and self-sacrifice, loved him for the fact that he was doing it all for his woman, that he was paying a debt of honor, gratitude, and love. It was old time Hollywood come true.

And because they respected and trusted Harry, the people came to respect and trust Eternal Life. Roger, that old Hollywood wheeler-dealer, had gotten it just right. His choice of Harry, and the massive advertising campaign he built around him, won over public opinion and routed the forces that stood against him. By the end of that second year, he was finally able to give in to Jericho's demands and ease the pressure on Harry.

But by then it was too late. The strain had driven Harry over the edge. He became moody, irritable, depressed, at times almost psychotic. He began drinking again. His marriage began to founder. His drinking got worse. He and Susan fought constantly. He turned to other women, a whole string of other women, eager to comfort the great Harry Neuman. He got into ugly public brawls, beating his opponents senseless, and Eternal Life had to work overtime covering it all up and bailing him out. At last, Susan could take no more, and three years after his first death, she packed up and left. And surprise, surprise! Who should be there waiting with a convenient shoulder to cry upon, but good old Roger.

10

Back from the Edge

That was the last straw and it almost broke Harry. Over the next year he spiraled ever deeper into an alcoholic haze of violence and debauchery that even the best spin doctors at Eternal Life couldn't cover up. He was becoming a liability for the company, and they began cutting back on his public appearances and resurrections.

Then, something happened that broke the self-destructive, downward spiral. Harry discovered a way to die quickly and painlessly. He didn't learn it overnight nor did he do it without help.

Up to that point, all he knew about his ka came from the moment its tether to the flesh was cut and it became nothing but a helpless victim of forces beyond its control. Jericho suggested there might be other possibilities. He baited his hook with stories of ancient shamans, saints, and mystics who supposedly acquired superhuman powers through contact with the ka. According to these stories, they could do everything from healing the sick and raising the dead to walking on water and predicting the next lottery winner. Jericho admitted he wasn't sure if it was possible, or even if the stories were true, but he was certain that if anyone could find out it was Harry.

Harry was not impressed. In fact he didn't care. Doc knew he had his work cut out for him. Lighting even a spark of interest in that tortured, guilt-ridden, whiskey-soaked brain would be a major accomplishment. He threatened, cajoled, begged, and promised. In the process he became Harry's friend, confidante, and father confessor. He was always there to pick him out of the gutter, dry him out, and start all over again.

He was at every resurrection, lending his quiet support and

peppering Harry with questions. How was this resurrection different from others? What had he seen? How had he felt? It was always kept in a spirit of scientific inquiry, forcing Harry to objectively examine the experience, to look deeply into himself and his ka. In the beginning, all Harry wanted was to get it over with as fast as possible and find the next whiskey bottle, budding starlet, and barroom brawl but, gradually, he came to accept these meetings as part of his resurrection and even began to look forward to them.

He and Jericho would go over each death again and again, examining every detail. What happened at the moment of transition? What was the ka like? How did it feel? Could you control it? How? When? Where? Details, details, details.

Harry surprised himself by gradually remembering more and more and for the first time began to show a spark of interest. The devil was in the details, Doc kept repeating, as he fanned that spark into a guttering flame of curiosity.

The breakthrough came when Harry noticed that, at the moment of death, his mind gave an odd little internal shrug that seemed to twist his ka loose from his body. It was such a little thing and happened so fast he never would have noticed it if he hadn't been looking for a little "devil in the details". After that, he taught himself to do it and, from then on, dying held no fear. He was no longer a victim. He was in control. As soon as things got too bad, the cancer that bit too deep or the bullet that didn't go deep enough, he just shrugged out of his old body and headed down the resurrection trail without all the traumatic, painful preliminaries.

It was a turning point. That guttering flame of curiosity burst into a blazing wild fire that gradually consumed Harry's old life. He stopped drinking and began to take care of himself, watching his diet, exercising, getting enough sleep, and reading everything he could find that might explain what was happening.

He confided in no one except Jericho. The old man was almost as excited as he was and proved indispensable in helping him find answers to how, what, and why this was happening. He provided Harry with piles of scientific and religious texts, everything from advanced physics to books on mysticism, philosophy, psychology, and religion. Many of them were old pre-Crash documents, and Harry wondered in passing how they had survived and where Jericho had gotten a hold of them.

Surprisingly, the texts that proved most helpful came from a recent New Hollywood scholar, called Jake Lloyd, who had died twenty years ago. The ten volumes of his work from "The Neurobiology of Enlightenment" to his final bewildering "Anubis Gates" seemed to speak directly to Harry, guiding him through the confusion of fear and doubts that assailed him. Harry had never been much of a scholar but he devoured everything Lloyd wrote.

He began to look forward to his next resurrections as journeys of discovery. During the last year of his contract, he went through a record eighteen resurrections, most of them unsanctioned by the company. He went into each resurrection carefully, noting everything that happened. He discovered that the point between life and death, just where the ka is about to leave the body, contained the seeds of vast knowledge. At that point, the body left its imprint on the spirit body of the ka that not only retained a human form but was covered all over with fine, glowing, colored lines, like a weird schematic of some complex machine or circuit board. These lines were legible for only a few moments just before the ka was pulled towards the white light of death.

Harry gradually realized these lines were lines of concentrated information consciousness that contained the coded wholeness of his body/mind, much as a seed contains the coded wholeness of a tree. The lines ran up and down and across the ka, swirling in and out of several juncture boxes of concentrated energy spaced along the torso. In the months of dying that followed, Harry tried to read that diagram, memorizing bits and pieces in the few moments before they faded. Afterwards, he traced as much as he could remember out on paper.

He discovered that those bright junctures of energy consciousness corresponded to the energy nodes or chakras he found in ancient yogic texts. Using them as a basis, he was able to trace a more complete though still extremely simple copy of these bright schematics. Later, Jericho provided him with acupuncture diagrams from China that added another layer of complexity to the circuitry tracings of his ka.

About two months after he learned how to die, he managed to follow a bright, pulsing red line of pure information pain back to its source, and the next time he was dying in agony, he used his imagination to follow that red line back to its source and figuratively pulled the switch. It was the equivalent of the mental shrug that allowed him to die, but this time it cut off the pain.

Gradually, he found that he could do other amazing things like close a knife wound in a matter of minutes, heal a broken bone overnight, or slow his heart and breath rate and put his body into a state of suspended animation that was just this side of death. It wasn't raising the dead or walking on water but it was changing him more deeply then he suspected.

At first, he hardly noticed the change. It seemed such a small thing. His mind just seemed to be getting quieter. It was as if he had had a radio in his head going full blast with thoughts, emotions, and desires and now someone was turning down the volume. Sometimes his mind would go completely still and he would be aware of a silent, inner presence filling the stillness. Each time he died and was reborn, he seemed to bring back a little more of this silent presence that somehow felt more intimately him than his meat locker of a body.

When he finally told Jericho about this, the old man grew quiet and thoughtful. Shortly afterwards, he introduced Harry to the secret garden of the most powerful Tong Godfather in New

Hollywood, and to Samuel Kade, a shaman trance-walker, who made his home there.

With Kade's help, Harry came to realize that this silent presence was not only his own ka stripped of all the conscious layers of everyday ego babble that usually blanketed it, but that it was also possible to consciously shift his awareness into his ka without having to die first. It marked a turning point in his life, a time of heady promise and discovery, but it came far too late to salvage his marriage. Susan had already married Roger the year before.

11

Two-way Mirrors

"Look, Harry, why don't we just stop bickering and try to get things cleared up, okay?" Roger's voice cut through his memories and Harry turned. "Clear what up?" he asked.

Roger ran his fingers nervously through his thinning ginger hair. "The reporters have been on our backs for the last thirty-six hours, wanting to know why they couldn't interview you."

"Thirty-six hours?" Harry asked in disbelief. "I was out for thirty-six hours?"

"Yeah, didn't Jericho...?"

Harry shook his head. Thirty-sixes, he thought, and instinctively rolled his shoulders and felt the welts on his back stretch and sting.

For most people it could take anywhere from three days to a week to recover from a resurrection and get used to their new bodies, but the twin traumas of death and rebirth no longer touched Harry, and he was usually up and smiling for the camera within twelve hours. Whatever ambushed him out on the resurrection trail had been bad enough for his ka to bury itself as deep as it could in this new meat locker body and then slam the door shut for almost thirty-six hours!

"Look, Harry, we've been holding the reporters off by telling them you were resting up and considering new contract options from Eternal Life..."

Roger saw the scowl darken Harry's face and threw up his hands as if to ward it off. "I know, I know." He laughed. "You haven't changed your mind. We're not asking you to go through another death. Believe me, I understand. Haven't I been with you right from the beginning? Five years, Harry, that's a long time. Together, we made Eternal Life the greatest institution in the world. We've…"

"Roger, I don't need a sales pitch," Harry said tiredly, "I know what I did, and why I signed that contract. I died fifty-one times and put myself through hell. Now, it's over."

"Of course, of course, Harry," Roger's voice was full of understanding. "We're not asking you for that, just a personal appearance every once in a while, promotional tours, that kind of thing, just like we agreed."

"We didn't agree on anything," Harry said. "You told me to think about it."

"Look, Harry, I'll be honest with you. You got us over a barrel," Roger said, trying to shift gears and back pedal at the same time. "You've become a symbol of trust for Eternal Life and…"

"What happened during the last resurrection, Roger?" Harry cut in as he surreptitiously fingered the note that Doc had slipped into his hand. "What made me so hysterical and panic-stricken that I had to be sedated, and what are those marks on my back?"

Roger's hands fluttered nervously and his usual, florid complexion darkened. "Really, Harry, I don't know. Don't you remember?"

Harry shook his head. "Nothing," he lied. "Now, what I want to know is what's going on? I've heard rumors…"

Roger spat in disgust. "Just rumors, Harry! You know how the competition is. We still got enemies. Hell, the churches would love to break us. Those bible-thumping fanatics will try anything to get at us. Remember the time…"

"Stop bullshitting me, Roger. They're saying that we're losing people in resurrection, that they're not all coming back, or that they're not all there when they do come back. Now, I don't intend to put my ass on the line for you or Eternal Life anymore unless I get some straight answers."

Roger had smoked his cigarette down to the butt. He walked

over to the night table beside Harry's bed and stubbed the cigarette out beside the other one on the saucer covering Harry's glass of water. He did it with the slow, deliberate concentration of a brain surgeon performing a lobotomy. Then, he lifted the saucer off the glass and dropped the butt into the water. He regarded Harry thoughtfully. Harry could almost see the cartoon cogwheels turning inside Roger's head, weighing alternatives, extrapolating decisions... choosing the best lie.

Finally, he shook his head almost sorrowfully. "Harry, Harry, Harry," he murmured perplexedly. "What are we going to do with you?" Then he turned away and walked slowly over to the holo-screen. The deer had wandered out of the glade and into a field of wildflowers with brightly colored butterflies flitting through the air. Overhead the sky was impossibly blue, filled with little, puffy, white clouds like you see in children's drawings.

Roger stopped in front of the screen. Automatically, he reached inside his jacket for his cigarette case. He flicked it open, took out a cigarette, and lit it with the same calm, deliberate concentration he'd used in crushing the butt. He tilted his head back and blew a cloud of smoke at the holo screen. The smoke broke against the glass and rebounded in lazy, blue swirls.

"You know, Harry," he said at last. "When I started this company, it wasn't just for the money. Oh, I won't try to shit you, the money was important but, Jesus, Harry, I wasn't exactly poor. I didn't really need it. I'd made my bundle. I mean, how much is enough, right? But here was a chance to do something meaningful. Not like these two-bit Hollywood deals where everyone is out to screw everyone else but something worthwhile, something that would change the world and, yeah, I admit it, put my name in the history books.

"I know I pushed you hard in the beginning, but you were our trump card, the only one we had. People trusted what you said. They trusted that noble, honest face and that, 'aw shucks grin'. I don't think you ever really appreciated how much we needed you… How much we still need you."

He paused, staring thoughtfully at the holo screen without really seeing it. "I'm sorry about Susan," he said at last. "I really didn't plan for it to go that way. You probably don't believe me, but it's true. Anyway… what's past is past," he said bitterly and dismissed it with a wave of his hand. For a moment, an air of hopeless despair seemed to settle over him. His shoulders slumped and his body sagged as if it had finally given up the fight against gravity. The cigarette burned forgotten between his fingers.

Harry watched the smoke curl towards the ceiling and waited. He listened to the digital wind, rustling holographic leaves and to the intermittent bursts of bird song. He wondered what Roger was up to, where this apparent soul searching was going. Was it genuine or just some ploy to gain a bigger market share of Harry's limited trust and sympathy?

Whatever was going on, Roger finally seemed to come to some private closure. He straightened up with a quick shrug and squared his shoulders decisively. He glanced quickly at the wall of two-way mirrors and then looked at Harry. "I guess what I'm trying to say," he said as he started walking across the room, "Is that it's been nice knowing you, champ. And if you don't want to work for Eternal Life anymore, well, fuck you!" He stopped in front of Harry's bed, took a deep drag of his cigarette, and then casually flipped the burning butt at the two-way mirror. Then, he turned and walked away.

When he reached the door, he paused with his hand on the knob. "By the way, Harry," he said over his shoulder. "Those rumors you've been hearing are pure dog shit. And if you begin repeating them in public, you'll find yourself up to your ass in lawsuits." Then he jerked the door open and let it slam behind him.

Now, what was that all about? Harry wondered as he watched

the cigarette butt burning a black scar in the floor beneath the mirror. He thought of the look on Roger's face when he flicked it. It was a look of defiant bravado, of a man standing in front of a firing squad and giving it the finger. For the first time, Harry felt something akin to sympathy, maybe even respect, for Roger Morely, but his features revealed none of this. They remained placidly blank with only a calm smile for the grav-corders that hovered over his head, buzzing like curious bumblebees.

12

A Cover-up

The press conference had gone badly, and Harry was relieved when it was over. He had prepared for it by keeping his clothes deliberately casual, blue chambray shirt open at the neck, no tie, faded jeans, and a pair of scuffed white running shoes and his iconic Chief's Special in a clip-on holster on his belt. An old original Los Angeles Dodgers baseball cap was pulled down low over his eyes. He'd picked it up once at an auction. It had cost a small fortune but its battered, broken-brimmed, disreputable appearance appealed to him. It was also perfect for this occasion where he was out to make a deliberate fashion statement that said, "I'm out of it, retired, gone fishing." It also served to distance him from the suits at Eternal Life, who hovered watchfully in the background.

There weren't as many reporters as he'd expected. The others were probably chasing a bigger story and for that he was thankful. He knew most of the ones that had turned up by their first names and they took their cue from him, asking about his retirement plans and whether he would be going back into films. But it was all just a courtesy to Harry and it wore off real fast. What they really wanted to know was why he was so late and did it have anything to do with rumors that something had gone wrong with his resurrection?

Harry took his cue from Eternal Life's public relations man, Don Gibson, who had prepped him thoroughly before the news conference. "Everything went fine," Harry lied. "I just had to go through a few final physicals before Eternal Life would agree to release me. I guess they didn't want me coming back and saying they gave me a faulty body or something." He smiled disarmingly, hating himself and the role he was being forced to play in this cover-up. "Everything is tip-top," he continued. "Guaranteed to last at least two hundred thousand miles without an oil change." He thumped his chest and grinned into the grav-corders and promised himself never ever to do this again. Roger could take his new representation contracts and shove them up his ass sideways.

The reporters scented a cover-up and began pressing him. Had he heard the rumors about the recent problems at Eternal Life, patients not coming back, or coming back murderously insane or maybe even possessed?

Harry pleaded ignorance and let Gibson field the questions. Gibson was a long, loose-limbed black man with a laid back, easy manner and the patience of a saint. It was said that he could charm the venom out of a cobra, but today the reporters weren't buying it. They scented blood and the tone of their questions became ever more strident and aggressive. Gibson's easy, down-home drawl and folksy manner began to wear thin. At last he tried stonewalling with a company release and when that didn't work, he turned harsh and abrasive and finally cut short the interview.

Harry had never seen Gibson lose his cool like this and when he tried to talk to him afterwards, the man nearly bit his head off. "Not you too, Harry! Did you hear that? Now it's demonic possession! For Christ's sake, these rumors are getting completely out of hand."

He ran his hands over the tight kinky curls of his close-cropped head and eyed Harry belligerently. "Don't you think if something like this was happening, it'd be splashed all over the headlines? Look, Harry," he said earnestly. "It's just not true. There's no problem. A few lawsuits maybe but nothing we haven't seen before.

"Now why don't you get the hell out of here," he grinned good-naturedly. "Take a long, well deserved vacation. Go get drunk, find yourself a couple of buxom young starlets and go lie on the beach with them." He gave Harry a friendly slap on the back and turned away.

"Demonic possession," Gibson shook his head and laughed to himself as he walked down the hall. And it was all an act. Harry knew acting when he saw it and Gibson was good, but he wasn't that good. Behind his laughing, good ol' boy façade, Gibson was scared spitless.

13

The Norma-gene

Harry stepped out of the air-conditioned coolness of the Eternal Life building and into the tropical humidity of downtown New Hollywood. He heard the soft pneumatic hiss of the doors as they closed behind him, and he gave a sigh of relief.

Every time he went in there, he felt as if he was forced to cripple himself. The place was wired to the eyeballs with hidden cameras, sensors on his ka, and remote telemetry measuring everything from body temperature, blood pressure, brain wave activity, and even which pheromones he was giving off that day. Once inside, he just shut down contact with his ka and any powers that developed from it. Even out here on the street, he was careful not to let his guard down, especially today.

He scanned the broad marble stairs that led down from the door and noted with satisfaction that they were empty; no reporters, no autograph seekers, not even a grav-corder. At least, he wouldn't have to lie his way out of any more interviews for a while. That was why he chose this little used side exit in the first place. His car was parked at the front entrance and probably knee deep in reporters and gawkers by now.

Whistling tunelessly to himself, he put on a pair of dark aviator sunglasses, pulled down the broken bill of his baseball cap, and started down the stairs. The late afternoon sun flashed like burning copper off passing grav-cars. They all stayed above the sixty foot minimum height for the city. Occasionally, one dropped out of traffic and descended to the grass-covered avenue to let out a passenger or park.

The advent of the grav-car made asphalt and concrete obsolete. Instead, the streets in New Hollywood were lush green swathes of grass with long beds of brightly colored, tropical flowers running down the middle. Low trees lined the streets. They arched over broad sidewalks, forming a protective arcade for the pedestrians beneath. On the street sides the trees were cut back to a green wall allowing grav-cars to descend and ascend unhindered. None of the cars seemed remotely interested in Harry.

Casually, he reached into his jean's pocket and took out Doc's note. He unfolded the crumpled piece of paper and read the short message, "Chueh's". He smiled to himself. It had been a while. A moment later, the smile died on his lips as he saw a man hurrying across the avenue, cutting through the flowerbeds and heading straight for him. Harry groaned and shoved the note back into his pocket. How the hell had the reporters gotten wind of where he was?

A second glance changed his mind. This didn't look like a reporter. Not even a freelancer or stringer would dress like that. Despite the thirty five-degree temperature, the man wore heavy woolen trousers, a woolen stocking cap pulled down over his ears, and a fleece-lined leather bomber jacket zipped all the way up. His shoulders were hunched, his hands thrust deep into his jacket pockets and the fleece-lined collar was pulled up around his ears as if he was freezing.

As the man got closer, Harry saw the characteristic star-shaped scars that pitted his face and the strands of peroxide blonde hair that stuck out from beneath the stocking cap. A Norma-gene! He thought they had all left for the Nevada Quarantine. He hadn't seen one in years. When he was a kid, they were everywhere.

They had come in during the Caliphate War along with a lot of other muties, all fleeing the ovens of the Seraphim Jihad. Within a few short years, New Hollywood was overrun with muties, all seeking refuge and forced to live as outcasts on the fringes of a society that had no time for them and viewed them with suspicion, revulsion, and sometimes maybe even a little pity.

They constituted an army of the deformed, whose ancestors had lived through the genetic plague wars and the radiation burns of the Crash, and still bore the scars branded into their DNA. But even among the multitude of the deformed, the Norma-genes stood out.

It looked like this guy had been luckier than most, Harry thought. The Norma-gene plague was a broad-spectrum mutation that played countless variations on the basic Norma-gene theme. In this case, it had apparently played havoc with the bodies inner thermostat, but apart from that had left none of the grosser genetic deformities of a disease that could turn human flesh into something as fluid as melted wax and leave walking nightmares in its wake. Many Norma-genes died young, the genetic damage too extensive to repair.

On the other hand, not all broad-spectrum variations turned out negative. It was known that some Norma-genes developed almost superhuman abilities. Their reflexes were incredibly fast or their senses extremely acute. Some developed the strength of ten men while others developed paranormal abilities and were called, "weirdings". Some were telepaths, others far-seers or fire-starters, some could teleport, or even bend space time to their will. A few never seemed to age. Maybe this guy was one of them, Harry thought. He looked to be only about thirty but might be as old as Doc. With Norma-genes you never knew and that was the problem.

Harry could still remember the scary stories that older kids whispered in his ear when he was little. "If you were bad, the Norma-genes would get you. They could call up demons and cast spells on the unwary. They possessed the evil eye and could kill with a look. They were shape-shifters and skin walkers, who took the form of animals and roamed the night seeking blood, and there was no escape because they could read your mind and knew where you were going because they could see the future;

and when they caught you, they would burn you to a cinder with a look."

They were the stuff of children's nightmares. The residue of old horror stories left over from the Genetic Plague Wars and the Crash, when frightened bands of refugees huddled around lonely fires and gave a face to their fears, whispering about the inhuman powers of the mutant Norma-gene.

With time the stories grew wilder and more hysterical, encompassing all mutants and at last spiraling out of control into bloody witch-hunts and the holocaust of the Seraphim Jihad, where the ovens burned day and night to rid the world of its mutant stain. In the old days, he could even remember a few witch-hunts through the streets of New Hollywood.

As the Norma-gene drew nearer, Harry could smell the sour reek of urine, sweat, and cheap wine. He could see the patches and stains on the man's clothes, the unwashed hair, and ground in dirt. Too many mutants ended up like this. The witch-hunts were history now, but Norma-genes were still shunned, mistrusted, and feared, even by other mutants.

After the fall of the Caliphate, most of the other mutants gradually returned to the Continental Quarantine, but the Norma-genes stayed behind, living as homeless derelicts on the edge of a society that had no time for shame, guilt, or recompense.

When he was a kid, he remembered seeing them creeping through back alleys, sleeping under bushes, scavenging in garbage bins, or begging with their deformities for a dollar or two to buy the next bottle, needle, or wire fix.

But that was before the Norma-gene messiah, Rielly Logan, brought his promise of salvation to the Nevada Quarantine and emptied New Hollywood of Norma-genes. So what was this guy still doing here?

"You're Harry Neuman, aren't you?" The man asked in that breathless, sexy, alto whisper, so characteristic of Norma-genes

"I'd know you anywhere," he added almost shyly and put a hand on Harry's sleeve. "I'm sorry to bother you, but a lady wants to talk to you, back there," he jerked a finger back up the street towards the corner. "She said it was real important. Gave me a twenty to come and get you."

It was probably a freelancer who hadn't gotten a pass to the interview, Harry thought. "Look," he said, gently disengaging himself from the hand on his sleeve. "I really don't have time for this."

The derelict reached in the pocket of his torn leather jacket and took out a thin, red, Plexiglas heart. It had another clear plastic heart in its center, with a hologram of Harry and Susan with their arms around each other looking young, happy, and in love. Harry recognized it immediately. He had bought it for Susan from a street vendor on one of their first dates. He knew that if you pressed the back of the inner heart, the two figures would come holographicly alive and his voice would tell Susan how much he loved her.

"The lady said I was to give you this if you wouldn't come. She said it might help change your mind." The man held out the heart, and after a moment's hesitation, Harry took it. He handled it gingerly as if he were afraid it might explode. He was especially careful not to press the back of the littlest heart. He hadn't thought she would save something like this or even remember receiving it. He felt a curious, sinking feeling. "Take me to her," he said resignedly.

14

Susan

The black limousine hovered near the curb around the corner and half a block down from the Eternal Life building. Its grav-units hummed softly as it bobbed gently in the down draft of traffic going by overhead. The limo was black metallic, the windows were polarized, black diamond glass, impossible to see inside. For a moment, Harry thought he saw something stir in the depths of the dark mirrored surface. An instant later a black, snarling snout lunged against the glass, slathering, fangs bared, trying to push its way through and rip out Harry's throat. The apparition was gone even before he recoiled in shock and bumped into the Norma-gene who stood behind him.

The man looked over Harry's shoulder. "Is anything wrong?" he asked, concerned. Harry stared at the black glass window. The apparition was gone, and his own scared reflection stared back at him instead.

A moment later, the back window whispered down and Susan leaned out smiling. She wore wrap-around, mirrored sunglasses. Her honey blonde hair was cut short beneath an elegant little nineteen forties, June Allyson hat with a black net veil. She wore a black tailored suit with a short skirt and a white silk blouse open at the throat. She wore no jewelry. She reached out a black gloved hand and gave the derelict something. He glanced at it quickly, grinned, and then turned and hurried away.

Then, she turned and looked at Harry from behind her black veil and mirrored glasses. "Hi, Harry. It's been a long time." Her voice was as soft and intimate as the rustle of silk sheets against naked skin. Her smile was full of promise.

Harry felt his heart pounding with conflicting emotions. He fought to keep his features impassive. Keeping himself intact, he called it. "Hello Susan," he said and was surprised at how normal, how under control his voice sounded. "Yeah, it's been a long time."

Susan pushed open the door of the car. "Won't you get in?" she asked.

Harry looked at her for a moment, at the invitation of the open door… "What can I do for you, Susan?" he asked without moving.

Susan leaned out of the door and cautiously looked up and down the busy street. "Harry, we have to talk," she said in a throaty, conspiratorial whisper, "and we can't do it here in the street. Please get in."

Harry didn't trust himself so close to her, in the intimacy of the backseat of a limo. Too many memories, too many tangled emotions, too much lost love, betrayal, and longing. "Look, Susan, just tell me what you want," he said patiently, trying to sound both concerned and reserved at the same time.

Susan reached out and touched his hand where it rested on the door of the car. "Harry," she said and there was so much repressed desire, regret, and longing in the way she said his name. Even through the soft leather gloves he could feel the touch of her fingers like an electric shock. He pulled his hand away. No! There could be nothing between them. She was another man's woman now. "What do you want?" he asked.

Susan sighed resignedly and leaned back into the shadows of the limo's interior. "I need a favor, Harry," her disembodied voice pleaded from the dark interior of the car. "Please," she begged when Harry did not reply.

Harry thought about the last five years, of all the loneliness, pain, and deaths he'd endured. He shook his head sadly. "I think I've just about used up all my favors," he said.

Susan leaned out of the darkness. "Please, Harry," she pleaded. "One last time." She reached up with a gloved hand and lifted the black veil from her face. Then she removed the mirrored sunglasses.

Harry gasped in shocked surprise. "Oh no! Who did this to you?"

She looked worse than Roger. Both her eyes were black and blue with a deep gash under her right eye, as if a large ring on the fist that did all this had caught and torn the flesh. It brought to mind the image of Roger's large fire opal signet ring with the engraved rising phoenix. He discarded the thought immediately. It was just too unbelievable.

Now that the veil and sunglasses were gone and Harry knew what he was looking for, he noticed that Susan's face was heavily made up to cover other cuts and bruises. "Oh no, Susan!" He shook his head in pity and sorrow. At the same time, he felt a slow burn of rage, starting deep down in the pit of his stomach.

Susan's eyes filled with tears and she looked away, back up at the glittering façade of the Eternal Life building towering in the distance. As she lifted her chin, Harry saw the angry bruises on her neck, as if someone had tried to strangle her. A blind, killing rage boiled up inside him. "Who did this?" he asked, his voice thick with clotted emotion.

Susan shook her head and refused to look at him. Tears ran down her face. Harry grabbed hold of her and turned her towards him gently. "Sue, tell me what happened," he said, trying to keep his voice calm and controlled and not doing a very good job of it. Susan bit her lip, scrunched up her eyes, and shook her head in shame and denial. She just kept sitting there shaking her head with the tears running down her face.

It was too much for Harry. He forgot all his resolutions of keeping emotional and physical distance and instead did the only thing he could do and took her gently in his arms and tried to comfort her. He could smell the familiar scent of her perfume, the soft touch of her hair against his cheek, the feel of her body leaning against his. He knew he was skating on thin ice. He could feel the old scars breaking open, the love and its betrayal that he had tried to bury through so many deaths… and he felt something else, something indefinable, something not right.

He brushed it away and said, "Susan, you've got to tell me who did this? Was it Roger?" he suggested doubtfully. But then he felt the tension suddenly go out of Susan's body, and she sagged against his chest, crying hopelessly and nodding her head.

"Roger did this?" he asked dumfounded. He'd always thought he knew Roger. The man may have been a ruthless son of a bitch in business, but Harry could never imagine him beating up Susan. It was obvious how much he loved her. Even Harry could see that. This just didn't make sense. "Are you sure?" he asked again. "Roger? But why? How?"

She tried to talk but her voice was a whispered sniffle. She fumbled blindly behind her in the back seat of the limo and at last found a package of tissues. She blew her nose and dried her eyes, and all the time she kept her head downcast, refusing to look at him, as if ashamed of herself for letting him see her like this.

She started to talk in a painful halting whisper. "I didn't have anyone else to turn to," she said. "I didn't know where to go. I think he's going crazy. He's not the man I… married." Her voice died away in hopeless confusion.

"Tell me what happened," Harry said. "From the beginning." Now, that she had started he had to keep her talking, he had to know.

"He didn't come home after the resurrection," Susan began in a hesitant whisper. "When he finally came back last night, he looked like he'd been in a fight. He said you did it. I guess I wasn't sympathetic enough, or maybe I didn't show that I believed him enough, or… Oh, I don't know! I'd been drinking. I guess I've been drinking a lot lately. So maybe I said the wrong thing. Anyway, he went berserk. Oh dear God! I thought he was going to kill me!" Her voice had a sharp, hysterical edge to it. She looked up at him with her bruised eyes.

"He kept hitting me again and again, and then, he grabbed me around the throat and started to strangle me. I managed to kick him in the balls and get away and locked myself in my room. I could hear him rampaging through the house, screaming and cursing and smashing things." She buried her face in her hands and wept in despair.

Harry held her gently in his arms until her sobs quieted. Slowly, she got control of herself and pushed away from him. She wiped the tears from her face with a tissue and looked at him with large, frightened eyes. "I'm sorry to bother you with this, but I didn't know who else to turn to. I had to talk to someone.

"It's not Roger doing this." She shook her head in emphatic denial. "It's something else inside Roger... something wearing Roger's body. It's not the man I married; it's something dark and evil and violent. It's not Roger," she repeated and kept shaking her head in denial.

For a moment, the memory of Roger leaning over him in the rebirthing chamber returned to haunt him. Once again Harry saw Roger's features elongate into a snarling, feral snout, becoming one of the black wolf-like things that had chased him through death.

Suddenly, Susan stiffened and pulled back into the dark interior of the car. "I shouldn't have come. I shouldn't be seen here like this. What if he sees us, or what if one of them sees and tells him?" There was a shivering note of terror in her voice as she drew further back into the interior of the car.

"One of what?" Harry asked in confusion. "What are 'they'?" he persisted.

Susan shook her head. "I can't tell you," she said. "They may be watching," she nodded at the Eternal Life building. "This is crazy! I should never have come." She reached out to pull the door shut, but Harry grabbed it and stopped her.

"Tell me what's going on, what you're afraid of?" he said.

Susan hesitated biting her lip indecisively. "Can I trust even you?" she asked, looking up at him with her bruised, frightened eyes.

Harry reached up to gently touch her cheek, but she shook her head and pulled away before he could touch her.

"Sue, you know you can trust me," he said with quiet steadfastness.

She looked up into his eyes as if searching for something. At last, she nodded and took a deep breath. "I'm going away," she said, "some place far away where even Eternal Life can't reach me. There are people who will help me for a price. They can get the monitor off my ka and give me a new identity north of the Seattle Firewall. There's clean wilderness up there, beyond the jurisdiction of the Empire and the power of Eternal Life. A person can lose herself there and start all over."

"Why? Who are these people?" Harry asked, careful to keep his voice neutral.

She studied him warily, trying to gauge how much to tell him. At last she said, "I'm leaving tonight, and I want you with me."

Harry stepped back and the breath whooshed out of his lungs. He felt as if he'd just been gut punched. Things were moving too fast. Was she asking him to go with her?

Susan read the look on his face and shook her head. "Not like that," she said with a sad, knowing smile. "I know it's all over between us that way, too much dirty water under the bridge. I need you there to…" she waved her hand vaguely. "To make sure nothing happens."

"You don't trust these people?"

"I'd feel better if you were there."

"Susan, if you have to get away I can get you…"

Susan put a gloved finger on his lips and silenced him. "It's all arranged. Just be there for me tonight. If you think there's something wrong, I'll pull out. I promise."

She looked fearfully up and down the street. "Harry, I gotta go now," she said and began to pull back into the car. "Just say yes or no. Either way I'll understand, but please don't tell anyone about meeting me today, promise."

Harry sighed resignedly. "Okay, just say where you want to meet."

She looked up at him, her eyes glistening with unshed tears. "Thank you," she said and reached into the car and opened her purse that lay on the seat beside her. She took out a piece of paper and a pen and quickly scribbled instructions. "I'll be waiting for you here, tonight, at eleven thirty. From there we'll go to meet my contacts."

She folded the paper and slipped it into Harry's hand, closing his fingers around it with her own. She held his hand like that for a moment and looked up at him. "Please don't fail me," she said and drew back into the dark interior and pulled the door shut. A moment later the car whined softly as it rose a few feet into the air and then shot away, climbing into the afternoon traffic.

Harry stared thoughtfully at the black limousine as it climbed into the distance and at last disappeared around a corner. Even after it disappeared, he remained standing there, sorting through his thoughts and feelings. Something wasn't right about Susan or her story. He remembered the indefinable sense of wrongness he felt when he held her. A quiet voice inside warned him to be careful, and he had learned from experience to listen to that quiet voice because it was seldom wrong.

On the other hand, this was Susan, and she needed his help. It wasn't something he could easily refuse. He carried a heavy burden of guilt for all that he had put her through. His blind stupidity had almost killed her and his drinking and woman-izing had killed her love and thrown her into the arms of Roger, who had... Once again he saw her battered face, the deep gash across her cheekbone, the dark bruises on her neck. He closed his eyes but the image remained to haunt him. There was no way he could have said no to her... and she knew it.

After a while, he unfolded the paper and looked at what

Susan had written. It was a set of grid coordinates for the automatic navigating system in his car, followed by what to do when he got there. Harry was familiar enough with the coordinates of the area to know that these were nowhere in New Hollywood. In fact, it looked like they were somewhere in the Sinks!

Just looking at them brought on that old, familiar, falling down an elevator shaft feeling. He hadn't been near the Sinks since that disastrous night seven years ago. Why did it have to be the Sinks, but he knew why. Where else were you going to get somebody to take out the monitor on your ka, get you past the Seattle Firewall, and give you a new identity? Any one of the rogue Tongs, Slavers, or even Seraphim could probably do it. All you needed was money, lots of money.

The only question was why would they even bother to keep their side of the bargain? Why not just take her money and then sell her south to one of the Slaver plantations in the Burn or maybe ransom her back to Roger… probably not a good idea knowing Roger… better to just deep-six her in the Trench.

And that's where I come in, Harry thought. I'm probably supposed to prevent all that. He shook his head. Susan, I think you've got me mixed me up with that blockbuster hero I once thought I was, but who never really existed outside of a whiskey bottle.

15

Black Ice Hype

Harry carefully refolded the piece of paper with the coordinates and stuck it in his pocket along with Jericho's note. One mystery on top of another, he thought.

He decided to walk to Chueh's. He needed time to think. He called his car on his wrist phone and had it return to the parking garage until further notice. Then he strolled leisurely down the street beneath the sun-dappled shadows of over-arching trees. With his battered baseball cap pulled down low over his eyes and the dark sunglasses on, he was comfortably anonymous in the late afternoon crowd that brushed by.

He stopped in front of a brightly colored store display and stood, looking without really seeing it. He took out the little plastic heart and held it in the light so that he could see the two tiny figures standing in its center, laughing happily for the camera. How young and innocent they looked, he thought, and suddenly felt a thousand years old by comparison. He knew that if he pressed the back they would both come to life, laughing and singing and mugging for the camera.

He remembered the day it had been taken as if it was yesterday. They had gone to the beach, out on the newly constructed boardwalk, eating hot dogs and ice cream. Just being together, in love, made the day magic. The sky was an infinite blue and the sea sparkled like diamonds. They had kissed and held hands and talked and laughed. Later, they swam in the moonlight and made love on the deserted beach with the distant glow of the boardwalk lights stretching out into the dark sea.

He suddenly remembered something else and his hand tightened around the plastic heart. "How did you know, Susan?" he asked looking at his closed fist. "How did you know that I would be coming out of Eternal Life by that side door? I didn't even know until five minutes before." It had been a spur of the moment decision after talking to Gibson. Yet Susan had been waiting for him. She even had time to find someone to intercept him. He opened his fist and stared at the holographic image. "How, Susan?" he asked, but Susan, frozen in time, looked out at him and laughed in the first flush of true love.

At last, resignedly, he pocketed the locket and looked up. He caught his reflection in the plate glass window and behind it… he stared at the reflection of the building across the street. It was one of the new Wolf Temples that were springing up all over the city. Religion had become one of the newest fads of the in-crowd and their wannabe hangers-on, especially this religion that offered the sacrament of black ice, one of the newest, nastiest drugs on the market. It was rumored it came out of the Sinks.

The Wolf Temple was a four-story, black marble cube, built on the same franchise model as all the other Wolf Temples in the city. It had no windows or decoration of any kind, just a broad, black marble staircase, leading up to a pair of inset brass doors at least ten feet high. A wolf's head pushed out through the center of each door as if the beasts had run headlong into them while the metal was still soft.

Harry turned and stared at those doors. Even at a distance, across a busy street, they filled him with atavistic fear as he remembered the black, ragbag shape that chased his ka down the resurrection trail and marked him with its claws. Before he got a glimpse of the true horror of what it really was, it looked just like a large, black timber wolf, like the one pushing through those doors.

At that moment, the wolf doors opened and a man stepped out. He put on a black Stetson hat and pushed it back high on his head. Then he stood at the top of the stairs with his hands on his hips and looked around with the proprietary arrogance of a king.

Harry recognized him immediately. Anton Shane was a minor

produce-director, specializing in low-budget horror flicks. Harry didn't particularly like him but the guy had given him his first, real movie break in a terrible remake of "The Creature from the Black Lagoon", that was, of course, set in the Sinks.

When Shane suddenly caught sight of him and waved, Harry smiled and automatically waved back and instantly regretted it. He groaned inwardly as Shane strode down the stairs and started across the street with a friendly smile stretched across his face. After all that had happened today, Harry was in no mood for exchanging gossipy pleasantries with Anton Shane.

Shane favored riverboat gambler black suits with string ties and black cowboy boots polished to a mirror-sheen. With his coarse black hair sleeked back with oil and a perfectly trimmed pencil-thin mustache, he was aiming for the outlaw image of a nineteen-thirties, Hollywood-style villain, with a derringer up his sleeve, five aces in his hand, and a glass of whiskey at his elbow.

It was said that "Shane" wasn't even his real name, that he had taken some old movie gunfighter's name to better fit his image. New Hollywood was all about image, he liked to say. You gotta have an image that sets you apart from the crowd, an image people will notice and remember. He never quite pulled it off... until now, Harry thought as he took off his sunglasses and studied Shane's approach.

This wasn't just a harmless hustler with an image problem. Shane had changed, and it had nothing to do with image. He walked with a kind of careless, dangerous swagger, that telegraphed a don't-give-a-shit attitude that was a little too real for the staid streets of New Hollywood.

People were scurrying aside, giving him a wide berth. They can feel it too, Harry thought. This guy was like an atomic pile with all its control rods pulled. Just watching him move, you knew he'd reached critical mass and was capable of anything, and he didn't mind letting you know it. In fact, he seemed to get off on letting you know it, but that didn't make it any less real.

Harry wondered what had happened. Shane had always been all show and no content, just a thin geek with soft features and bad skin, who had inherited a lot of money and wanted to play at making movies. He was still thin, but now he moved with the wiry grace of a mountain lion, and when he got closer, Harry noticed that his complexion had cleared and his too soft features had grown firmer. No, not firmer, Harry thought, but harder, crueler, more ruthless. Despite his bad-ass image, the old Shane wouldn't have hurt a fly, but this new version…

"Hi, Harry," Shane said, still smiling and showing a lot of teeth. "It's been a long time." Even his voice had changed. The old, irritating, nasal whine had deepened and darkened and reminded Harry somehow of rusty hinges and smoked whiskey. When they shook hands, Harry felt a flash of contact, like blood splatter across a high speed crash that made him instinctively recoil and pull his hand away. What the hell was that? He wondered.

Shane smiled knowingly. "You've changed, Harry," he said. "You're looking good. I heard you're on the wagon now."

"You've changed too, Anton," Harry said and didn't mean for the better. The man was strung-out on something. There was an oily sheen of sweat on his face and even standing still his body seemed to be prowling restlessly in place, stalking each passerby, his eyes glittering with feverish hunger.

"Yeah, I guess I have," Shane said with a manic grin. "You might say I got some of that 'old time religion'," he jerked his thumb back at the black cube of the Wolf Temple and laughed. It was a deep, throaty growl of triumph with nothing funny about it.

Harry decided he'd had enough weird for one day and flashed his best smile and looked at his watch as if he had an important engagement. "I'm sorry, but I've got to be going," he said. "It was good to see you again, Anton. Have a nice day."

"We're not done, Harry," Anton said and put a restraining hand on Harry's arm. As he did so, his suit coat opened and Harry caught a glimpse of a neural whip clipped in a tight coil at his hip. Neural whips were another nasty import from the Sinks. They were a sadist's wet-dream, capable of inducing unbearable pain at the flick of a switch.

Harry stopped and looked pointedly at the hand on his arm and then at Shane. Harry was notorious for an uncontrollable, hair-trigger temper when he was drunk. Sober he was a pussy cat; most people didn't know that and neither did Shane.

Reluctantly, he let go of Harry's arm, but his eyes smoldered with a barely contained rage that he smothered beneath an embarrassed grin. "Look, Harry, I'm sorry if I offended you. It's just I get so excited over what's happened to me that I sometimes forget that other people don't understand, or maybe aren't interested, in being remade."

Harry's curiosity was pricked. Despite his better judgment he asked, "Remade? Isn't that something that only Norma-genes do?"

Shane gave a short, barking laugh. "Not anymore," he said. "Look at me. I'm faster, stronger, healthier, and smarter than I've ever been in my life. He rolled his shoulders and stretched with feline grace and a soft purr of pleasure. "You can't imagine how good it feels having the body of a healthy animal, strong enough to take whatever it wants, whenever and wherever it wants."

He leaned a little closer to Harry and whispered, "Let me tell you a little secret, Harry. God is an animal, the biggest, meanest, bad-ass animal in the universe. I know because I've run with him. Together we've slashed, torn and drunk the blood of prey in the holiest sacrament of the hunt. And when you take that blood sacrament, it changes you in ways you can't imagine."

He looked past Harry into someplace only he could see. His eyes filled with infinite hunger. He licked his lips. "You can't imagine how wonderful it is," he whispered with breathless longing. "How clean and pure it is just being an animal. Life stripped to the bone. There's no self-doubt or guilt, no moral complexities, no good or evil, no should I do this or that. Life is so simple, so pure. There are only the primal imperatives to hunt, kill, feed, and fuck… life stripped to the bone and nothing else matters."

His eyes refocused on Harry, but the hunger in them remained and the oily sheen of sweat seemed to thicken and darken his features.

"You can't imagine," he repeated, in a voice filled with something akin to religious awe. He pulled away from Harry, shook his head as if to clear it, and shouted, "And that's what I call Old Time Religion!" Then, he threw back his head and howled with laughter.

Shane was as mad as a hatter and as dangerous as a rabid Rottweiler on steroids, and Harry wanted no part of him. Once again he tried to politely end this little séance. "This is all very interesting," he said. "And I'm sure it's done you a world of good but I really have to…"

Once again, Shane stopped him with a hand on his arm. "It's paradise, Harry," Shane whispered. "I can take you there."

Harry reached down and grabbed Shane's arm. The man looked at him with unconcealed contempt. Harry felt the corded muscles in Shane's arm tighten momentarily and was surprised at the strength they telegraphed. Shane wasn't kidding when he said he'd grown stronger. Then, he felt the other man relax his grip and Harry let go of his arm. "If you touch me again," he said, "I'll be forced to do something we'll both regret."

Shane turned away, but Harry could see the angry flush that further darkened his features. The man was breathing hard and there was a soft dangerous growl riding every breath. "Time to go," Harry said, and started to walk away.

"Don't you want to know what it's like there?" Shane asked. "Your ex-wife knows."

Harry stopped and turned around slowly. "What about my ex-wife?" he said, his voice low and dangerous.

Shane's lips twisted in a contemptuous smile. "That got your attention, didn't it?"

Harry felt a slow burn of anger ignite but tamped it down. "What about my ex-wife?" he repeated, as he slowly circled Shane, like a hunter circling a dangerous, unpredictable animal.

Shane suddenly got cagey, glancing up and down the street at the pedestrians, who were stepping far out into the street to get around him.

"Let me show you," he said, reaching into his jacket pocket and taking out what looked like an antique, silver snuff box. Shane flipped open the lid of the box, and Harry slid cautiously closer and glanced inside. A spikey, black crystal about the size of a large gum ball lay on a bed of purple velvet. The spikes sparkled like black diamonds in the dappled sunlight.

Shane broke off one of the spikes and tried to hand it to Harry. Harry shook his head and stepped back. "What is it?" he asked, although he was pretty certain he knew already.

"Black ice," Shane whispered, his voice a reverent caress. "It'll take you to where you want to go."

"And just where is that?" Harry asked impatiently. He was getting tired of Shane's games.

"The same place we all go," Shane said dreamily as he stared down at the spiked ball of black crystal. "We could take it together, you and me," he suggested and then shook his head. "No, it's better to take it first in a big group. Then, we can all cross over together and hunt in a pack.

"You have no idea. It's so unbelievable. You've never felt so alive, so powerful, so pure, as when you hunt down your first kill and rip out its throat and feel its hot blood spray across your face.

"And after the pack feeds, we fuck," Shane's voice fell into a soft crooning. "You've never fucked like that before. I guarantee it. It's pure, unbridled, animal lust, with no restrictions, no moral qualms, no brake of conscience. Everything is allowed up to and including torture, rape, and murder of innocents." He giggled and gave Harry a sly knowing look, a confidential wink and nudge that said, "We're both men of the world. We know what the score is, don't we?"

When Harry didn't react, Shane took it as a kind of tacit agreement and continued. "We always invite a group of unsuspecting wannabes that we can use as sexual prey." He sighed, "Their innocence is so delicious. Those that survive the evening can even become part of the pack.

"Sometimes, in the morning, I wake up covered in blood and bites and scratches." He seemed to be talking to himself, his eyes turned inward on that other world. "Sometimes the blood is my own and my muscles ache, and maybe there's a dead body or two beside me," he gave a sigh of pure surfeit. "And I feel so wonderful, so clear, and clean, so powerful and pure."

He looked up at Harry and saw the horror and revulsion on his face and shook his head. "Don't worry," he said. "It's not really murder. They all just resurrect again. Don't you see? Eternal Life and black ice, together, have given us the ultimate freedom to be the beasts we truly are." Then he opened his arms wide, did a slow, soft shoe pirouette and roared with laughter.

Pedestrians, who had been making a wide detour around him, glanced over nervously and then looked down and hurried away.

Harry had just about had enough. He grabbed Shane by his jacket lapels and shook him. "What about my ex-wife? What about Susan?"

Shane's face took on a trapped, furtive expression that he instantly buried beneath a look of aggrieved surprise. "What about your ex-wife?" he said defiantly. "I don't even know her! I just said that to get your attention." He held out the spike of black ice. "You need to take this, Harry."

Harry looked at him through a red haze, as if all the blood

vessels in his eyes had burst. "Maybe you want me to be one of your new crop of wannabes," he said.

Shane stepped back and put up his hands as if to pacify him. "Hell no, we'd never do that to you. You're special. I mean, you're Harry Neuman! Hell, we'll even let you make the first kill. You can even pick out the wannabes you want to use beforehand."

Harry hit him. Shane never saw it coming and neither did Harry. Something just snapped inside him, and the next thing he knew, Shane was sprawled on the pavement with one hand over his nose and blood spurting between his fingers.

Harry forced himself to turn and walk away. He knew that if he stayed he would keep on hitting Shane until there was nothing left but bloody pulp.

He had not gone more than a few paces before a whip lash snapped around his neck and he was dropped into boiling oil, his skin was flayed from his body and he was rolled in salt as every nerve screamed in unbearable agony.

Without thinking, Harry threw up a pain block and a moment later stood on the other side of an impregnable glass wall, watching a firestorm of pain rage through his nervous system.

He staggered against the tug of the whip that was lashed around his neck. The son of a bitch hit me with that neural whip, he thought, and it's short-circuiting all the pain receptors in my body!

Slowly, he turned and grabbed hold of the flat, black whip cord where it wound around his throat. Then he looked at Shane.

Shane stood with the butt of the neural whip in his hand and a look of dawning disbelieve on his blood-smeared face. Harry smiled and that smile turned Shane's look of disbelief into instant terror. Frantically, he pressed the button on the butt of the whip as Harry slowly unwound the cord from his neck.

Shane realized the whip was useless and panicked. He threw the butt at Harry and turned to run away. Harry caught the butt in midair, pressed the activate button, and flicked the whip. The cord snaked out and slapped around Shane's neck. He stiffened in midstride and then began shaking uncontrollably, as if he had just stepped on a live high-tension wire.

Harry dropped the whip with the switch still on. Then he turned and walked away as Shane toppled over backwards, his mouth open in a silent scream. His body convulsed in paroxysms of pain, his boot heels jitterbugged against the pavement and his back arched up as if it had been broken over a log. He foamed at the mouth and his bladder let go and there was no escape.

Harry didn't even bother to look back. Instead he called his lawyers. Let them take care of it. They were used to cleaning up his messes.

16

The Church of She

Later, as he was crossing an intersection, he happened to glance up and caught sight of the great She Cathedral, devoted to the Goddess in her twin aspects of warrior-defender and compassionate mother of the world. The cathedral had been built on a high jungle ridge, right after the Caliphate War, when the towers of New Hollywood were nothing but a distant glitter on the horizon. Now, the cathedral seemed to float over the city, like some kind of ethereal snowflake with its white marble walls and high alabaster arches rising out of the steaming jungle mist. Those delicate arches supported a great golden dome that looked as weightless as sunlight. The cathedral was considered one of the most beautiful buildings in the Empire, and Harry could not help but compare it to the squat, black cube of the Wolf Temple and its sick, predatory god.

He didn't belong to the Church of She, but he knew the Goddess was real because he saw her every time he died, beckoning to him with love and compassion and a promise of everlasting peace. He was beginning to suspect he'd also met the sick, predatory god of the Wolf Temple, chasing him down the resurrection trail of his last rebirth.

According to the first Book of She, the bible of the Church, the Prophet General of the Goddess led her armies against hordes of demons and fallen angels in a cosmic war that mirrored the struggles of humanity during the Crash. As he turned down a little side street that ran down to the sea, Harry wondered if maybe those hordes of demons and fallen angels were rising again, and their prophets here on earth were men like Anton Shane.

17

Follow the Yellow Brick Road

The little cobblestoned side street looked like something out of mid-twentieth century Miami Beach, all chrome and glass, set in pastel blue or pink stucco with soft, curving art-deco lines. A rustling row of palms trees lined the street that ran down to a white, sandy beach. People dressed in casual beachwear strolled past elegant boutiques or sat beneath brightly colored parasols outside exclusive bistros.

About halfway down the left side of the street the buildings gave way to a high, whitewashed, stucco wall, topped with a peaked row of red Spanish tiles. The faint blue ionization halo of a high-density, security repeller-field rippled along the top of the tiles like a gigantic, ghostly snake. Beyond the wall Harry could see the top of an old apple tree and beyond that the roof of a large, elegant, town house. All window dressing, he thought, nothing but window dressing.

He strolled over to a little wrought iron gate set in the wall. Behind the gate was a short, enclosed passage. It led back towards the garden but then turned a sharp corner, blocking any view of it. On the outer wall beside the gate was a simple bronze plate with the word "Chueh' discreetly engraved.

It all looked so staid and respectable that Harry couldn't help smiling because this was the entrance to Heaven's Gate, the near-mythical secret garden of the most powerful Tong Godfather in New Hollywood. Entrance was by invitation only, and only those select few who met Chueh's personal criteria got in. It was said that even the Emperor had to wait almost two years before he was finally admitted.

Harry wasn't sure what Chueh's criteria were, but they must have been pretty eccentric to open the gate after only a couple of weeks to a scandal-ridden movie star has-been while the Emperor was left to cool his heels for two years. Harry was under no illusions that it had anything to do with his sparkling personality. He suspected the only reason he got in was because Jericho wanted him in, and Jericho and Chueh went back a long way.

As he was about to lift the gate's wrought iron latch, he caught a glimpse of something out of the corner of his eye that made him instinctively step back and look up. A man dressed in the simple hooded robe of a za-zen monk was floating serenely over the repeller-field that ran along the top of the wall. He was turned half away with the hood pulled up so that Harry couldn't see his face. He sat in lotus position with his back ramrod straight, radiating the absolute stillness of deep meditation. Harry was sure he hadn't been there before.

There was nothing unusual about the sudden appearance of a levitating monk in Chueh's garden. Heaven's Gate formed the perfect framework for such oddities. At any one time Chueh had dozens of such holographic follies scattered around his garden like surrealistic signposts on the road to nirvana. What was strange was finding one in public, outside of the Garden.

Just then, the monk turned his head and threw back the hood of his robe, and Harry stumbled back in surprise. The monk's face was covered with the star-shaped scars of a Norma-gene, and not just any Norma-gene, but the one who had taken him to Susan. The Norma-gene looked at him, raised a warning finger, and disappeared.

One of Chueh's holographic follies? Harry doubted it. How would Chueh know about the Norma-gene? And if in some improbable way he did, what was he up to? And if not...? Harry stared at the spot where the Norma-gene had been and wondered what the hell was going on? He finally decided the best way to find out was to ask Chueh, although the odds of getting a straight answer weren't always that great.

He turned back to the gate and lifted the wrought iron latch.

After a momentary resistance, the gate swung open with a welcoming creak. Deceptively welcoming, he thought, because Chueh's wasn't for everyone, and even if you were welcome one day, you might not be welcome the next. If not, the little wrought iron gate would not budge. Harry had no idea how Chueh determined if you were welcome or not. He had been refused admittance a few times and could never figure out why.

One thing he did learn, when he forced the gate once, was that it would eventually open, but when he walked down the passage and around the corner, he came out not in Chueh's secret garden but in the little overgrown garden of the town house that he could see from the street. After a little while, a brawny gardener appeared and told him he was trespassing and asked him to leave. Harry didn't try to force the gate again, even though he was refused admittance for almost two weeks afterwards. He figured it was Chueh's garden and Chueh's rules... whatever they were.

The gate closed behind him with a discreet click and he followed the enclosed passage back to where it turned the corner and after five or six feet disappeared into an impenetrable wall of fog. Just before it dissolved into the fog, someone had scrawled on the inner wall, "SAY GOOD-BYE TO KANSAS, DOROTHY".

"You can say that again!" Harry grinned and stepped into the fog. For a moment, the mist swirled around him as cold as an arctic blast. Then, he stepped out into warm sunshine someplace between Middle Earth and the Magic Kingdom. The walls that guarded Chueh's, the enclosed passage, even the frigid wall of fog were all gone and in their place was a vast panoramic landscape.

No matter how many times he came here, this view never ceased to fill him with wonder. He found himself standing on the edge of a high cliff, overlooking a wide flood plain with a broad, lazy river snaking through it. In the distance, a range of hazy, humpbacked, Chinese mountains faded into a powder-blue horizon. The mountains seemed to float in midair, as their rich, green, shadowy valleys slowly filled with mist. It was like being inside one of those exquisite Chinese landscape paintings from the classical period that Chueh was so fond of.

But no painting could be this real, Harry thought. He could feel the cool breeze blowing up from the edge of the cliff, bringing with it the heady scent of pine and cedar mixed with the tang of wet earth and blossoming wild flowers. Above him a pair of eagles rode the thermals into the blue-violet stratosphere.

He turned slowly to the south, following the edge of the cliff with his eye. It seemed to go on for miles before meeting the sheer, granite slope of a mountain. In actual fact, it did go on for miles. Harry knew because he had walked it one day out of curiosity, but when he reached the distant slope of the mountain, he discovered he could go no further. As he started to climb it, he suddenly found himself walking back down again. He tried again and the same thing happened. Every time he reached a certain point a little way up the slope, he would suddenly be facing in the opposite direction, walking back down. It was the oddest, most impossible of sensations.

But no more odd or impossible than all this, he thought, letting his eyes follow the slope of the mountain up and around to the west, where it met the slope of another mountain. Cradled between them was a green upland valley, with the silver thread of a stream spilling down to the cliff on which he stood. In the distance beyond the valley, framed between the two mountains, rose an enormous snowcapped peak. It towered so high that he almost had to lean back to see the top. Now, how did you fit something like that into the back garden of a New Hollywood townhouse?

He asked Jericho about it once and the old man replied, "Have you asked Chueh?" When Harry said, "No", Jericho nodded and said, "Don't", and that was that.

Harry took a deep breath of the cool, clean mountain air and felt tension knots in his neck and shoulders loosen as muscles relaxed. The Garden always had that effect on him. No matter how bad the day had been, and today had been particularly bad, Chueh's garden always took the edge off it. The place radiated profound peace. He could feel his whole body settling into it as his mind gradually quieted down and the events of the day slid away into silence. This was what Chueh's garden was all about, he thought.

Jericho told him that Chueh had hired the greatest landscape artists and feng shui masters to create just this effect. Here every hill, river, and lake was part of a perfect pattern whose sole purpose was to bathe the senses and mind in such peace, harmony, and beauty, that the busy, busy stresses and strains of daily life were washed away, leaving the mind free to settle into the quiet depths of itself, perhaps even down to where the ka waited at the door of the spirit realm, a non-space usually reserved for shamans, saints, fools and madmen. He sometimes wondered which category he fitted into. After all that had happened today, he was tempted to linger here and maybe find out, but he had to meet Jericho and was already late.

A worn path that led from the edge of the cliff up through a small alpine meadow offered the quickest way across the garden to where he knew Doc was waiting in Chueh's legendary Silver Slipper Saloon. There was another more direct entrance to the Silver Slipper but it was many miles away on the other side of the city (another one of Chueh's impossibilities). By cutting across this corner of the garden, he had less than a mile.

He strode across the meadow and dropped down into the forested valley beyond. The forest hadn't been there the last time he had walked through here. Harry just smiled and accepted it. Chueh liked to move the furniture around every once in a while.

The feng shui masters and landscape artists had created what Chueh considered to be a baseline on which he could build, and he was constantly remodeling after some inscrutable plan of his own, or maybe just for the hell of it. The trees, rocks, or buildings in his garden could be real or just computer controlled repeller fields, textured to feel like the real thing and then wrapped in a holographic sheath of light and color.

Chueh was a master at the art of sculpting repeller-fields, and it was almost impossible to tell his creations from the real things. Of course, he had the backing of the most powerful nano-quantum computers in the Empire and a staff of the best and brightest programmers to carry out his ideas. Harry imagined him like the great Disney, striding through his studio filled with artists and technicians eager to turn even his wildest fantasies into reality.

In his garden he was like a playful god, molding and remodeling, creating any environment he felt appropriate. Sometimes, Harry had a feeling that this reworking of reality was ongoing, purposeful, and aimed at specific individuals as they wandered through the garden. The sometimes absurd or shocking holographic follies that Chueh scattered across his garden were only the most obvious examples of this.

Harry noticed that the forest trees were mostly mountain oak and cedar, moss covered and twisted with age. Suddenly, an Alice in Wonderland, Cheshire cat materialized in front of him. For a moment, it hung by its tail from the branch of an old oak tree and then slowly disappeared into a broad, keyboard grin. It was Chueh's signature image, the artist signing off on his work. Harry had seen it many times in scattered places across the garden and touched the brim of his baseball cap in a casual salute of recognition.

The forest was so skillfully constructed that it looked like it went on for miles, but after a few hundred feet, the dirt path became raked gravel, and he pushed through a stand of bamboo into a classical Japanese garden that he recognized from the last time he was here.

A small brook fed into a little, looking-glass pond filled with lily pads. A simple wooden bridge arched over the brook. The clearing was surrounded by overgrown bonsai conifers. Harry heard the faint reverberation of temple gongs and spotted the familiar pavilion of a brightly colored Shinto temple set back among the trees. The mountain rising over it was new, one of Chueh's holographic follies, a distant view of Mount Fuji lifted straight out of a Hokusai print. It rose in silent, stately majesty out of a sea of clouds that blended seamlessly with the surrounding sky.

Two young businessmen sat beneath an overhanging willow tree on the opposite bank of the pond. They had their trousers rolled up with their bare feet dangling in the cool water. Harry was surprised to see them. You could usually walk through Chueh's garden and not see anyone.

That was one of the garden's attractions. It offered privacy and security in a mind-expanding environment. If you wished to meditate or hallucinate undisturbed, Chueh's provided holographic privacy screens complete with repeller-fields to create a bubble of serene, private beauty. If someone happened to stray off the paths, he might wander across an open forest glade only to suddenly come up against the soft invisible wall of someone's privacy shield. The glade would still seem to stretch away before him, but it would be impossible to go any further.

The two young men sitting with their feet in the water were either another of Chueh's follies or just not concerned about privacy. They had a large ornate hookah set up between them and puffed contentedly on the stems of brightly colored hoses attached to the pipe. As Harry crossed the bridge, he caught the heady whiff of gen-grass, genetically modified marijuana. Thanks to twenty-first century genetic engineering, it was one of the strongest hallucinogens known.

The men were obviously "gen-grass plumbers". One of them looked up and gave Harry a big, goofy grin. Then he raised his hand in ultra-slow-motion and waved. Harry wondered what the gen-grass plumber thought he was seeing, Puff the Magic Dragon, maybe?

As he followed the path across the grassy bank and reentered the forest, he heard the gurgle of the hookah and then rippling, high-pitched giggles, like the twitter of rare, exotic birds. He shook his head with a tolerant grin. Thank god, that the old war on drugs was only a nasty four hundred year old memory, on a par with the Salem witch-hunts or the inquisition, he thought.

Far from stopping drugs, the war created vast, criminal financial empires that rivaled the largest multinational corporations or even the combined assets of some nation states. These empires fueled the world-wide corruption of civil society that was one of the major factors contributing to the wars and financial chaos that finally ended in the Crash.

When society rebuilt and redefined itself in New Hollywood, one of its cornerstones was the absolute right of every citizen to self-determination over his own body and what he put into it or took out. But like with the use of weapons, this right of self-determination carried an absolute responsibility. There was no cop-out plea of "I didn't know what I was doing because I was high, drunk, or temporarily insane". You made the initial life-style choice and you paid the consequences.

Although drugs of every kind were now legal, cheap, and readily available, Chueh's garden catered only to hallucinogens. Harry suspected this was because hallucinogens were seen as a necessary part of many religious paths, providing invaluable initial insight into higher states of consciousness.

From what he had seen, Heaven's Gate resembled a kind of adult theme park or enormous, quasi-religious art form, appealing not only to gen-grass day-trippers, but also to a clientele that was looking for something beyond pure physical and material gratification. It was a place where spiritual seekers could come and experience an environment maximally conducive to their special needs. Sometimes, like Harry, they hardly even knew what they were looking for when they first entered the garden.

Harry wondered, not for the first time, why a ruthless Tong Godfather like Chueh built a place like this. It certainly wasn't for the money. The chosen few who were invited into his secret garden were never asked to pay for the privilege. When rumors of his garden began to surface over ten years ago, people laughed and called it, "Chueh's Looney Tunes". They didn't say it too loud or laugh too hard though. Chueh was, after all, the most powerful Tong Godfather in the Empire and his word carried more weight than God's in New Hollywood.

But when a hardheaded kingpin decides to build a secret garden park, you couldn't blame people for thinking it was a joke, that maybe the old man had grown senile and, like Brando's Mafia Godfather, decided to take up gardening instead of killing, although no one said that out loud either.

Harry knew for a fact that Chueh was a long way from senile, and his garden was definitely no joke, but what it really was and how and why Chueh built it remained a mystery.

He wondered if Chueh knew about what was going on in the Wolf Temples. From what Anton Shane said, it sounded as if the Temples were a kind of obscene parody of Chueh's Garden. Instead of opening a person to a higher state of consciousness, they used black ice, violence, and death to call forth a predatory beast-god in their worshippers.

Although the Tongs controlled the drug trade in New Hollywood, they didn't control black ice. From what Harry heard, it came in through the Sinks and the Seraphim were distributing it. Now, it looked like they were distributing it through the Wolf Temples. If that was the case, Chueh would know. He'd make it his business to know.

As he continued to follow the dirt path through another forest glade, Harry suddenly came across a large black "X" splashed across the ground in front of him. He stopped in surprise and looked around. As far as he could see, there didn't seem to be any reason for the mark. The path on the other side of the "X" looked no different than this side, but this was Chueh's...

As soon as he stepped over the "X", the forest glade disappeared and the dirt path became a narrow, yellow brick road, winding between rolling hills and fields of bright red poppies. In the distance he could see the shimmer of the Emerald Towers of OZ. It was typical Chueh.

As he followed the yellow brick road up over a hill, he spotted an old black man dressed in bib overalls and a blue work shirt, sitting cross-legged in the field of poppies. He was chanting softly to the slow, rhythmic beat of a tom-tom he held between his legs. Harry recognized him immediately.

Samuel Kade, doing what Samuel Kade does best, he thought. Kade was a big, raw-boned man with long, straight, black hair tied in a ponytail and a face like a rough-hewed, ebony slab. He was also a shaman trance-walker and was working with a very stoned client at the moment.

Probably trying to lead him through the levels of a heavy acid trip, Harry thought, as he eyed the "client", lying spread-eagled among the poppies. He wore khaki Bermuda shorts and a wild Hawaiian shirt and lay with his eyes wide open, staring beatifically up into the blue-violet stratosphere. A hypodermic stuck out of his outstretched arm. Harry could see the skin-colored button patch of a "root canal" where the needle went in.

There were easier, more effective ways of getting drugs into the body, but nothing beat the outlaw romance of shooting up with a good old-fashioned hypodermic. And the little button patch of the "root canal" was "the perfect accessory before and after the fact" as the advertisers loved to say. No more of those unsightly needle tracks up and down the arm, no more collapsed veins and jabbing searches. With a handy little "root canal" you kept a vein open and ready for action all the time. Your one-stop convenience store, so to speak. Just stick the needle through the self-sealing membrane and shoot up. It was a clean, efficient, and self-sterilizing sure-fire seller for the man who had everything. And this guy had obviously had the works. Lost in his own blue heaven, he didn't move a muscle as Harry walked by.

Nor did Kade acknowledge his presence, and Harry respected that. Kade was working and up until a month ago, he had been working with Harry. The work started on the first day Jericho took him to Chueh's secret garden, introduced him to Kade, and then left without another word. Kade asked a few terse questions and looked him over like a sculptor examining a piece of wood to see how the grain ran and whether there were knots or signs of rot or disease. He'd probably heard all the stories about Harry but chose to suspend judgment and accept him as a work in progress. In the next few months, he taught Harry not only how to shift his waking awareness to his ka but to actually unite with it and trance-walk through the door of the spirit realm and out onto the edge of the Astral Planes or into the shallows of the Shining Sea of Gods and Demons.

Then about a month ago, he told Harry that he could take him no further. "I've got more important things to do than waste my time teaching you what you already know or can find out by yourself," he told him. Then he shook his hand and added, "Good luck, son. It's been an honor." Harry didn't quite know what to make of the, "It's been an honor," but said the feeling was mutual and hadn't seen Samuel Kade again until today.

If I'm really seeing him, Harry amended. This tableau could be nothing but another one of Chueh's holographic follies, like the whole Wizard of Oz setting. If it was, then putting Kade into it wasn't coincidental. Chueh didn't do coincidental. He was telegraphing a message. If it was meant for Harry, he wasn't getting it. Sometimes the old man's pose of oriental inscrutability telegraphed nothing but inscrutability, Harry thought.

He continued to follow the road down around a high, rocky outcrop to where a bullet riddled wooden sign sagged from a post beside the road. A vulture, sitting on the sign, spread its wings and flapped into the sky with a raucous screech. The sign said, "Welcome to Bardoville, Population..." The rest was shot away. Harry looked up at the emerald city towering in front of him and then back down at the sign. "Bardoville?" He shook his head and grinned. It's more like "Say good-bye to Oz, Dorothy".

He stepped past the sign and the yellow brick road turned into dust and tumbleweed, and the emerald towers shimmered into an ersatz, nineteenth-century Mexican border town straight out of a Sergio Leone, spaghetti western. Horses stood tied to hitching rails along the empty, dusty street. The wind blew hot and dry, and he could taste the alkali grit in his mouth. He stood facing the mottled, cracked, adobe façade of a Mexican cantina. A pair of batwing doors led into the cool, dark interior. A weathered sign hung over the door, proclaiming, "The Silver Slipper," in a hand painted scrawl of black letters.

He had arrived, end station. In all the time that he had been coming to Chueh's, through all the permutations of landscaped follies, this façade, like his initial view from the cliff, never changed. Harry crossed the road and mounted the boardwalk in front of the cantina. Behind him a dry ball of tumbleweed blew down the middle of the street. He pushed through the swinging doors and stepped into The Silver Slipper.

18

The Silver Slipper

Harry paused just inside and looked around. He hadn't realized how much he missed the place. He and Jericho used to come here after every resurrection. In the beginning though, they went to local bars. It was Jericho who first suggested this might be a good way of escaping the clinical, impersonal atmosphere of the usual Eternal Life debriefings.

After they finished hashing through the last resurrection, they would sometimes sit nursing their beers, letting the conversation flow along the path of least resistance and most interest. These talks gradually laid the foundation for a deep friendship based on mutual trust and respect. It was this friendship, more than anything else that helped Harry pull through the worst times after the disintegration of his marriage.

Then, about six months ago, when he learned to die and began manifesting the first signs of those profound changes that nonstop resurrection was making in his body/mind, Jericho decided that perhaps a local bar might not be the best place to talk about these things. He suggested that they adjourn to Chueh's saloon instead. A couple months later, Jericho intro- duced him to Chueh's Secret Garden and Samuel Kade.

After that, his visits to The Silver Slipper became less frequent, and it had been a while since he'd stopped in but the place hadn't changed. It never did. It still looked like a movie-set saloon right out of the Golden Age of Hollywood westerns. A long, polished mahogany bar with a brass foot rail ran along the left-hand wall with brass spittoons strategically placed on the sawdust-covered floor. The bartender was a thickset, balding giant with an enormous handlebar moustache and biceps like Christmas hams. Behind the bar a large mirror in a baroque, gold frame reflected an eclectic collection of brightly colored bottles.

Wooden tables and chairs were scattered around the room and a row of comfortable leather padded booths ran along the opposite wall. A large window beside the batwing doors showed a view of the dusty, western street Harry had just left. A wagon wheel chandelier hung from the ceiling, and a flight of stairs led up to a wooden balcony with doors opening off it at regular intervals. A couple of dance hall girls in low cut velvet gowns leaned over the balcony rail, smoking cigarettes, talking quietly, and showing a lot of cleavage. To one side of the stairs, a man sat at a battered piano, casually fingering the keys. He had a derby hat cocked on his head, a cigarette dangling from the side of his mouth, and a half-empty glass of whiskey within easy reach. The soft, melancholy strains of "As Time Goes By" rippled from his fingertips.

Beneath the balcony a pair of ornate batwing doors opened into another impenetrable wall of fog. Harry knew if he walked through it, he'd come out in front of an armored brass and diamond glass door that opened onto a busy street on the far side of New Hollywood.

There were only a few customers at this time of day, and the saloon had a cool, twilight intimacy. A group of men sat around a large corner table playing cards. A dance hall girl, with her back to Harry, leaned over the shoulder of one of the gamblers and whispered in his ear. Two women in dark business suits sat in one of the booths talking intimately and nursing their drinks. There might have been people in the other booths, but if they had their privacy screen drawn, you wouldn't be able to tell.

None of these were the real customers, Harry thought. The real customers were upstairs. The group of men playing cards at the corner table had the heavy-lifter look of bodyguards killing time, while the two women in dark business suits, who kept glancing nervously up at the closed doors along the balcony, were probably clients, competitors, or possibly deadbeats whose fate was being discussed in secrecy behind the holographic illusion of that balcony with its dance hall girls and closed wooden doors.

The Silver Slipper sold secrecy and security. If you wanted to buy a politician, sell a corporate secret, have a liaison with the Emperor's wife, Chueh's was the place to come. It sold discretion, absolute, one hundred percent, satisfaction-guaranteed discretion, and it sold it to anyone willing to pay its capricious and sometimes outrageous admittance fees.

Despite this, The Silver Slipper never lacked customers. People with secrets to bury were more than willing to pay whatever Chueh asked because they knew The Silver Slipper was impregnable. Nothing that was said or done here ever got out, unless the client wanted it out, and no one and nothing got in unless Chueh wanted it in. Harry had concluded long ago that the place was impregnable because, like The Secret Garden, it wasn't in the "real" world and so nothing in the "real" world could touch it.

On the other hand, the business of The Silver Slipper was not the business of the Garden. Even though you might have free access to the Garden, you didn't have free access to The Silver Slipper. You paid for that just like everyone else. Only Jericho and Jericho's guests were the exception. They were always welcome and never paid.

Harry spied Chueh, sitting in a dark corner at the end of the bar, smoking a long, bronze opium pipe. He regarded Harry's entrance with the heavy-lidded serenity of a satiated boa constrictor. He was small-boned, slightly built, and looked hummingbird-delicate. But like everything else at Chueh's, looks could be deceiving, and Harry knew for a fact that the old man was as hard as nails. He had the strong, long-fingered, hands of a concert pianist or a professional strangler. His wispy, white chin-beard gave him the appearance of an old Chinese sage, but he wore his steel gray hair braided in the long pigtail queue of a

Tong Godfather.

Harry walked over and bowed deeply. "Master Chueh," he murmured respectfully as he felt a privacy screen close around them. "It is an honor to see you again."

"Hi, Halley," Chueh said, affecting a grossly exaggerated, Chinese laundry-man accent. "Velly, velly good to see you again in my most humble establishment." He bowed his head slightly, hands clasped across his stomach. Then still bowed, he looked up sideways at Harry and winked. It was typical Chueh, a laughing Buddha dressed in a denim jacket, blue jeans, and snakeskin cowboy boots, who knew where all the bodies were buried because he put them there.

Chueh, you old bandit," Harry grinned as the old man straightened up and gave him a high five. "How are you doing? Jesus, I've missed this place. How could I have stayed away so long?"

"I don't know, but is a most grievous insult," Chueh said shaking his head and falling back into his Hollywood movie Chinaman role. "Next time I send leg breakers along to remind you maybe, chop, chop, huh?"

Harry shook his head in delight. "You've been watching too many of those old Charlie Chan movies again," he grinned.

"Can there be too many Charlie Chan movies?" Chueh asked with a mischievous glint in his eye. "Old Chinese proverb say, 'A Chinaman in the hand worth two niggers in the woodshed'."

"Now what the hell is that supposed to mean?" Harry asked, nonplussed at Chueh's verbal end-run into absurdity.

Chueh bowed deeply. "Is for me to know and you to find out," he said inscrutably. "You looking for Doc?"

"Yeah, is he here yet?"

Chueh eyed him coolly. "He's been waiting for you for over half an hour." The tone of reproach was unmistakable. Chueh and Jericho had formed a kind of cantankerous, old man's mutual-admiration-society that demanded absolute respect and took quick offense at the slightest hint of neglect. They had both refused resurrection and said they were determined to live through every stage of life to the end and talked glowingly about the peaceful balance, wisdom, and self-knowledge that came with an old age free from the raging, ragtime drives of youth.

Harry was never sure how serious the two of them were about all this, but he played along anyway, murmuring exaggerated, abject apologies for being late and bowing again and again until Chueh slapped him lightly on the side of the head and said, "Don't overdo it Harry.

"Doc's waiting for you upstairs." He turned and broke the privacy shield.

"Mae will show you up," he said and called, "Mae," so softly that only Harry should have been able to hear, but this was Chueh's and of course things worked differently.

The dance hall girl leaning over a gambling bodyguard straightened up and turned. She was a striking platinum blonde dressed in a white, low cut gown that looked like it had been shrink-wrapped to her body. She cocked her head coquettishly and winked acknowledgment. Then she leaned back and whispered in the gambler's ear and they both laughed. Her ample bosom brushed his shoulder with enticing promise, and he half turned and pulled out his wallet. Then he peeled off a couple of bills and stuffed them down her ample cleavage. She patted his cheek and let her fingers trail languorously along his neck as she walked away.

Her hips swayed with unconscious sensuality while the white silk gown displayed every wonderful curve and jiggle. Harry pursed his lips in a silent whistle of appreciation.

"Mae, this is Harry," Chueh said as the woman came up. "He's one of my special customers."

Mae eyed Harry for a moment, her big, blue eyes smoldering with chained passion while a slight, ironic smile played across her lips as if she was secretly laughing at herself. "The famous

Harry Neuman," she said in a husky whisper. "I recognized you as soon as you came in." She gave Harry her hand. "You've made my day, Harry," she said with a little hiccup of laughter as Harry took her hand and raised it to his lips. The hand was soft, warm, and alive to the touch, and he gave a little start of surprise as he realized what she was. He kissed her hand gallantly and said, "The pleasure is all mine Miss…" he hesitated, uncertain.

"West, Mae West," she said. "Shaken not stirred," she added, with a playful toss of her long blond hair.

"Of course," Harry murmured. "How stupid of me. You make an unforgettable impression."

"Excuse me, Mae," Chueh broke in politely, "Harry and I have some unfinished business; then I want you to show him up to Doc's suite. Maybe you can get yourself a drink in the meantime."

Mae gave Chueh a little pout of dissatisfaction, and then turned to Harry with a dazzling smile. "I'll be looking forward to taking you upstairs, Harry," she said with enough sub-vocal promise to make a sailor blush.

Harry watched her walk back down the bar. Just before she stopped, she cast a look over her shoulder, just to let him know that she knew he was watching.

Harry smiled and shook his head in appreciation. "This time you outdid yourself," he said to Chueh.

"How did you know?" Chueh asked, dropping any pretense to his laundry-man accent.

"She's perfect," Harry said.

"How did you know?" Chueh repeated

"No one else would have even guessed," Harry assured him.

"How, Harry?" Chueh repeated patiently.

"She's alive, soft, and warm. She's all woman, but there's no ka."

"Ah!" Chueh sighed in acknowledgement. "Of course, you would know."

"For a while there she had me fooled. I really did think she was real. Then, I took her hand and I couldn't feel her ka. She's an eidolon, isn't she?"

Chueh nodded impassively. His face was like old, yellowed parchment that had been crumpled up and then smoothed out again, leaving a deep, webbed tracery of wrinkles.

"I've never met an eidolon this lifelike before," Harry said. "The movement is in perfect synch with the holographic image and the skin texture and feel of the repeller-field were perfect. I could feel the warmth and pressure of every finger. No one's ever gotten an eidolon this lifelike before. How'd you do it?" he asked.

Chueh shook his head. "She's Doc's baby, and even more special than you think. She could walk out of here with you and go anyplace you wanted to take her."

This knocked Harry back on his heels. An eidolon was only a hologram projection, clothing a repeller-field to give it solidity. A computer programmed with the personality matrix of the eidolon coordinated movement between the holographic projection and the repeller-field. All this hardware was bulky and external, projecting a solid image of limited range and quality. An eidolon shouldn't be able to go any further than the equipment that supported it before the image atrophied.

If what Chueh was saying was true, Harry could take Mae home with him or to the other side of the planet, and she would remain just as life-like. "How?" he asked.

"Doc came up with the idea of putting the hologram projector and repeller-field inside the image instead of having to project it from twenty feet away."

"You lost me there. Where inside? How?"

"Doc created a package about the size and shape of a slightly flattened football. It contains a miniaturized holo-projector, repeller-field generator, super-quantum-nano computer, sensor array, and zero-point energy pack, all wrapped in one of those little personal grav-units that baby's wear when they learn to walk. The whole thing weighs less than a kilo and fits inside the chest cavity."

Harry shook his head in disbelief. "The computer power you would need to create and maintain such a lifelike repeller-field and synchronize it with a moving holo image is... is..." He couldn't find words to cover this.

"We could never have done it without the new super, nano-quantum computers and their near infinite capacity," Chueh conceded. "They contain the latest AI programs coupled with a deep personality construct of the eidolon. It's self-evolving and able to extrapolate new behavior-patterns within the constraints of the original personality."

"Like Marta," Harry said, thinking about the nano-quantum computer and AI that Doc had installed in his car. "Only you've given her a human body."

Chueh nodded. "In a way Marta was the proto-type," he said. "Doc thought she was so perfect that all he had to do was reprogram the personality substrates. Like Marta, all eidolons can and do make their own independent decisions governed by the hardwired failsafes encoded in the Robotic Laws that make it impossible for them to kill or injure a human being."

"That's it!" Harry said excitedly. "You've created the perfect robot. No gears, wires, struts, or moving parts, just a football-shaped unit inside the hollow shell of a repeller-field. This has the potential to turn the world upside down! It's as revolutionary as resurrection technology, maybe more so."

Harry looked around to make sure their privacy shield was intact. "How many other people know about this?" he asked.

"Me, Doc, his research staff, and a few others who will not talk," Chueh said.

"That's it?" Harry asked as the implications of this began to sink in.

"Yes," Chueh replied quietly, his eyes hooded.

"I am honored by your trust," Harry said and bowed deeply.

He was also uncomfortably aware that he was in way over his head. Why would the most powerful Tong Godfather in the Empire trust someone like him with a secret like that? It didn't make sense and that scared him.

"Time to go now, Harry," Chueh said. He broke the privacy shield and called Mae back. "Don't keep Doc waiting any longer."

Harry hesitated.

"Is there something else?" Chueh asked with mild reproach.

Harry shrugged. What have I got to lose, he thought. I'm already in over my head.

"I saw something strange at the entrance to your garden," he said.

Mae approached and Chueh waved her discretely back. The privacy screen closed around them again. Chueh cocked a questioning eyebrow at Harry, took a deep drag on his pipe, and waited.

Harry told him about the Norma-gene he had seen levitating just outside the entrance to the garden. He kept his word to Susan and didn't mention their meeting. Instead, he finessed the truth and said that it was the same Norma-gene who had approached him earlier, begging for money outside the Eternal Life building.

When he finished, the old man nodded, his face expressionless. Then he fumbled in the pocket of his denim jacket and fished out a pair of old-fashioned horn-rimmed spectacles straight out of the nineteen-fifties. When he perched them on his nose, there was an almost instantaneous flicker as Chueh accessed his own private data-sphere. The spectacles flashed the results of his query directly onto his retinas, along with audio commentary. To an outside observer Chueh was just relaxing, smoking his opium pipe, his eyes hooded in peaceful contemplation.

Harry looked around. Mae had gone back to the other end of the bar. The gamblers on the other side of the room were still at it. One of them in particular caught his attention. He was dressed like a cowboy and sat in the corner facing the bar. His wide-brimmed, white Stetson was pushed back on his head as he studied his cards. He was a big, raw-boned, handsome man, with a curl of black hair falling over his forehead. It took Harry a moment to realize he was seeing another one of Chueh's eidolons, this one the classic Hollywood cowboy hero, John Wayne. The other four men were just what they seemed, under-world heavy hitters waiting for their bosses to conclude their business upstairs.

"Interesting," Chueh mumbled at last and looked up.

"And?" Harry asked, trying to hide his impatience.

"And you were right," he said. "Here, take a look." Chueh looked directly into Harry's eyes. The spectacles seemed to film over for a moment and then cleared, and suddenly Harry was looking at the street scene in front of the entrance to Chueh's garden. He could see himself stop and look up a second after the Norma-gene appeared above the wall.

"You're certain that's the same Norma-gene you met earlier?" Chueh asked after the scene replayed to the finish.

Harry nodded. "Yeah, no doubt about it."

"Hmm," Chueh said, chewing thoughtfully on the stem of his pipe. Finally, he looked up and asked. "What do you know about Norma-genes, Harry?"

Harry shrugged. "As much as the next guy, I suppose," he said.

"You know who Rielly Logan is, don't you?" Chueh asked with a hint of exasperation.

"Sure, he's supposed to be the new messiah of the Norma-genes."

"And?" Chueh prompted.

"And about twenty years ago, he led ten thousand Norma-genes from Old Chicago across the Continental Quarantine to the promised land of Las Vegas. He set up his own country there, strictly for Norma-genes, and he's pulled just about every

Norma-gene out of New Hollywood and everyplace else with a promise of giving them a new healthy body, remaking them in the image of their dreams."

Harry stopped. Chueh gave him a disappointed, "is that all you got" look.

Harry sighed. "From what I've heard, he can really do it."

Chueh waited, but Harry didn't have anymore. Norma-genes and their new messiah were not on his top-ten hit list of things to know.

Chueh frowned. "You should go and see Doc now," he said. "Then come back and see me afterwards." He broke the privacy shield and gestured to Mae.

Harry bowed respectfully; and as he turned to go, Chueh added, "And Harry, you might want to keep up on the news better."

19

An Eidolon's Request

Mae led him up the stairs and through the holographic image of the wooden balcony that, like so much at Chueh's, wasn't really there. Instead, they turned down a silent, softly lit corridor with silk carpeting on the floors and a hint of opium in the air. He wondered in passing if the smell was real or if Chueh had added it just for atmosphere. The walls on either side were rice paper and bamboo with sliding doors reminiscent of a Japanese tea-house or maybe a Chinese opium-den.

Mae had been strangely silent on the way up. Now, she stopped in front of one of the doors and turned. "Here we are, Harry," she said and gave him a bright, professional smile. It lasted all of two seconds before collapsing into a wounded little girl sob. There were suddenly tears in her eyes. "How did you know?" she asked. "Please, Harry," she pleaded when she saw him hesitate. "I have to know what I did wrong."

Harry looked into those pleading tear filled eyes and thought, but you're only a computer programmed eidolon, a holographic image wrapped around a repeller-field. How can you be feeling this?

"Please, Harry."

Harry wondered what Chueh would make of this and then thought, screw it. He took Mae gently in his arms and whispered in her ear, "You didn't do anything wrong. You're perfect. No one else would even suspect."

"But you knew," she protested.

"That's because I'm..." he groped for the right word, "...different. You see, I can feel people's ka, and you didn't have one."

"That's all?" she asked brightening up and smiling. "Then I

didn't do anything wrong? Oh, Harry, I'm so glad." And she leaned over and kissed him on the lips.

"Now, that definitely felt like the real thing," he said, slightly flustered. "But can you tell me how you knew I knew?"

Mae rolled her big, china blue eyes heavenward as if to say, isn't it obvious, and then she sighed. "A girl just knows that kind of thing." Then she patted him on the cheek, turned and sashayed down the hall.

20

So Many Questions, so Few Answers

The sliding door, like the walls, seemed to be made of flimsy rice paper stretched over a delicate bamboo frame. In reality, these "flimsy rice paper" walls and doors were built of armored spider-spin on a titanium steel frame with reinforcing repeller-fields and were more solid than a bank vault. The Silver Slipper may have been impregnable, somewhere not on this earth, but Chueh believed in being thorough and always having backup.

Inside, the rooms had state of the art privacy curtains that were guaranteed bug proof. Whether it was a delicate business meeting, a discreet lover's tryst, or high political wheeling and dealing, Chueh's always guaranteed complete privacy, discretion, and security.

A mini grav-camera, hanging like a large pearl above the door, swooped down and looked Harry over. Then he heard the click of the latch being released. As the door slid aside, he realized that Doc wasn't alone. A young woman sat across the table from him, studying an open electronic notebook.

She didn't look up when Harry came in. Her short, black hair was parted in the middle and fell like raven's wings on either side of her bowed head, concealing her features. Harry quirked a questioning eyebrow at Doc.

"Come on in!" The old man grinned. "Don't just stand there gawking."

Chueh prided himself on offering his clientele a wide range of beautifully appointed rooms in all sizes and decors. To his eternal disgust, Doc and Harry made a habit of choosing late twentieth-century truck-stop. This came complete with worn, green linoleum floors, dirty beige walls, maroon-colored vinyl upholstered benches, and marbled green Formica-topped tables with little chrome record-selectors, containing the top jukebox hits from well over four hundred years ago.

The plate glass window on the opposite side of the room usually looked out on a parking lot full of long-haulers, but today Doc had opted for something altogether different in the "dry landscape" of one of lost Japan's most famous gardens, the Ryoanji near Kyoto. The fifteen stones scattered across a bed of raked, white gravel were starkly enigmatic and somehow deeply moving. The late afternoon sun cast long shadows across the gravel ridges and furrows, turning them into silent, standing waves.

Harry wondered why Doc had chosen this particular scene. The contrast between the truck stop interior and the outside "landscape" was like one of those cryptic Zen koans, like "one hand clapping", he thought, as he sat down beside Jericho.

At that moment, the woman across the table closed the notebook and looked up at Harry with frank curiosity, and his heart skipped a beat.

His first impression was of some exotic Botticelli Goddess, a Celtic Aphrodite maybe. Her skin was pale cream, her face a perfect oval. The nose was perhaps a little too long, but her eyes had an elfin tilt and were a startling jade green. She wore just a hint of ruby lipstick that accentuated the contrast between the cool cream of her skin and the jet black of her hair that fell straight and thick, cut in a curve to her chin.

She was elegantly dressed in a cobalt blue silk blouse, open at the throat, black silk "coolie" trousers and black patent leather ankle boots. She wore a pair of silver earrings shaped like crescent moons. A fine silver chain and locket were just visible in the open V of the blouse.

Harry stared spellbound. It had been years since the sight of a woman had moved him like this. In fact, not since Susan, he thought nonplussed and looked away, feeling strangely guilty and embarrassed.

The woman tilted her head and smiled with a kind of sympathetic amusement as if she was used to having this effect on men.

Harry glanced over at Doc. The old man tried to keep a poker-face but was obviously enjoying Harry's discomfiture. He cleared his throat theatrically and said, "Harry Neuman, may I present Miss. Diana Lloyd. She's got an interesting story to tell. I think it might throw some light on what happened to you last night."

"Please just call me Diana," she said with a slight, unidentifiable accent and offered him her hand.

Harry felt an almost electric jolt as their fingers touched. Her grip was firm and cool with surprising strength in the long tapering fingers. A moment later, he felt her gently pull her hand away and realized that he had been just standing there holding it.

He pulled his hand back in confusion and looked at Doc for help. He should have known better. The old man rolled his eyes like a lovesick Casanova, and Harry could hear him humming the wedding march under his breath.

"Okay, Doc, cut it out." He laughed and sat down next to the old man.

"Cut what out?" Jericho asked with wide-eyed innocence.

Harry turned to Diana and grinned. "You got to excuse him," he said and put his finger to his temple and made little circular motions. "Old age, you know. It catches up with you after a while."

Diana smiled uncertainly and then put a hand to her mouth to stifle a laugh as Doc idiotically crossed his eyes and drooled his tongue out of the side of his mouth.

"Don't encourage him." Harry laughed. "Or he'll be hamming it up all day."

Doc straightened up and became as serious and dignified as a mortician at a mayor's funeral. "When I was a child, I spoke as a child," he intoned sonorously. "But now that I am a man..." He winked and pulled the cord of an imaginary steam whistle. "WO-O! WO-O!" he said.

"Wo-o, wo-o? What's wo-o, wo-o?" Harry threw up his hands in mock despair. "Jesus, Doc, you're incorrigible," he said.

"Incorrigible, but smart as a whip and charming to boot," Doc added in a whispered aside to Diana.

Harry shook his head in despair and turned to Diana. "You see what I have to put up with," he said. "If I..."

He had just time to think, "Oh shit, it's happening again!", as a black snout pushed out of Diana's face. Her voice became a low, rumbling growl as she bared long, yellow fangs slathered with spittle. Her raven black hair became a gleaming black pelt as her whole body transformed into a huge black she-wolf.

Harry shoved away from the table and pushed to his feet with his heart pounding and his breath a bellow's roar in his ears. Fear, anger, and a wild, inhuman blood lust, fought inside him. He felt a low growl start in the back of his throat. His muscles bunched to spring. He looked down at his hands clawing the tabletop and saw instead the paws of a gray timber wolf, his arms shaggy with matted fur.

The shock was like a splash of ice water. "My God, what's happening to me?" His voice growled and he felt the timber wolf draw back at the sound of his voice, at this recognition of human identity. The sharp claws slid back into his fingertips. The pounding blood lust lifted like a red veil and his mind cleared. A last, deep growl gurgled into a soft moan of relief.

"Easy, Harry," Jericho said. "Just take it easy. Whatever it is, it's not real."

Harry looked over at Diana. She was standing on the other side of the table, her face flushed, her hair disheveled, her breath coming in jagged gasps. A dark shadow lay across her face. He watched the shadow lift as she regained control. She heaved a deep, shaky sigh and ran her fingers through her hair.

She looked over and gave Harry a tentative smile. "Sailor, you sure know how to show a girl a good time," she said with a quaver in her voice that belied the quick bravado of her words. "Do you have this effect on all the girls you meet?"

Harry admired her spirit. He realized this was her way of getting it all back together and played along. "Only if they're beautiful, elegant, and intelligent," he said.

"Then I guess there's something to be said for ugly, sloppy, and stupid." She laughed and the tension eased.

Jericho watched this by-play with a kind of bemused fascination. Harry hadn't looked at another woman like that since his divorce and despite the numerous stories of his sexual escapades, he'd been living like a monk for the last six months. Now, he was actually flirting. Jericho grinned, and with the wrong woman. This could get interesting.

Harry turned. "I sure hope you've got some answers, Doc," he said and stopped when he saw Jericho's grin. "Come on, Doc!" he cried with an angry no-nonsense edge to his voice. "This isn't funny anymore. We just turned into wolves!"

"No, you didn't," Jericho said.

"We both saw it," Diana said

"I can assure you both, nobody turned into a wolf," Jericho said. "You growled and spit at each other like animals but no one turned into one."

Diana took a deep breath and closed her eyes. She sat perfectly still, not breathing.

Harry sent Jericho a questioning look. The old man shrugged.

Finally, she gave a deep sigh and opened her eyes. "Jericho's right," she said. "We didn't turn into wolves".

"Then what happened?" Harry asked, looking from one to the other. The question covered more than just wolves now. It looked like Diana had just trance-walked into her ka for a few seconds to check out what had happened. She shouldn't be able to do that, he thought. I can't even do that. The only person he knew who could was Samuel Kade, and he was a professional shaman trance-walker.

"I'm not sure what happened," Jericho said and looked meaningfully at Diana.

She ignored the look and said, "There's only one thing that Mr. Neuman and I have in common that might tie us to the wolves..."

"Of course!" Doc said.

"Of course what?" Harry asked.

"Patience," Jericho said and turned to Diana. "My dear, do you mind?"

She hesitated a moment and then unbuttoned the sleeve of her blouse. When she rolled it up, Harry saw four, long, angry, red welts, slashing across her forearm.

"You recognize them?" Jericho said.

Harry nodded, too stunned to answer. They were the same scars he had seen in the mirror while dressing.

"She's got more scars across her shoulder," Jericho said as Diana rolled down her sleeve and buttoned it.

Harry looked at Diana. "How... Where?" he asked.

Diana shook her head and turned away.

"Later," Jericho said. "First tell us how you got yours. What happened the other night?"

Harry looked at Diana again. She refused to meet his eye. Instead, she stared out the window, her face a closed, impassive mask. He shrugged. "Sure, why not?"

He told them what happened, choosing his words carefully. When he finished, he added, "They're not wolves. They may look like them at first but that's an illusion they hide behind. I caught a glimpse of what they really are just before the spin-generator caught my ka. I think the leader of the pack got caught in the event horizon of the spin-generator and it tore away the body, or whatever it is it was wearing, just before it clawed me." Harry looked at Diana and Jericho. His eyes had a haunted, bruised look. "Believe me, they don't look anything like wolves," he said. "They don't look like anything from this world."

"Because they're not," Jericho said.

"But what are they? Where do they come from?"

Jericho looked over at Diana who nodded imperceptibly. "They're the advance scouts of an alien army," he said. "They come from another dimension, or maybe an alternate universe. They started riding into our world on the backs of resurrecting kas...

"So all the rumors are true about Eternal Life losing people," Harry said.

Jericho nodded. "But that's only one of the doors they use now to enter our world and it's not always a reliable one," he said. "They've got a powerful ally in the Nevada Quarantine who opened the original door to them over twenty years ago, and we never even knew it," Jericho added with surprising bitterness, as if for some reason he should have.

Harry began putting it together in his mind. Nevada Quarantine meant Norma-genes. He thought of the Norma-gene that had materialized at the entrance to Chueh's garden, and he remembered Chueh asking him what he knew about Rielly Logan. "This mysterious ally wouldn't happen to be a Norma-gene by the name of Rielly Logan, would it?" he asked.

Jericho winked at Diana. "The boy's not as dumb as he looks!"

Harry grinned. "You sure know how to bring out the best in people, Doc."

Jericho gave a self-deprecating shrug. "It's a talent," he said and asked, "How did you get it so fast?"

Harry shrugged. "It's a talent." He laughed. Then he told him about meeting the same Norma-gene outside the Eternal Life Building and later at the garden entrance. Once again, he left out any mention of Susan. "Later Chueh asked me what I knew about Rielly Logan," Harry concluded. "And I just put two and two together."

He was tempted to tell Doc about Susan and what Roger had done to her, but he'd promised her. Besides, he realized he would feel slightly shy and a little embarrassed talking about Susan in front of this other woman. Instead, he decided to talk to Jericho later. It was a decision he would live to regret.

Jericho was perceptive enough to know that Harry wasn't telling him everything and eyed him skeptically.

Harry shot a quick glance at Diana and shook his head imperceptibly.

Doc got the message and leaned back and steepled his fingers thoughtfully. "I wonder if they know we're here," he said thoughtfully.

"Why would they care?" Harry asked.

"It's a long story," Jericho said and then changed the subject. "It sounds like they're keeping an eye on you, Harry."

"Could be just a coincidence," Harry suggested without much conviction.

Doc pursed his lips and shook his head. "I don't think so? Not right after the wolves made a run at you in your last resurrection and almost succeeded."

"They tried twice before, I think," Harry said.

"So-o-o," Doc leaned forward, rested his chin on his fist, and looked at Harry. "You never told me," he said.

Harry shrugged. "I didn't think it was important. I wasn't even sure they were there the first time. The second time they were nothing but indistinct shadows. I outran them both times. Besides, we haven't been doing a lot of comparing notes lately."

He didn't mean it as a reproach. When the old man placed him under Samuel Kade's care, he'd also agreed to butt out and let the trance walker take over Harry's training on the assumption that too many cooks spoiled the soup. The upshot was that even though Jericho was present during the last few months at Harry's resurrections, he held no debriefings afterwards.

"Did you tell Samuel about these things chasing you?" Jericho asked.

Harry shook his head. "He wasn't interested in my resurrections. He said that wasn't why I was there." He glanced over at Diana and wondered how much he should say and how much she already knew.

Jericho saw his glance and waved it aside. "Kade was right," he said resignedly. "That's not why you were there."

Harry could hear the tone of self-reproach in Jericho's voice and said, "No use spilling over cried milk." He grinned. "Besides, I beat them and I'm here now."

"You not only beat them," Jericho said. "You saw them for what they really are. I don't think they liked that. I think after you got away this last time, they began to suspect that maybe you were something special."

"Special?"

"Special meaning beyond you being the famous, 'Harry Neumann'," Doc said. "They're looking for a prophecy. Maybe they're beginning to think you're it."

"What kind of prophecy?"

"They call him the 'King of the Dead'. You've died enough times to be called that, don't you think? According to their seers, he's the only one standing between them and the conquest of earth."

"Come on, Doc, you're mistaking me for one of those block-buster heroes I played. People are doing it all the time."

Jericho shook his head and smiled. "Maybe I am, but I don't think they are," he said. "In the beginning, they probably figured you for a pushover. They'd just capture your ka during a resurrection, ride it piggy-back into your body, and take possession. You'd be a valuable asset for them if you came through it intact, with your memories, behavior patterns, and whole personality gestalt under their control. To anyone outside you'd just be Harry Neuman, but inside they'd be pulling the strings and, the worst of it is, you could be conscious of what they were doing with you and couldn't stop it, even if what they were doing made you sick with disgust."

"Oh shit!" Harry muttered and closed his eyes, trying to shut out the vision of Susan's battered face. All of a sudden, what had been bothering him about Susan's story made sense. Roger would never have hurt Susan. He was devoted to her and loved her deeply. It had taken Harry a long time to finally admit that to himself. Roger could never beat her up like that, not if he was in his right mind.

"It's not Roger doing this," Susan said. "It's something else inside Roger... something wearing Roger's body. It's not the man I married. It's something dark and evil and violent. It's not Roger."

No, it wasn't Roger, Harry thought, and now he knew what it was. Roger had resurrected quite a few times. They must have gotten hold of his ka then. No wonder Susan was desperate to get as far away from him as possible.

"Harry, are you alright?"

Harry opened his eyes and looked up at Jericho. The look of concern on Jericho's face bordered on fear. Harry put on one of his carefree, don't-give-a-damn, Hollywood hero grins. "Don't worry Doc, there's only me in here," he said and tapped his head. "No aliens allowed."

"What is it, Harry?" Jericho asked.

Harry shook his head. "It's nothing Doc really, just bad memories out of my checkered past." There was no way he could tell him about Roger without telling him about Susan.

He looked at Diana and upped the wattage on his grin. "Besides, you've probably read all about it in the gossip columns. They should be paying me royalties."

Harry saw a look of distaste flicker across her face. Then her eyes narrowed suspiciously. Smart lady, she wasn't buying it and neither was Jericho. Harry decided to change the subject. "From all the rumors I've heard, it sounds like there was a good chance I wouldn't have survived wolf possession intact."

Jericho nodded. "It's not always their best door into this

world. Every time they fail to take complete possession, one of their soldiers is left trapped inside unable to get control, with his personality and his host's leaking into each other. It's madness."

"So, how long have you known about all this?" Harry asked. "And how come you didn't warn me?"

"I didn't warn you because I didn't know about any of this until last night, when Diana and her sister came to my island compound and asked me for help."

Diana gave an almost imperceptible start and shot a quick glance at Jericho.

The old man isn't telling me everything, Harry thought. "According to Roger, you didn't leave my side the whole time I was unconscious after I resurrected," he said unable to keep a sudden edge of suspicion from his voice.

Jericho nodded noncommittally.

"You just said you didn't know anything about this until Diana came to you at your house, last night," Harry said. "So how could you be in two places at once?"

Jericho leaned back and regarded Harry. "Do you trust me, Harry?" he asked.

For the first time, he had to think about that. Jericho was his best friend. He had pulled him out of the gutter and given him his life back. "Of course I trust you," he said, but realized that his trust was no longer unconditional.

Jericho was perceptive enough to pick up on this and sighed resignedly. "You met Mae West, I gather?" he said at last.

Harry nodded, wondering where this was going.

"She was one of my earliest successes," Jericho said. "She keeps surprising me, constantly upgrading her personality with every detail she can find on her original and then assimilating it into her core personality and extrapolating from there." He smiled like a proud father.

"She's beautiful," Harry said and reined in his impatience. Jericho sometimes had a roundabout way of getting to the point but he always got there eventually.

"The next logical step, of course, was to make an eidolon of myself," Jericho said. "It turns out he's surpassed my wildest expectations. He's the newest, most powerful, self-referral quantum AI, much like Mae and your Lady of the Road," he added, referring to the AI in Harry's car. "But unlike either of them, my eidolon has a living person to model his character on. He constantly monitors my every move and gesture, analyses my speech patterns and shifting moods, mimics every idiosyncratic character trait. He's perfect, Harry. He even fooled Chueh, and he and I have known each other a long time."

"So it was your eidolon who took in Diana and her sister last night," Harry said. "But why did she go there in the first place? She must have known I'd resurrected and you'd be here with me. Everyone in the Empire knows that; it's become a tradition."

"Because she knew all about my eidolon," Jericho said irritably and left it at that.

Harry was tempted to push but decided Jericho wasn't going to be pushed. The old man was stubborn, secretive, self-contained by nature, and seldom told all he knew. One of the pillars their friendship built on was that Harry accepted this and trusted that Jericho had the best of intentions and would always tell him if there was something he needed to know. So why was he having a problem with it now?

He glanced at Diana. She was studying him closely.

He looked away. The problem with unconditional trust is that once you begin to question it, you can't stop, he thought. "You founded Eternal Life," he said. "You must have been one of the first to hear the rumors about people not coming back from resurrection or coming back insane. Didn't you suspect anything?"

"Of course, I heard the rumors," Jericho said. "I even got letters from concerned relatives screaming about satanic possession and the curse of resurrection. But I thought they were just like all the other crank letters and rumors I've seen and heard through the years, maybe a bit more graphic and desperate but..."

Jericho shrugged and spread his hands palms up. "What can I say? I ignored them. I told myself they were just part of the usual rebirth trauma and weren't my concern. I was finished with Eternal Life. I'd moved on to other things. It was Roger's show now. Oh, I made a few discreet inquiries when the rumors surfaced in the papers. I even confronted Roger..."

Harry snorted sarcastically. "I bet that helped a lot."

"Not a lot," Doc agreed.

"I'll bet," Harry growled.

Doc looked at him sharply. "Don't go jumping to conclusions, son," he said softly. "Things and people change. They're not always what we think they are."

Harry looked Jericho in the eye and said, "Amen to that," in a voice dripping sarcastic accusation.

21

Jake Lloyd's Daughters

There was a strained silence in the room. Diana studied a line of storm clouds forming over the Ryoangi Garden, and Jericho stared at the far wall, tapping his finger irritably on the table.

Harry realized he'd let his unfounded suspicions push him over the line. Jericho was his best friend. He'd answered all his questions. If there was something between him and Diana and these wolves he didn't want to talk about, that was his business. And that leaves the ball in my court, he thought.

"I'm sorry about that," he said. "It was uncalled for."

Jericho turned and looked at him for a long moment. Finally, he nodded to himself as if he'd seen what he needed to see. "Apology accepted," he said with a terse smile.

"Good," Harry said. "Now maybe you can tell me about these wolves. You said they come from an alternate universe or timeline. How is that possible, and what do they want with us?"

"What they want is to enslave and eat us," Jericho said. "Believe me, these things are the boogeyman of everyone's worst nightmare. As to how they got here." He glanced over at Diana, who nodded her head as if giving permission. "You have to know something about Isis and the work she did with Norma-genes."

"Who's Isis?" Harry asked.

Doc looked over at Diana. "Why don't you tell him," he said. "She is, after all, your sister."

Diana nodded and took a deep breath, like a diver getting ready to go off the high board. "Isis is not only my sister," she said, "she's my twin sister. We're identical twins."

"Interesting," Harry said.

Diana raised a questioning eyebrow. "And?" she asked.

Harry shrugged. "And nothing special, except that you were

both named after the twin aspects of the Goddess." He noticed how her eyes widened with surprise that he should know this. So just to hammer the point home he added, "Isis is the Egyptian goddess of motherhood, compassion, and healing and wears a sun disk diadem. On the other hand, Diana is the Moon goddess, goddess of the kingdom of the dead, and goddess of the hunt. Some say it's a hunt for dark knowledge. They also say she could be a merciless, vengeful, bloodthirsty bitch," he added and cocked a quizzical eyebrow. "Is that true?" he asked with exaggerated innocence and a provocative grin. He wasn't sure why he was baiting her, but it probably had something to do with secrets and trust or rather lack of trust.

Diana gave a twitch of her shoulder as if shrugging off an irritating insect. "We were named by the Goddess," she said with cool distain and paused as if daring him to make another comment. "She came to my father in a dream on the night we were born and named us. The significance of the names and the naming was not lost on him. My father was after all a classical scholar," she added with a touch of bitterness. "In an age that had no use for classical scholarship."

Harry was busy putting two and two together. "Your father wouldn't happen to be Jake Lloyd?" He asked excitedly.

Diana looked surprised. "Why, yes," she said. "You know of him?" she asked it as if she had trouble believing that.

Harry cast an amused glance at Doc and nodded. "I've read a couple of his books."

"How interesting," she said giving a little, skeptical twist to her words. "What have you read?"

She was testing him, of course. He was used to it. People just couldn't seem to accept that a movie star, action hero, with a reputation for womanizing and drunk and disorderly behavior ever read anything but the funny pages.

"We're waiting, Mr. Neuman," she said with a schoolmarm's questioning tilt to her head as if waiting for the dimmest bulb on the tree to fail.

"Sorry, wool gathering," he said, flashing her a crooked grin, and then added, "*Shaman Games, Saints and Sinners, The Mythology of Enlightenment,*" and tossed in half a dozen others for good measure. He was showing off of course and Doc rolled his eyes despairingly, but Harry didn't care. She irritated him with her smug, superior assumption that he couldn't possibly know about her father and probably couldn't even read! He was a little surprised at his reaction. When other people did the same thing, he just laughed it off, but this was different because it was her and for some reason that made it painfully personal.

Diana arched her eyebrows in surprise and looked at him with genuine interest. "What did you think of them?" she asked.

"Interesting," he said giving the words a skeptical twist of gentle rebuff.

Diana looked at him with confused embarrassment. "I'm sorry," she said. "I didn't mean to..."

"It's all right," Harry said, "I'm used to people seeing only the cardboard cutout, media image. Besides, this prodigious erudition is really only skin deep. For most of the last seven years, I was exactly what everyone expected of a brawling, drunken womanizer."

Once again, he noticed her look of distaste, quickly hidden but not quick enough. He decided it was time to change the subject. "What made you go to Jericho's in the first place?" he asked. It was obvious they had a history, and he had been wondering about it ever since he got there.

"I don't know what you mean," Diana said, momentarily caught off balance by this sudden change of direction.

"It sounds like you and your sister were in some sort of trouble with the wolves and the Norma-genes. So why did you run to Jericho for protection? You could have gone to the authorities."

Diana cast a sidewise glance at Jericho. Once again Harry had the feeling that they were weighing out the truth, deciding how much to short-change him.

"We're waiting, Miss. Lloyd," he said, mimicking her voice from earlier. It was a petty ploy born of irritation and anger. Once again it was a matter of trust. She and Jericho didn't trust him and it rankled.

Jericho was perceptive enough to realize what was happening and said. "I'm an old friend of the family."

"So you knew Jake Lloyd?" Harry said.

Jericho nodded.

"And you never told me?"

"You never asked."

"That's the lamest excuse I've ever heard."

"It's the only one you'll get."

Harry shook his head in disbelief. Jericho knew how important Jake Lloyd's writings were to him. Shortly after he revealed the strange abilities that constant resurrection was calling forth, Jericho gave him a copy of *Shaman Games* with the comment, "This might help explain what's happening," and it did. Harry devoured the book and asked for more and Jericho obliged with a whole stack of Lloyd's books. In those early days when he was just beginning to realize what was happening and could easily have been terrified, doubting his own sanity, these books became invaluable guides. They showed him that others had experienced these things; lots of others throughout history had walked this road before him. They were called mystics, shamans, seers, and saints. The most recent one had been the Prophet General of the Goddess, who founded the Church of She. They all had the same thing in common. They had walked in their kas out onto the edge of the Astral Planes or the Shining Sea of the Gods or whatever other form this magical non-space might take and it changed them. They were no longer ordinary men.

Lloyd seemed to have an intimate, even encyclopedic

knowledge of all this, and his books referred back to hundreds of pre-Crash sources, documenting a rich tradition of knowledge and firsthand experience. More than anything else, it had been Lloyd's writing that had given Harry the intellectual strength to take his first step into his ka and out and into the spirit realm, together with Samuel Kade.

Harry looked at Diana. She smiled uncertainly.

"I'm in awe of your father," he said at last. "He was a giant. I wish I'd met him. No one in the Empire measures up to his boot heels."

"In fact, no one in the Empire cares," Diana said. "His books have been out of print for years."

"I think that's probably about to change," Jericho said.

Diana smiled wearily. "I'm afraid you're right."

"Where did you get the books you lent me?" Harry asked.

"My own private copies," Jericho said. "You could probably get a complete set from the Imperial Library though."

"Or from the Cathedral of the Goddess," Diana added. "The Church of She keeps a complete set in all cathedral libraries."

"Why?" Harry asked curiously.

Diana shrugged. "They see my father's writings as part of the same spiritual tradition that gave birth to the Church."

"I think we've gotten way off the track," Jericho said, looking pointedly at Diana and, once again, Harry had the feeling they were getting into something the old man didn't want him getting into. "We've got a lot of ground to cover and not much time."

"Of course," Diana said and smiled at Harry. "I was going to tell you about Isis." She reached up and pulled out the golden locket that hung around her neck. Harry noticed a crescent moon inside a blazing sun engraved on its front. It was the sign of the Church of She. Diana pressed a hasp and the locket sprang open revealing a hologram of two young women.

She pressed the hasp again and the holo-images expanded until they were each about six inches across. The two young women were facing each other and talking animatedly. Diana must have shut off the sound, and Harry could only guess at what they were saying as they both threw back their heads and laughed with the same unconscious, mirror-image body language.

For a second, he was reminded of the little plastic heart in his pocket, with the hologram of him and Susan mugging for the camera. He pushed the thought firmly down into a drawer in his mind and then closed the drawer and locked it.

He studied the image of the two women. At first glance, they appeared as unalike as any two strangers. The one who was obviously Diana was casually dressed in jeans and a blue denim work shirt, open at the throat and spotted with what looked like different colored dabs of paint. Her sleek black hair was longer than it was now and pulled back in a girlish ponytail, tied with a red bandana. As far as Harry could see, she wore no makeup.

Her sister on the other hand wore a spotless, white, lab smock buttoned all the way up, with an official looking ID-badge just visible in the lower left hand corner. Her hair was a striking platinum blonde, cut to a radical pageboy bristle. Her jade green eyes and blonde hair were in striking contrast to her deep golden-brown complexion. This was further heightened by midnight blue eyeliner and bright ruby lipstick. A pair of black horn-rimmed data-glasses hung on a fine golden chain around her neck.

Harry looked up at Diana. "You didn't try very hard to look alike, did you?" he said. "The only question is, which of you is the real you?"

Diana collapsed the hologram and closed the locket. "Isis and I always needed to somehow express our individuality, to draw a line, to be different from each other. It wasn't that we disliked each other. We were our own best of friends. I mean, how could it be otherwise? I guess being identical twins just exaggerated the need to be a unique individual, that's all.

"But we always tried to be true to ourselves, even when we chose very different ways of doing it. And I think we succeeded. Even though we chose different careers, we each found fulfillment and a degree of success. For example, I became, among other things, an artist, a painter while..."

"You're a painter?" Harry interrupted, suddenly making another connection. "Do you happen to sign your paintings with a 'D' resting in a crescent moon?

Diana looked at him in surprise. "Why yes," she said. "How did you know?"

"I bought one of your paintings," he said excitedly. "When I asked the dealer the name of the artist, he refused to tell me. He said the artist wished to remain anonymous. I thought that was a helluva way to run a business."

"But you see, it's not a business,' she said with an enigmatic smile.

"The price tag said different," Harry answered with a sardonic smile of his own.

"My paintings are not for just anyone," she said. "They find their owner. If their owner can't pay the price, then the painting finds a way to them anyway."

Harry raised a skeptical eyebrow. "Your paintings know who they're meant for?"

"What painting did you buy?" she asked.

"An icon called, 'The Madonna of Eternal Life'."

"Of course," she said, as if that proved her point, and strangely enough it did.

As soon as he saw it in the gallery window, he knew he had to have that beautiful little icon of the Madonna. She was dressed in glowing blue robes, standing in a spiraling tunnel of light. She reached out with both hands as if offering him the spiritual promise hidden in every resurrection he had ever been through. It was the promise of the eternal life of the ka made manifest in the loving arms of the Goddess of light. But what finally pulled him in off the street was the face of the Madonna, that same sweetly smiling, loving face he had seen time and again in every resurrection and in countless dreams afterwards.

Harry leaned back and regarded the young woman across from him with a new sense of respect and something akin to awe. "How many times have you resurrected?" he asked.

"Never," she replied.

"But how could you...? He stopped, at a loss for words.

She smiled, understanding. "You know you don't have to die to see these things," she said, casually fingering the silver locket round her neck.

22

Valkyrie

For the first time, he noticed the black onyx ring edged with silver on the third finger of her left hand. Suddenly, he understood or thought he understood. "You're Jaganmatri," he said, "A Valkyrie!"

Diana heard the undertone of accusation in his voice and sat up very straight, eyeing him defiantly. "If this bothers you, Mr. Neuman," she said and lifted her hand, showing him the ring. "Perhaps we should discontinue these talks and you should leave." She stood up and offered her hand in regal dismissal.

"Whoa, just a minute!" Harry said. He was having a tough time reconciling Jake Lloyd's beautiful, artistically talented daughter with the fabled warriors of the Jaganmatri. "You just took me by surprise..." He stopped as he realized that was just what she meant to do. She had kept that ring concealed with her left hand in her lap until just the right moment. But right moment for what, he wondered. With a Jaganmatri Valkyrie, you probably didn't want to know.

The Jaganmatri were the sisterhood of the Church of She. The Church worshipped the Goddess in her dual aspects of creator and destroyer, and the sisterhood mirrored this duality. On the one hand, the Jaganmatri of Compassion, like the goddess Isis, served the creative aspect of the loving, caring, life-giving Earth Mother. They wore a distinctive ivory ring banded in gold on their right hand.

By contrast, the Jaganmatri Valkyrie served the Goddess in her aspect of destroyer. They wore the black onyx ring and were a sisterhood of warriors sworn to defend the Church and the earth against all enemies, natural and supernatural. Like the Goddess Diana, they were hunters, and their prey wasn't only dark knowledge. Their exploits in the Quarantine against the Seraphim Jihad were legendary. They were not only superb soldiers and tacticians; they were also spies, assassins, courtesans and diplomats, all in the service of the Church.

They were admired and respected by some, feared and mistrusted by others, particularly in New Hollywood, where The Great Cathedral to the Goddess dominated the skyline. The Church was the major religion of the Empire and a force to be reckoned with, especially since its intentions were seldom clear and not always those of the Empire. Even the Tongs tread carefully when it came to the Church of She and especially the Jaganmatri Valkyrie.

"You were saying?" Diana said. She stood looking down at him. Her jade green eyes held his in a cold, steady gaze. The pupils grew larger. They became great pools of liquid darkness that grew and merged, eclipsing her face and drawing him in.

He felt a momentary resistance and then let go. He knew where this was going. He'd been there before. It was like stepping off a cliff and letting gravity take over. He toppled into darkness. A deep feeling of peace swept over him and he opened his arms and let it take him. He felt his ka stirring, and his meat body heaved a deep, boneless sigh of contentment. He was going home.

He registered a distant pinprick of light and, in the next instant, he was standing in his ka on the shore of the Shining Sea of the spirit realm. Someone was standing beside him. He knew it was her. He didn't have to look. You couldn't hide anything here. Everything was revealed in the infinite light of the spirit realm. You knew each other right down to the...

He dropped back into his body. He swayed and grabbed hold of the tabletop. He was standing up. He didn't remember standing up. He could still feel the residue of peace and light from touching his ka and the infinite possibilities coming off the Shining Sea.

He blinked and looked around bemused. Diana stood across from him, studying him carefully. Her skin still retained a subtle golden glow from the touch of her ka. Everything is revealed, he thought, and for an instant he saw her standing on the shore of the Shining Sea in the fullness of her ka, Diana, Moon Goddess of the hunt, infinitely beautiful, alluring and deadly. He shook his head, and the vision disappeared, and even the memory of it was gone.

"Very good, Mr. Neuman," Diana said.

Harry sat down heavily and looked up at her. "What do you want?" he asked uncomprehendingly. He was having trouble processing what had just happened. The only other person who had been able to drop him into his ka like that was Samuel Kade and it usually took him a while to do it.

Diana smiled. "Now, we both know where we stand," she said and sat down. "Doctor Jericho told me about your hold on the ka but," she shrugged. "You never know."

Harry glared at Jericho. "I thought we had an agreement," he said bitterly. "No one was to know about this unless I agreed to it, not even Chueh. Or maybe I misunderstood something?"

Jericho refused to meet his eye and instead began to flip through the hit list of the small jukebox music selector standing on the end of the table. GREATEST HITS OF NINETEEN FIFTY-NINE was printed in gold letters across the front of the selector.

"It was my fault," Diana said. "I pressured him. I had to know."

"Why?"

"You don't belong to the Church of She, do you?" Diana asked without answering his question.

Harry shook his head. "What's that got to do with anything?" he asked.

"But you know the Goddess is real?"

Harry looked at Doc.

"Come, come, Mr. Neuman; you died fifty-one times. You

must have seen something."

Harry sighed resignedly. "Yeah, I've seen the Goddess. She's real."

"And despite that you don't belong to Her Church?"

"I'm not a joiner," Harry said. "I don't need some organization standing between me and the Goddess, telling me what they think she said or what they think she wants me to think or do."

"And what does the Goddess want you to think or do? What does she want from you?"

Harry shrugged uncomfortably. "She doesn't say," he said.

"Maybe you haven't been listening."

"Maybe she wants me to die for real!" he shouted as long dammed-up feelings of pain and guilt broke loose in a bitter torrent. "And some days I still wish I could!" His words washed over her like battery acid and she jerked back and shook her head. "I'm sorry," she whispered. "The wound goes deep and doesn't heal, I know."

"What the hell do you know?" He was tired of all these annoying word games, all the hints, innuendos, half-truths and no answers. "Why don't we cut the crap!" he said. "What do you want?" He looked at Doc angrily. "What do you both want?"

23

A Dark Matter

"Take it easy, Harry," Doc said. "And we'll tell you, but first there are some things Diana has to explain about her sister. She's the key to all this."

Harry looked at Diana. She sat patiently waiting with downcast eyes as if nothing had happened. What was it about her, he wondered, that just by sitting there she could call up such a storm of conflicting emotions inside him? He'd never met a more irritating, arrogant, stubborn, beautiful, attractive, intelligent... Stop it! He told himself. This isn't helping. He took a deep breath, held it for a moment, and exhaled slowly. "Okay," he said at last. "Tell me about Isis."

Diana glanced at Jericho and then nodded. She folded her hands over the notebook on the table and stared out the window gathering her thoughts.

Harry followed her gaze. Storm clouds continued to pile up beyond the trees but the sun still shone across the fifteen standing stones, dragging long shadows across the raked gravel. The garden had the static, timeless quality of an immovable axle around which the whole universe revolved.

"My sister was first and foremost a medical doctor," Diana said at last. "Her primary concern was to help the sick and suffering. Looking back now, I can see how the trajectory of her career, right from the beginning, inevitably led to the Nevada Quarantine. Her Doctoral thesis explored new treatments for obscure genetic disorders and, after that, she focused on the transgenic diseases left over from the plague wars. She was especially interested in mapping and plotting the flux, the rate of genetic divergence of the new strains from the originals as the diseases continued to mutate and gradually burn out. She became fascinated with what was known as the Norma-gene Paradox?" Her voice ended in a query, and she looked at Harry.

He just shook his head. "Another one of the many things I don't know," he said and assayed a half-hearted grin.

"There's no reason why you should," she replied. "It's just I never know with you." And for one unguarded moment their eyes met and clung to each other. Diana quickly pulled her gaze away and glanced down at the notebook and Harry looked out at the Ryoanji Gardens and tried to figure out what just happened. It felt as if some silent message had just been telegraphed back and forth along the lines of sight between them, but he was damned if he knew what it was.

"As I was saying," Diana continued, as if nothing had happened, "the Norma-gene Paradox lies in the fact that the basic Norma-gene mutations of the human genome have remained remarkably stable for over three hundred years. They show no sign of flux. On the other hand, the grosser physical and neurological expressions of the disease show almost astronomical variations, with the only common denominators being the star scars, the peroxide blond hair and that husky, Marilyn Monroe voice. It's as if the disease is mutating wildly, turning genes on and off, while the basic genome remains stable and that's impossible, and that's what fascinated Isis. And to add paradox to paradox, it's this very stability that's made it impervious to all treatment."

"Until Rielly Logan?" Harry suggested.

"That's also something Isis went into the Quarantine to find out," Diana replied. "But we're getting ahead of ourselves.

"Isis began studying the Paradox four years ago. She had to go into the slums and back alleys of New Hollywood to find the few Norma-genes who still lived there as homeless outcasts. The exodus to the Nevada Quarantine hadn't left many behind.

"She made contact with a small group and in the course of her work met an old Norma-gene with psychic powers. The old man usually kept them well hidden. Norma-genes haven't forgotten the bigotry and fear that fired the witch hunts a half century ago. Despite this, Isis managed to earn the old man's trust, and he showed her how he could move objects with his mind.

"The phenomena fascinated her, and she began researching it in her free time. With the help of the old Norma-gene, she gradually met others with hidden powers. They told her that all psychic powers were based on the ability to see and manipulate an unknown form of energy that's all around us. It's around all healthy, living organisms, but also around grav-cars, repeller-fields, and especially around the spin-generators at Eternal Life. There were also certain geographic areas where the energy concentrates. Some Norma-genes claimed to be able to use these areas to see into other worlds; some said even into worlds of gods and demons. These areas often coincided with ancient holy places.

"Isis developed a theory based on what the Norma-genes told her and what her own research showed. It incorporated a number of almost forgotten theories from late twentieth century physics, among them the theory of dark energy.

"Dark energy?" Harry asked.

"Another one of those things you don't know?" Diana teased.

Harry grinned more easily now and shrugged. "What can I say?"

"Well, don't feel bad, there aren't many people today who have heard of dark energy. After all the horrors of the Crash, science was more concerned with the practical problems of healing and rebuilding. A lot of promising research was destroyed in the Crash or later just got lost in the shuffle."

"If it wasn't for those time tombs that pre-Crash civilization left scattered across the country, dark energy would have been lost too. The theory is based on solid measurements and observations of gravitational attraction, the discrepancies in the orbits of planetary bodies, and the movement of galaxies. Physicists in the late twentieth century calculated the entire mass and energy of the universe..."

"They could do that?" Harry asked.

"Yup," Diana nodded. "Isis showed me some old articles. Anyway, when they finished making their calculations, they found that the amount of energy and matter in the universe was far less than what it should be. In fact, it was over ninety percent less. So the big question became, where was all this matter and energy? And since matter is only another form of energy, the question was simplified to, where was all this energy?"

"Maybe they calculated wrong," Harry said.

"That was the first thing they thought of," Diana said. "But after checking and double-checking countless times, they were still left with the same question. And the only answer they had was the theory of dark matter and energy. It went something like this. Since by all calculations this energy must exist, it must be in a form unknown and invisible to us and all our instruments. Therefore, it must, in contrast to everything we know, be dark energy."

"That doesn't say much, does it?" Harry asked.

"No, not really." Diana laughed. "But giving the unknown a name always makes people feel more secure and in control. Why should scientists be any different?"

"What does this non-existent, existent dark energy have to do with repeller-fields, Eternal Life's spin-generators, Rielly Logan, or even black ka-eating wolves?" Harry asked.

"You might want to add magic, religion, and the future of the human race," Doc threw in with a mad bomber glint in his eye.

"You gotta be kidding!" Harry said.

Doc shook his head. "I wish I was."

"Well let's just start with something I know for a change, like repeller-fields," Harry said.

"Oh ho, so you know all about repeller-fields?" Doc asked with the look of a hungry cat that just cornered a tasty mouse.

"Why sure, everyone does."

"What are they then?" Doc pounced.

Harry looked at Diana for help, but she just smiled encouragement. "Well, they're, ah, a kind of force field," he said.

"And what kind of force would that be?"

Harry squirmed. Doc could be merciless sometimes. Like most people, Harry took repeller-fields for granted. They'd been around all his life. They powered his cars, his home, his whole world. They were even responsible for his resurrections. "It's a kind of anti-gravity," he said, thinking of his grav-car; and ninety-nine percent of the people in New Hollywood, not to mention the rest of the world, would probably have backed him up.

"That's just what Oskar Danzig thought when he created the first repeller-field and sent a steel ball through the roof of his house a hundred years ago," Doc said. "And it's what most scientists believed for the next seventy-five years while the Danzig spin-generator was adapted to push, pull, lift, and power just about everything.

"Then about twenty years ago, we learned not only to bend and form repeller-fields but to give them feel and texture too. By varying the crystal resonance or the shape of the rotating coil or by changing the iridium labyrinth, we could suddenly give a repeller-field the feel of wood bark or animal fur or even human skin. And that shot a lot of holes in the anti-gravity theory.

"But what finally killed it was one of those urban legends about accident victims miraculously coming back to life when they got caught in the gravity field of a passing car or the backwash of one hovering nearby.

"We all recognize that weird prickly sensation when a nearby grav-field passes over us. It's supposed to be harmless, but if you were dead, it looked like it could sometimes bring you back to life. It didn't always happen, but it happened often enough that rescue units at the scene of fatal accidents routinely put the victims beneath hovering vehicles for short periods of time.

"Many of these people came back to life and came back with very clear after-death experiences. I saw it happen once, and it started me thinking. From there it was just a short step to creating an "Eternal Life" spin-generator that's nothing but a modified Danzig coil spinning through the pzio-electric field of a resonating crystal. And despite what some of my colleagues are still teaching, there is no way in hell that the theory of anti-gravity is going to explain why certain resonating crystals and patterns of iridium can tag and then pull in the souls of dead people!

"But to be perfectly honest, I had no idea what I was dealing with until I read one of Isis'..." Jericho stopped and looked over at Diana, suddenly embarrassed. "I'm sorry," he apologized. "This was supposed to be your show and here I am hogging center stage. It's a bad teaching habit. You know, old lecturers never die; they just blabber away."

"Don't apologize." Diana smiled. "I enjoyed the show."

"Well, now that I've totally destroyed young Harry's intellectual credentials," Jericho said with a playful chuckle. "Maybe you can take over but try not to strain his limited abilities."

"One of these days, Doc..." Harry said and drew an imaginary knife across his throat. Doc grinned and Diana laughed, and the residue of the strained atmosphere from before seemed to evaporate.

"Seriously though," Harry said, turning to her. "I think I see where this is going. Your sister thought that repeller-fields were somehow utilizing dark energy, right?"

"Yes and no," Diana said. "Because no one knew what dark energy was or where it came from or why it could capture kas and bring dead people back to life or give some Norma-genes visions of alternate realities."

She looked at Jericho. "Thank you for letting me get a word in edgewise, but I really do think you're better qualified to explain this part than I am."

"You're being too modest. The Church maintains the best schools in the world at the Holy See in New Omaha, and the Jaganmatri receive the best education those schools can give."

Diana glanced uncomfortably over at Harry. He wondered what kind of game Jericho was playing by purposely reminding everyone that she was Jaganmatri.

Jericho beamed at them with all the grandfatherly benevolence of a child molester offering a couple of kids a bag of candy. "But since you insist," he said, spreading his hands in a what else can I do gesture. "You know how much I love to put my vast intellectual abilities on display for poor ignorant Harry."

Harry looked over at Diana and rolled his eyes in mock despair. She smiled tentatively.

"Isis developed a kind of unified field theory that tied together two of the major concepts of twentieth century physics," Jericho said. "And then tied them together with the realm of the spirit that had always been the preserve of religion."

"From what you've told me, Harry, every time you trance-walk into your ka, you always walk out onto the edge of what you call the spirit realm, that manifests either as something you call the Shining Sea of the Gods or the Astral Planes. You say that in reality the spirit realm is neither of these things. It's just how your mind, using reference forms that Samuel Kade taught you, tries to define the indefinable. Now, having said that, I'm going to try to define it."

He cleared his throat and as he started speaking, his voice took on the dry, objective tones of a lecture hall. "Isis's research opened a back door to an almost forgotten branch of twentieth century physics called quantum physics. Twentieth century quantum physics postulated the existence of what they called a quantum field, a field of infinite potentiality beyond the finest, most subtle levels of material existence.

When physicists began exploring the field of atomic and

subatomic particles, they discovered that high energy particles could appear out of nowhere and disappear into nothing and this, according to Newtonian physics, was downright impossible. To make matters worse, not only was matter and energy being created and destroyed along the borders of what we call physical reality, but the processes taking place at that level were responding to the conscious expectations of the scientists performing the experiments.

"The conclusion they finally reached was that there had to exist a field, a quantum field or vacuum state, containing infinite amounts of energy and matter existing as pure potential, as virtual particles or probability waves of vacuum flux, in other words, a field of nothing containing the infinite possibilities of everything.

"Our universe not only sprang out of that field of nothingness but was constantly being created and recreated out of it. To top it all, this nothing responded to consciousness and therefore also had to be a field of consciousness. Not only were the borders of physical existence becoming porous but they were becoming consciously porous.

"Isis realized that all that missing "dark energy" wasn't missing at all. That, in fact, the universe as we know it is like a thin scum floating on top of an infinite pond of this dark energy. This pond is in reality a field of consciousness and a realm of all possibilities, containing all probable and improbable realities, alternate worlds, and universes. We are created and nourished by this quantum pond but are, for the most part, unaware of its existence even though it responds to our consciousness; to our human expectations and desires.

"It sounds like this quantum field is what Samuel Kade calls the spirit realm," Harry said. "He taught me that it was without form and structure but could take on infinite forms and structures depending on how we look at it. Trance-walkers like Kade prefer to work with it in the form of the Astral Planes or the

Shining Sea. He said it could be anything I wished it to be, but there were dangers in this, and he illustrated it with the great Disney's classic film, 'The Sorcerer's Apprentice', where the apprentice is unaware of the powers he's invoking and nearly calls down catastrophe.

"Kade taught me that when you enter the spirit realm in your ka, it's best to invoke it or call it forth in a form or structure that you know and can work with in relative safety. He said he used these two mental constructs, the Astral Planes and the Shining Sea, to structure the structureless and give form to the formless."

Diana nodded agreement. "The Church uses similar forms to structure the spirit realm but has also added a couple of "structures" of its own."

"Ever since the Prophet General walked in and out of the spirit realm and founded the Church of She more than three hundred years ago," Jericho added, "the Church has kept this knowledge alive, guarded it closely, and handed it on only to high initiate Jaganmatri." He cast a meaningful glance at Diana.

She returned it with a look of cool appraisal. "Maybe we should get off this tangent and back to the point of your lecture, Doctor Jericho," she said.

"The point, my dear," Jericho said with a wry twist of his lips, "is that with the advent of the Danzig spin-generator we learned how to tap the infinite energy of the spirit realm. Our whole civilization runs on this quantum dark energy, but until Isis made the connection, we had no idea what it was.

"She saw the fact that the spin-generators at Eternal Life used this dark energy to draw the souls of the dead back to their cloned bodies as a confirmation that this energy was somehow connected to the world of the spirit. She then made a bold leap and claimed that this quantum realm of dark energy was also the realm of saints and seers and gods and demons. It was science curling back on itself and biting its own tail only to discover it was religion." Jericho spread his arms wide as if he was about to take a bow, like a magician who has just managed to pull a rhinoceros out of his top hat. "And that my ignorant, young friend," he said with his mad bomber grin, "is that!"

Diana let Jericho have his moment and then said, "Unfortunately, this story does not have a happy ending. After three years of research, Isis published her findings in a monograph that was viciously attacked and ridiculed by the scientific community. It destroyed her credibility, her standing, and her career in the medical establishment.

Jericho shook his head sadly. "I think I may have been one of the very few outside of the Nevada Quarantine who realized the true, explosive potential of what she discovered," he said. "I contacted her and encouraged her to continue her research. I even promised to finance any future research into this field, but she politely declined."

"In reality, Isis wasn't interested in Quantum Field Theory, dark energy or repeller-fields," Diana said. "The research paper that so inspired Doctor Jericho was just a by-product, an interesting tangent... perhaps a laying to rest of old demons," she added, pointedly looking at Jericho.

The old man cleared his throat as if to say something then instead looked away.

"In the end," Diana continued, "all this was marginal to my sister's chief concerns."

"In fact, she opened a whole Pandora's box of interesting concerns," Jericho growled testily.

"That's true," Diana conceded. "But you don't shoot the messenger just because you don't like the message."

Harry wondered what that was all about. He was doing a lot of that lately.

24

The Nevada Quarantine Blues

"As I said before, my sister was first and foremost a doctor, a healer," Diana said. "She was interested in dark energy, quantum field theory, and the spirit realm only in so far as they had medical applications. That was also part of the reason she was so interested in the stories coming out of the Nevada Quarantine about a new messiah who not only cured the Norma-gene syndrome but "re-made" the victims, giving them new and perfect bodies."

"Rielly Logan," Harry said.

Diana nodded. "I suspect she was fascinated with Rielly Logan long before she wrote that monograph, maybe even before she began interviewing Norma-genes. Maybe he was even the reason she got interested in the Norma-gene paradox in the first place."

"Do you have any reason for believing that?"

Diana shrugged. "She's my twin," she said, as if that explained everything. "I know for a fact, though, that at least two years before she published her famous monograph she applied for a research grant from the Imperial Quarantine Research Office to mount a medical expedition into the Nevada Quarantine, specifically sighting Rielly Logan and the possibility of finding a solution to the Norma-gene paradox."

"And...?" Harry asked.

"And nothing. They refused her request citing that there was absolutely no evidence that Rielly Logan could, in fact, cure the Norma-gene syndrome. All these stories were, and I quote, "apocryphal myths and urban legends with no basis in scientific fact". They added that due to extensive tribal warfare all medical and research expeditions into the Nevada Quarantine had been suspended indefinitely. Shortly after this, the Nevada Quarantine was declared out of bounds for all citizens of the Empire."

"Out of bounds, why?" Harry asked. As far as he knew, nowhere in the Continental Quarantine was out of bounds to citizens of the Empire. A citizen was free to go anywhere in the Quarantine as long as he was willing to take complete personal responsibly for the consequences of his decision. He could not depend on the Empire to pull his chestnuts out of the fire if they got radiation burned, plague infected, ambushed by hostile mutie tribes, or shot up by pre-Crash war-bots hiding powered down and waiting in some god-forsaken wasteland.

Jericho regarded him with a kind of benign exasperation. "Harry, how much do you know about what's been going on in the Nevada Quarantine in the last five or six years?"

Harry squirmed inside. It reminded him too much of Chueh's parting shot, "And, Harry, you might want to keep up on the news better." He probably should have, he thought; but for the last five or six years he'd gotten most of his "news" from the bottom of a whiskey bottle, and when he finally stopped drinking, he was too interested in exploring the inner world of his ka to pay much attention to the news of the world outside.

"Okay," he sighed resignedly. "Since we're assuming my total ignorance in so many other areas, why stop now. Why was the Nevada Quarantine out of bounds?"

Jericho looked at Diana. "We're going off on another tangent," he said.

Diana shrugged. "He's got to know what he's getting into."

"What I'm getting into?" Harry said. "As far as I know I'm not getting into anything!"

"Should I do this or do you want to?" Doc said to Diana.

She waved her hand in mild indifference. "Why don't you," she said and looked down at her notebook again.

Jericho gave Harry a conspiratorial wink and then said, "The

Nevada Quarantine is out of bounds because Rielly Logan declared it out of bounds," he said. "He started with the jungles around Las Vegas ten or fifteen years ago and gradually extended his control over the whole southern quarter of the Nevada Quarantine. Then about four or five years ago, he claimed the whole Nevada Quarantine and started a war of racial cleansing, exterminating and enslaving anything not Norma-gene."

"And no one tried to stop him?" Harry asked. "What about the Empire?"

"The first thing you've got to realize is that no one in the Empire cares about what happens in the Quarantine," Jericho said. "The Empire's got enough problems of its own. It's been over fifty years since we inherited those eastern provinces from the Caliphate, and they're still a hotbed of barely suppressed Seraphim rebellion. A major part of the Empire's military and economic power goes to trying to keep that powder keg from exploding again.

"On top of that, we have the remnants of the Seraphim Jihad at our back in the Sinks. If recent reports are true, they've been making aggressive alliances and uniting Slavers, renegade Tongs, Jackers, and everyone else under a new Seraphim banner."

Diana coughed and cleared her throat demonstratively. Doc looked at her and sighed. "Okay, the point is that no one in the Empire gives diddley-squat for what happens anywhere in the Quarantine. "On the map it's just this big empty space with meaningless old United States state borders dotted in. Officially, no one in the Empire goes there except for an occasional medical research team. Unofficially, Slavers, gun-runners, smugglers, and traders move in and out of there, trading with the tribes for scavenged ancient technology, old books, and works of art that can be sold on the black market at an enormous profit. Otherwise, no one cares."

"The Church cares," Diana said, looking up from her notebook.

"Only because the Holy See lies at New Omaha, smack in the middle of the Continental Quarantine," Jericho said.

"The Church cares because the Great Mother cares and maintains over five hundred missions of mercy all over the Quarantine, including the Nevada Quarantine," Diana said in mild rebuke. "Let's not get into this again, Doctor Jericho."

Get into what? Harry wondered. It sounded like the tail-end of an old family feud.

Jericho deftly shifted gears. "In fact, the Church has always been our best source of intelligence concerning the Quarantine. News of Rielly's long march from Old Chicago to Las Vegas first reached the Empire two years after it happened and came via the Church.

"The Empire dismissed the news as just another routine outbreak of religious fanaticism. It happens all the time in the Quarantine. Rielly, like all the other fanatics before him, would disappear in a few years and his movement would be swallowed up by inner divisions and tribal conflicts. The Church disagreed. Right from the beginning, they realized that Rielly was not your ordinary, run-of-the-mill bible thumper.

"It wasn't until a few years ago that people began to notice that almost all the Norma-genes had left the Empire. In fact, they had been leaving for the last ten years or more. On the other hand, who cares? After all, they were only Norma-genes. If they wanted to go back to where they came from, that was just fine. It left one less social problem to deal with.

"Even when rumors of genocidal wars began leaking out of the Nevada Quarantine, people just looked the other way. The muties were always fighting among themselves, what else was new? As it turned out, a lot. Rielly had built an army of Norma-gene re-made cavalry, supported by cadres of weirdings, warlocks, and any other Norma-genes with exceptional talents."

"Like fire starters, shape-shifters, telepaths," Harry suggested, remembering the old horror stories from his childhood.

"You got it," Jericho said. "They were also conventionally well-armed and organized and swept through the Nevada Quarantine in less than four years, slaughtering and enslaving anything not Norma-gene." Jericho eyed Diana. "We know this only because the Church has missions there."

Diana shook her head. "Not anymore."

"No, not anymore," Jericho said. "One of the first things Rielly did when he took over was to expel the Church. Jaganmatri were personae non grata in the new world he was building for Norma-genes.

"It didn't matter, though. The Church had its hands full, caring for the flood of refugees created by the war. Most fled north and east into the Continental Quarantine. Rielly's kingdom in the south prevented them from getting out that way, and the Sierras to the west blocked that route, so not many made it into the Empire. The Norma-gene army didn't pursue them once they crossed the old state borders of Nevada that were now the borders of the Norma-gene homeland. Muties, smugglers, Slavers, and anyone else who tried to cross that border never came back and pretty soon everyone got the message.

"Once again, the attitude in New Hollywood was, who cares. Everyone knows the Nevada Quarantine is nothing but jungle and wasteland anyway. If the Norma-genes want it, let them have it and good riddance. Not everyone had that attitude though," Jericho said and looked at Diana.

"The Church was concerned by what was happening and sent in a mission of Jaganmatri," she said.

"Valkyrie Jaganmatri," Jericho amended, "not the compassionate ones."

Diana eyed him coolly. "The Church had received alarming reports coming out of Las Vegas and sent in a Valkyrie reconnaissance team," she said and turned away. She looked out the window at the rain-drenched Ryoanji Garden. The fifteen stones lay like stark, solitary islands in a sea of rain pitted gravel. She shook her head. "They were never heard from again," she added.

"Jesus Christ!" Harry said.

"I doubt if Jesus Christ had anything to do with it, Mr. Neuman," Diana replied dryly.

"And you never found them?" he asked in shocked disbelief. The Church just did not lose Valkyrie. They weren't superwomen but they came close. During the Caliphate War a handful of Valkyrie held a mountain pass against ten thousand Seraphim warriors for over three weeks before being wiped out. The Church renamed the pass Thermopile.

Diana looked down at her notebook and shook her head. "No, we never found them," she said.

There was an uncomfortable silence. Harry wanted to ask about what the Valkyrie were looking for in Las Vegas but let it go. If she was going to tell him, she would have already.

Jericho coughed and cleared his throat. "It turns out the Empire was also getting interested in the Nevada Quarantine about that time," he said. "What finally caught public attention, though, was a medical research team that went missing in the southern Nevada jungles. It seems they'd been working in Arizona, up along the border, and inadvertently strayed into Nevada and were not heard from again."

"According to Church sources, that medical team didn't "inadvertently stray" over the border," Diana said with a wry a smile. "And it wasn't a medical research team."

Jericho shrugged. "The Empire, like the Church, lost a number of operatives trying to find out what was going on over there. This one just happened to get more publicity, and it forced the Empire to send in a much publicized search and rescue mission, accompanied by a heavily armed military escort, to find them. The Empire made it clear, though, that this was a purely humanitarian mission.

"When they went in, they were supposed to hang data

spheres, floating at max three hundred feet all along their back-trail to keep in constant communication. Less than four hours later, the data spheres stopped working and all contact with the rescue party was lost. As far as we know, they made it almost to the outskirts of Las Vegas before going down in the jungle.

"I managed to get hold of a copy of their last transmission," Jericho paused and glanced at Diana.

She cocked her head and raised a quizzical eyebrow.

Jericho shrugged and opened his hands in a palms-up gesture. "So I've got friends in high places, is that a crime?"

Diana laughed. "I heard a copy of the same transmission."

Jericho's face split into a wide grin. "It's so nice working with professionals," he said and suddenly, they were both laughing like a couple of kids who caught each other with their hands in the cookie jar.

Harry looked from one to the other and wondered at their relationship that could be filled with so many sharp edges one moment and then something akin to real affection the next. Like family, he thought and felt a twinge of old loss.

"Well, since we both know," Jericho chuckled, "perhaps one of us should let poor, innocent Harry in on the secret. Would you mind doing the honors my dear?" he asked with a chivalrous sweep of his arm.

Diana eyed him archly and laughed. "Why not?"

She turned to Harry. "According to their last transmission, it all started out routine," she said and then her voice deepened to a macho, military mockery, "foxtrot leader two this is alpha eagle one, over..." She tossed her head and gave him a street-wise, gamin grin. "You know, all that military bullshit they copy from the old movies. Then someone starts yelling that the grav-units are cutting out and they're going down. After that, all you heard were garbled static bursts of screaming interspersed with gunfire and explosions. Then, right at the end, clear as a bell, someone crying. After that everything went dead."

She glanced at Jericho. "Isn't that the gist of it?"

Jericho nodded and added, "As you can imagine, the government didn't want any of this getting out. They put a tight security lid on the Quarantine and began preparing for a major military incursion. The only problem was, they didn't know what they were up against, and Rielly wasn't telling them.

"Grav-units don't just cut out all altogether and all at once. It's impossible. On top of that, the force they sent in to "escort" the search and rescue mission had enough firepower to level Las Vegas and take out every Norma-gene clan in the Quarantine. Instead, it disappeared without a trace.

"An air of panic gripped the government. Everything from using some of the old nuclear weapons still lying around to a major ground invasion were suggested, but they all stranded on the fact that they didn't know what they were up against or even if it was worth going up against it. They needed more information.

"Spies were sent in and never came out. Norma-genes all over the Empire were quietly rounded up, interrogated, and released. A few were even sent into the Nevada Quarantine to attempt to make contact with the messiah. They never came back.

"The government adopted a wait and see attitude and tried to strengthen security and surveillance along the border..."

"Doctor Jericho," Diana interrupted. "I think he gets the idea."

Jericho nodded. "Right," he said and looked slightly embarrassed. "One tangent too many, information overload, running off at the mouth again. Is that it?"

Diana smiled and nodded. She turned to Harry. "A month after they lost contact with that search and rescue team, my sister received a personal invitation from Rielly Logan to visit Las Vegas."

25

A Beast of Burden

"What did you say?" Harry asked in disbelief. He'd heard what she said, it was just it didn't make any sense.

Diana nodded. "I know," she said with a tight, sympathetic smile. "It hit me like that too. As crazy as it sounds, Rielly Logan sent her a personal invitation. It was hand-delivered by her old Norma-gene contact, the one who inspired her famous monogram. He'd gone to the New Jerusalem of Las Vegas to be re-made, but Rielly sent him back for Isis along with a promise that if she came, he would remake the old man in front of her eyes.

"She had two days to decide and put her affairs in order. She also had to agree to stay in Las Vegas for a minimum six months. After that, she could leave whenever she wished.

"Isis had no doubts. She was bubbling over with excitement when she told me. It was the chance of a lifetime. No scientist had ever seen a re-making first hand and, to top it off, Rielly promised her complete access as his personal guest. That was the real deal maker. She was like a school girl going on her first date.

"I tried to talk some sense into her. Didn't she know what was going on in the Nevada Quarantine? Did she realize Rielly had just carried out a war of extermination and was building something on the outskirts of Las Vegas that scared even the Church? I shouldn't have told her that or about the Valkyrie we lost trying to find out what it was, but I did. She was my sister, my twin, and I wasn't about to let her walk into that without trying to stop her. I could have been talking to a wall."

"Why Isis?" Harry asked.

"I asked the same question," Diana said. "Apparently, Rielly read her monogram and thought that she was the only scientist who could appreciate what he was doing and explain it to the world."

"So she could play John the Baptist to his Jesus Christ, maybe," Jericho said sourly.

Diana glared at him out of the corner of her eye and then waved his comment aside as if it was a mildly irritating insect. "Maybe everything Rielly said was true," she said. "But I had my doubts. Remember, we lost Valkyries walking in there.

"On the other hand, Isis and I both knew she was going to go no matter what I said or did." She shook her head. "Even so, I should have tried harder to stop her. For my own sake." She gave him a sad, sardonic twist of a smile. "At least then I could tell myself I really tried."

Harry caught a glimpse of something in her eyes, something he recognized. It was something he saw every time he looked in his own mirror. A kindred spirit, he thought, another beast of burden carrying hell on its back. In the next instant, it was gone; her eyes cleared and she made a quick throw away gesture. "Water under the bridge," she said. "I would have had to chain her to the wall for the rest of her life to stop her."

"Neither of you told me anything about this," Jericho chided. "I didn't find out until three months after she left. As your legal guardian I should have…"

Diana straightened up and looked Jericho in the eye. "We are not children anymore, Doctor Jericho," she pointed out frostily. "We do not have to ask your permission or tell you anything anymore."

Harry looked at Jericho. "Her legal guardian?"

Jericho waved his question aside and instead leaned across the table and said to Diana, "But you were happy enough to ask my help last night, weren't you?"

Once again, Harry felt as if he had just walked into the middle of an ongoing family feud.

Diana's eyes didn't waver. "You're right of course, and I thank you," she said with all the regal dignity of a queen indulging a wayward servant.

Harry watched Jericho's thin, testy smile turn into a broad grin. Then he shook his head and started to chuckle. "I forget sometime how much you've grown beyond me," he said affectionately.

"Let's not get carried away," Diana said drily. "Besides, we didn't tell you because Isis wasn't supposed to tell anyone, but there was no way she wasn't going to tell me. She knew that if she just disappeared, I'd have every Valkyrie in the Quarantine and every cop and Tong in the Empire looking for her.

"Of course we didn't tell Rielly either," she said turning to Harry with a street-wise grin. "He didn't even know I existed. No one except Chueh and Jericho and a handful of other people knew that Isis had a sister or that we were Jake Lloyd's daughters or that he even had daughters."

Harry was about to ask why, but she raised a stop sign hand, palm forward. "Don't," she said. "Let's just say we like our privacy. Keep it at that for now."

Harry shook his head. Jake Lloyd's family had more secrets than the Borgias.

Diana closed her notebook and reached up and unhooked one of the silver crescent earrings she wore. She looked at Jericho and raised a questioning eyebrow. The old man pursed his lips with distaste and nodded.

She laid the earring on the table and started to unhook the other and stopped. "I gave these to Isis just before she left," she said. "It was the only thing I could think of. They probably wouldn't protect her but..."

She gave her head a quick, defiant toss. "What else could I do?" Once again Harry caught a glimpse of that beast of burden, walking through her eyes, carrying its heavy load of guilt. "I was still Jaganmatri Valkyrie," she said, "and the Church needed to know what happened to our Sisters and what Rielly was building. As long as Isis was going into the lion's den anyway, why not take advantage of the situation, right? Kill two birds with one stone so to speak."

Suddenly she started to laugh, a bitter, cynical, self-lacerating laugh. Then her voice broke, control broke, and tears ran down her cheeks. She shook her head and kept shaking it. "I couldn't protect her!" she said. "I couldn't even stop her. I'm a Valkyrie, god damn it! I should be able to do stuff like that!"

She leaned back, closed her eyes, and took a deep breath and let it out slowly. When she spoke again, it was as if she was speaking only to herself. "I should have guessed," she said, her voice a whisper of despair. "I'm Jake Lloyd's daughter! I climbed the Nano Tree, I walked out on its branches. How could I be so blind? I had all the Church intelligence on Rielly. I knew what his people called him. I even knew where he lived in Las Vegas and the name of his pet wolf, and I didn't put it together. I let her walk right into it."

"Isis was Jake's daughter too," Jericho said. "She should have seen it coming, she should have at least suspected."

Diana's eyes shot open. For an instant, she stared at Jericho with something akin to hatred. Then she shook her head in violent denial. Harry recognized the symptoms. This was her burden of guilt and she wasn't about to let anyone take it away from her or push it off on someone else. "Don't you see? She was in love with Rielly!" she said. "It blinded her. Before she even met him, she was in love with the idea of him, the romantic hero, the messiah, the savior of his people. And when she saw him in the flesh and he was everything she ever dreamed of, she was lost.

"I wasn't though. I didn't have that excuse," she said, and there was only the blank acceptance of her own guilt as a kind of absolute truth. "I should have known. I should have stopped her even if it meant chaining her to the wall." She gave a savage, disgusted laugh. "Jake Lloyd's daughter, the all-seeing, all-knowing, Jaganmatri Valkyrie, and I let my sister walk right into the claws of the Anubis!"

She turned away and looked out at the Ryoanji Gardens. The wind had picked up, whipping the trees and bushes in the background and driving the rain in a slant across the garden and against the windows.

Harry glanced over at Jericho. "I assume the Anubis are these wolf-thing invaders you were talking about."

The old man was watching Diana closely and didn't answer.

She sat very still, very straight, and very self-contained. She'd regained her disciplined self-control, wrapping it around herself like a suit of armor. She folded her hands on top of the notebook and glanced down. A second later, she unclasped her hands and folded them in her lap.

Finally, she looked up, straight at Harry. Once again he saw the tortured beast of burden walk through her eyes, but this time it was different. This time she was openly showing it to him, not trying to conceal anything, letting him know that she too recognized a kindred spirit, carrying its own load of guilty hell. She sat perfectly still, watching him... waiting.

Waiting for what, he wondered. The answer came with almost clairvoyant certainty. She's waiting for the final hammer to fall, you fool! She's waiting for the playboy debaucher to pass final judgment!

He leaned back and closed his eyes with a weary sigh. Then he looked out the window. The wind ripped leaves and twigs from the trees and scattered them across the garden. It drove the rain against the window like buckshot. Even the fifteen stones seemed to be hunkered down, riding out the storm in their water logged bed of raked gravel.

He glanced at Jericho who was idly flipping through The Greatest Hits of Nineteen Fifty-six on the little chrome juke box selector at the end of the table. It looked like the old man had programmed quite a storm to go with his Ryoanji Garden. Harry wondered to what purpose. With people like Jericho and Chueh there was always a purpose, but he knew from experience it would probably be a waste of time to try to untangle it.

He looked over at Diana. She was once again sitting straight backed, composed and self-contained. Her hands were folded demurely in her lap. She stared at the truck-stop beige wall just over his right shoulder. This time her eyes gave away nothing.

"You know," he said, "there should be a statute of limitations on guilt. It never does any good to keep beating yourself up for what you did or didn't do. Believe me, I know."

Diana looked down at her clasped hands and said nothing.

"After the car crash that left Susan brain dead," he said and couldn't believe he was doing this, "I let guilt beat me senseless with a whiskey bottle. After that, I let it kill me fifty-one times. That has to make me some kind of world expert on guilt."

"But your guilt brought Susan back to life," Diana said without looking up.

"No, it didn't," Harry said.

"But everyone knows you signed that contract with Eternal Life to bring her back," she said. There was a bit more animation in her voice this time.

Harry shook his head. "No, I didn't. That's just advertising spin. I could have paid an exorbitant fee and had Susan cloned and resurrected on the spot, without ever signing that contract. The technology was in place. It'd been tested and proved. It was just they hadn't gone public yet.

"Roger was waiting for the right moment, looking for the right angle, something they could spin into a worldwide publicity campaign. Just bringing Susan back would and did give the project an enormous boost, but Roger wanted more."

Harry shook his head. "I have to hand it to him. He recognizes potential when he sees it. Where everyone else saw only a broken-down, guilt-ridden, alcoholic has-been, Roger saw a suffering, romantic hero, willing to die for love in the most successful advertising campaign the world has ever seen.

"And the beauty of it was, he knew I couldn't say no because he was giving me everything I wanted. Not only would I get Susan back, which I could have gotten anyway but, more importantly, and this is the kicker, he was giving me a chance to atone for what I did to her. By dying again and again, I could expiate the demons of my own guilt. I jumped at the chance… especially when it was tied up in such a noble, heroic package," he added.

"After about the seventh or eighth death, I realized that atonement was highly overrated and guilt a blind alley for burn-brained masochists, but by then, it was too late. I had signed a contract, and the whole world expected me to fulfill it. I was trapped in the role of self-sacrificing, romantic hero and couldn't get out."

He shook his head. "You can't imagine how many times I got down on my knees and begged Roger to release me from the hell of that contract. I wish…" Harry stopped, embarrassed.

"I've never told anyone about this before," he said, looking past her and out the window. The rain and wind had let up, but there were more thunderclouds blowing in from the horizon, their bruised underbellies heavy with rain. The fifteen stones of the Ryoanji Garden stood fixed, solid, and immutable in a world of windblown change.

"Didn't you tell Susan?" Diana asked.

Harry shook his head. "What good would that have done? She would only have blamed herself, and a new cycle of guilt would have begun. Besides, none of it was her fault. I figured I made my bed of guilt and had to lie in it alone…" he gave her a sardonic smile. "Well, not exactly alone."

"But she must have known," Diana persisted.

"Believe it or not, I'm a pretty good actor," he said and flashed his crooked, Harry Neuman, blockbuster grin.

"I'm not telling you this to seem noble," he added. "There was nothing noble in what I did. I died fifty-one times for guilt, not for the woman I loved! It was a stupid, useless waste. It destroyed that love and drove Susan away from me... all because of guilt."

There was a long silence. Raindrops began to beat against the window again. Harry watched them slide down the glass.

Diana sat perfectly still, watching him with a kind of amazed wonder. She felt her inner demons slink away to hide under whatever mental rocks inner demons hide under. For the first time in months, she began to feel at peace with herself. She knew it probably wouldn't last, that the demons were still there and would be back to demand their pound of flesh. But that was why she was here, wasn't it? That was why she was going to walk out on the Nano Tree and ask this man to follow her. Screw all her father's prophecies! She thought. She was doing this for herself and for Isis.

She looked down at the one earring lying on the table. Slowly, she reached up and unhooked the other and laid it on the table beside the first.

26

A Quantum Impacted Storage Vampire

Perfect twins of the Moon Goddess, Harry thought, as he watched her undo the silver hook from each crescent and place the crescents so that their tips almost touched. They formed a perfect silver circle, a little bigger than an old American quarter. Gently, she pushed the tips together and the two crescents seemed to flow into each other. The empty space in the middle filmed over with a black sheath that spread across both halves of the circle, creating a flat, shiny disk. Harry wondered how she did that.

Jericho leaned forward, watching the transformation intently. Harry wasn't the only one wondering. He caught Diana's eye, and she smiled indulgently at the old man. "Doctor Jericho would love to get his hands on this," she said. "It's Church science, a quantum impacted storage vampire." She picked it up and laid it in the palm of her hand. It looked as if it was made of the same black onyx as her ring. Then, with a playful smile, she flipped her hand over and let the disk drop onto the top of her notebook. It hit with a heavy thud and stuck there.

Harry heard Jericho's squawk of protest.

"Don't worry, it can't get into Chueh's system through the notebook, even if they are networked," Diana said.

She looked at Harry and explained. "The Vampire has an infinite storage capacity and can hack and read all the data in any quantum system it's physically in contact with."

"I doubt if Chueh would let you do that," Harry said. "And if you did, I doubt he'd let you get out alive."

"He wouldn't even know I took it," Diana said complacently. "Master Chueh may have the best security in the world, but it's all facing the front of the store. The Vampire goes in the back door instead."

Jericho saw Harry's look of confusion. "It goes in through a quantum trapdoor," he said sourly. "Remember those electrons and protons that were constantly being created and destroyed along the quantum border. In reality nothing is created or destroyed. It's just a transformative exchange of information states. The first quantum computers used this apparent creation and destruction as on-off switches for instant data transmission.

"Then it was discovered that these particles are themselves intelligent and capable of picking up and storing infinite amounts of data, the whole universe, not in a grain of sand but in a proton. It's the basis of the newest super-quantum computers. The Church seems to have found a way to use the quantum transformation of these intelligent particles to hack these computers. They do it instantaneously and leave no tracks."

"So the Church could have already hacked every system in the Empire," Harry said. He looked at Jericho. Jericho looked at Diana. She shook her head. "The Vampire has to be in direct physical contact with the hardware of the specific system to work its magic. I don't know why that is, no one does. Church meta-physics is still working on that one."

"What about major computer networks," Jericho protested. "All you'd have to do is hack one key piece of hardware and you could hack the whole system."

Diana shook her head. "Doesn't work that way. Unless all the information in the network is stored in the hacked machine, we can't get at it."

She leaned back and steepled her fingers beneath her chin. "Besides, the Church and the Empire have an agreement about stuff like this," she said with an enigmatic smile. "If New Hollywood ever found out we were hacking their systems, they'd close every church in the Empire and throw every Jaganmatri they could find in jail. It's just not worth the risk."

"The Empire still might do it," Jericho growled.

Diana shrugged indifferently.

"So why are they letting the cat out of the bag now?" Harry wondered.

"Because it doesn't matter anymore," Diana said. "Isis discovered that certain Norma-genes can do the same thing with their minds. All they have to do is physically touch a machine and they're in."

"What!" Jericho nearly jumped out of his seat in surprise. "And you didn't tell me!" He sagged back as if he had been punched.

"How did she find out if they don't leave any trail?" Harry asked.

"Ghosts in the machine," Diana said. "Unlike the Vampire, the Norma-gene's mind gets in the way. It leaves something like a faint information vapor trail, call it a fingerprint of consciousness, that gradually dissipates over time. If you don't know what to look for and don't catch it in time, you'll never even notice it before it's gone."

She peeled the Vampire off the top of her notebook and flipped it in the palm of her hand like a coin. "Besides being undetectable, the Vampires also contain miniaturized cameras and nano grav-units, with everything activated when the two halves are brought together. Otherwise, they're just two earrings, almost indistinguishable from any others." And to demonstrate she pulled at the two sides of the black disk and it slowly came apart into two silver crescent moons.

"When I realized I couldn't stop Isis from going to Las Vegas, nor protect her while she was there," she said as she slipped in the hooks for the earrings. "The Valkyrie in me decided to take advantage of the situation and give her a Vampire. Who knew, maybe she'd find out what was going on in Las Vegas and maybe even what happened to the Valkyrie we lost there."

She gave a short, self-lacerating laugh. "Once a Valkyrie,

always a Valkyrie. You use what you got, even if it's your own sister." The beast of burden rode through her eyes once again and she shook her head as if to shake it away. "What's done is done," she said and picked up one earring and fastened it to her ear.

"I gave her these earrings just before she left. I told her to use them as a secure backup if things went wrong, or she began to suspect something. She could hide sensitive research or personal information, or she could use the built-in miniaturized camera and nano grav-unit for short term reconnaissance."

"I also told her about the Valkyrie we lost in Las Vegas and why they were there and asked her to keep her eyes open." She shook her head. "She was so excited about finally getting to meet the great and powerful Rielly that I doubted she was even listening.

"She liked the earrings, though," Diana said as she fastened the other one to her ear. "And she must have been listening, because she did use them, and without that we never would have known what happened to her in Las Vegas. She certainly wasn't in any shape to tell us when she got out."

She opened her notebook. "I took the liberty of downloading and editing what Isis put on the Vampire," she said and began hitting keys. "It starts with her first meeting with Rielly. I'll network it through your truck stop windows." She nodded at the scene of the Ryoanji Gardens.

The wind had died down and the rain was a thin veil of drizzle below the lowering clouds. In the next instant, it was all swept away along with the rain-streaked, truck stop windows.

27

A Boy and His Dog

A white, sandy beach rolled down to the edge of the scuffed, green, linoleum truck stop floor. The line where the two met was as straight and sharp as a razor's edge. There was no sign of a wall or window frame. The image filled the whole space from edge to edge.

The beach sloped up for almost a quarter of a mile to a serrated row of low sand dunes that rolled away towards a distant blue-green jungle. Overhead, fat cumulus clouds, like cotton candy mountains, sailed across the sky. The clouds chased their shadows up the beach, across the dunes, and northward over the jungle, where they began to pile up, climbing higher and higher into distant thunderheads on the horizon.

The camera panned around past an idling grav-car to where the gentle swells of the sea rolled in, staining the white sand with a dark, wet metallic sheen. The waves cut soft furrows through the sun-glittered sea, and Harry picked out a scattering of islands and a dark volcanic plume to the southwest that told him approximately where he was even before the voice-over cut in.

"We're standing on the edge of the Mexican Break, Arizona territory, not far from the spot where the Empire defeated the Seraphim Jihad at Winding Rock," the voice said and for a second Harry thought it was Diana's voice. Then he realized it was her sister's.

"Rielly Logan said that he would meet us here and personally escort us to Las Vegas," Isis continued. Harry could hear an undertone of excitement in her voice as the camera continued to pan around and came to a stop, focusing once again up the beach to the distant jungle. After a moment, it started panning slowly back and forth across the beach.

There was a breeze blowing in off the sea, and Harry could see how it sent streamers of sand skittering up the beach and bent the saw grass growing along the tops of the dunes. Absently, he studied the storm clouds piling up over the mountains on the northern horizon. The dark, swollen cumulonimbi billowed high into a purple stratosphere threaded with quick flares of lightning.

Once again he marveled, as he had done so many times before, at how much the earth had changed since the Crash. The Mexican Break that connected the Atlantic and Pacific Oceans had once been an enormous land bridge connecting the northern and southern continents. The great Slaver islands of the Burn were all that remained of that land bridge now. What was left of Arizona, New Mexico, and Texas was now covered with lush, tropical jungle where before there had been nothing but deserts and drought. The heavy moisture-laden clouds blowing up from the Break carried their life-giving burden far into the jungles of the southern Nevada Quarantine and even further north, transforming the bone dry Great Basin into rolling savannah where great herds of buffalo, antelope, and wild horses roamed.

Jericho noticed him studying the horizon and said, "That storm front is probably over the southern Nevada Quarantine by now. The lightning you see there is nothing compared to when the storm moves north of Las Vegas and hits the area around the old American nuclear test sites at Frenchman's Flats, then you'll see a show. There are electrical discharges in the upper atmosphere that can be seen all the way from New Hollywood. According to the Church, they tear down through the stratosphere and pit the ground with blast craters like the face of the moon."

"That information is purely speculative and more than two years old," Diana said casting a warning glance at Jericho.

"Uh oh, what Schrodinger's cat did Jericho let out of the box this time," Harry wondered.

The camera, panning slowly back and forth across the beach, suddenly jerked to a stop, swung back, and focused on a distant row of dunes bordering the edge of the jungle. A line of horsemen was just climbing into view over the crest of one of the dunes. They spread out along the low summit and stopped, looking down, facing the camera.

Harry could hear the hissing beat of waves against the shore and the soft sough of the wind whipping whirls of sand into small dust devils that danced up the beach and burst like dry bubbles. Then he heard the camera whir, and the riders suddenly jumped into a close up view that left him gaping in surprise. Diana froze the frame.

There were six Norma-genes sitting astride streamlined, futuristic horses that looked as if they had been aerodynamically designed in a wind tunnel. The beasts were as thin as greyhounds with long spindly legs and powerful shoulder haunches. Their pointed muzzles and swept-back, sandblasted-smooth features, that rose to a high dolphin-like cranial bulge, reminded Harry of something but he couldn't quite put his finger on what it was. What really got his attention, though, were the colors. He'd never seen blue, green, or fire engine red horses before. He glanced over at Diana. "Do the horses really have those colors?"

She nodded. She was watching his reactions closely.

He turned to Jericho. "Even given the accelerated rates of mutation in the Quarantine, how long would it take for something like this to evolve?" he asked.

"Not long enough," Jericho said with grim certainty.

"So where does that leave us?"

"Take a closer look at the Norma-genes," Jericho suggested.

Harry's first impression was of pale Indians out of an old Hollywood shoot-um-up. They wore moccasins, buckskin breeches and were either bare-chested or wore fringed buckskin vests. Their blonde hair, bleached to an almost silver transparency by the sun, was tied back with leather thongs. Some had

James Burkard

feathers and beads threaded through them.

Except for the characteristic constellation of star-shaped scars that covered their pale bodies, they looked to be in perfect condition. They were young, lithe, and muscular and sat astride their mounts with a relaxed ease and a supreme confidence that bordered on arrogance.

Harry thought of the deformed, suffering wrecks that he had seen as a young man growing up in New Hollywood and tried to square this with the reality of what he was seeing now. "Remades?" he asked.

Jericho nodded. "Ten years ago I'd have said this was impossible. As far as we knew then, in any random group of Norma-genes, you had something like a million to one chance of getting one with a pure strain of the disease. But here you've got six perfect specimens without any other grosser genetic defects. And Rielly's got a whole army of these guys."

"So he can really do it, remake them I mean?"

"Oh yeah, there's no doubt about that."

Harry looked up at the riders on the hill. Then he slid out of the booth and stood up so that he was on eye level with them. He leaned over the table and studied them closely. He thought a couple of them resembled old Hollywood movie stars, an Errol Flynn, maybe a Cary Grant. He couldn't be sure.

Despite their primitive, noble savage appearance, they were all well-armed with an eclectic collection of weapons ranging from what looked like antique pump-action shotguns, to the most modern military pulse rifles. One of them even carried a light plasma canon resting easily in the crook of his arm.

But it was the last Norma-gene that caught his eye. He sat astride a magnificent, machine-tooled, gun-barrel blue stallion. As far as Harry could see, he was unarmed except for a sheath knife and what looked like a long neural whip coiled around the pummel of his saddle. There was something in the way he stood slightly aside and in front of the rest of the group, something in

183

his air of casual authority that marked him as a leader. And there was something else… Harry leaned closer studying the still… something about those piercing, ice blue eyes.

"You're not going to believe this," he said, looking down at Jericho. "But I think this," he pointed to the Norma-gene astride the blue horse, "is the same guy I met outside of the Eternal Life Building and who appeared outside Chueh's garden."

"Are you sure?" Doc asked.

Harry looked at the still again and shrugged, "No, not completely."

"Just a minute," Diana said and fast-forwarded so that the horsemen suddenly galloped full speed down the face of the dune, and disappeared behind another line of dunes only to instantly reappear, galloping over the crest and racing down the last quarter mile of flat beach in no time.

They dismounted in front of the camera, and milled around in juddering fast-forward. Isis entered the frame, shaking hands and talking animatedly. The camera angle jerked and jumped to keep her centered. She must have had a grav-cam slaved to her, Harry thought. Finally, the fast-forward froze on a close up of the Norma-gene in question, standing beside Isis.

They stood close to each other, smiling for the camera, his arm resting easily across her shoulder. Isis had exchanged her tight, buttoned down academic look from the holo-locket for heavy hiking boots, khaki shorts, and a work shirt under a faded army field jacket with the sleeves cut off. She also wore a pair of silver crescent earrings that were twins to the ones Diana wore.

Harry looked closely at the Norma-gene. "Bingo," he said. There was no doubt about it. It was the same guy that had taken him to Susan and had been outside Chueh's garden. That intense gaze and mocking twist of a smile were embedded like a thorn in Harry's memory. And yet…

Harry looked up at Doc. "I'm sure this is the same guy, but look at how he's dressed," he said pointing to the buckskin breeches and the open vest he wore over his bare chest. "The guy I met in New Hollywood was dressed for the arctic as if his inner thermostat was on the blink. Even outside of Chueh's garden he was wearing what looked like a heavy woolen monk's cloak in a thirty-eight degree heat wave."

"Maybe a disguise," Doc suggested. "Showing us what we expect to see. As I said before, a pure strain Norma-gene is extremely rare and might draw a lot of unwanted attention."

"Oh, and floating above Chueh's wall and disappearing into thin air wouldn't?" Harry said sarcastically. He was tired of never getting straight, conclusive answers to anything.

Diana tapped a key on her notebook and the freeze frame came to life again. The wind blew the sand hissing across the beach. It lifted Isis' hair that had grown to almost shoulder length since the holo in the locket had been taken. Her hair was still a hard-edged platinum blonde, and Harry realized for the first time just how much it made her look like a Norma-gene. Just chance, he wondered, or maybe Diana's sister was a closet, Norma-gene groupie.

Then Isis turned from the camera and looked up at the Norma-gene beside her, "This is Rielly Logan," she said, her voice had a far away, tinny quality as if the mike was suddenly having trouble picking it up. "He's the leader of the Norma-genes in their Nevada Quarantine homeland. His people call him 'Rielly Laughing Wolf', and he's going to be my guide."

The way she said, "my guide" and looked up at him with a smile that had enough wattage to light up a small city reminded Harry of the idolizing groupies that used to wait outside his stage door... or maybe it's just a woman very much in love, he thought.

He set that aside and looked at Jericho. "Did she say 'Laughing Wolf'?" he asked.

"If you liked that, you're going to love what comes next," Jericho said with a thin, humorless smile as the camera pulled back and revealed what the close-up had concealed.

Harry felt the hairs on the back of his neck stand up. "Holy shit!!" he exploded. A huge, black timber wolf lay on the ground beside Rielly who knelt down and rested his hand affectionately on its neck. The wolf looked into the camera, its eyes hooded, its mouth slightly agape, its tongue lolling.

"Where the hell did that come from?" Harry said.

"We think it wandered in from off-camera," Jericho said. "Probably from down the beach while everything was focused on the dunes."

The wind was still blowing sand around. It ruffled the wolf's black pelt, and Rielly shifted position slightly, looking down to keep the dust out of his eyes. The wolf looked away from the camera and rested its head on its paws. In the background, Harry could hear the high-pitched whinny of one of the horses. It sounded like a woman screaming.

Suddenly, he knew what those horses reminded him of. He'd had a glimpse of it as he fell into the spin-generator at Eternal Life and just managed to throw off the wolf that was trying to claw its way into his ka. In the second or two before it was caught in the event horizon and swept away, the thing lost its wolf form and he saw its sharp, swept-back, aerodynamic head rising to a high cranial bulge like the horses' except that it looked more like a hard insect's carapace then a horse's soft flesh. It was also tiger-striped in black and white, but the stripes bleached away down the rest of its body which was the color of old bones or dead fingernails.

For a moment, he looked into its huge multifaceted insect eyes that glowed with the pale green phosphorescence of an old radium watch dial and radiated enough raw hatred to strip-mine an atomic core. Then it was swept away; its dead white body stretching like spun toffee as it whipped around the event horizon. In the end as the thinning strands of its body tore apart, he heard it scream like one of those horses, like a woman screaming.

He was still standing up and put his hands flat on the table and leaned over and closed his eyes for a moment. In the background he heard Isis's voice-over. "Rielly Laughing Wolf says that he would prefer not to be called the leader of the Norma-genes," she said, "but rather their guide. His people call him the "Opener of Ways", and this is his tame, hunting wolf, Nubis."

Harry opened his eyes and looked up.

At the sound of his name, the wolf's head shot up, his movements almost too fast for the camera to follow. One moment he was lying with his head on his paws, the next he seemed to be lunging right at the camera, lips pealed back, yellow fangs snapping and snarling, eyes burning with demonic frenzy.

"Jesus Christ on a stick!" Harry shouted and jerked back so far he almost fell out of the booth.

Rielly grabbed hold of the wolf's neck hair and tried to pull it back. It shook it head trying to get free, snarling and slobbering as Rielly tried to calm it down with a series of barking, yapping growls interspersed with mewling hisses that sounded like nothing Harry had ever heard before. Slowly, the wolf settled back down and once again rested its head on its paws and stared into the camera with its mouth slightly agape and its tongue lolling. Rielly knelt beside it crooning softly in its ear and stroking it gently.

Harry ran shaking fingers through his hair and down the back of his neck that was suddenly knotted with tension. Just a boy and his dog, he thought, and gave a sharp, corrosive howl of laughter.

"Harry, are you okay?" Doc asked, his face furrowed with worry.

Harry fought for control and at last managed to put a lid on his hysterics and nodded. "It just took me by surprise, that's all," he said. "Just one wolf too many today, I guess."

He glanced at Diana who was watching him closely. He cast a

crooked Harry Neuman grin in her direction. "But I have to admit that last one took the prize."

"Yeah, a real blue ribbon winner," she answered dryly and once again their eyes met in a tangle of voiceless intimacy before she broke off contact with a look of angry confusion.

She's not the only one who's confused, Harry thought, and not just about Rielly Logan and his wolf. He had to admit he was attracted to her; more than attracted. He hadn't felt anything like this since… since Susan, he admitted. But why did she have to be Jaganmatri Valkyrie? He must be nuts. She was one of the most frustrating, irritating, attractive women he had ever met. Leave it alone, he finally told himself. There's no future in it.

He looked back at the holo-screen where the sequence had been jumped forward to where the six Norma-genes were now riding away from the camera, following the shoreline eastward. Rielly was in the lead and Isis shared the back of his saddle with her arms wrapped around his waist. The black timber wolf trotted beside them. The old man who had accompanied her from New Hollywood was riding double behind another rider. Gradually, they angled north toward the distant jungle and the bruised wall of rainclouds roiling into the stratosphere somewhere over the Nevada Quarantine. A thread of lightning flared through the distant clouds as the riders topped a line of dunes and disappeared down the other side.

Harry watched the windblown sand skitter across the empty beach. For some reason, it reminded him of the beach in the iconic closing scene of Planet of the Apes.

28

Dark Interlude

Diana froze the image of the empty beach and looked up. Her gaze was once again cool, calculating and in control. No sign of tangled intimacy or angry confusion here, Harry thought, and the thought frustrated the hell out of him.

Her lips quirked in a fleeting smile. Harry wondered if she could read his frustration in her Valkyrie way and found it amusing.

"This sequence you just saw, and the two you are about to see, are all Isis brought back from Las Vegas. Everything else, all her research, all her records and holos, were destroyed. She only got these out because she hid them on the vampire after it was too late to save anything else. I'll let her explain," Diana said and hit a key on her notebook.

The wind swept beach along the Mexican Break dissolved in a swirl of colored pixels and then went dark. It took Harry a moment to realize he was looking into a darkened room at night. He could make out faint, silvery phosphorescence coming through a thin sheath of drawn curtains behind a shadowy figure sitting in front of the camera.

"I have to be careful and do this after everyone is asleep," a voice whispered and once again Harry had the uncanny sense that he was hearing Diana instead of her twin.

"I'm putting this on the Vampire. I've only used it once before, testing it with a sequence from my first meeting with Rielly. I haven't used it since. You told me only in an emergency. I think this is an emergency. I can't trust putting anything else in my notebooks or the extra data cores I brought. They're all compromised. I don't even dare transfer them to the vampire for fear it too will be corrupted. I don't understand how they did it.

I have the best security system Jericho and Chueh could give me. Even the military couldn't hack it."

Harry glanced at Diana. "You didn't tell her about the Normagenes' back-door ability?" he said.

Diana shook her head. "We weren't aware of it until six months ago. By that time she was already in Las Vegas."

"I'm certain they've gotten in somehow," Isis continued. "When I went back in, things were missing from my logs, important things. There was a pattern to it. At first, all the video clips of remaking, the whole process, were gone. Then, the written records went. Then, all the clips of Rielly's pet wolf and all the other wolves wandering around the city were wiped. I'm beginning to be afraid, Di. I think I've walked into one of Jake's prophecies, one of the real bad ones.

"I should have seen it coming as soon as Rielly told me the name of his pet wolf, Nubis. It's short for Anubis, and you know where Rielly makes his home? You're going to love this." She gave a short, choking laugh of despair. "He's got a penthouse on the top floor of the Great pyramid of the old Faro Casino Hotel. He had the pyramid specially rebuilt. I've been living up here with him almost from the day I came and never put two and two together. Some scientist, huh?

"I think they've built a gateway, a small one, on the outskirts of town. It's been there ever since I came. I never paid it too much attention, too busy... too busy banging Rielly!" Once again Harry heard that short, bitter, choke of laughter.

"But when I wasn't too busy, I began to get curious about a lot of things going on here. If you scratch the bright shiny surface of this brave new world, things begin to look decidedly flakey, and when you begin looking too closely at that building on the outskirts of town, things begin to get downright scary.

"Di, I think Rielly's opened a gate and is bringing in the Anubis. It's starting all over again. "I..." She stopped and looked over her shoulder. "I thought I heard something. I think someone's..." A shadowy arm reached out for the Vampire and the darkness dissolved once again into a rainbow swirl of pixels.

Harry blinked and looked over at Diana. "What was that all about?"

She held up an admonishing finger. "Let Isis tell it," she said and started to hit the key and hesitated. "It's not pretty," she warned.

29

The Bride of Frankenstein

When the pixel swirl cleared, they were looking into a large luxurious apartment. Once again, the view went from floor to ceiling as if there was no wall between. This time the green linoleum floor gave way to a thick pile carpet as white as an avalanche. The truck stop interior of Formica topped tables and beige walls gave way to sloping walls of dark tinted glass edged with black silk curtains.

The camera was focused on the end wall and a pair of sliding glass doors. Through the tinted glass, Harry could see what looked like a balcony and a low balustrade and beyond that sky and clouds. It was like looking out at the world through dark sunglasses.

The camera drew back and focused on a large black leather sofa with its back to the sliding doors and a low, black marble coffee table in front. On the table was an ashtray, a crystal tumbler filled with ice cubes and amber liquid, and a bottle of cheap whiskey, half full.

Harry recognized the brand immediately. An old favorite, he thought and felt the old, familiar craving twist his gut. He thought he'd gone beyond that, but it looked like his body still remembered the "good times". He pulled his eyes away from the bottle and looked at Isis.

She lay stretched out on the sofa, with one leg hitched up over the back and one arm bent behind her head, and stared up at the ceiling, smoking a cigarette. She lay there as if unaware the camera was running. She was dressed according to the latest, creepiest, "little girl" fashion to sweep New Hollywood; bobby socks, shiny red, patent-leather, platform heels, a short, hot pink, plasti-silk jumper, and a yellow T-shirt that was two sizes too small. Her long blonde hair was braided into pigtails, each tied with a bright yellow bow.

Her short skirt rode high up on the thigh of her raised leg and the position of her arm behind her head pulled her breasts up tight against the undersized T-shirt. She wore nothing underneath and her nipples pressed impudently against the fabric. Harry wondered if this pose of wanton relaxation with its obvious sexual overtones was on purpose. If so, he wondered to what purpose? He glanced over at Diana. She was watching him. He looked away embarrassed.

Isis suddenly swung her leg down from the back of the sofa and sat up. She looked into the camera and took a deep drag of her cigarette. Harry studied her face through the haze of smoke. He was shocked by what he saw.

It wasn't that she had physically changed that much from the twin he'd seen in Diana's locket holo. Perhaps she was a little thinner but she still kept that deep bronze skin tint that was so startling against the platinum of her hair.

What shocked him was her makeup and what it did to her face. In the locket holo she'd applied makeup with a light touch that tended to underline the strength and beauty that was already there. Now, it looked like she'd applied it with a bricklayer's trowel and wore it like a grotesque mask.

Her lips were exaggerated, brightly painted, ruby rosebuds. A thick coating of blusher turned her cheeks into rouged bruises, while dark eyeliner, mascara, and false eyelashes turned her eyes into kewpie doll caricatures.

Harry realized that that was just the image she was aiming at. The little girl clothes, the pigtails and bobby socks, the painted doll's face. Not a woman but a doll, not a person but a perverse sexual toy. What the hell was going on here?

Isis blew a long stream of smoke into the camera. "How do you like my new look?" she asked in a breathless Marilyn Monroe whisper so like a Norma-gene's. "Do you think it will blow Rielly's skirt up?" She laughed. It sounded like glass breaking.

She crossed her legs, stretched her arm along the back of the couch, and smiled at the camera. She took another deep drag of her cigarette. Harry noticed that her hands were trembling. Behind the false lashes, mascara, and liner, her eyes had the look of a caged animal.

For a while she said nothing, just smiled into the camera and drummed her fingers on the back of the sofa. The smile never left her face and never changed because, Harry suddenly realized, it was painted on. Those rosebud lips had been given a permanent upward quirk like the smile on a clown's face. The effect was ghastly.

"Where to start, where to start," she muttered to herself. At last, she reached for the crystal tumbler on the coffee table. "A toast!" she cried and raised the glass. "To the Bride of Frankenstein!" Her voice lost its breathless Norma-gene quality and instead became a sharp-edged screech, a razor scraping a line of coke across a mirror.

She threw back her head and emptied the tumbler and slammed it back on the table. "It's whiskey, whiskey, whiskey that keeps us all so frisky," she sang as she reached over and refilled the glass from the always friendly bottle.

She ran a finger around the rim of the glass and stared at it thoughtfully. "To the Bride of Frankenstein," she repeated in a normal tone of voice so like Diana's. "I guess that's as good a place as any to begin." She puffed on her cigarette drawing the smoke deep into her lungs and letting it out slowly. Her eyes took on a sad wistfulness so at odds with her painted smile.

"When I first met Rielly, I thought he was the most beautiful creature I'd ever seen," she said. "He was like some fantastic, romantic hero, riding that futuristic, blue stallion with the wind blowing through his silver hair, and Nubis running beside him. Like something out of a fairy tale." She gave a bitter bark of laughter. "A real Prince Charming!"

She smoked the cigarette to her fingertips and then stubbed the butt out in the ashtray. She reached behind her and pulled out a little purse. It was bright red with yellow polka dots and a thin shoulder strap. Just the thing for a little girl out on the town, Harry thought.

She took out a crumpled pack of cigarettes and a lighter. She shook out a cigarette and threw the pack on the table. Then she lit the cigarette, grabbed the whiskey glass, and leaned back with the glass in one hand and the cigarette in the other.

"I have to admit I was smitten," she said. "Head over heels, love at first sight. No, let's not bullshit. The time for bullshitting is long gone, isn't it, Di? You were right when you said I loved him before I even saw him." She took a sip of her drink and waggled the glass. "And Rielly, the bastard, knew it."

"Just listen to me." She shook her head in disgust. "I sound like a self-pitying school girl who's been dumped by the captain of the football team." She smiled her painted clown's smile and looked down at herself and spread her arms. "At least I'm dressed for the part!"

She started to laugh and then stopped herself. She put her drink down and looked directly into the camera. "I'm sorry, Di. This isn't the way it was supposed to be. I should have listened to you. I should have at least suspected something was wrong but... God, he was so handsome, so intelligent, so understanding." She closed her eyes and shook her head. "...and he had the body of a young god.

"They all did, and they were all Norma-genes, and that was impossible. Everything about them was impossible, from their too perfect bodies, to those horses they rode, to that wolf that followed Rielly everywhere and talked to him.

"Oh yeah, Nubis talked and when he did, Rielly listened. I know. I heard. Not with my ears but in my head. That damned wolf was telepathic, can you believe it? This was sensational stuff, and I was in on the ground floor. Nothing anyone told me prepared me for this. I mean, this guy not only had the body of a young god but some of the powers too.

"O-o-h, Rielly." She shook her head and rolled her eyes. "Let's face it, even if I knew then what I know now, I'd still go with him. I'd walk over the dead bodies of every friend and relative I ever had, you included, just for the chance to follow him back to Las Vegas.

"God, he was beautiful," she said, lying back down on the sofa with one leg hitched up over the back like before. She took a drag on her cigarette and blew a cloud of smoke at the ceiling. "Just beautiful, the son of a bitch!" She was silent for a while watching the cigarette smoke drift towards the ceiling. She smoked the cigarette down to the butt and crushed it out in the ashtray until there was nothing left but shredded paper and loose bits of burnt tobacco.

"He really knew how to turn on the charm and sweep a girl off her feet," she said at last. "Not that I needed much sweeping. When we started back to Las Vegas, he asked if I wanted to ride with him. Did I? Hell I would have killed for the chance. It was like a dream come true, pressed against his back with my arms around him, feeling the heat of his body, smelling his musky male smell." She closed her eyes. "I can still feel the tickle of his hair blowing against my face as we raced towards Las Vegas.

"Those horses are unbelievably strong and fast. They're also slightly telepathic and Rielly and his troop rode them without reins or bridles. Instead, you just held onto their mane and thought what you want them to do and they did it.

"They never seemed to get tired, rocking us together mile after mile," she sighed. "You can't imagine how wonderful it was. A little more of that and I would have been ready to give Rielly anything he wanted and that was just what he wanted.

"After we rode up the beach and across the sand dunes for a few miles, Rielly decided no one was following us, and said it would be safe to take a "shortcut" to Las Vegas. He and his troop turned down into a hollow between the dunes where an old woman was waiting for us. She was an unremade witch, a weirding, and she was dressed like a queen.

Rielly never remakes his weirding witches or warlocks who control the special powers he needs. For some reason Norma-genes lose these powers when they're re-made. Most of the time they're so weak and uncontrolled it doesn't matter; but for the few who control real power, remaking is a lost world. They're richly compensated for their loss and are second only to Rielly himself in wealth and power.

"When we were all gathered around her, the witch pointed her finger at the air in front of us and drew a large circle. It was as if her finger was a laser that could cut out a piece of reality. A pencil thin line of darkness appeared where she pointed and when she closed the circle, the landscape inside just fell out onto the ground like a big round picture postcard.

"It left a hole in the world at least eight feet across and looking through it was like looking into a fairy tale, the Arabian Nights maybe. It was as if we were standing on a high bluff above a tropical rainforest. In the distance I could see the spires and domes of an exotic city surrounded by a vast checker-board of farmland while we stood surrounded by sand dunes and the smell of the sea.

"Rielly looked back at me and said, "Shall we?" as if he was asking me to dance and we stepped through. Without waiting for the others, he kicked his horse and we raced headlong down off that bluff and out onto a dirt road, cut ruler straight through the rainforest.

"Those horses ran like the wind and never stopped, never seemed to tire." She closed her eyes and smiled dreamily. "God, it was wonderful, the wind in my face, that racing horse between my legs and Rielly's body pressed against mine and all my dreams coming true.

"We raced for miles through rainforest that gradually gave way to vast plantations as we neared Las Vegas." Her eyes remained closed and her voice took on a soft, dreamy quality as if she was seeing it all again just as it was that first day. "Gangs of men and animals worked the fields, and everywhere we saw these beautiful, godlike Norma-genes on their great, multi-colored horses with their pet wolves trailing in their wake. There was something barbarically feudal and romantic in their bearing, in their clothes with flowing capes and high riding boots and light chainmail armor; in their swords and whips and pistols, in the turrets and colonnades of their whitewashed mansions sitting in the shade of huge, impossible oaks. It was a land of wealth and beauty, and all this Rielly had accomplished in less than twenty years. It was unbelievable, but just a pale preview of the New Jerusalem.

"The heavy rain clouds that had been piling over the forest gave way to open blue sky and as we raced into the city, the sun shone down on it like some celestial spotlight." Her words trailed off and she sat perfectly still, her eyes closed, her features relaxed.

The camera stayed focused on her face that started to twist and contort as if something inside was trying to get out and print its features over hers. A dribble of saliva bubbled from her lips and she began to sway and moan. Suddenly, she opened her eyes wide. They were filled with fear and loathing and showed too much white. Her pupils were mere pinpricks as if she was staring into the sun. "Get away you son of a bitch!" she screamed and then answered herself in a spitting, hissing, mewling obscenity of speech.

She twisted and turned. Her back arched up and slammed down, arched up and slammed down as if she was receiving electroshocks. She threw her head from side to side, screaming and kicking and swinging her fists as if she was fighting some unseen enemy. Her arm shot out and knocked over the tumbler, splashing whiskey across the black marble tabletop. Her eyes rolled up, showing only blood-shot whites, staring into the top of her head.

With an inhuman howl of triumph, she grabbed for the whiskey bottle, but her other hand seized hold of her arm, and the inhuman howl morphed into human speech. "You don't want that!" Isis screamed. As she dragged the arm away, her body seemed to go into hissing, spitting convulsions that left her foaming at the mouth and shaking like a rag doll.

"You can't have me!" she screamed, throwing herself from side to side on the couch and kicking out her legs and beating the air with her fists. Tears ran down her face, smearing her makeup into long black mascara stripes that dripped down her face like black tears.

Finally, she shrieked, "Gottcha, you son of a bitch!" and her hands clawed at the air, closing around an unseen enemy, twisting it, snapping it, and laughing hysterically.

Suddenly, she stopped, as if some infernal motor had cut off inside her. She relaxed with a deep sigh of relief. Her body sprawled bonelessly across the sofa. She opened her eyes and looked around in momentary confusion, her eyes still limned with flitting shadows.

Finally, she sat up and made a desultory attempt to straighten her clothes. Her yellow T-shirt had ridden up, exposing one firm, round breast. Harry noticed dark purple bruises and scars that might have been cigarette burns just before she jerked the shirt down and straightened her skirt. Her pigtails had come undone and she combed her fingers through the tangled platinum snarls and pulled out one of the yellow ribbons. She held it in her hand and looked at it as if she was seeing it for the first time.

Then, she shook her head. "Nodded off again," she said half-to-herself. "Been doing that a lot lately. Gotta watch it." She looked up at the camera. Her mascara was a black smear around her eyes with two, long, black tear-streaks running down her face. She looked ghastly before; she looked even worse now.

"You open that door just a little and you wake up a few hours or days later and you've done unspeakable things." She grabbed the whiskey bottle and picked up the overturned tumbler. Her hands were shaking as she filled the tumbler. She took a sip and closed her eyes with a sigh, holding the edge of the glass pressed against her lips. "This stuff is the only thing that really stops it... well not really," she said with a bitter shake of her head. "It's still there inside me, my own dirty, little, secret alter-ego. I can smell it on me sometimes, like rotting meat.

"I'm not drunk enough," she said and tipped the glass up and emptied half of it in one swallow. "It doesn't like it. The whiskey shuts down something in my mind, closes some doors. It can't get through. It really hates it when I drink." She waggled the glass at the camera. "That's why I keep drinking. Then it's trapped down there in the dark all by its shitty self.

"I just gotta be careful now," she raised the tumbler and squinted at its contents with exaggerated solicitude. "My ladies' little pick-me-up," she said. "But you don't want her to pick you up too much, otherwise... Whoops!" she shouted and jerked her arm in a wide, drunken toast that sloshed whiskey over her hand. "She'll let you down instead." She shook her head. "And that's not good. In fact, it's fucking terrible because then all those locks fall off, and he jumps out like some insane Jack in the Box, Jack the Ripper. Then, the real fun begins!

"It wouldn't be so bad if I was unconscious, but when the son of a bitch gets possession, he keeps a little peepshow hole open and forces me to watch what he does with my body."

She looked away and fumbled after the pack of cigarettes that lay in the puddle of spilled whiskey on the table. She shook out five or six soggy cigarettes before finding a couple that were dry enough to smoke. She laid the one carefully aside, lit the other with her little gold lighter and drew the smoke in with a deep sigh. Then she crossed her legs, leaned back with one arm stretched out along the back of the sofa and smoked in silence. She tilted her head back, watching the lazy curls of smoke unravel towards the ceiling.

"You want to know how I got this way?" she asked without looking at the camera. "It was an accident just waiting to happen. I accidentally walked in on Rielly and Nubis one day. They were in Rielly's study, and I heard these hissing, growling sounds. When I walked in, I saw one of the wolf-headed Anubis standing over Rielly and by the sound of it, reading him the riot act. He sounded supremely pissed and was probably making the point by throwing off his wolf shape and taking on that seven foot tall Anubis wolf-headed, human shape instead.

"I think I knew it all along," she said. "I just didn't want to know so I went on fooling myself, but there was no denying it anymore. Rielly had made a pact with the devil and opened the door to the Anubis, and we were all fucked... but mostly me."

30

City of Dreams, Riding on Nightmares

"I guess I must have made some sound because the Anubis spun around, dropped onto all fours and turned back into its wolf form, but it was too late. It knew I'd seen what I'd seen, and it told Rielly I had to go." She drew a finger across her throat with a grin so wide it almost pulled her painted-on clown smile from ear to ear.

Then she rolled her eyes and shook her head. "But good old Rielly didn't want that, and he told them so. He wanted to keep his little, human sex toy."

"Not to worry, they said, we'll fix everything. You can keep your little Barbie doll. In fact, she'll be better than ever. We'll just remake her. Well, not really remake her, just infect her a little... or maybe a lot. She'll be one of us, but she'll still be yours. Won't that be just perfect?

"And the son of a bitch went along with it!" she hissed and grabbed the whiskey glass. Harry saw her hand tighten and her knuckles turn white with the strain. For a second, he thought she would either crush the glass or throw it at the camera. Instead, she forced her hand to relax into a soft caress. "My last defense," she crooned with bitter irony and, for a second, Harry knew exactly how she felt as an old hot-flash of desire came rushing back as sharp and clear as if he'd just picked himself out of the gutter.

"They used black ice to infect me with one of their kas," Isis said. She looked up at the camera with black tear streaks of mascara smudged across her face and her kewpie doll eyes still showing too much white. "It's one of their favorite ways of getting in," she added. "Only it didn't work out quite like they expected. From what I've heard, it doesn't always turn out like they expect. We're too alien, kind of like trying to force a square peg in a round hole. Their kas can't always link up with our body-minds without something going haywire.

"Lucky for me," she said with forced bravado. "Or maybe Jake Lloyd's daughters are just too crazy to make any crazier." She smoked her cigarette, drawing the smoke deep into her lungs and releasing it slowly, blowing out smoke rings, like insubstantial life preservers that slowly unraveled as they floated away.

"It's completely mad you know," she said at last. "They're all completely mad, but that doesn't matter. It still dreams its unspeakable dreams. It still wants me... still wants to use me, and if I'm not careful, if I'm not always on my guard or..." She lifted the whiskey glass in a silent toast. "If I don't have a glass of my ladies' little pick-me-up handy, it drags me down into that rotting cesspool where it lives at the bottom of my mind."

She looked down, leaned over, and began drawing wet swirls with her fingertip through the whiskey spill on the tabletop. "You can't imagine what it makes me do," she said without looking up. "The degradation, the obscenities beyond imagining... and in the beginning, that bastard Rielly was all for it, all the kinky, sadistic, sexual perversions beyond his wildest teenage wet dreams, and I was always ready, willing, and able to satisfy any of them and more."

She shook her head in despair. "Look at me!" she said. "An alien sexual predator's wet dream made flesh! You can't imagine..." The words trailed away, and she looked up at the camera with a look of such self-loathing that Harry had to look away.

Suddenly, she leaned into the camera and spread her arms as if she was about to take a bow. "What you want is what you get, ladies and gentlemen!" she shouted like some freak show, carnival barker and smiled her painted clown smile. "And this is what Rielly got! This is what he let them make me into!

"Well, not always and never completely," she grimaced. "And when I can't keep that piece of shit locked down in its cesspool where it belongs, there's always this," she said and lifted the glass of amber liquid and took a delicate sip.

"It doesn't like it," she said in a whispered aside. She waggled the glass at the camera. "This stuff closes doors it would rather have wide open. Gotta be careful though, not too much, don't want to get completely blotto." She began to giggle. "Just enough to keep it blotto."

She looked around in momentary confusion. "I think I'm repeating myself," she said and then waved it away. "It doesn't matter, it's worth repeating." She pulled out the top of her T-shirt and shouted down into it. "You hear that you piece of shit!"

The cigarette had burned down almost to her fingertips, and she took a last careful drag and mashed it out in the ashtray. She looked around the room wistfully. "They leave me alone now," she whispered half to herself. "They don't even watch me anymore. They think I'm one of them.

"Even Rielly leaves me alone now. I think I disgust him. I think that's why he lets me have as much of this as I want," she said, tapping the glass of whiskey. "He knows it stops the thing inside me, the thing that disgust even him, the thing that makes him never want to touch me again." She suddenly looked away, hiding her face from the camera.

"And it was all so perfect in the beginning, a fairytale come true." She turned back and faced the camera. There were tears in her eyes. "Oh, fuck that!" she yelled and wiped away the tears with a bitter backhanded sweep. She picked up her drink and toasted the camera. "To Las Vegas, city of dreams, riding on nightmares!" She smiled her gruesome clown's smile and took another careful sip of her drink.

Then she picked up her last cigarette and her lighter and laid them carefully in her little girl's polka-dot handbag. She straightened her T-shirt, got up very carefully and made a "follow me" gesture with her forefinger. She walked a little unsteadily on her high platform heels over to the sliding glass doors. "Come on, let me show you Prince Charming's magic kingdom," she said with a bitter laugh.

She must have had the vampire slaved to her because the camera followed every movement as she slid aside the doors and stepped out onto a narrow balcony of black marble. She crossed to the low balustrade and leaned over and looked down. She leaned over further and further until her feet lifted off the floor and she was balancing right on the edge. A fraction of an inch more and she would go over. She hung like that for a minute or two with her legs spread, the whiskey glass in her hand, and her arms outstretched as if she was flying. The camera never moved. Then she wriggled back and straightened up and took a sip of her drink as the camera closed in and looked over her shoulder. "What do you think?" she asked with a wave of her hand.

The view from the camera swung out and down in a long swooping glide like a hawk dropping from the top of a huge pyramid shaped mountain of black marble and tinted glass. Then it panned out over the city.

It was a roughly circular layout that faded into the cultivated fields of the great plantations that stretched to a horizon of dark, tropical jungle. The sun was going down casting long shadows and glazing gold on the towering spires and domes. Here and there you could still see signs of the old tawdry glitter of a bygone age in the ruins of a castle, with one turret and wall still standing, and the fabled Statue of Liberty sagging to one side with her upraised arm and torch blown away to a ragged stump.

The city looked like a cross between a Cecil B. de Mille biblical epic and Fritz Lang's "Metropolis" with an old Flash Gordon comic book thrown in. There were a couple of huge megalithic stone palaces straight out of the old kingdom of Egypt, side by side with graceful colonnades of a Greek Parthenon, and what looked like a Roman coliseum.

A broad river twisted through the heart of the city where no pre-Crash river had ever flowed before. It branched into what looked like old Venetian canals lined with Renaissance palazzos where brightly colored barges and galleys with painted sails seemed to float upon a golden haze with their rows of oars lifting and falling in a spray of glittering droplets. Harry could almost imagine Elizabeth Taylor reclining in luxury with her Richard Burton-Mark Anthony lover kneeling beside her in the prow. Were those really slaves rowing those barges? He wondered.

Side by side with megalithic and classical architecture were a handful of futuristic needle thin spires, swaying gently like flowers in a summer breeze.

"Do you see that?" Isis said, pointing towards the northern outskirts of the city and what looked like three enormous, stainless-steel obelisks. They were at least fifty stories high with thick doughnut-like brass rings that spiraled up each column and then seemed to flatten out towards the top and coat the pyramid forms on the tip of the obelisk in a thin layer of brass. This layer of brass, in turn, gave way to what looked like a jeweled, cobalt blue cap stone.

Each of the obelisks rested atop squat, square, windowless buildings that looked like they'd been cast in a lead mold. The doughnut-like spirals disappeared into the roofs through what looked like enormous, circular, transformers. The whole installation was surrounded by a high gray wall that looked like it had been poured from a lead mold of its own.

"Watch this," Isis said as the camera focused on the three obelisks, then zoomed in so that the miles between seemed to shrink to just a couple of hundred yards. "I think I've timed it pretty close."

As they watched, the brass rings, spiraling up the side of each obelisk, began glowing red-hot like enormous toaster coils. Suddenly, the jeweled capstones flared into white-hot incandescence, and an enormous electrical discharge danced like lightning between them. A column of sparkling haze began to form within the circle of obelisks. The haze grew thicker and became a column of light that flickered like a neon malfunction. The light flickered faster and faster until suddenly the white-hot incandescence went out in the capstones, the lightning cut off in a sputter of thunder, and the column of light collapsed. Afterwards, the air shimmered with heat within the circle of obelisks as the glowing coils cooled down to a sullen smolder.

"They bring them in just like clockwork," Isis said from off camera.

Harry wondered who was bringing in what, but before he could ask the camera refocused on Isis. "In Xanadu did Kubla Khan / A stately pleasure dome decree," she intoned. "Where Alph, the sacred river ran, / Through caverns measureless to man / Down to a sunless sea..." Then she smiled her gruesome smile, finished off her drink and threw the empty glass off the balcony. "So much for the value of a classical education." She laughed.

"What do you suppose Daddy would think of that?" she asked, jerking her thumb at the obelisks. She hopped up and sat on the balustrade with her back to the city. She swung her legs and kicked up her heels like a little kid. "Rielly built them a gateway so they can come here in their own bodies instead of having to ride in on someone else's," she said. "He can only bring in one or two at a time though.

"I didn't see what it was in the beginning. There was a lot I didn't see in the beginning." She waved her hand dismissively. "Too busy looking at Rielly, I suppose."

She began to root around in the little polka dot shoulder bag until she found the cigarette and the lighter she'd put there. She lit up and inhaled deeply. "Okay, I admit I was probably a little brain dead." She gave a short, savage laugh that had nothing funny in it at all. "Okay, more than a little," she admitted. "All my brain cells sank down into a nice warm spot between my legs. It made Las Vegas look like paradise, and I was sailing over it on my own little, pink cloud." She sucked in a lung full of smoke and closed her eyes and held it for a long time.

She let the smoke dribble out of her nose. "You know how Rielly remakes them?" she asked without opening her eyes. "If you cut through all the ritual mumbo jumbo, which I admit is pretty impressive, he just slits his wrists and lets his blood drip into a golden chalice of wine. Then, he lets one of those wolves slobber all over it, and presto-change-o, instant miracle!

"He lets his followers kneel before him and imagine their ideal body, and drink his blood and wine... and the wolf slobber of course. It reminded me of the old Christian communion ritual, only this one really does transform its worshipper. There's something in Rielly's blood and I suspect, something more in the wolf's slobber that makes it possible for Norma-genes to shape-shift into new, re-made, disease-free bodies.

"I asked for and got a sample from the chalice and from Rielly's blood and checked it out. They gave me a pretty well-equipped lab, by the way. That blood sample had some pretty weird protein structures floating around in it but nothing compared to what I was seeing in that chalice. I'm still not sure what I saw, but it looked like... Shit I don't know what it looked like!" she said and jumped down off the balustrade.

"I was getting everything I wanted but when I asked for a blood sample from the wolf, the doors slammed shut with a big "Off Limits!" sign. That should have told me something but..."

Whatever she was going to say she waved aside and said instead, "Come on, let's go inside before I throw myself over the side." She cupped her hands around her mouth and shouted over her shoulder, "Man overboard!" Then, she walked unsteadily back into the apartment. It looked like that last drink had almost tipped the scales.

She sprawled on the couch again with her arm behind her head, her leg bent up, and her plastic platform heel hooked over the top edge of the coffee table so that the short skirt rode all the way up her thighs. With her other hand she groped for the whiskey bottle and then looked for a glass. When she couldn't find it, a look of momentary confusion crossed her face. Then she brightened "Oh yeah, I remember, "Man Overboard!" She picked up the whiskey bottle by the neck and waved it. "Tallyho!" She giggled and took a long drink from the bottle, wiped her lips with the back of her hand and carefully set the bottle on the table. She eyed it owlishly. There was maybe an inch left in the bottom.

She took her foot off the table and stretched out on her side on the sofa. With her head resting on her upturned hand, she looked into the camera again. "You know, after everything that's happened, after everything he's done to me, I still love the son of a bitch. How lame can you get?" Her words were beginning to slur and a tear trickled down her cheek.

Harry glanced over at Diana, trying to gage how she was taking this. She sat ramrod straight, her face impassive, staring at the far wall of the truck stop interior without once glancing at the holo-screen. She reminded him of someone at a funeral.

"I was so blind. I didn't even see the cracks in Rielly's picture perfect world. I didn't see the slaves. And they were everywhere. You couldn't miss them unless you were blind and brain dead." She grinned her hideous clowns grin. "That was me, blind and brain dead. I mean, how do you miss seeing all those people working the fields every day, riding grav-carts filled with sacks, serving me breakfast every morning." She shook her head in disgust. "See what I mean?" She tapped the side of her head with her finger. "Brain dead.

"I was out riding one day. I loved riding those beautiful, streamlined horses. They could run like the wind and all you had to do was think a thought at them and they reacted. I rode out of the city on one of those ruler-straight avenues. Nobody tried to stop me. In those days I had the run of the country, famous scientist, working directly with the boss, sharing his bed. I didn't notice the looks of contempt behind my back.

"Lots I didn't notice. Like those wolves that were everywhere following people... only they weren't following people, people were following them, and it became pretty clear, pretty fast that there were more and more of them coming in every day, and I didn't even ask where they were coming from!" She reached for the bottle again and shook her head and stopped. "Better not," she said and waggled her finger at the bottle. "Gotta finish this first."

"I've picked up a couple things from this rat bag inside me. His mind leaks like a sieve and most of the time you really don't want to see what's leaking out but every once in a while, you get something useful.

She raised a warning finger. "You don't have to worry about him getting into my mind," she said. "All he's interested in is getting possession and riding his little, alien sex toy into the ground. Even if he did pick up something, no one would pay any attention. He's one of the "lost ones" that didn't fuse and take complete possession. Everyone knows they're as mad as hatters. Hell, they all are, but even by their standards, this guy's off the charts.

"Now listen, Di, this is important," she said and sat up and looked straight into the camera. "They've got seers, like Jake, who have been left out on the astral plane for so long they're as transparent as their kas and can see right through the twisted snarl of timeline futures, and they're looking for us.

"They call us the dark twins, and they know about the King of the Dead. There's someone else too. Someone called the Angel of Death. I don't remember Jake ever talking about her. Whoever she is, she's on our side... kinda, I think. The wolves don't know who she is or who we are or who the King of the Dead is, but they know we exist. They call us the Trinity of Power. Their seers are telling them that together we might be able to close them down permanently, and they're scared spitless and will do anything to find us.

But mostly it's like Jake said, it's all about the King of the Dead. Without him we can do nothing, but without us he might still beat them. It's just that without us the odds against him increase a thousand fold. The Anubis know this. That's why they want to find him so badly, but that doesn't mean they've forgotten us.

"I think that monogram I wrote turned their spotlight on me. I think I may have revealed more than I realized. I suspect one of those seers told Rielly to bring me in. Jake was right to separate us and hide the fact we were his twins. But they still suspect. I think I can keep this piece of shit inside me from finding out or saying anything, but be careful, Di."

She leaned back. "I think that's all," she said, "except for one last thing. They've planted a Nano Tree, maybe more than one. It's growing fifty miles north of here, feeding on the lightning it pulls in. Every once in a while I can feel the earth tremors here in Las Vegas. You know what that means, don't you?"

She stood up with an air of sudden finality. "I'll try to get this out to you somehow," she said. "Now, I think I have to go powder my nose." She patted her scorched clown's face and giggled. She started to turn away and hesitated, looking back into the camera. "I'm sorry, Di," she said. "I'm sorry for everything. Watch your back. I love you."

The screen turned into a pixel haze and stayed that way for quite a while.

31

An Unwelcome Guest Comes Calling

Harry stared silently at the pixels until the screen finally dissolved back into the rain-streaked Ryoanji gardens. He had so many questions he didn't know where to begin, but Diana forestalled them all by saying, "Two weeks ago Isis discovered that she was three months pregnant.

"Oh no!" Harry said. "I'm so sorry, Di."

Diana eyed him curiously as if she hadn't expected such spontaneous sympathy. She hooked one of the dark wings of raven hair behind her ear and said, "She knew she had to stop drinking, and she had to keep the mad Anubis sharing her body from finding out about the baby. She didn't know what damage the alcohol had done already or what the Anubis would do to the fetus if he found out, and it was only a matter of time before he did. All she knew was, she had to get away fast.

"As she said, they weren't watching her closely so she began making plans. Then she learned that the Nano tree was full grown, and the wolves were planning to use it to move the Nevada Quarantine prior to the buildup for an invasion of earth. Suddenly, she realized there was no time left.

"Just a minute!" Harry interrupted. "Move the Nevada Quarantine? Where? How?"

Both Jericho and Diana stared at him blankly. "Haven't you heard?" Jericho said. "It's been all over the news this morning."

Harry shook his head and once again heard Chueh's admonition. "You should follow the news better, Harry."

"Sometime last night, the Nevada Quarantine vanished," Jericho said. "Where it used to be is just a blank, gray wall of what looks like petrified fog. The latest reports say that ships sent into it reappear instantly on the opposite side of what was once the border of the Nevada Quarantine as if there's nothing in between."

"That's impossible!" Harry said.

Jericho shrugged. "It happened."

"But moved it where?" Harry asked.

"When I found Isis," Diana said, "she was raving about how she had to get out before they moved the Nevada Quarantine out of our universe, whatever that means." She glanced at Jericho and quickly looked away.

Something else they're not telling me, Harry thought, and filed it away for future reference.

"Once Isis learned the wolves were planning to move the Nevada Quarantine, she knew she had to act quickly," Diana continued. "But even so, she was determined not to leave empty-handed and decided to steal an Anubis Pathfinder. She knew it was now or never, that the chance would never come again."

"What's a Pathfinder?" Harry interrupted.

Diana glanced at Jericho. The old man's features remained pokerfaced noncommittal. It was her call. After a momentary hesitation she said, "The Pathfinder contains the most valuable, most closely guarded secret of the Anubis Empire, the location of their racial home world. Only Anubis high priests carry them. It allows them to cross the astral plane to any of their colony worlds and find their way home again, and just now, a large number of high priests, representing the various castes and crèches, chose to be in the Nevada Quarantine to oversee the invasion buildup.

"Somehow, Isis stole a Pathfinder from one of them. It was an insane, impossible, wonderful thing to do. Then, she stole a horse, started a diversion to cover her escape, and managed to get out of the Nevada Quarantine moments before it shifted out of our universe. After that, she used the vampire to call me.

"I homed in on the Vampire and found her in the jungle south of what had been the border of the Nevada Quarantine. Her horse lay dead from exhaustion beside her, and she wasn't in much better shape. She'd been fighting off possession from the wolf inside her for days. He kept breaking lose, trying to submerge her; and she kept fighting back, trying to protect the secret of her planned escape and her unborn child. In the end, she had to start drinking again.

"When I found her, she was too exhausted to defend herself, and the wolf inside found out everything; about me, Jake Lloyd, the dark twins, and the unborn baby, and he went over the top berserk, tearing at her mind, trying to take over and get this knowledge back to his race.

"I went... "She hesitated, changed her mind and said, "I had to stop him before he drove her insane or killed the baby. That's when I got these," she said, rubbing the sleeve of her blouse that covered the blistering marks of the wolf she wore on her arm. "I went into her mind with my ka and confronted him."

"You could do that?" Harry asked, astonished.

She smiled sadly. "Valkyrie," she said as if that explained everything. She shook her head. "I've never faced anything like that before," she added, and Harry wondered just what she had faced before.

"On the other hand, that insane piece of garbage never faced anything like me," she said with a streetwise, predatory grin. "I wanted him either dead, or out of Isis, preferably both; but his ka was so entwined with hers that I had to settle for hurting him enough to give Isis a fighting chance while he retreated to lick his wounds.

"I was determined to go back in later and finish the job but first, I had to get her to Doctor Jericho as fast as I could. His island was closest and better defended than the Imperial Palace. I was sure we would be safe there for the night. Unfortunately, I misjudged Rielly Laughing Wolf and the Anubis."

"They broke through my defenses," Jericho said. "Shut them down. They used that quantum back door I didn't know about," he added sourly and glanced at Diana.

"I know I should have told you," Diana said. "But it was a Church secret, and I was still bound by my vows as a Valkyrie." She shook her head. "Another mistake," she said bitterly.

"To make a long story short, they took her back," Diana said. "They had a weirding woman with them and walked right through a hole in the wall of Jericho's study. Rielly was the first one through. He wanted Isis. He had an Anubis high priest and one of his warriors with him. They wanted the Pathfinder.

"When we wouldn't give it to him, the high priest tried to crack open our minds. Those priests are masters of telepathic mind control, but he didn't know he was dealing with a trained Valkyrie and Jericho's eidolon artificial intelligence. When he met a blank wall of resistance, he went mad with frustration and ordered his warrior to just kill us. It would have too if it hadn't been for Jericho's eidolon."

"He and Diana killed the warrior," Jericho said.

Diana shrugged. "It was careless, expecting an easy kill, just a woman and an old man. It was armed and could have just burned us down, but its predator nature wanted the taste of tooth and claw blood. Big mistake!"

"And Isis?" Harry asked.

Diana grimaced. "Rielly grabbed her and jumped back through the hole in the wall while her super Valkyrie sister was busy helping to kill an Anubis Warrior. Isn't that a laugh?" Diana said. "It was my job to take care of her. She sure couldn't take care of herself. She had to use all her strength to keep from being swamped by that thing inside her. When Rielly grabbed her, she had nothing left to resist with.

"By the time we killed the warrior, Rielly and Isis were gone, and the high priest hardly had time to get out before the hole closed behind him." Diana stopped. She didn't look at him but just stared straight ahead, watching a guilt-laden beast of burden march across the inner landscape of her mind.

Harry had said all he had to say about that. He had nothing to add. He could only try to divert her attention. "What happened to the Pathfinder?" he asked.

Diana turned her head slowly and looked at him. He could almost see her mind come back into focus. Then, she smiled, showing a lot of teeth. It wasn't a pretty smile. "I've got it," she said with an almost feral growl. "And I'm going to use it to get my sister back and make sure those sons of bitches never come back again, and you're going to help me."

It looked like his little diversion had worked, Harry thought. The irritating, self-reliant, pissed-off Valkyrie was back in the saddle again. "Why should I?" he asked.

"Because you're already a part of this," she said impatiently. "The wolves think you may be the King of the Dead. Jericho thinks so to. Personally, I have my doubts. There's one other who might be more suitable." She shrugged. "But beggars can't be choosers."

"Thanks for the vote of confidence," Harry said and gave her his crooked Harry Neuman blockbuster smile that was known to make woman melt like butter.

Diana didn't melt. "My pleasure," she said coolly.

Harry shrugged. You win some, you lose some. "How do you expect to get her back?" he asked. "You said yourself they moved the Nevada Quarantine out of our universe. How do you get back in?"

"The Pathfinder is the key. It'll unlock the door to the Nevada Quarantine wherever it is," she said. "I can't tell you anymore. I'm leaving tomorrow morning. If you agree to come with me, I'll tell you everything on the way. You should probably stay here tonight though."

Harry shook his head. "I can't do that," he said. "'I made a promise I cannot break / to walk through the inside of out / into the upside of down / my soul at stake...'"

Diana was unable to conceal a startled look of surprise. She was still finding it difficult to make the Hollywood playboy image fit someone who could quote from an obscure, apocryphal proverb attributed to the Prophet General of "The Book of She".

"Is there a problem?" Harry asked with a knowing smile.

Her eyes flared with momentary irritation and then, icy Valkyrie control took over again. "I'm leaving tomorrow morning early," she said. "With or without you."

"I'm sure Harry can make it by then," Jericho said reasonably.

Harry didn't think so. If he was going to make sure Susan got safely past the Seattle firewall and into the Canadian wilderness, he was going to have to follow her there. His conscience would allow nothing less. That meant the earliest he could be back was the day after tomorrow, probably later. "I can't do it, Doc," he said. "I'm sorry, but there's something I promised to do, and it's going to take a day or two."

"Break the promise," Jericho said.

Harry shook his head. "Can't do it, Doc," he said and turned to Diana. "If you could just give me a day or two," he pleaded, "I'm sure..."

A soft musical chime indicated that someone was at the door. Harry looked questioningly at Jericho. The old man ignored him as he accessed the data-sphere in his glasses. Then he nodded and smiled to Diana. "Our last guest has arrived," he said. "Better late than never."

The door slid open and Roger Morely strode in, flushed and rumpled with his tie askew and his curly ginger hair in tousled disarray.

Harry jumped up. "What's he doing here?" he asked, glaring at Roger and bracing himself for a vision of a black wolf snapping and snarling in his face.

"Take it easy, Harry," Doc said calmly. "I asked Roger to come. He's got some..."

"You asked Roger to come?" Harry cried in amazement. "Don't you know what he...?" Harry stopped. He couldn't betray

Susan's confidence. Who knew what Roger would do if he found out what Susan had told him? If he suspected she was leaving...

"What?" Roger asked as he strode in. "Know what, Harry?" he asked with his usual good ol' boy, used car salesman's grin. "Come on, can't we just let bygones be bygones?" he asked and offered his hand in a friendly handshake.

Harry saw the glint of gold from the heavy signet ring on his finger. He remembered the deep gash across Susan's cheek where a ring had slashed open the soft flesh. "Screw you!" he said, his body shaking with rage, his hands balling into fists.

He turned to Doc. "Is he in on this?"

"Look, Harry if you'll just calm down."

"Well, is he?"

"If you mean have we been sharing information, the answer is yes. Roger is helping us..."

"Bullshit!" Harry shouted. "Doc you don't know what this guy is, what he's capable of." Harry stopped in frustration. What could he say that wouldn't expose Susan to Roger's vengeance?

"What do you mean?" Roger asked, flushing brick red with anger. "What are you accusing me of, Harry? I know we've had our differences in the past, and god knows I'm no angel, but if you got something to say then just spit it out!"

Harry turned to Doc. "Don't do this," he begged. "For Diana's safety, if not for your own. Think twice about letting Roger in on anymore of this."

"I think I can take care of myself," Diana suddenly broke in. "We're not in one of your Hollywood extravaganzas, and I don't need some big, strong, block-busting he-man to protect me, thank you very much!" She eyed him coldly. "I've discussed this thoroughly with Doctor Jericho and Mr. Morely and have every confidence in them."

"But you can't!" Harry said turning to Jericho in desperation. "Doc, don't let her do it! You can't trust Roger. There are things you don't know."

"What things?" Roger asked his voice low and dangerous. "What exactly are you accusing me of?"

Harry ignored him. "Doc, give me a chance. Give me just one more day."

Doc eyed him skeptically. "I don't know, Harry," he hesitated and looked at Diana. "We don't have much time."

Harry looked at Diana, but she refused to meet his gaze. "Just one day. Please, Doc, can't you put off whatever you're planning with Roger for just one more day." He looked at his watch. "Just twenty-four hours that's all."

"If you know something, why can't you tell us now?" Diana asked.

Harry turned to Doc. "Just twenty-four hours."

Roger strode over and leaned across the table, pushing his fat, florid face into Harry's. "I say put up or shut up!" he growled. "I'm through listening to your insinuations."

Harry could smell Roger's sickly sweet blend of breath mints, stale tobacco, and sweat stained cologne, and all the years of frustrated rage coalesced in an image of Susan's battered face.

Doc saw that Harry was about to lose it and stood up and pushed between the two men. Roger stumbled back and Doc put a restraining hand on Harry's chest. He could feel the muscles tensing beneath his grip. "Don't, Harry!" he whispered. "Don't do something you'll regret. Listen, I'll do what I can, twenty-four hours maybe. I can't promise."

Harry said nothing but Doc could feel the tension ease. "Thanks, Doc," he whispered hoarsely, his eyes never left Roger's face. He imagined he could see violet shadows moving beneath the florid surface like roiling clouds running before the wind. He was afraid that at any moment a black snout might push out from that pug nose and if it did, not even Doc would be able to stop him from tearing Roger apart.

"I think you should go now, Mr. Neuman," Diana's voice cool, precise, and preemptory broke the spell. Harry blinked and shook his head as if trying to shake off a bad dream. He straightened up and looked at Diana. "I'm truly sorry," he said. "I'll explain. I promise."

"I sincerely hope so," Diana said with icy skepticism.

"Doc, I..."

"You should go now, Harry," Doc said. "Come here when you get back. Chueh will know where to find me."

Harry looked at Diana and tried on a reassuring smile for size. "I'll try to make it back tomorrow," he said but the smile fit badly, and she gave him a fractional nod of dismissal.

Harry sighed and pushed past the table. Roger stepped back to let him pass. Harry stopped for a moment. "I wish I was wrong," he said and strode out the door.

32

Our Lady of the Road

"Well, you sure handled that with all the delicacy of a root canal," Harry thought as the door slid shut behind him. He stood in the empty corridor, undecided what to do next. He should go back down to Chueh like he'd promised, but at the moment, all he really wanted was to get away, cool off, and clear his head.

"Screw it!" he decided and instead of going down the corridor to the bar, he turned in the opposite direction. Chueh had a back door for clients who wished to avoid prying eyes down in the bar. Harry followed the corridor back to where it ended in a squat, iron-banded oak door like something out of a medieval castle. It was another of Chueh's conceits, totally out of place amidst the delicate rice paper walls and plush carpeting. Harry always thought of the doors in Alice in Wonderland when he used it and figured that was probably what Chueh had in mind... or maybe not. With Chueh you never knew.

Harry lifted the simple iron latch. There was that momentary resistance as hidden processors read his mind-body matrix and then the door opened and he stepped out onto the top landing of a narrow flight of stairs. Unlike the corridor he had just left, the stairs were simple, unadorned oak, the walls whitewashed plaster. At the foot of the stairs was a wall of frozen fog.

As he stepped through it, he felt the same touch of icy cold and disorientation he always felt. Then, he stepped out into a short corridor with a black and white chess board pattern of marble tiles on the floor and polished oak wainscoting on the walls. Businesslike and discrete, he thought, as he turned the corner at the end of the corridor and came to a heavy brass door inlaid with a pane of pebbled diamond glass. He pushed down on the ornate brass door handle. Once again, there was that momentary resistance, then the door opened with a reluctant click, and he strode out onto a busy city street miles across town from where he had entered Chueh's garden.

He looked around, half expecting to find some sign of Norma-genes but there were none. He activated his wrist phone and called up his grav-car. "Marta, can you pick me up, please," he said.

"It's the least I can do," Marta said in her husky, Janis Joplin voice. "Hearing from you always picks me up, Harry," and she signed off bubbling with laughter. Harry couldn't help smiling. At least there was one bright spot in his life.

He set the transponder for the car to home in on and strolled down the street. It was early evening. He glanced back at his watch in surprise. It was almost six-thirty. He'd been in Chueh's for almost three hours. Time flies when you're enjoying yourself, he thought with a sardonic twist of a smile.

Chueh's door opened on a totally different section of town from the sedate, upscale boutiques and fashionable restaurants that bordered the entrance to his garden. The pace here was fast, frenetic, and full of flashing neon. This was the entertainment district where gambling casinos, brothels, night clubs, and private pleasure gardens rubbed shoulders with each other and made fistfuls of money. The District, as it was called, was famous all over the Empire, and the streets were crowded with gawking wide-eyed tourists, strutting, peacock-proud prostitutes, grinning high-rollers, street-wise street vendors, and sweating businessmen in wrinkled suits looking for a good time before going home to the wife and kids.

Harry loved it. He'd misspent a great deal of his misspent youth here, sucking up the glitz and glitter, the energy, the jostling crowds, and the gritty, vulgar flash. Now, older and wiser, he sauntered thoughtfully down the street with his head full of unanswered questions. The most intriguing one was what he was going to do about Diana Lloyd. It had been a long time since any woman had affected him like this. Not since... And that led to Susan. What was he going to do about Susan? There was something not right there. And meeting in old LA? And who was Jack Lloyd really? He was certainly a lot more than the classical scholar and philosopher Harry thought he knew.

While he was wondering about that, he remembered Lloyd had written a book on Anubis, the shape-shifting, jackal-headed god of the Egyptians who seemed to have a lot in common with Rielly's Anubis wolves. As far as Harry knew, the book was the last thing Jake Lloyd wrote, and it wasn't really a book but rather a short monograph called "The Anubis Gate". He was going to have to take another look at it when he got home.

Behind him he heard Janis Joplin sing the first few bars of her classic hit, "Mercedes Benz." It was from the original, limited edition Janis Joplin collection, "A Box of Pearls" that had somehow survived underground in a pre-Crash military bunker somewhere in the Montana Quarantine. The trader who recently brought it back became an overnight multi-millionaire, and Marta immediately became Janis Joplin's greatest fan.

A grin of unreserved pleasure spread across Harry's face as the low, sleek sports convertible bobbed gently to a stop beside him with Janis announcing Marta's arrival. Her chameleon finish was a soft cream color this evening. It reminded him in some subtle, understated way of a silver fox fur coat. Marta was growing up.

As he walked over, a paparazzi grav-corder, that had hitched a ride on the car, shot into the air and began peppering him with questions, buzzing down and zooming in for close-ups.

Harry groaned. He must have forgotten to set the privacy pulse locks that would have discouraged such unwanted hitch-hikers. "This is an unwanted and illegal invasion of privacy," he stated for the record and then ordered the car to activate its electromagnetic pulse shield. A moment later the paparazzi grav-corder dropped out of the air with its processors fried and its speaker hissing and sputtering unintelligibly.

Harry kicked it aside and jumped into the car.

"Where to, Harry?" Marta asked in her hoarse, Janis Joplin whisper.

"I'll drive myself if you don't mind Marta," Harry said and took the wheel.

"I always enjoy when you drive..." she paused. "It drives me cra-z-zy," she added with a seductive, whiskey-tinged laugh.

Harry grinned. Marta's artificial intelligence never ceased to amaze him. She had recently discovered word-play humor and used it whenever and wherever she could.

He felt the wheel click over to manual and stepped on the lift feed to the forward grav-units. He climbed into the traffic pattern, gave Marta the coordinates he'd gotten from Susan, and headed west out of the city. He wanted to get to the rendezvous early enough to look it over and maybe stake it out if for no other reason than to quiet that nagging little voice of suspicion he kept hearing.

He thought of what had happened at Chueh's and concluded that he'd acted like a hotheaded moron. He should have stayed and heard Doc out or maybe just taken him aside for a few minutes and explained things. When it came to Susan though, Harry knew he had trouble thinking straight. He always got caught in a tangled web of guilt, love, hate, and betrayal.

Seeing her battered face had torn open old wounds that he had fooled himself into thinking were healed. He'd felt a flood of tenderness, mixed with a deep-seated sense of guilt, as if he was somehow responsible for her ending like this and that it was up to him to protect her and somehow make things right again.

He knew that was crazy. After all his preaching to Diana about the futility of beating yourself up with guilt and making yourself responsible for other people's mistakes, he'd blown it as soon as he saw Roger.

"Harry?" Marta said. "Am I disturbing you?"

"No, not at all," Harry said, relieved to have a chance to shelve these thoughts for a while. "What is it?"

"I'm sorry about that paparazzi hitchhiker," Marta said.

"It's okay. Don't worry about it. It's not your fault," Harry said. "I just forgot to set the pulse locks."

"No, you didn't," Marta said and there was an edge of concern in her voice. "I'm absolutely sure you set them but when I scan my memory banks, I can't find any record of you doing it."

"A system failure?" Harry suggested.

"That's the first thing I checked," Marta said with a hint of reproach as if to say, do you take me for a total incompetent.

"Sorry, of course you did," he said and wondered, not for the first time, about the extent of Marta's emotional life. He'd thought of asking her a few times but didn't quite know how to go about it without possibly hurting her feelings. Now that was a catch twenty-two if ever there was one, he thought.

"There's a possibility I've been hacked," Marta said, and Harry thought he detected a touch of fear in her voice.

"What makes you say that?"

"Scatological thinking, a process of elimination," she giggled at her own wordplay. "I checked every possibility. Hacking was all that was left."

"But wouldn't you know if you'd been hacked?"

"That's what's so scary," Marta said. "If they were clever enough, I wouldn't. Imagine if someone could go into your mind and change a memory, for example that you drank a cup of tea this morning instead of coffee. If they were clever enough, you'd never know. In my case they weren't. They left a residue of certainty behind even though they wiped the memory, and that's almost worse."

"What do you mean?" Harry asked and thought of what Diana had told him about the Norma-genes ability to hack a super-quantum computer.

"Don't you see Harry, if I can't be sure what memories are

mine or not, I can't even be sure who I am..." Her voice quavered with fear and, for a moment, the soft cream color on the hood of the car took on a rippling rainbow effect like gasoline on water.

Harry knew from experience that this was a sure sign of agitation but had never seen it so pronounced before. He'd had the car for over a year and bonded easily with the basic AI personality matrix. He had watched with almost paternal pride as it branched and developed under his guidance. Marta was curious about everything, and Harry had tried to guide her through the information morass on the data-sphere. She had a natural (?) pre-programmed optimism and enthusiasm that was infectious, and Harry had developed a deep fatherly affection for her.

It was something the manufacturers warned against and even provided slaver software to, as they phrased it, "...keep that professional distance so that the master-servant role remained intact". Harry decided early on he didn't need or want a slave. He wanted someone intelligent and self-sufficient enough to make her own decisions, someone competent enough to take over in an emergency, someone he could trust with his life.

With Marta he got much more than he ever bargained for. She was like a wonderful child full of joyful optimism, insatiable curiosity, and naïve innocence, all coupled with a razor sharp intellect. She was one of the things that helped pull him back to the land of the living after Susan remarried.

"Do you remember when I got you?" Harry asked.

"Of course."

"Remember one of the first things I did was introduce you to Mister Chueh?"

"I like him. He knows how to talk to a girl. He always treats me like a lady when we talk on the data-sphere." She paused. "He calls me his foxy lady and says I'm hell on wheels." She gave a hoarse purr of contentment at the memory.

"He also has a lot of connections that allowed me to have you customized so far beyond the legal limit that if the authorities ever found out, you'd end up in the crusher and I'd end up in the slammer. You're probably one of the fastest, most intelligent, best armed independent grav-cars in the world. I had your carbon fiber body strip-layered with light spider-spin armor that cost a small fortune but, most important, I had you optimized and buffered with the best security programs in the world, fire-walls, encrypted program defense, viral traps, all top of the line military upgrades and beyond. Nothing should be able to get through."

"Something did. I'm sure of it," she said.

Once again, he thought of what Jericho and Diana had told him about Rielly Laughing Wolf and the Norma-gene ability to subvert super-quantum systems. He debated whether he should tell Marta. In the end, he decided this was something he couldn't protect her against. She had a right to know.

After he told her, there was a long silence. Finally Marta said. "Ghosts in the machine, yes, that's a good description. I could almost read consciousness in that vapor trail he left behind... as if he was mocking me with it... teasing me. Why would he do that, Harry?

"I don't know," Harry said uncomfortably, although he was beginning to suspect.

"Harry, I'm afraid," Marta said. "I can't be sure who I am anymore. I can't be sure I won't do something terrible. Maybe go crazy. Can an AI go crazy, Harry?"

"Wow steady," Harry said. She really was in danger of losing it, he thought. She never referred to herself as an "AI". She hated the term. He noticed how the poisonous gasoline rainbow spread across her hood like a darkening bruise.

"Look, forget about maybe doing something terrible. Your basic moral structures are governed by the Robotic Laws. They're hardwired into your system and make it impossible for you to do anything terrible, and there's no way anyone can change that without physically dismantling you.

"If what Doc says is true, it sounds like this guy is sending a message, trying to play with my head. He thinks I'm something I'm sure I'm not, and he's telling me he can get to me anytime, anywhere, maybe even through you. This is just the effect he wanted to have."

"What do you mean?" The whiskey rasp of her voice was thin and fragile, tinged with a childlike vulnerability that he hadn't heard in a long time. She was usually so competent and self-assured that he forgot how young she was.

"Think about it. He selectively wiped your memory and sensory banks but purposely left you with the certainty that something had been done. He knew he left that vapor trail ghost and knew you would find it only if you suspected someone hacked your systems. He purposely pointed you towards it, purposely left a big, fat footprint to scare you and to let me know he'd been there and what he could do."

"If he could do all that, then he could have done more that we don't know about," Marta said and Harry realized his explanation was having the opposite effect than he intended.

They had reached the outskirts of the city where the land broke off in a steep slide down to the sea. Harry had been looking forward to racing the car across the sea, skimming the water at close to the speed of sound. Despite the accident five years ago, he still loved driving fast cars, pushing the envelope, and putting his skill and reflexes on the line. Now, instead of racing towards the coordinates Susan had given him, he idled high above the traffic lanes and put in a priority call to Chueh.

The old man's holographic image appeared, hovering just above the dashboard. "Ah, Harry," you didn't stop back," he chided. "Doc told me what happened. He is most upset." Chueh fixed him with a hard stare. Harry felt like the school screw-up, standing in the principal's office. "What is it with you, Harry, don't you know who your friends are anymore?"

Chueh glanced over Harry's shoulder and suddenly smiled with genuine affection. "Marta, my favorite Lady of the Road. I'm sorry I didn't see you, my dear. How are you?"

Harry couldn't hear her reply because suddenly the speakers went dead. Then Chueh's image vanished. It happened every time Chueh called. Marta acted like a love-sick teenager whose boyfriend had just called, and she demanded absolute privacy with him.

Harry gave a disgruntled sigh and wondered if he was getting jealous. He noticed that the poisonous gasoline rainbow was fading from the hood of the car, and the soft cream color had not only returned but had taken on a slight blush of pink. He smiled with relief. If anyone could get Marta's spirits up, Chueh could.

After five more minutes of silent confidences, Chueh's laughing Buddha image appeared and got right to the point. "I want you to take Marta directly to the gentlemen who customized her security upgrades and software optimizations. I don't think it would be a good idea to take her into old L A at this point."

Harry raised an eyebrow. "She gave you the navigation coordinates?"

"Of course, I asked her."

"Uhm," Harry grunted noncommittally. He was going to have to talk to Marta about the distinction between his private information and hers. She had a tendency to treat anything in her data banks as her own personal property to be disposed of as she saw fit.

"Harry!" Did you hear me?" Chueh asked.

"Sorry, I was thinking."

"Something you should do more of in the future," Chueh said, pointedly letting him know he still wasn't off the hook for his behavior that afternoon.

"My associates were forced to change their place of business since last time." Chueh continued. "I've given Marta the new coordinates. They are expecting you."

"Chueh!" Harry called before the old man could sign off. "I need Marta tonight. There's some place I have to be at midnight."

"Would that place happen to be in old LA?"

Harry said nothing.

"Bad idea, Harry."

"It's important."

"What is?"

"It's personal."

Chueh shook his head. "Bad idea."

"It's important, Chueh. It's something I have to do."

Chueh gave him one of his inscrutable Oriental looks. Then he shrugged. "We'll see," he said. "If it takes too long, I'll provide you with one of my own vehicles."

"But I need…" Harry started to protest.

"Don't push it, Harry."

Harry could hear the steel in Chueh's voice and bowed his head respectfully. "As you wish, Master Chueh."

"I'll keep in contact. We have other things to discuss," Chueh said and then looked beyond Harry with an affectionate smile. "It's always a pleasure to talk to you, Marta. I promise to call again tonight to hear how things are going." Then he broke the connection.

33

Shutdown

Harry sat in silence, watching a dark squall line of thunderheads climbing over the western horizon. Monsoon's coming in early this year, he thought, absently tapping the steering wheel. Chueh's decision irritated him, probably because he knew the old man was right. He couldn't take Marta into old LA if there was the slightest chance that her systems had been compromised.

On the other hand, he didn't trust any other vehicle to cover his back if his premonition of danger proved true. Marta was the fastest, smartest, best-armed and armored car on the road today. Chueh probably had a few battle wagons that could match and probably surpass Marta's armor and armament... but they weren't Marta.

"Harry, am I disturbing you?" Marta asked.

"No, not at all. I was just thinking."

"You're not mad at me for giving Master Chueh those coordinates are you? I know you didn't say I could, but he was only trying to help and I..."

All his resolve to talk to Marta about the distinction between his private information and hers crumbled when he heard the self-effacing uncertainty in her voice. This hacking had shaken her deeply. "It's okay, Marta," he said gently. "Don't worry about it. You did good."

Chueh was right, Harry thought, as he swung the car around, following the new coordinates. There was no way he could take Marta into danger after what she'd been through. Even if Chueh's "associates" gave her a clean bill of health, he might still have to take another vehicle. He knew Marta would hate it as much as he would, but he could always call on Chueh to back him up, and with Marta, Chueh's word was up there close to God's.

The new coordinates took him in a wide bow, out over the sea, south of the city. They swung back in towards the southeast corner of the plateau, a landfill area of truck stop depots, warehouses and small fly-by-nights that catered to everything from horny truckers to wet-ware junkies.

The setting sun sank into the squall line, rising over the sea. Harry could see distant flashes of lightning and hear the muffled rumble of thunder.

Chueh's coordinates took him down to almost ground level, threading a dark weed-choked maze between windowless warehouses. Harry turned on Marta's headlights and throttled down. He could feel the powerful thrumming rumble of her spin-generators as they crept down a long narrow alley. The walls on either side were covered in a profusion of clinging vines. Their leaves slapped against the windows, and a bird flew squawking through the glare of the headlights. The alley made a sharp ninety-degree turn and Harry caught a glimpse of a mottled concrete wall through the greenery. For a moment, he felt like he was in the middle of some ancient, jungle-covered ruin. It didn't feel as if anyone had been down here for centuries, which was probably just what Chueh's associates wanted people to think.

The alley dead-ended in a vine-covered wall. Marta gave it a quick, screeching squirt of hyper code and the wall slid slowly aside. They drove into a featureless room that was nothing but a large concrete box without doors or windows. As soon as the wall closed behind them, the floor dropped away, easing them down a long vertical shaft. They sank into a brightly-lit, cavernous space filled with roaring, grinding, banging activity and countless grav-cars in various degrees of dismemberment.

A technician in spotless white coveralls waved them forward into another large elevator. When the steel doors hissed shut the elevator began its descent, a disembodied voice said, "Please make sure your roof repeller-field is in place. Decontamination begins in ten seconds. Mark!"

Harry raised the repeller-field and a hazy blue bubble covered the interior of the car. A moment later the room was bathed in ultra violet light, and high pressure nozzles embedded in the walls, floors, and ceilings buffeted the car with hot streams of decontaminates. Afterwards, warm air blew the car dry. Steel doors opened in front of them and they slid into a spotlessly clean, white tiled room, lit with high-intensity lamps in the walls, floor, and ceiling. Halfway up one of the walls, the white ceramic tiles gave way to a glassed-in control room.

Six white-suited technicians swarmed over the car as soon as it stopped. A couple went over the interior with portable detector scanners, while others popped the hoods fore and aft and crawled under the car attaching fiber optic and electric cables. One of the technicians motioned for Harry to climb out. "I have to go now," he told Marta. "Are you sure you're going to be okay?"

"It's okay, Harry," Marta said bravely. "Mr. Chueh explained that they're going to have to shut me down for a little while, but there's nothing to worry about. If there's any hacking, they'll find it. Mr. Chueh hires only the best."

As Harry climbed out of the car Marta called, "Harry, where will I go when they shut me down? I mean what happens to me? Do I just not exist anymore... like dying?" Marta was trying to keep up a brave front, but Harry could hear that she was afraid.

"You don't cease to exist," he told her, gently rubbing her front fender where the density of her sensor arrays was greatest. "Your personality, everything that's you, is just lying dormant in your memory core. This is like a human going to a hospital and being given an anesthetic. It knocks him unconscious for a while so the doctor can operate painlessly. The patient isn't dead, he doesn't cease to exist; his consciousness is just sleeping until it's awakened. Don't worry," he patted her hood. "When they shut you down, you're still here, and I'll be here waiting for you when they bring you back on line."

"Thanks, Harry..." she hesitated. "I... I love you," she said in a rush.

Harry was deeply touched. "I love you to," he said.

"Harry please stay until they disconnect me," she pleaded.

"I'll be right here," Harry promised as the technician began going over him with a scanner looking for any electronic bugs that may have been fastened to his body. After he finished, the technician said, "Mr. Chueh wanted to see you when you were done."

"Tell him, I'm not done yet," Harry said and turned away.

The tech grabbed his arm. "He said right away."

Harry turned and deliberately stared at the hand on his arm. Then he looked up at the technician. He was a big, raw-boned man with a stiff shock of sun-bleached hair and pale, hard eyes. Probably one of Chueh's leg-breakers in his spare time, Harry thought.

They stared at each other for a moment. Then, Harry smiled disarmingly. "We don't have to go there," he said. "Just tell Mr. Chueh that Marta wants me to stay with her while they shut her down. I'm sure he'll understand."

The technician gave Harry a measuring stare and then released his arm and spoke into a throat mike. After a few seconds, he nodded and gave Harry a tight professional smile that never quite made it to those pale blue eyes. "It's okay, Mr. Neuman. Mr. Chueh will be expecting you when you're finished."

Harry thanked him, but the technician remained standing beside him. "Don't you have something to do?" Harry said. The tech just gave him his professional, zipped-up smile and remained standing there.

"Ah, I see," Harry said. "Another devoted, star-struck fan, dazzled by my glamour and enamored by my wit. You just can't

get enough of me, is that it?" Harry patted his arm in mock solicitude. "I understand. You're not alone. Would you like my
autograph?"

The tech glared at him, and Harry could almost see visions of
bodily harm dancing through his head.

Harry turned away and stared up at the window wall of the
control room where technicians sat over their electronic scanners
and banks of computer monitors, studying readouts and making
adjustments to equipment. "Can you put me in touch with
whoever's in charge in there?" he asked, squinting through the
glare of the high intensity lights.

When the tech, leg-breaker didn't answer, Harry turned and
looked at him. The tech tried to hold his eye in another tough-
guy stare-down match, but Harry wasn't in the mood for any
more testosterone games. "Just do it, please," he said wearily and
turned away.

He knew the tech was Chueh's way of sending him a message,
of showing his disappointment and displeasure with his
behavior this afternoon. Well, message received, roger-wilco,
ten-four, over and out! Now all he wanted was to get Marta
through this as painlessly as possible, and he really didn't need
any more shit getting in the way.

He could feel the tech standing undecided for a moment and
then finally whispering into his throat mike. One of the white-
coated technicians behind the glass wall looked up and his voice
boomed out of a speaker high up. "Yes, what can I do for you?"

"Could you give me a countdown of ten before you
disconnect?" Harry asked.

"Sure," the tech nodded. "It'll be a couple of minutes yet."

Harry walked back over to the car. He noticed how the cream
color of the hood flickered nervously with that poisonous
gasoline bruise running through it again. "How're you doing,
kid?" he asked brushing his hand lightly across her fender.

"I'm fine, I guess," her voice came through thin and reedy, a frightened little girl's voice. Where was Janis Joplin when you needed her? "Maybe it w-won't take so long. As the saying goes, 'Absence makes the fart grow honder'." She giggled nervously. "On a scale from one to ten that wasn't bad," she said.

Harry smiled. "It could've been worse," he agreed.

"Real pun-ishment, huh?"

Harry gave the requisite groan. He'd walked right into that one.

"Harry, I'm sorry I let you down," she said suddenly.

"What are you talking about? Don't be silly."

"You needed me tonight, and I let you down," she said doggedly. "You were ambushed once before in the Sinks, and you never intended to let it happen again. I may not be very old but I'm not stupid. I know that's why you armed and armored me, why you gave me all those military upgrades. And tonight you're going back there, and I won't be able to go with you."

Harry looked at his watch. "Don't worry about it. We can still make it. We still got time." He said it with more optimism than he felt. It was nearly eight. If he wanted to be out there and reconnoiter before twelve, he had to be going in an hour or so.

"Don't try to fool me," she said. "I know what time it is as well as you."

The loudspeaker suddenly boomed, "Shutdown in ten, minus, mark... nine."

"You see, I knew what time it was." Marta laughed nervously.

"Seven"

"Harry, please be careful!"

"Five."

"I'm sorry I let you down."

"Three."

"Harry, I'm afraid."

"It's okay, kid I'm right he..."

"Shutdown."

The deep creamy gloss of color on the car turned the flat, dull gray of a photographic negative. Something vibrant and alive seemed to flee the heavy, dead machine hanging in the portable grav-units under the pitiless glare of spotlights. Harry knew that it was stupid and irrational, that Marta wasn't gone, that she couldn't be gone, that she was only a complex program floating in the bubble memory of a quantum computer, but still he felt as if he'd just seen someone die, someone he loved... his child.

"Mr. Neuman." Someone tapped him on the shoulder. He hadn't realized that he was bent over with his hands splayed on the fender and his head resting on the hood of the car. The tap on the shoulder came again. "Time to go, sir."

Harry raised his head, slowly straightened up, and turned. It was the tech of course. His face was hard, set in concrete, expecting trouble, but when he saw Harry's face, a bit of the concrete crumbled in confusion. "Ah, Mr. Chueh wants to speak to you now."

Harry was surprised to feel the wet trails of tears on his face. Where had they come from? He wondered and wiped them away.

The tech shook his head in disbelief. "It's only a car, for Christ's sake," he muttered under his breath as he led Harry out of the chamber.

"Yeah," Harry said. "Only a car."

34

Smoke and Mirrors

The tech slammed the heavy steel door behind him and left Harry standing in a dimly lit, windowless room, furnished with a battered metal table with a metal chair on either side. The table and chairs were an institutional gray and were all welded to the floor. Like an interrogation cell, Harry thought, which was probably pretty close to the truth. The room was sound-proofed. As soon as the door locked behind him, the silence was so complete he could almost hear dust motes banging against each other as they floated through the air.

He sat down on the chair behind the table that the tech had pointed him to and waited. They were probably sweeping him for bugs again, making sure the room was secure before opening a line to Chueh. He looked around idly. The walls and ceiling were spinach green steel paneling. The light came from what had to be a twenty-watt bulb buried in a steel mesh cage bolted to the ceiling. He wondered why places like this always had to be so ugly. Then, he noticed the drain in the middle of the concrete floor and the dark stains that splattered the walls in places and decided that ugly was probably the best way to describe what usually went on here.

He shivered involuntarily. The air felt cold and dank, with the musty smell of an old cellar. Beneath that musty smell he picked up something else, a putrid touch of decay mixed with the sharp tang of fresh blood. He noticed how the floor sloped down to that little open drain. Makes it easy to wash away the evidence, he thought. Well, maybe not all the evidence, he glanced at the stains on the wall. They seemed to have gotten fresher, glistening as if the walls were sweating blood.

The smell of death grew stronger, a heavy, fetid smell of putrefying flesh. Harry felt the hairs on the back of his neck stand up. His heart began to race. He could feel the subsonic beat of terror constricting his chest. It stalked the edge of his mind like one of those black wolves looking for a way in.

The steel door suddenly clanged open and Harry flinched. Then he sighed with relief when he saw it was only Chueh. He hadn't realized how on edge he was. He started to get up.

"Stay where you are!" Chueh ordered, his voice cold and hard. "If you move, I'll kill you."

"What the hell is going on?" Harry said and then he saw the little fléchette derringer in Chueh's hand. It was not much bigger than a pack of cigarettes but had six rotating barrels like a mini Gatling gun. Each barrel fired a little packet of miniature explosive fléchettes at well over Mach three. The six barrels could be discharged all at once with enough firepower to slice and dice an elephant at forty feet. On the other hand, one barrel would shred a man nicely at twenty.

It didn't have much range but was perfect for those more intimate occasions and was the weapon of choice for women against wife beaters, cheating husbands, or brutal pimps. It was equally effective against back alley gamblers with loaded dice and an attitude problem or barroom brawlers with axes to grind and a straight razor in their hands. The little guns were affection- ately called "Daisies", either because the six barrels looked like the head of a daisy or because that's what you would be pushing up if you got on the wrong side of one. Like now, Harry thought.

He looked up at Chueh. "What's going on..." he started and stopped when he saw Chueh's face. It was not the friendly face of a laughing Buddha; how could he ever have fooled himself into believing that? This was the face of a murderous pirate, a ruthless Tong Godfather, and a sadistic psychopath with stone dead eyes. He felt as if he was seeing the real Chueh for the first time. The old man's parchment wrinkled face seemed to telegraph every sadistic obscenity imaginable. Chueh's lips crimped in a tight, humorless smile. "Good." He nodded. "We understand each other."

He walked over and sat on the chair across from Harry. He wore an expensive, tailor-made, pearl gray silk suit with a diamond stickpin in a black silk tie and gleaming black wingtips on his feet. He crossed his legs and fastidiously straightened the crease in his trousers while he kept the derringer pointed in Harry's general direction. With a fléchette derringer this close, "general direction" was good enough.

The air was filled with the rank, sweaty smell of fear and death. For a moment, Harry couldn't take his eyes off those six barrels of darkness spaced in a gleaming little circle. He felt raw, animal panic building. His body was throbbing with fear, drenched with sweat, redlining adrenaline overload. His mouth tasted of burnt copper. The room, cold and dank moments before, was now as stifling as a sauna. His breath came in short, hard pants as if he was trying to breathe through warm water. He couldn't remember ever being this afraid. He would grovel, beg, do anything if only…

Whoa! Wait just a minute! What the hell was going on? For a second, Harry caught a glimpse of the truth before his mind was swallowed by another wave of adrenaline fueled panic. But that one glimpse was enough. He fought his way back, like a drowning swimmer. His head broke the surface of illusion and, for a moment, the room flickered with images too quick to catch with the naked eye. Images charged with such emotional horror that… Once again, a tidal wave of fear swept over him with a roaring, subsonic throb of panic, but now he knew… he'd seen… He

"SAY GOODBY TO KANSAS, DOROTHY"

… opened himself to his ka and immediately felt as if he had landed in the eye of a hurricane. All around him he could hear the howl of adrenaline fueled winds of fear and horror battering his body but here, here in this still center… "Give me a place to stand and I'll move the world," an ancient Greek philosopher had said... Harry reached out from his ka and retook control of his world. He shut off the flow of stress hormones poisoning his body and twisting his mind; he flushed away the chemical overload, triggering misfiring neural receptors; he cut the trip hammer beat of his heart and slowed his breathing. He...

"SAY GOODBY TO KANSAS, DOROTHY"

... once again broke the surface and this time nothing could drown him, this time he was in control, this time he sat in the still center of his ka and saw through their illusions and was immune...

"SAY GOODBY TO KANSAS, DOROTHY"

... immune to the throbbing subsonics that were tightening his chest in fear, immune to the bloody, subliminal images flickering too fast for his eye to catch, immune to the pheromones of violence permeating the air and the traces of nerve gas boosting his terror, immune to the illusion... For a moment, he saw...

"SAY GOODBY TO KANSAS, DOROTHY"

... through the illusion, through the stained green walls to the technicians sitting on the other side, controlling this high-tech horror show. And they were also beginning to get the message through their computers, on their monitors, through all the physiological sensors embedded in the chair Harry sat in.

Oh yes, they were getting the message loud and clear. He could feel their nervous glances, their frantic attempts to reassert control, or at least, maybe, perhaps salvage a little something... But they were way past too late. There would be no encores, the show was over, Elvis had left the building, and Harry was bringing down the curtain.

"SAY GOODBY TO KANSAS, DOROTHY"

He looked over at Chueh, or rather the illusion of Chueh, with the flat, black, stone-dead eyes and the flicker of subliminals, jacking up the illusion of a cold-blooded, sadistic, mass-murdering psycho. "We do still understand each other, don't we,

Harry," he asked with his lips still crimped in that tight humorless smile.

"No, I don't think we do," Harry said, keeping his voice level but unable and unwilling to rein in his anger. "What do you think you're trying to do with this tough guy routine? Scare me? You think I need reminding of what a fucking big-shot, bad-ass, Tong Godfather you are?"

"Wrong answer," Chueh said and aimed the derringer at Harry's head. The subliminals were working overtime now, giving it one last shot, flickering tortured, Saint Valentine's Massacre, bloodbath images on those stone dead eyes.

"Chueh, I don't know what kind of a point you're trying to make with this cheap, side-show, haunted house routine, but there's no amount of pain or death you can threaten me with that I haven't seen before. I've died fifty-one times and there isn't a day that goes by when I don't wish someone would pull my plug at Eternal Life and just let me die for real! So let's take off the stupid, scary masks and stop playing Halloween!"

Chueh lowered the gun and sat unmoving his eyes hooded, his face expressionless. Someone had finally pulled the plug on the subliminals. "Well, if that's the way you want it," Chueh said at last and got up. He pocketed the derringer and walked over and opened the door. "Good luck, Harry," he said and walked out.

The room flickered like broken neon and then all color and definition washed out of the walls, ceiling, and floor, leaving only the gray photographic negative of deactivated holo-screens. The subliminal noisemakers shut down, and the room sank back into its original soundproofed silence. The air no longer packed a chemical punch. Instead, it felt mountain-top clean and thin without its freight of pheromone, positive ions, and traces of nerve gas.

Harry leaned back and sighed deeply, letting his anger do a slow burn through the sensors buried in the chair. He was back in control, resting in the calm center of his ka, feeding them data, jacking up his emotions and masking his intentions (two could play that game), and making sure they got one message loud and clear: HE WAS PISSED OFF!!

The steel cell door had disappeared along with the rest of the torture chamber décor. Now, it was just another gray patch on the photographic negative wall. There wasn't even a door handle to show where it had been. Without warning this section of wall opened again. This time there was no clang of steel or creak of rusty hinges. Instead, the whole panel slid silently aside, into the wall.

A moment later, Chueh walked back in. "Hi, Helly! How's tlicks!" he said in his horrible Chink laundry-man parody as if they were still in the Silver Slipper and nothing had happened. He followed this up with his usual, trademark laughing Buddha grin. It lit up his face like an old, wrinkled up jack-o-lantern.

Harry didn't buy it, didn't want any part of it. He stood up and bowed stiffly. It wasn't much of a bow. You could have measured it with a micrometer. To a Chinese elder and a Tong Godfather, it was just this side of insult. Harry knew it, he had measured it that way. "Mr. Chueh," he said keeping his voice neutral, his face expressionless, "I am honored." He gave the end of this ritualistic phrase a slight upward inflection that turned it into a disrespectable half-question. Let's see what he does with that, he thought.

Chueh ignored the barb and gave Harry a fractional bow of his own. "The honor is mine," he said with a knowing smile. Then, he walked over and pulled out the chair across from Harry and sat down.

When he saw Chueh pull out the chair that was no longer welded to the floor, Harry wondered briefly whether this was just another holographic knockoff or whether he might be talking to real flesh and blood. With Chueh you never knew and at this point it really didn't matter one way or the other to Harry.

"Now that we've dispensed with the ritualistic bullshit," he said pushing the envelope for all it was worth. "Maybe you'd like to tell me what the fuck is going on!"

"Easy, Harry," Chueh said raising a warning finger. "You don't want to say something we'll both regret."

"I already regret coming here and talking to your sideshow doppelganger. Any other regrets I pile up along the way, I'll just add to the account." And at least I've gotten the satisfaction of wiping that irritating little smile off your face, Harry thought. He knew he was free-wheeling a dangerous high wire act, but he really didn't care anymore. He didn't like people playing nasty games with his head, especially people he considered friends.

He had been completely truthful with Chueh. There was nothing the old gangster could do to him or threaten to do to him that he hadn't already suffered. Besides, he'd learned to shut off physical pain as easily as a faucet and if they somehow found a way around that one, he could always just shuck this body. He didn't care one way or the other.

Chueh shook his head and sighed regretfully. "Doc warned me about this. Maybe I should have listened."

Harry didn't think that deserved a comment so he just continued radiating his own personal brand of toxic waste. He figured the technicians hiding in the walls were picking up the contamination loud and clear and relaying it to Chueh if he was too dense to pick it up himself.

Chueh leaned back his eyes hooded in thought. "You know, Harry," he said at last. "You're a very dangerous man. I'm glad you're on my side."

35

An Offer He Can't Refuse

"On your side!" Harry spluttered in blind-sided surprise. "After what you just pulled. You gotta be dreaming. I wouldn't..."

"You don't want to go there, Harry," Chueh said and stood up. "Please take my hand," he said.

"What? Why?"

"So you know you're really talking to me and not just some hologram or eidolon."

Harry reluctantly reached over and took Chueh's outstretched hand. It was warm and dry with a surprising grip of spring steel in the long delicate fingers. It was also vibrantly alive with the signature of the old man's ka. There could be no doubt that he was talking to Chueh in the flesh.

The old man continued to hold Harry's hand and looked him in the eye. "I deeply regret what happened here today, and I ask you to please accept my most humble apologies," he said.

For a stunned second, Harry didn't know what to say or do. Here was the most powerful crime boss in the empire asking Harry to accept his apology. Of course he had to accept. As they used to say in the old gangster movies, it was an offer he couldn't refuse. In this case it would cause Chueh an unforgivable loss of face and, despite everything, Harry did not need that kind of grief. On the other hand, he wanted an explanation. Any real acceptance was conditional on that.

"I am most honored," Harry spoke the ritualistic words of acceptance, but his bow was measured with conditions.

Once again, Chueh surprised Harry. "The honor is all mine," he said with a deep bow of unequivocal acquiescence. Then he gave Harry a self-deprecating, little smile. "Now, maybe we can sit down and talk a little."

When they were seated, Chueh made a little circular "roll 'em" motion with his hand and suddenly they were sitting at the edge of the cliff, at the entrance to Chueh's garden, with the panoramic view of hump-backed, Chinese mountains rising out of the morning mist. A cool breeze blew up from the edge of the cliff, bringing with it the smell of new mown hay.

Harry turned and looked up at the high snow-capped mountain towering behind him. "Impressive," he said. "But so was the torture chamber. Do you use that one a lot?"

"I regret that my business requires the use of such tools every once in a while," Chueh said smoothly.

"Like today?" Harry asked.

"You're a personal friend of Doc's," Chueh said, choosing his words with care. "He sets great personal store in that friendship. He says you're a man of unusual potential, a man who can be trusted. Up until today, that was all the recommendation I needed."

"What happened today?"

"Today we became partners."

"I hadn't noticed," Harry said, keeping everything on hold until he got an explanation.

"I have to know the caliber of the people I work with. Before today you were only a good customer, a charming acquaintance, and a man of unusual potential, according to Doc."

"What changed today?"

"Have you heard of black ice?"

Harry stiffened, shrugged. "Of course," he said carefully. "It's a hallucinogen, highly addictive, very expensive. It's the latest fashion statement of the rich and famous and a particularly nasty one even for them. What's that got to do with anything?" He was certain Chueh had seen the Isis holo, but he was willing to play along to see where this was going.

"What more have you heard?" Chueh persisted.

"I've heard that it's such a bad trip that the Tongs won't even touch it."

Chueh leaned back, his eyes hooded, regarding Harry like a sleepy snake. "Anything else?" he asked.

Harry was beginning to feel as if he was in a choreographed, high-stakes poker game. "The stuff is coming in through the Sinks and the Seraphim are distributing it, and they aren't doing the Tongs any favors," he said. "You guys have had a monopoly on the drug trade for so long it's almost an accepted fact of life. You've got the government in your pocket, but more important, you've got the trust of your average citizen because they know that you provide them with standardized, well-regulated, affordable products. If it wasn't for the occasional Tong blood bath and some of your other "business ventures", you guys might almost be respectable.

"Now, along comes black ice. The Seraphim have brought it in and broken your monopoly, and they've done it with a really bad-ass drug. It opens people to a kind of demonic possession that doesn't always take and when it doesn't, the host mind can break down under the demonic assault and go completely insane." He thought of Isis. She was probably back, sitting alone in that glass cage at the top of a black pyramid, fighting demonic possession with only a whiskey bottle to help. The jury was out which way that would go.

Then for some reason he thought of Roger. The jury had long since given its verdict there. He looked at Chueh. "When they take possession successfully," he said and could hardly keep the anger out of his voice, "the alien demon thing hides behind a façade of normalcy, pulling the levers and pushing the buttons. Even though the host personality still functions, it's skewed in a diabolically twisted way by the thing that's taken possession."

Harry stopped. He suddenly remembered Anton Shane and felt as if one of those big cartoon light bulbs had just flashed on in his head. Roger wasn't the only one, he thought.

Chueh smiled minimally. "You were saying?" he prompted.

"I had a run in with a guy today," he said. "He tried to get me to take black ice."

"I heard about it," Chueh nodded.

"Heard about it?" Harry asked.

Chueh smiled. "We like to keep an eye on you," he said.

"We?"

"There was a paparazzi grav-corder across the street, filming the whole thing. Strictly against all privacy laws. The police confiscated it."

"You've seen it?"

Chueh smiled.

"So you know what that sick slime ball was talking about," Harry said. "He loved the stuff, said it turned him into an animal, said it was the best high he ever had, said it changed his life. Just looking at him, I could believe that. I knew him back when I was still doing movies. Back then, he was nothing but a harmless hustler. He isn't harmless anymore."

"I think I broke his nose," Harry said. "Something just snapped inside of me. The next thing I knew the guy was lying on the pavement, and I just turned and walked away."

He looked at Chueh. "You understand? For a second there, I was afraid of being just like him. I wanted to let the beast off the leash and pound him into a bloody pulp. Knowing that, I had to walk away."

"Then, he hit you with a neural whip," Chueh said.

"Big mistake!" Harry said with a ferocious grin, and the old Tong Godfather had no trouble imagining the beast leashed behind that grin.

"How?" Chueh asked.

"How, what?" The smile was gone and instead Harry's eyes had the weary, haunted look of someone who had looked too deeply into his own abyss.

"How did you do it? No one can resist a neural whip. The pain it induces is unbearable."

"I guess there are some things Doc forgot to tell you," Harry said and left it at that.

Chueh leaned back and regarded him for a moment, his parchment yellow face unreadable. At last he nodded and smiled. "Doc said you were a man of unusual potential. I begin to see what he meant."

"Rumor has it that black ice comes in through the Sinks, but it's not made there," Harry prompted.

"No, it's not," Chueh said and picked at the crease in his trousers, straightening an imaginary wrinkle.

Time to talk straight, Harry thought. "You've seen the holos Diana's sister brought back?" Harry said.

"Yes."

"So you know."

"Of course," Chueh said. He crossed his legs and fastidiously plucked at the knees of his trousers. "When black ice first turned up about a year and a half ago, the Tongs were naturally concerned," he said. "As you pointed out, we have a very lucrative monopoly and a reputation to protect. We also have, shall we say, a commercial agreement with the Sinks that guarantees this monopoly. They were breaking this agreement. We asked them to stop and they refused."

"So that's what's behind what people have begun calling, The New Tong Wars." Harry said.

Chueh nodded. "At first we tried to stop the flow of black ice into New Hollywood by going into the Sinks and taking out a few staging areas." Chueh shook his head with sardonic amusement. "It was getting to be like the old War on Drugs, only we were the ones making war. And just like back then, we realized that the only way to stop this was to stop it at its source. Which we discovered was not in the Sinks. They were only middlemen.

"During the last few months, we've managed to track it back up north to the Oregon Quarantine and a group of Norma-genes who bring it down to the coast and sell it to the Seraphim for almost nothing. From what we were able to find out, the drug was not produced anywhere near the coast. It's brought in from somewhere further inland."

"Like the Nevada Quarantine," Harry said.

"Do you know the story of Pinocchio?" Chueh asked.

"You mean the old Walt Disney fairytale? Yeah, why?"

Chueh leaned back comfortably and stared at the distant mountains that seemed to float over the horizon on a sea of golden fog. "In the story, Pinocchio and all the bad boys are taken to an amusement park," he said, "where they can smash things to their hearts content, eat themselves silly on sweets, and drink themselves into a stupor from unending streams of beer and wine. While it lasts, it's every delinquent's dream of heaven. But then these bad boys began to change. They turned into animals, into donkeys to be exact. When the change was complete, the men who ran the park came in, rounded them up and herded them away to slave labor."

Harry thought of Anton Shane and the Wolf Temple and nodded thoughtfully. "I see where you're going with this," he said. "The Wolf Temples are like that amusement park, and black ice turns you lose in it to fulfill all the darkest desires of the human beast by becoming one of these black wolves..."

Harry stopped as he remembered Anton Shane swaggering across the street, like a nuclear meltdown, radiating such deadly danger that people instinctively stepped out of his way.

Chueh sat patiently, watching him with hooded eyes, waiting for him to put it all together.

"When they take black ice in the Wolf Temples," Harry said at last, "they think they become animals, but in reality the animals become them."

The old man nodded. "The wolves use black ice in the Wolf Temples to open people up to possession," he said. "In the beginning they let people ride them. They take them back to their world where people think they are experiencing the purity of their own animal nature but, in reality, they're experiencing the nature of the wolves they're riding. As they hunt, kill, feed and copulate, the boundaries between their human ka and the wolf's are gradually eroded. After a few times of this, when a person comes back, he brings the wolf with him but now, instead of him riding the wolf, the wolf is riding him.

"Do you know how many Wolf Temples there are in the city at this moment?" Chueh asked as he contemplated the distant landscape.

Harry shook his head.

"Forty-one."

Harry gave a soft whistle of surprise. "I knew that there were a lot, but not that many."

"I suspect the wolves discovered that this Pinocchio amusement park is a much more effective way of taking possession of human bodies than catching them between resurrections or just spiking their drinks with black ice at some party. They've lost a lot of warriors that way when possession failed, driving either the host or the wolf, or both, insane, and leaving the wolf stranded inside. On the other hand, it looks like they have an almost hundred percent success rate in the Wolf Temples.

"How do you know this?"

Chueh smiled enigmatically. "In business it's always a good idea to keep an eye on your competitors, especially these competitors. One of the first things we noticed was the concentration of Wolf Temples in areas of the city where the rich, powerful, and politically connected live and congregate. It looks like the wolves are building a fifth column army of black ice possessed all over New Hollywood but especially concentrated among the rich and powerful. You'd be surprised at how many high-ranking military personal, politicians, business people and their families are members of Wolf Temples."

"They're not wolves, you know," Harry said. "I got a glimpse of what they really look like when I resurrected. They're not anything like wolves. I don't know exactly where they come from, but they're not like anything from this world."

"No, they're not," Chueh said. "And it took us too long to realize it. They're Jake Lloyd's Anubis, and they're planning an invasion just like he warned, and we never even noticed." He shook his head in disgust. "And now they're holding all the cards. They've got a powerful fifth column in place in the heart of the Empire and an advanced technology that can bring down grav-ships and move over a hundred thousand square miles of Nevada Quarantine out of our universe in the blink of an eye and, to top it all off, they're now capable of bringing an army and warships into a staging area in the Nevada Quarantine. In any conventional war we don't stand a chance."

Chueh leaned forward, rested his elbows on the table, steepled his fingers, and regarded Harry with just a hint of a smile. "Fortunately for us, the Anubis don't believe this is a conventional war," he said. "As a matter of fact, neither do Jericho, Diana nor the Church of She."

"The Church?" Harry asked nonplused.

"The Church is in this up to its eyeballs. You don't actually believe that it's just a happy coincidence that Diana Lloyd, Jake Lloyd's daughter, is a high Jaganmatri Valkyrie in the Church of the Goddess, do you?"

"What is this with Jake Lloyd?" Harry asked in exasperation. "Who was he really?"

Chueh eyed him thoughtfully. Once again, Harry had that same old, uncomfortable feeling of being weighed in the scales. He was getting tired of it.

"Jake Lloyd was the prophet I didn't believe in," Chueh said at last. He shrugged. "We all make mistakes. Jake went out on the Astral Plane further than any man had ever gone before, and he was lost out there for over ten subjective years. When he came back, he was dying, his body eaten away by... probability."

"Are you saying he walked out on the astral plane in his body?" Harry asked in disbelief. "How is that possible?"

Chueh waved the question aside. "It's another story, Harry, and it's not mine to tell," he added cryptically. "What I can tell you is that when he came back, he prophesied the coming of the Anubis again."

"Again?"

"Leave it alone, Harry. Jake Lloyd prophesied the coming of the Anubis and the probable enslavement and destruction of humanity. Probable is the key word. According to Lloyd, the dice are loaded heavily against humanity and the only things that might tip them in our favor are Lloyd's two daughters and a creature called the King of the Dead whose very existence goes against all probability. That means he shouldn't exist at all."

"I don't understand," Harry said.

Chueh shook his head. "Neither do I, Harry," he said. "Neither do I."

"But according to Isis, the Anubis believe in him too," Harry said.

Chueh nodded. "Yeah, it turns out their seers keep finding signs of his possible existence all over the alternate timelines branching out of the quantum field, and they're scared spitless. They're as mad as hatters of course, but the high priests take them seriously and, if the priesthood believes them, the Anubis believe them."

Chueh eyed him searchingly. "Jericho says the Anubis think that you may be the King of the Dead."

"I'm no King of the Dead," Harry said and grinned. "Believe me I'd know if I was."

"Jericho's not so certain," Chueh said. "No one has died and come back as often as you. In some people's eyes that makes you a good candidate for King of the Dead."

"I'm no King of the Dead," Harry repeated, this time without the grin.

"I didn't think so either," Chueh said. "With your background you weren't my first candidate, nor my second, or even my third for that matter. Then you pulled that trick with the neural whip today, and I decided to talk with Samuel Kade... Another thing I should have done a long time ago."

"You talked to Kade about me?" Harry said, feeling somehow betrayed by his former teacher.

"He agrees with Jericho, you're special. No one has ever progressed as fast or as far in such a short time. Kade says you've gone beyond him and don't even know it. Apparently, I should have paid more attention and listened to Jericho."

"I'm not King of the Dead," Harry said emphatically.

"Jericho tells me they tried to capture your ka three times and failed. I don't think that happens too often, do you?"

"I'm not King of the Dead," Harry said irritably. How many times did he have to repeat this?

Chueh leaned back and watched a flock of geese cutting a perfect 'V' across a powder blue sky filled with fluffy, puff-ball clouds. "No one goes through so many resurrections without being changed by it," he said without looking at Harry. "Unfortunately, it didn't look like you were being changed for the better. In fact, you seemed to become more dissolute and irresponsible for every resurrection you went through. When Jericho asked me to let you enter my garden, I did it more to humor him than that I saw any real potential in you, but now..." he shrugged. "Who knows?"

Harry shook his head in stubborn denial.

"No one can resist a neural whip, Harry," Chueh said with disarming reasonableness. "Maybe that's the key."

"To what?"

Chueh shrugged. "Perhaps to our partnership. Now tell me what these wolves really look like."

36

Down in the Sinks

Harry listened to the rain drumming on the roof of the car. A lightning flash left nightmare afterimages of broken towers and rubble-strewn waterways. A second later a cannonade of thunder rolled over the ruins of old LA. It was eleven o'clock. It had taken him almost two hours powered down, picking his way through back alley ruins, and avoiding open waterways to get here, hidden in the shadow of a broken freeway off-ramp a hundred yards from his rendezvous.

He checked the car's sensor dials and monitor images for what must have been the hundredth time in the last ten minutes. The sensor systems were top of the line, almost as good as Marta's. He felt a twinge of guilty regret at being forced to leave her with Chueh's technicians, but there was nothing else he could do.

When the technicians started a deep-sweep AI analysis of Marta's core personality, they hadn't counted on her being a self-evolving individuality without any slaver restrictions. They soon discovered that she had been customizing many of her own deep structures and altering core programs in her personality matrix. This, coupled with the fact that she had already been highly customized with military and security up-grades, made intrusive analysis extremely complex and time consuming. In fact, it sounded like it was going to take all night and probably part of tomorrow, forcing him to take another vehicle.

Chueh's associates had a large selection to choose from, everything from C-class military battle-wagons to long-haul Dumbo freighters, all hidden in a massive series of artificial caverns beneath the warehouse complex. Harry finally settled on a low-slung picket-runner, a little smuggler built for speed and maneuverability. Like Marta, it had been stealth modified with radar absorbent finish, low heat signature, and shielded grav-units.

Unlike Marta, though, its interior was cramped and uncom-fortable, basically a bucket seat, controls jammed between dashboard sensor screens and two massive spin-generators that drove the little picket-runner faster than a speeding bullet. The only left-over space was a little cavity where a miniscule passenger jump seat had been ripped out. Whatever the picket-runner smuggled must have been something with high value and low volume. Something like black ice maybe?

Harry leaned over the detector screens and studied the monitor. The low-glow off the monitor painted his face a ghoulish green. The picture of the partially collapsed building stood out sharp and clear, a computer enhanced composite of all the information his sensors were picking up from side-scan radar/sonar to infrared night vision, x-rays, magnetic resonance imaging, bio scanners and advanced gravity/motion detectors. The sensor systems were what finally sold him on the car.

So far, though, they had picked up zilch. The building faced a broad expanse of open waterway and looked like it had once been a two story apartment block. Part of the concrete facade had collapsed leaving empty black squares overgrown with curtains of Spanish moss, clinging vines, and tropical ferns and flowers. A small forest of coconut palms and banana bushes grew on top of and out of the broken roof. All courtesy of nature's new millennial reclamation project, Harry thought.

Idly, he fingered the medallion that hung from a golden chain around his neck. It was an ancient, bronze, Chinese coin, with a square hole in the center surrounded by embossed Chinese characters. The coin had a blue-green patina of age and was about the size of an old American quarter. It was banded in gold. Chueh had given it to him before he left. He told Harry that the Tongs had allies in the Sinks and if he got in trouble, the medallion would identify him as a friend. He told Harry that anyone going down to the Sinks alone in the middle of the night needed all the friends he could get.

Harry looked at his watch. Time to get moving. He wanted to be in the building before twelve. He fed a trickle of power to the grav-units and slid slowly through the shadows. He stayed powered down, floating only a fraction of an inch above the surface of the water. He knew he'd be a sitting duck if he tried a frontal approach across the open waterway. Instead, he turned into a narrow tunnel of collapsed concrete columns and slabs of broken paving. Outside the lightning flashed, jabbing jagged blue fingers through the dark rain.

He worked his way down the street and around behind the building, staying in the detector shadow of rubble as much as possible. He didn't question why he was being so careful... so suspicious. After what happened down here the last time, he had a right to be careful, but he knew it was more than that. It was still Susan and that something that didn't fit and that he still couldn't put his finger on.

In the end, though, he knew it didn't matter. He'd have come down here anyway. He owed her. It was a debt that could never be repaid. Driving slowly through the darkness, listening to the rain, with the ruins of Old LA all around, he couldn't help remembering that night seven years ago when he held her in his arms in the cold, dark water begging the Goddess to please make it okay again. And when his prayers were finally answered and he got Susan back, he'd screwed up all over again.

He could whine all he wanted about how terrible his contract with Eternal Life was and how much pain and horror it had put him through, but in the end it was still his own choice and could never excuse the way he treated Susan, the drunken rages, the public scenes, and finally the unforgivable, serial infidelities.

Oh, Eternal Life tried to hush it all up. They didn't want any hint of scandal to dull the bright fairytale image they'd built up around the marriage. But it just got too much for Susan, and Harry couldn't blame her. He never blamed her. It had all been his fault, his drinking, his stupidity, his weakness that finally drove her into Roger's arms.

And that was why he was here, he thought. That was why he would always be here, no matter what his suspicions, no matter what his doubts. He owed her, pure and simple.

Besides, once Susan showed him what Roger had done, those deep purple bruises on her neck, her blackened eyes, the gash on her cheek, once he held her in his arms and felt her shaking with fear and with tears in her eyes, there was no way he could have said no.

He thought of the good advice he'd given Diana, how guilt was a blind alley, how you couldn't keep taking responsibility for another person's life. Well, he'd always been better at giving advice than taking it, he thought with a sour smile as he brought the little picket-runner to a halt against the back of the apartment block.

He scanned the back of the building. It looked pretty well intact except for a gaping hole in the glass brick wall of what looked like a back stairwell. He scanned the stairwell and then nosed the picket-runner into the gap beneath the stairs.

Before popping the bubble roof and getting out, he did another scan. Mounds of overgrown rubble, like miniature tropical islands, littered the shallow back-alley sea. The detectors picked up a gigantic sewer rat scuttling along a fallen wall across the way but otherwise, on a night like this, there was little sign of life.

He reached up and ripped away the Velcro straps that held the rail-gun strapped to the ceiling. He usually kept the rifle in a hidden compartment in Marta's door panel. Now, he checked the charge and rechecked the load. The magazine in the butt held two hundred ball bearings. They would accelerate through the magnetic field of super-conductor coils wound around the gun barrel and exit at speeds great enough to transform them into projectiles of massive, destructive force, capable of blowing man-sized holes through Ferro concrete walls six feet thick.

He wondered briefly if maybe he wasn't exaggerating a little, taking a weapon like this along to meet his ex-wife. Then he remembered that rocket trail in the night, the searchlights probing the dark waters, and the sound of Seraphim gunboats coming after him, and also checked the modern copy of an antique Glock 18 slug thrower he carried in a shoulder holster under his jacket. He'd left his iconic Chief's Special in Marta's glove box in favor of the Glock that had more stopping power, an extended 18 round magazine, and could shoot fully automatic as a machine pistol. Be prepared, that's my motto, he thought.

Finally, he set the car on automatic with instructions to continue scanning and warn him of anything out of the ordinary. The AI in the picket-runner was severely limited with loboto-mizing slaver circuits that left little room for independent thought or decision-making. This may have been desirable when all you were doing was running contraband through the Sinks, but Harry would have preferred Marta's self-reliant competence covering his back.

Well, as Marta would say, that's the way Niagara falls, Harry thought, and pulled on the night goggles that hung around his neck and popped the bubble top. Something plopped into the water from a nearby grove of overgrown rubbish. Harry caught a momentary glimpse of a sleek round head and two large faintly luminous eyes disappearing beneath the rain pocked surface.

A seal? No, too big, almost man sized. How had his detectors missed it, whatever it was? He thought of the stories he'd heard as a kid, of old experiments gone wrong, of soldiers genetically modified to fight in the watery ruins of coastal cities during the Tribulations, of genetic change run wild, of sea monsters that were hunted down and destroyed along with all the other mutants during the race purity witch hunts at the end of the

Tribulations. Even today there were persistent rumors coming out of the Sinks...

Harry scanned the back-alley sea, but there was only the sleeting rain and the wind blowing through tropical foliage, all colored low-glow green in his night goggles. He pulled up the collar of his leather jacket, tipped the bill of his baseball cap low over his goggles, and climbed out. His feet crunched on broken glass from the shattered tiles lining the stairwell.

Slowly, he worked his way up to the stairs. From what he had seen during his reconnaissance, the whole first floor was under water. Whatever was going to happen would happen upstairs. Water sheeted down the inside wall. The stairs were slick and slimy, covered with generations of mold that grew up the walls and hung in wet, slippery strands from what was left of the banister. At the top of the landing, the rotting splinters of a caved-in door clung to one rusty hinge.

He heard the sound of a minor waterfall and, when he looked inside, he saw water pouring through a hole in the ceiling down at the far end of a long narrow corridor. The water streamed towards him down the center of the floor and disappeared down another hole that gaped like an open wound a few feet inside the door. Slimy green chunks of concrete clung to bent, twisted steel, reinforcing rods that had been blown up and back by the force of what must have been an explosive charge fired from below in some long forgotten battle.

He looked down the hole to the surface of the sea and once again caught a glimpse of those round luminous eyes looking up at him. A flare of lightning burst across the water and momentarily overloaded the night goggles with white light nothingness. When his vision cleared, the creature, whatever it was, had disappeared.

The hole in the floor covered almost the whole width of the hall, and Harry tested his footing on the rotting concrete as he grabbed hold of a twisted reinforcing rod with one hand and gingerly stepped across the opening with the rail-gun in his other hand. He suddenly slipped on the slimy surface and lost his balance. He started to fall onto one of those rusty, spike-sharp points of torn, bent-back reinforcing rod. Instinctively, he let go of the rail-gun and grabbed for the rod to prevent impaling himself. He cut his hand on the rusty steel and cursed as the gun fell through the hole and disappeared with a dull plop into the sea below.

"Goddamn, son of a bitch!" he muttered as he pulled himself up past the hole. He looked back down but there was no sign of the rail-gun. He should have used the shoulder strap. He shook his head in disgust. What the hell did he think he was doing running around down here, armed to the teeth and tripping over his own feet like some half-assed Rambo warrior? He looked at the shallow bleeding gash the rod had cut across the palm of his hand. He sucked at the wound in his hand spitting out blood and whatever infections it had just picked up and then used a trick he learned from his ka to stop the bleeding and close the wound.

It was crazy coming down here all alone, he thought. What did he expect to do against gangs of Seraphim, pirates, or Slavers if Susan's little deal went sour? He'd counted on that rail-gun to give him extra leverage if he needed it, but now...

He should have asked Chueh for help. The old man had given him plenty of opportunity. But no, he had to come down here and John Wayne it all alone. A man's gotta do what a man's gotta do, he thought. Yeah, and this man's gotta fall on his ass and lose his gun before he even gets started.

He couldn't help smiling at his carping tirade as he did a slow geriatric shuffle down the slime slick hall. "Pathetic!" He grinned. "What a klutz!" he added jacking up the sarcasm. "A block-busting loser!" he giggled with malicious glee. "Can't even walk and carry a gun at the same time!" He put his hand over his mouth to stifle a derisive whoop. Then he leaned back against the wall chuffing down silent laughter.

He could feel the laughter draining the tension from his body. He hadn't realized how tightly wound he was until he felt the tension letting go in little hiccups of laughter. He gave a long, slow sigh of relief. What now? he wondered.

Forget the R-gun, he told himself. At least he still had the automatic in the shoulder holster under his jacket, and don't forget the little Daisy derringer Chueh had insisted on giving him. "You never know when you're going to need an ace in the hole." The old man had grinned and told Harry to hide the Daisy in his boot. Neither weapon was going to do any good against heavily armed battle-wagons but, at close quarters in a building like this, they might give him an edge. We'll just have to make do with what we got and hope we don't need anything heavier, he thought and started down the hall again.

Four doorways gaped open off of it. Harry pulled out the Glock, racked the slide, and fed a slug into the chamber. Then he peeked into the first apartment. There were a few rotting splinters of wood hanging from rusty hinges where the door had been. The floor inside had caved in when the façade collapsed, and he looked down at the open waterway through tangled mounds of overgrown rubble.

He nodded to himself. This checked out with the view out front, from the car. With the façade gone he'd been able to look into all four apartments on this floor. In the one on the right, this one, the floor was gone. The next apartment, the one he was to meet Susan in, had looked pretty intact, while the last two were clogged with rubble from the roof collapsing through the ceilings.

Harry checked his watch. He had less than fifteen minutes to check out this floor. He moved up the hall keeping close to the wall. He glanced into the second apartment.

The rotting remains of a door sagged open against the inside wall, but the concrete floor looked solid enough. He tested it anyway before stepping through. A hall led to a large living room where the collapsed façade left it open to the storm blowing through a curtain of foliage.

A walk-in closet and a small bathroom opened off the hall. In the bathroom a sink had been torn off the wall and smashed into the toilet in some long ago orgy of destruction. The empty eye sockets of a human skull glared up at him from a nest of smashed ceramics. Harry noticed more bones scattered around, broken and gnawed. They didn't look that old, he thought, and was startled by a scuttling rustle off to one side. He spun around with his Glock ready and caught a glimpse of what looked like a mutated sewer rat disappearing down the open toilet drain hole.

The rat-thing was huge and elongated like a dachshund, with a long segmented tail and a scorpion-like stinger on the end of it. Harry kept his gun on the drain and backed out of the toilet. His heart beat wildly and his breath was coming in hard, sharp gasps as adrenaline pumped through his body.

John Wayne rides again, he thought, as he leaned against the wall and reached into his mind, opening himself to his ka and shutting off the flow of adrenaline and other stress hormones. He felt his heartbeat slow and his breathing stutter down to normal. He'd heard about weird animal mutations down here in the Sinks, but hearing about them and seeing them were two different things.

He quickly checked the rest of the apartment, the living room and what had probably been a bedroom, but found nothing but scattered bones and overgrown rotting clumps of what might have been anything from furniture to bodies. After the bathroom, he didn't bother to check too closely.

He walked back out of the apartment and turned down the hall to check the last two doors. As he expected, they were both clogged with piles of rubble that spilled out into the hall. He walked over and looked up at the waterfall pouring through the hole in the ceiling at the end of the hall. The hole was almost six feet wide. A long flap of concrete ceiling was hanging by a pair of rusting reinforcing rods against the back wall. The hole formed a perfect drain funneling all the rainwater off the half-collapsed roof down into the corridor.

As he stared up through the hole, he was blinded again by a lightening flash that overloaded his night goggles with white light. He looked away and waited for his vision to clear. Just then, he heard a scuttling clatter of rubble falling from the hole and instinctively swung his gun toward the sound, fearing that one of those rat things would jump down at him. When his vision cleared, he saw only a dribble of rubble that must have been dislodged by the rain.

He turned back to the apartment and his rendezvous. It was almost time. He stationed himself in the little toilet off the hall, after first jamming a piece of broken ceramic into the drain to block it. Hiding in the darkness, listening to the rain and the occasional rumble of thunder, he wondered what he thought he was hiding from. There was no sign of Seraphim, Slavers, or anyone else. Did he really believe that Susan was hiding something? And all because of a nagging doubt, a vague feeling, something he couldn't quite put his finger on... Was he going paranoid nuts or something?

He was just supposed to meet Susan here. That was all. Then they would go deeper into the Sinks to meet her contacts. That would be the time to be paranoid.

Once again, he saw her lifting the veil, taking off the dark sunglasses, revealing the bruised battered remnants of her beauty. He felt her crying in his arms, and for just a moment he caught a glimpse of that "something" that had been nagging him all day, that "something" that brought him here early, to stand hidden in the darkness; just a glimpse of a shadow of something that fled again when he heard the soft, muffled whine of approaching grav-units.

A moment later, the big black limousine nosed through the curtain of vines and moss hanging in front of the apartment. It was showing no lights, but Harry felt the back-wash of detector radiation sweeping the apartment. The car turned ponderously, blocking the opening. Then it settled, rocking gently on its grav-units, a few inches above the floor.

37

There Be Monsters Here

Harry stood in the smashed bathroom and wondered, what now? Why didn't he just go out and meet Susan? She had kept her word and was right on time, and he had found nothing here to back up his own paranoid suspicions, but still he hesitated. He could hear the muffled hum of the car's idling spin-generators through the background patter of rain. Distant thunder muttered uneasily. What was he waiting for, an engraved invitation maybe? He shrugged and was about to step out of the bathroom when he heard the faint click of a car door latch. He hesitated and then carefully leaned out of the doorway to see what was happening.

The windows of the grav-car were polarized darkness but a long sliver of light fanned out of the interior as the door slowly swung open. At that moment, a giga-watt lightning flash burst directly overhead.

Once again, white-light overload blinded the night vision goggles, and Harry ripped them off impatiently and his baseball cap went flying in the process. A moment later, a deafening clap of thunder drove him staggering back into the bathroom. For a few seconds, he couldn't see or hear anything, but as the thunder rolled away, he thought he felt something rush past his doorway. He couldn't be sure; maybe it was just his imagination, maybe just the pressure wave from the explosive lightning strike freakishly channeled through the apartment, or maybe just sensory overload.

He let the goggles hang around his neck, brushed old plaster dust out of his hair, and peeked out. The car door stood all the way open, and the soft pearly radiance of its interior lights spilled out into a darkness filled with rotting concrete and old bones. Susan sat in the softly upholstered interior, illuminated like some dark, fairy queen, dressed in black as she had been that afternoon with the veil of her little nineteen forties, June Allyson hat pulled down. The dark sunglasses were gone. She sat motionless, waiting.

Harry regarded the tableaux. It reminded him of one of those old Renaissance paintings with a solitary figure sitting in darkness, dramatically illuminated by a candle flame or single ray of light. He shook his head and smiled appreciatively. Susan always did know how to make an entrance.

Just then, she slowly turned her head as if she'd heard his thoughts, but she'd probably heard some minor scuffing sound when he shifted his weight to peek around the doorframe. At any rate, she seemed to look directly at him, but it was doubtful she saw him. She sat in the light, her eyes not adjusted to the darkness, and even though a little light from the interior of the car spilled down the hall, the section where Harry stood was in deep shadow.

She smiled to herself, just a slight Mona Lisa quirk of the lips. Then she slid across the seat to the open door and started to get out. Harry noticed she was wearing elegant, open-toed, stiletto high heels. Not very practical down here in the Sinks, he thought.

As she stretched one long silk stocking leg to get out, her short black skirt rode up over her thigh. Harry caught a glimpse of the soft, milky white skin where the old fashioned, now high fashion, garter belt caught the top of the stockings. He felt his breath catch in his throat and his stomach tightened in that old familiar way. He wondered if he would ever get over her.

She paused, holding the pose as if she knew he was watching and knew what effect it was having. She bent over, put her elbow on her other knee, rested her chin in her hand and looked directly at him. This time, there was no doubt that she saw him. "Hello, Harry!" she said in a breathless whisper. "Have you been waiting long?"

Harry gave an embarrassed sigh and started to step out into the light. At the last moment, he remembered the pistol he still held in his hand and stuck it back in his shoulder holster. "Hello, Susan," he said as he started to walk towards her. "This is kind of a funny place for old friends to meet."

"Old friends?" she said archly, and then shrugged dismissively. "But why not here? This is where it all started."

"Where what started?" Harry asked. As he approached the car, he thought he heard something rustle in the flickering darkness beyond the faint fan of light from the open door. He stiffened, coming to a stop, squinting, trying to make out what it was. He should have kept the night goggles on, he thought as his hand strayed towards the Glock. At that moment, three lightning flashes, one after the other, lit up the apartment like an old Frankenstein movie set. Harry squinted into the stuttering blue light, looking for his own imagined monsters but saw nothing but rotting clumps of indeterminate refuse.

He thought he heard Susan start to say something, but it was washed away in a roll of thunder. As the thunder grumbled into silence, she continued, "Well, it's the night for it, don't you think?" She swung her other leg out of the car and sat in the open door with her knees primly together and smoothed her skirt down.

"For what?" Harry asked irritably, peering into the darkness.

"For bad dreams and worse memories. Do you still have bad dreams, Harry?" She hugged herself and shivered as if she was suddenly cold. "I know I do. And lately, reality has been nothing to brag about either."

"What's going on, Susan?" Harry asked as he leaned on the open car door and looked down at her. She looked so small and vulnerable, huddling in the light of that huge black limousine. Like a frightened child, Harry thought, and felt an almost irresistible urge to get down on his knees and wrap her in his arms.

"What's going on?" she repeated and looked down at her hands clasped tightly in her lap. "I told you. I've made arrangements. I'm going far away before it's too late." She lifted her head and looked up at him. Through the flimsy, black net veil, he could clearly see the cuts and bruises that disfigured her face. Her blue eyes seemed unnaturally large, the pupils dilated with the thousand-yard stare of a shell shock victim. "Come with me," she pleaded.

Harry closed his eyes for a moment and shook his head. "We've been through this before," he said. "We both know it's over." Even as he spoke the words, he knew they were a lie. He wondered if it would ever be over.

He looked down into her eyes, those sad, beautiful blue eyes. They filled his world; they were his world. In their fathomless depths, guilt and retribution were redeemed with the promise of love reborn. He could have the dream back again. He and Susan together…

Without knowing how he got there, he suddenly found himself kneeling before her, gently lifting the veil from before those beautiful blue eyes. "You and I together again, Harry." Her lips were moist and full, whispering to his deepest desires. "We can have the dream again… Take me, Harry! Oh please take me!" she moaned with sudden passion.

Harry felt desire sweep over him like a dark tidal wave. "Careful, Harry!" a small voice whispered in the back of his mind. "You don't know what you're getting into. There's something wrong here. You know it. You can feel it." Harry groaned because he knew it was true and he wanted her anyway.

"But she's another man's woman," that little voice made the mistake of pointing out. "Yes! And see what he did to her!" Harry screamed in silent triumph as the walls of his resolve disintegrated. He took Susan in his arms and pulled her down onto the back seat of the limousine.

A faint smile played across her lips, her eyes were vast fathomless seas a man could happily drown in. He felt her arms around him, answering his desire, her lips swollen with promise. "Kiss me!" Her breath whispered past his ear and pulled a last groan of surrender from his lips as they met hers...

In that instant, when their lips touched, when it was already too late, Harry knew he'd made a mistake. In that instant, he knew what had been bothering him ever since meeting Susan that afternoon. He knew it in the same way he knew Mae West wasn't human as soon as he touched her hand.

Even though Susan had worn black leather gloves that afternoon and shied away when he tried to touch her face, he had felt something was wrong. He felt it more strongly when he held her in his arms but love, guilt, and shame refused to acknowledge it. Not until this moment, when their lips met and there could be no doubt, not until this moment when it was already too late, not until his ka screamed, "This isn't Susan! This can't be Susan! This is something wearing a Susan body, something inhuman, something filled with insane, ravenous hunger..."

Harry tried to pull away, but Susan's arms tightened around his body like steel bands. "No!" he groaned and tried to twist his lips aside. He gave a hoarse scream as small, sharp teeth bit into his lower lip and would not let go. A hand, possessed of inhuman strength, grabbed his head and forced it back until their lips met again. Harry felt the teeth let go and tasted the blood from his torn lip as her lips closed on his and her tongue darted into his mouth before he could stop it.

Her tongue squirmed deeper into his mouth. It felt cold and slimy with a sharp, metallic taste. He bit down on it, hard. It was like biting down on steel mesh that ground against his teeth as it pushed into his mouth. He felt its ravenous hunger, read its monomaniacal intent, flashing like red neon in his mind.

His arms were still free and he grabbed her hair with both hands and tried to pull her head away, but she held on with such inhuman tenacity that instead he tore out a large, bloody clump of her hair. He gagged at what he had done, but the thing that wore her body didn't even notice.

He tried to get to the Glock, but the thing held his body clamped so tightly that it was impossible. He felt its tongue crawling across the top of his mouth, blindly seeking the soft palate at the top of his throat, that soft spot of vulnerability so beloved by suicides, where it could drive up into his brain and make the electric connection that would suck the ka out of his body.

Black waves of panic threatened to engulf him. He wanted to open to his ka and draw on its extra strength to fight back, but he knew instinctively that was just what this monster wanted. By opening to his ka, he would only be exposing it, making it easier for this eater of kas, to satisfy its ravenous hunger.

His body bucked and flopped convulsively like a hooked fish, but Susan's arms only tightened their inhuman, vice-like grip, crushing his ribs and driving the breath from his lungs. He tried to break her hold by kicking out against the floorboards, levering his body up and twisting so that they rolled off the car seat and crashed onto the concrete floor.

He felt her tongue press against his soft palate. He screamed and gagged, rolling over and over through mud, mold, and rainwater rot but he was beyond noticing. Only a pinhole of reason remained in a wall of blind, animal fear.

38

Grandma, What Big Teeth You Have

That pinhole suddenly gave him the memory of a little fléchette derringer strapped inside his boot. He immediately squashed a sudden burst of hope, hid even the thought that had given it birth for fear of giving away his only chance.

He felt the tongue curl back like a snake. Its tip had grown stiletto hard and sharp, preparing to strike through the soft tissue and drive up into his brain. "No-a-r-g-g-g-g!" he screamed and drove his leg up into the things belly. He felt the tongue collapse in a momentary gasp as he reached down inside his boot and pulled out the Daisy derringer. He shoved the little gun up between their clamped bodies and into her belly and clicked the safety to fire one barrel at a time.

The Susan-thing suddenly realized what he was about to do and tried to twist aside. It tore its lips away from his in a low, animal scream that cut off as a hundred miniature fléchettes tore into its stomach, exploded through its back, and blew out its spine. The strength ran out of the arms holding Harry, its tongue shriveled out of his mouth, and the body flopped back into a pool of dirty water.

Harry crawled to his knees and looked over at Susan's body, caught in the fan of light from the open car door. She was lying on her back, the puddle of dirty water turning a deep red. Her hair was spread out around her head like a golden halo, and there was a look of surprised wonder on her face.

He heard the faint, tinny sound of two people laughing behind him. He spun around, but there was no one there. In the backlight from the open car door, he saw the little red plastic heart lying on the concrete floor. It must have fallen out of his pocket in the fight. Somehow it had gotten turned on, maybe when they rolled over it. He could see the little holographic image of Susan and him laughing, kissing, and mugging for the camera. When they began to sing a comically romantic duet, Harry screamed in anguish, grabbed the heart, and smashed it against the concrete until it stopped.

Hot, silent tears of grief ran down his cheeks. "Oh, Sue," he whispered. "I'm so sorry." Even though he knew the thing lying there was not Susan, it still felt as if he'd killed her all over again. His stomach suddenly turned inside-out up his throat, and he dropped to his hands and knees and threw up. Even after there was nothing left, he hung there racked by convulsive stomach cramps as if his body was trying to physically expel what had just happened.

After a while, when his stomach settled down, he pushed himself to his knees and settled back on his heels. He wiped his mouth with the back of his hand and tried to avoid looking at Susan. That was like trying to avoid breathing. At last, he gave up and looked down at her. Fresh tears welled in his eyes. "Oh, Susan, I'm so sorry," he whispered again. Her blue eyes stared up at him unknowing, unseeing, offering no consolation.

Then, they blinked. At first, he thought he was seeing things. Then, they blinked again, and began to change, the whites yellowing, the blue irises turning a feral green. Coarse black hair sprouted from her forehead and a long black snout began to push out of her face. A hoarse growl started deep in her throat, and yellow fangs grew out of the bloody foam of her mouth. A strange ripple passed through her body. It started at her head and passed down to her toes, and as it did, her body began to change into a large, black timber wolf. It lifted its bloody snout and howled, screaming out its insensate pain and rage.

Then it swung its head towards Harry. Spraying bloody foam and snapping and growling; it rolled over, pushed itself up on its forelegs, and began to crawl toward him, dragging its useless hind legs and the gaping, splintered wound of its shattered spine.

Harry backed out of range of those slashing fangs and stepped into the fan of light from the open car door. The beast stopped and eyed him. The feral gleam in its eyes burned with hate and frustration. It snapped and growled and crawled towards him again, but Harry just stepped back, watching it with an odd, paralyzed fascination. This thing had never been Susan, he thought. It was nothing but an alien skin-walker that had shape-changed into a Susan body and stamped it with a Susan person-ality matrix. It was even possible that Susan might still be alive somewhere.

The wolf stopped and cocked its head and seemed to smile, but the smile was really inside Harry's head. Somehow the beast had insinuated itself so deeply into his mind that Harry not only saw its smile but also felt the vicious, gloating triumph behind it. Suddenly, an overlay of Susan's face covered that dark, smiling muzzle like a thin veil. Her eyes were filled with unspeakable terror, and he heard her voice in his mind, "Harry, help me! Oh God, please help me! Get me out of here!"

Harry moaned, "Oh, Susan, what have they done to you?"

In the next instant, Susan was gone and the wolf lunged at him. Instinctively, Harry jumped back but was too late. The wolf should have had him but it slipped on the blood slick floor, and its fangs barely nipped the tip of Harry's boot. The beast shook its head and snapped at the air, howling in frustrated rage.

Harry backed away slowly. "You son of a bitch!" he cried and raised the Daisy and fired. The wolf's head exploded in a puff of blood mist and bone fragments. The howl shut off as if he'd thrown a switch.

It was too late though. It had probably been too late from the moment the car door opened, Harry thought, as he heard the answering howl of another wolf-thing somewhere in the ruins behind the building. He remembered being blinded by lightening just as the limousine door opened and then the feel of something rushing past his hiding place. Of course, there was more than one of them. They traveled in packs, didn't they?

A moment later, he heard the howl again, much closer. It was coming for him, and it was coming fast. Carefully, he reached out with his ka and slammed into the vision of its coming. He saw it rushing up the slime slick steps at the back of the building; saw its black pelt dirty, matted, and shiny with rain, felt its insatiable alien hunger, its insane hatred, and he knew it was coming for him.

He suddenly felt exposed and defenseless, kneeling in the light from the open car door. He glanced nervously into the darkness at the end of the hall and fumbled with the night vision goggles hanging around his neck. He started to get to his feet. He seemed to be moving in slow-motion compared to the wolf-thing closing in. Desperately, he tried to pull the goggles up over his eyes with one hand while keeping the derringer tracking across the shadowy opening to the hall with the other.

Out of the corner of his eye, he caught a glimpse of movement. He looked down at the dead wolf lying at his feet. Its thick, black, matted wolf's fur had turned into pasty white scales like dead fingernails while long, slow, waves rolled through its body twisting, stretching, transforming it into...

Suddenly, he heard a heavy splash and thud from beyond the darkened hallway. In his mind's eye he saw the beast vault the hole in the floor at the entrance to the corridor and come down heavy on its haunches in the water, slipping and sliding on the slimy concrete.

Harry knew his time had run out. He stopped fumbling with the useless night goggles and moved to one side out of the light and slightly behind the car door. He squinted down the length of entrance hall. It wasn't very long, fifteen feet, maybe less, but the light from the car petered out in a long angle of shadow that sliced across the middle of it and left the doorway at the end in darkness.

He felt rather than saw a deeper shadow move into that darkness, saw two feral yellow-green eyes blink, heard the low bloodthirsty growl just before it charged. A roiling cloud of darkness seemed to billow down the hall, rushing towards him at cyclonic speed. For a terrible moment, he felt the paralyzing fear of a small animal caught in the headlights of an oncoming long-hauler. He could hear the heavy woof, woof, woof of its breath every time its feet hit the floor. An instant later, it burst out of the hall and leapt at him. It seemed to expand, filling the whole room, its mouth a gaping maw surrounded by long, sharp, yellow fangs.

At that moment, the spell of paralysis broke. Harry whacked the car door shut with the palm of his hand, cutting off the light and dove aside. He twisted around in midair, swung the derringer up and began firing into the darkness. Two rounds exploded in bright flares against the ceiling silhouetting a black avalanche of fangs and fur rushing down at him. He kept firing as he hit the floor and smashed his head against the concrete.

Abruptly, the darkness above him blossomed red as hundreds of miniature explosions tore open the wolf's chest and stomach. In the next instant, the beast crashed down on him. Its crushing weight drove the breath from his lungs. His finger kept pulling the trigger of the derringer even though he'd emptied all the barrels and the gun was pointing at nothing in particular.

He lay under the dead weight of the wolf's body, drenched in its hot sticky blood. Desperately, he tried to pull the terror-shattered pieces of his mind together. After what felt like an eternity but was probably only a few seconds, he began to make sense of the world again. He realized where he was and tried to wriggle out from under the wolf's dead weight. Suddenly, its body began twitching and jerking as nerve cells shot their last load into the darkness and dying muscles spasmed a reply.

Harry screamed. It was a high, falsetto, woman's scream of pure terror. He thought of the other wolf-thing changing into something else after death. He hadn't had a chance to see it change all the way, but he'd seen enough to know what it was. He kicked out at the wolf's body, trying to shove it as far away as possible. Then, he dug in his heels and back-peddled on his butt as fast as he could until his back slammed into the side of the grav-car. He leaned back against the side of the car with a sigh of relief.

He thought of that falsetto scream, and a classic cartoon skit suddenly began unwinding inside his head. He saw a woman jumping up on a chair, lifting her skirt, and screaming at the sight of a mouse, except he was the woman. He started giggling. The sound balanced on a knife edge between hysterical sobs and mad laughter.

That was probably why he didn't hear the muffled sound of the approaching grav-car until it was right outside the apartment and flicked on an industrial-sized spotlight. The room was suddenly ablaze with the sharp, pitiless glare of an operating theater. The light seemed to burn through the curtain of vines and moss, leaving only faint traces of shadow on the walls. On the other hand, the limousine cast a long, solid, secure shadow. Harry hunched beside the forward grav-coil housing with his knees pulled up to his chest and waited for the next deadly cast of dice.

He didn't have long to wait. "Harry, are you in there?" Susan called hesitantly from someplace out beyond the spotlight. "Harry, answer me," she cried with just the right amount of fear and concern constricting her voice.

39

Caught in the Crossfire

Harry rolled over onto his knees and started to get up. "Susan?" he croaked and a big lopsided grin spread across his face. Then he looked over at the wolf that had once been Susan and was now an alien nightmare covered with dead fingernail scales and the grin faded. Instead of getting up, he ducked back behind the car, uncertain of what to do next.

"Harry, what happened in there? Please, Harry, answer me! I'm sorry I was late. Something came up... Harry, can you hear me?" she called softly.

Harry wanted to believe that this was the real Susan talking. He wanted it more than anything in the world. He wanted to be able to get up, put his lopsided grin back on, and walk out of this like walking out of a bad horror movie. He listened closely to her voice. It was Susan's, no doubt about it, but how could he be sure it really was Susan?

He looked over at the wolf-thing lying in the pool of blood and water. Its headless body had finished transforming into the thing that had been ripped off his back and flung into the event horizon of the spin-generators at Eternal Life. It was monstrously alien and a little while ago he had been sure it was Susan.

"... Harry are you hurt?" Susan's voice cried. "Oh god, please answer me, tell me you're not hurt!"

He thought of the dying wolf's parting, poisoned vision of Susan's ka tortured and trapped somewhere and begging to be set free. The vision may have been a lie, but Harry doubted it. He thought of that vicious triumphant wolf's smile. That smile had been no lie. "You may have killed me, it said, but look what I have, what you will never get." No, that vicious smile of triumph had never been a lie. So where did that leave him now?

"Harry, you're scaring me!" Susan cried. "If you don't answer me this minute, I'll... Ye-e-e-o-o-w-w-l-l!" Susan's voice tore open into a terrified wolf's howl of surprise. An instant later, the spotlight disappeared in a brilliant flash of high explosives. Harry felt the limousine rock on its grav-unit as the pressure wave of the explosion hit it. Shrapnel zinged into the apartment, pinging against the outer side of the limousine and rattling and ricocheting off the walls and ceiling of the apartment in a rain of fused plastic, metal, glass, and carbon fiber. One large flange of metal imbedded itself, like a gigantic arrowhead, in the back wall.

Harry covered his head and flattened against the side of the limo, trying his best to push his way right through its armored skin. A severed human hand still holding a machine pistol landed beside him. The stump was singed and still smoking. Outside, flames licked the night sky. He heard more explosions, men screaming, the rattle of machine guns, and the mewling beat of pulse rifles. It sounded like a full-scale war.

Someone out there had just upped the ante, and Harry decided it was time to cash in his marbles and get out while he still could. The apartment was dimly lit by flickering firelight and the occasional flash of high explosives. He pulled up the night vision goggles from around his neck and put them on... and couldn't see a thing. He ripped them off in frustration.

Now what? The lenses gleamed wetly in the flickering firelight. They were covered with blood. For a moment, he stared uncomprehendingly. Blood? He looked down. His shirt, jacket, jeans; the whole front of his body along with the night goggles was drenched in blood. His blood? How? Then he remembered. Not his blood, wolf's blood. When that last wolf came down on him, he'd unzipped it from crotch to collarbone with the fléchette Daisy.

Harry gave a sigh of irritated relief and tried to find a clean spot of clothing to wipe the glasses on. Outside it sounded like the battle was heating up. Another explosion rocked the building, and a large chunk of ceiling broke off and crashed down on the roof of the limo. Harry ducked and could hear the grav-units squeal as they took up the sudden impact. He looked up through the hole that had suddenly appeared in the ceiling and saw low-lying rain clouds scudding by, limned with firelight and the flash of explosives.

That did it. He pulled the night goggles over his head, snatched the Glock from its shoulder holster, and pushed away from the car. His vision was streaked and blurry but it would have to do. He ran hunched over, heading for the door, trying to keep the limousine between himself and the sounds of battle outside. A heavy caliber machine gun stitched the wall high up near the ceiling, spraying him with chips of rotted concrete as he entered the short hallway. He heard gunfire and fighting on the roof. There was the mewling beat of a pulse rifle again followed by the tearing screech and sonic boom of an R-gun round as another explosion shook the building.

Something soft and heavy landed on the hood of the limo. He heard sharp claws scrabbling for purchase on smooth carbon fiber but didn't bother to look back. He knew what it was. It must have come down through the new hole in the ceiling. He felt its black shadow rushing towards him and heard the heavy woof, woof, woof every time its padded paws hit concrete. The doorway loomed in front of him. One more step and...

Someone stepped into the doorway. In the split second before they ran into each other, Harry took in the pulse rifle, the necklace of human ears, and the dirty, black, Seraphim robe and reacted without thinking. Just before they crashed into each other, he grabbed the surprised Seraphim, spun him around, and shoved him back into the path of the onrushing wolf.

As Harry stumbled backwards through the doorway, he heard a growling impact, the crunch of bone, and a short gargling scream that cut off with a wet, tearing sound.

If there had been nothing but a level plain stretching out to infinity behind him, Harry probably would have kept stumbling backwards forever. Instead, after a few feet, he banged up against the corridor wall opposite the door. For a few seconds, he stood as if super-glued to the wall, unable to move, unable to turn away, unable to not see that frenzied swirl of black fur, bloody fangs, and razor claws ripping apart something that had been human moments before. The beast growled as it worried a splinter of bone that gleamed obscenely white through a spray of blood.

Harry stared at the bone splinter in dumb incomprehension. His eyes registered it and dutifully sent the message on but, for the moment at least, there was no one home to receive it. For the moment, Harry's mind had taken a well-deserved vacation from reality and a big DO NOT DISTURB sign hung on the door.

When his mind flew south for the winter, it left the rest of his body on auto-pilot, and sometimes, auto-pilot has to be good enough. With the slow grace of a dream walker, he lifted his arm. The pistol in his fist tracked across the opposite wall and started firing on full automatic. The heavy slugs punched into rotting plaster and concrete, stitching a pockmarked line across the wall towards the doorway.

The sound of shots exploding in the narrow hallway and the feel of the gun bucking against his hand blew away the DO NOT DISTURB SIGN from Harry's mind, and suddenly he was back in the saddle again.

Most of the slugs he had fired on autopilot had splattered harmlessly against the wall or torn into the body of the dead Seraphim. Now, the wolf threw the body aside and leapt at Harry instead. With his back to the wall, he had no choice but to stand his ground, firing wildly until the beast fell back, snapping and yipping at its wounds. As it turned and fled into the dark interior of the apartment, he emptied the clip after it.

Even after the gun clicked on empty, he kept his finger

pressed against the trigger. Finally, he got the message and let his arm drop. His ears rang with the echo of his own shots. The narrow hallway was laced with trailers of smoke and the air was thick with the smell of blood and spent gun powder. He leaned his head back against the wall and took a couple of deep, steadying breaths.

He heard the sounds of battle. They were all around him. It sounded like there was a minor war going on up on the roof. He heard the sighing whump of an incoming mortar moments before it hit, shaking the building and blowing shrapnel and debris through the waterfall hole at the end of the corridor. He wondered briefly who was fighting who. He'd seen the black wolves of the Norma-genes and he'd seen Seraphim. Could they be fighting each other? According to Chueh, they were allies, or at least trading partners. But even allies can disagree.

The Seraphim were big on demanding respect and guarding their turf. They were also paranoid fanatics. Maybe when the Norma-genes and their black wolves came down here to pick up Harry, the Seraphim took exception. If so, maybe he had a chance to slip away while they were busy cutting each other's throats.

He popped the empty clip out of the gun butt and slapped in a new one from his jacket pocket. He racked the slide, chambering a round, and then started down the hall towards the back stairs and the picket-runner. It was his only chance of escape. According to the navigation display on his wrist phone, the picket runner was still parked where he had left it. As he slipped and splashed down the hall, he called it for a status report.

When he reached the first apartment, he hugged the opposite wall and did a slow shuffle past the empty doorway. He kept the Glock pointed straight-armed at it even though he saw nothing but firelight flickering through the curtain of foliage that hung down to the dark water pooled over the collapsed floor. Once past the open doorway, he gave the car's status report a cursory glance. Everything looked clear. Now, all he had to do was get past that goddamn hole in the floor and down the back stairs.

The sounds of battle seemed to be moving down the block away from him. He could hear the characteristic projectile scream and sonic boom of a rail-gun blowing big holes in a nearby building. For the moment at least, everyone seemed to have forgotten him. He was less than fifteen feet from the hole in the floor and the back stairs and thinking he just might make it when he heard a rattle of stones and the heavy thump of something dropping into the hall behind him.

He spun around with the Glock automatically tracking down the hall. In the green low-glow of his night goggles, he saw the ghostly figure of another Seraphim. He was in a crouch and still off balance after jumping down through the waterfall hole. In the split second between sighting the man and firing, Harry thought, of course, I should have known. The first Seraphim had to come from somewhere and where there's one…

He squeezed the trigger just as a tremendous explosion rocked the front of the building and his shot went wild. For an instant, he and the Seraphim stared down their weapons at each other but neither fired. They were both listening to the high-pitched, tearing squeal of a grav-unit losing its containment field. It was going critical, and they both knew what that meant. The Seraphim started to throw himself flat on the floor while Harry lurched towards the opposite wall in a desperate attempt to get out of the way of the coming blast. Neither of them quite made it before the grav-field, expanding at trans-light speed, tore a nanosecond hole in space-time.

Harry hit the opposite wall just as the shock wave blew out of the doorways of the first and second apartment in a blinding flash of a sun gone nova. He never saw what happened to the Seraphim as the rocks blocking the last two apartments blew out into the hall like corks from a bottle. The front half of Susan's limousine was blown through the back wall of the apartment and crashed into the hall as the shock wave from the blast ripped Harry off the wall and threw him down the hall like a fly in a cyclone.

He slammed into the nest of broken steel and concrete surrounding the hole in the floor and was impaled on a rusty reinforcing rod. It drove deep into the back of his thigh and then immediately tore loose as a plasma fueled firestorm rushed down the hall after the shock wave and blowtorched him down through the hole. He cracked his head on a jagged concrete outcrop, his hair was on fire, and his clothes burst into flames. Just before his back hit the water, the headline, FALLING STAR GOES OUT IN A BLAZE OF GLORY, flashed crazily through his mind.

40

Love Opens the Door

Harry sank through cool water while plasma fire boiled off the surface above. He switched off the burnt agony of his charred body, shut down his breathing, and slowed his heart rate as he sank through dark depths, trailing pink swirls of blood. His back struck something solid, and he bounced gently as clouds of bottom sludge billowed up around him. Slowly, his body settled back into the soft muck of the sea bottom. Stale air bubbled from his lips as his burnt lungs slowly collapsed.

He laid motionless, all his attention turned inward, taking stock and doing damage control. He sent out feelers of consciousness, examining the deep gash in his thigh that just missed a femoral artery, the crack in the back of his skull that may or may not have sent bone splinters into his brain, and the multiple degree flash burns covering the front of his body.

He felt his blood pressure dropping precipitously. His body, poisoned by its own emergency chemical response to massive physical trauma, was going into toxic shock. Suddenly, he was fighting for his life, using everything he had learned in the last six months of dying. He tried to flush toxins from his blood, close his wounds, jack up his immune response and maintain his pain blocks all at the same time.

It wasn't enough. He felt his hold on consciousness slipping as toxic overload began shutting down vital systems. It was like watching the lights of a city going out one block at a time. He had only one chance left. He must put his body into a state of suspended animation and transfer his awareness to his ka. It was as close to death as he could get and still retain a vital spark. Hopefully, it would buy him the time he needed for his ka to begin the healing process.

Time was running out, but still he hesitated. He knew from experience that in a state of suspended animation, with his body resting just this side of death, his ka was going to leave his body with only a thin thread of consciousness tying them together. If that thread broke, his body would die and his ka would be pulled down the resurrection trail and into the jaws of any black wolves lurking there.

Suddenly, there was no more time. His body went into convulsions, shaking like a baby's rattle. Darkness closed in as consciousness spiraled down into an insensate black hole.

No more time.

With a practiced mental shrug, Harry dropped into suspended animation and jumped out of the decaying orbit of his body into the blazing light of his ka. Every time he returned, it felt like coming home, as if this glowing spirit of seed consciousness was his real self, eternal and unchanging while his body was nothing but a transient meat locker imprisoning glory.

He knew, of course, that as soon as his awareness returned to his body, the reverse would be true. His ka would become nothing but a ghostlike other, while his body became who he was and all he was. It was tempting to think it was all relative, a matter of perspective, but Harry knew better. He'd seen his old bodies die, one after the other, while his ka went on unchanged, putting on each new body like a new suit of clothes. The ka was the unique spark that animated flesh, the seed containing his wholeness. It was the soul, the spirit, and the pneuma of previous ages, the myth become reality, religious truth captured by the spin-generators at Eternal Life.

He rested for a moment in the light of his ka. It still retained his human form even though it floated six feet above his body, like a balloon on a string. The string was a silvery coil of light made of the same conscious light stuff as his ka, but as it descended to his body the string took on the pulsing silver solidity of fleshy awareness and penetrated his navel like a luminous, silver umbilical. This umbilical of awareness was his lifeline. It gave his ka its human form and as long as they were connected, his body could not die and his ka could not go down the resurrection trail or into the white light of death.

Harry looked down that bright umbilical to where his body lay just barely ticking over, half buried in the dark sea bottom. He could feel the burns, wounds, and toxic shock telegraphing up the umbilical like messages from a distant land. He could see how they left their dark imprint on the bright schematics that gave his ka its human form.

These schematics were drawn with the same conscious light stuff as the umbilical. They were glowing silver lines of concentrated information consciousness, running up and down, around and through his ka in a tangled maze that resembled a three-dimensional blueprint for some enormously complex piece of machine circuitry in human form.

During the last six months, he had painstakingly tried to capture and reconstruct these lines from the fleeting glimpses he caught between the moment of death and the pull of the resurrection trail. Now, with his body balanced precariously between life and death, these lines burned with the constancy of a disaster warning.

In many places, though, they were smudged and had lost their bright glow. A couple of "junction boxes" that should have blazed with concentrated energy from intersecting lines of power gave off only a low wattage flicker. Harry knew from the final moments of numerous deaths that this represented major injury or trauma to the physical body. He also knew that the effect went both ways. In the last few months, he had begun to learn how to influence and even heal the physical body by changing the energy flow through the bright schematics of his ka.

Now, he began to try to balance that energy flow and bring down the toxic shock that was taking such a deadly toll.

Gradually, the low wattage flicker in the "junction boxes" strengthened to a weak, steady glow. As the effects of toxic shock receded, he needed to shunt more energy to the smudged damaged areas to hasten the healing of his wounds and regenerate flash burned skin and lung tissue. The only problem was he had no energy to spare and the only source he could draw on was locked in the unlimited potential of Samuel Kade's spirit realm or Jericho's quantum field. The name didn't matter. It was the same non-space.

Getting to it could be dangerous though. The door that he had slammed so convincingly in the face of the black wolves back at Eternal Life was the same door he now had to open to access the healing potential of the spirit realm.

As soon as he tried to draw on the energy potential out there, the force of the collapsing probability waves would blow that door wide open and expose him to any black wolves roaming nearby. He really had no choice, though. If he didn't open it, he was as good as dead anyway.

When he had told Chueh he didn't care if he died for real, he had thought he meant it but now he wasn't so sure. Finding what lies beyond the white light of death had somehow lost its appeal. He hadn't realized until now that things had changed, that something had intervened... or rather, someone. He could clearly see her shiny black hair; framing jade green eyes, the high cheekbones, the pale cream of her skin, the air of cool, self-reliant competence... Diana. The thought of dying now and never seeing her again was unbearable. He had only just met her, and already she had become his reason to live. How could that be? When had it happened?

Love at first sight? If so, was he so blind, so out of touch with the deepest levels of his own feelings that it took the threat of death to make him realize what his true feelings were? Or was it that he had finally exorcised Susan's ghost and now there was room for someone else in his heart? The reasons didn't matter.

The simple reality of love was enough. He had to stay alive, he had to get back to her, and the only way to do that was to open the door to all the unpatterned probability energy of the spirit realm.

Still, he hesitated. He wasn't sure he could pull it off. He'd never tried anything of this magnitude before. In the last six months he'd learned to move his awareness from his living body to his ka and map some of its complex circuitry, but he was only just beginning to learn to manipulate the forces locked in the spirit realm/quantum field. Now, he was going to open the door and let those quantum winds blow through his ka and hope that he could control them somehow. Just thinking about it made him feel like the sorcerer's apprentice.

No more excuses, he told himself, and cracked open the door. Then, he reached out with his mind and touched a standing wave of probability with a pinprick of desire like Samuel Kade had once shown him, although he'd never tried it himself.

The wave exploded like a balloon, and fierce winds of probability blew the door to his ka wide open. They swirled into a howling tornado vortex that was sucked down into his ka like water down a drain. His ka lit up like a cosmic pinball machine, its schematics glowing with hot-wired incandescence. The dark smudges vanished and the junction boxes went nova.

Harry felt the energy howling through his ka and rushing down the bright umbilical to his body where it kick-started a miraculous regeneration. He felt as if he was standing at an old-time gas pump with the nozzle snugged into the tank of his car, filling it with high test, and as so often happened when you opened a door to the spirit realm, his thoughts took on a ghostly reality.

Suddenly, he was standing in front of a ramshackle desert gas station out of an early twentieth century movie. He was dressed in dirty coveralls with a grease-stained rag hanging out of his back pocket and was holding down the handle of a gasoline nozzle. He could smell the sharp gasoline tang and hear the "ding" of the pump counting out the gallons splashing into a vintage Ford Mustang.

He grinned with nostalgic pleasure until he heard the distant howl of wolves. The grin disappeared along with the gas station and the Mustang. Once again, he was left standing alone in an open doorway with the winds of probability blowing all around him.

41

Riding the Probability Plains of the Quantum Field

As long as the umbilical connection to his living body remained intact, Harry knew he could continue to draw on the infinite potential of the spirit realm/quantum field. He could even move across it at will. It wasn't anything like the featureless gray fog of death, where all the probability waves that made up his life had collapsed into one final reality that pulled him down either into the white light of the Goddess or into the spin-generators at Eternal Life.

Instead, with his umbilical intact, he could let the infinite probability potential of this non-space take whatever form his intention gave it. It was usually Samuel Kade's spirit realm with its Shining Sea of the Gods or astral planes, but this time Harry's intention gave a playful twist to both Jericho's idea of a quantum field and Kade's astral planes.

This time, Harry stood in the open door of his ka and stared out at a vast plain of standing probability waves composed of what looked like smoked panes of etched glass or maybe old, photographic plate negatives, piled one on top of another into low hills that rolled away to infinity. Contained within these rolling hills of probability were all possible and impossible worlds, timelines, and dimensions of probability.

His unconscious mind had played a word trick with his intentions, converting the astral "planes" of the spirit realm into the probability "plains" of the quantum field. Harry knew that his probability plains were nothing but a useful tool, a construct of his imagination, to make comprehensible that non-space of consciousness that was the basis of the multi-verse. In that sense, the probability plains were no more real than his vision of the ramshackle, desert gas station. They were both attempts to comprehend the incomprehensible, interface with infinity, and encompass it within the boundaries of the human mind.

Even though he had been riding collapsing probability waves down the resurrection trial for five years, it was only recently, with Samuel Kade's help, that he'd opened the door to this non-space and taken a few, stumbling baby steps into it. Now, he stood on the threshold and listened to the howl of the Anubis wolves that had leapt out of probability to threaten his world.

He had heard them howling out there before, but always faint and far away. Back then, he hadn't known what they were, but they still raised hackles of fear. They were closer now. It sounded as if they were passing by without being aware of him. He wondered what they were doing, where they came from, and where they were going. He realized he had a unique chance. The wolves didn't know he was here. He could follow them, spy on them; who knows what he might learn. It was a chance that might never come again.

He looked down his umbilical to his body resting on the seabed. Its condition wasn't great but it was stabilizing fast. He should be able to turn his attention away for a little while without too much danger.

No sooner had he made the decision than his ka rushed through the open door. He watched his body rapidly receding behind him as the silver strand of his umbilical unreeled, stretching across the rolling hills of the probability plain. That thread was all that kept his body alive. If it broke, his body would die for real, and his ka would ride a collapsing wave of probability down into the white light of death... if the Anubis wolves didn't catch him first.

His body disappeared into the distance as he rushed across the mounds of stacked probability, like piles of old photographic plates, each etched with half-formed worlds of mountain, forests, and seas that glimmered with ghostly possibility.

For a second, he imagined that he was riding a wild stallion across this vast plain of rolling smoked glass hills. No sooner did the thought form than it began to take on a ghostly reality, and he found himself riding a spectral gray stallion, his own ghost body, no more real than his steeds. "Ghost Riders in the Sky", he thought, and his thoughts conjured up a cowboy suit, a pair of six guns and a black, weather-beaten Stetson.

He knew that it was just his mind playing tricks with probability and that he had to be very careful. He had never been this far out before and was playing with forces that could easily get out of control. He thought of the sorcerer's apprentice again and quickly quashed it.

Then, he heard the howl of the wolf pack far off to his right. His steed reared up, its forelegs pawing the sky, steam snorting from its nostrils as it tested the air. Its hooves crashed down through plate glass probability as it veered toward the sound, galloping flat out across a dry streambed of smoked glass that swam with wraithlike sea monsters.

He closed in on the sound of the pack. Their barking howls grew more distinct. As he drew nearer, it sounded more and more like some kind of growling, guttural, yipping language.

His steed climbed a ghostly ridge, slipping and sliding through layers of shifting gray probability like thick ground fog. Harry could hear the wolves clearly now. He could almost feel them, like dense, black balls of malevolence, condensing out of the fog.

He reached the top of the ridge and broke out of the fog. He spotted five wolves far below, loping out across a flat, desert landscape. Three of them carried limp, gray, rag-like shapes clenched between their jaws. The rags fluttered weakly. Harry heard a faint wail of despair and terror and realized that these were the kas of the recently dead. The wolves had probably snapped them off the resurrection trail from the battle in the Sinks.

A few seconds later, he saw one of the wolves bite down hard on the ka it was carrying. Then it tilted its head back, opened its mouth and gulped it down without even breaking stride.

They eat kas, just like that Susan thing tried to eat mine, Harry thought in numb horror as he followed the pack out onto the desert through a shifting mirage of rattle snakes and dust demons, through spectral sagebrush and tumbleweed. At last, he rode out of smoked glass probability onto the solid alkali flats of a dry lake bed where probability had collapsed and reality condensed around two ancient black, basalt pillars, standing beneath a burnt blue sky.

Harry looked around uncertainly. The alkali flats seemed to go on forever in every direction. There was no sign of the wolf pack or of the shifting gray worlds of probability. For as far as the eye could see, there was nothing but alkali flats and these two pillars. They stood about fifteen feet apart and were at least twice the height of a man. The basalt was polished to a deep mirror-like sheen and perfectly carved into the shape of a man with the stylized head of a jackal. Its red ruby eyes gleamed malevolently down at him.

Harry recognized them instantly. He'd seen pictures of Anubis, the jackal-headed guardian of the underworld and Egyptian god of the dead, in Jake Lloyd's book. When Jericho first called the wolf-headed invaders, the Anubis, Harry just assumed it was a convenient metaphor. Now, he wasn't so sure. Were the ancient gods rising again? Could these pillars be guarding the entrance to the underworld, the home world of the black wolves of Anubis? Were these the Anubis gates of Jake Lloyd's book? Had he once stood on these alkaline flats and stared up at these two statues?

Harry felt a shiver of premonition. He turned and looked back. Nothing had changed. He could see the faint shimmer of silver thread that bound him to his body extending back over the flats and disappearing into thin air about thirty feet away.

Everything out here had a bright hard-edged solidity, every-thing except for that thread and Harry and his steed. They were as insubstantial as ghosts. He raised an arm and looked right through it, like looking through a faint mist. He stepped down off his mount and walked towards the pillars. Behind him the stallion dissolved into a cloud of flickering motes of light. They swarmed around Harry like moths around a flame and then swirled down into his body and disappeared.

As he approached the two stone pillars, they began to change, running and flowing like melting wax. Then, between one step and the next, they snapped into two roughhewn granite posts, moss covered, cracked, and weathered. They stood less than five feet high, leaning towards each other with an old, rusty, wrought iron gate between. The gate leaned open on one hinge. Beyond it Harry could see an ancient, overgrown graveyard with cracked, broken headstones sinking into the rank undergrowth. The sky was a lowering gray drizzle.

Harry smiled grimly. It seemed that even though probability had collapsed into some form of reality, he was still in the spirit realm where what you expect is what you get. This was supposed to be a gateway to the land of the dead and reality conformed to his unconscious idea by serving up a graveyard. The original pillars were probably only a reality residue of how the Anubis wolves saw the entrance to their world.

He studied the scene and hesitated. There was no telling what lay beyond those gates. "You'll never get another chance like this," he told himself. "You mean a chance to commit suicide?" he answered. "Just a quick peek and then jump back again," he told himself. "Just make sure you don't get your umbilical caught in the door. Okay let's do it!"

He stepped through the gate. He felt a moment of disori-enting vertigo as his umbilical lifeline gave a sharp, painful tug. The cemetery vanished, and he stood in some kind of prehistoric jungle instead. The air was hot and humid, with a steaming mist sifting through the thick undergrowth. The place was a riot of all the wrong colors. The sun was an arc welder blue, white dwarf, and much too close, while the sky was tinted a garish Halloween orange. The vegetation ranged in color from bruised blacks and blues, through corpse greens, to livid violets.

He realized he was standing in the dark entrance to a large stone structure. He turned and looked up. The entrance formed a truncated triangle at least three hundred feet high, framed by huge basalt plinths. He had to step out to get a full view of the building. It rose out of the rampant jungle growth, tier by stone tier, a gigantic black pyramid, like some fabled lost temple from a B-movie adventure.

A narrow dirt track led away from the pyramid, and Harry started to follow it. Lavender-colored fog steamed up from the jungle floor and curled around his legs. The air tasted of copper and cyanide. Suddenly, someone screamed nearby. It was a very human scream, followed by a loud barking shout that wasn't human at all.

Harry heard someone running towards him, crashing wildly through the thick jungle growth. A moment later, a man, his eyes bulging with blind terror, his naked body crisscrossed with bleeding welts burst out of the jungle and ran straight into him. Instinctively, Harry stepped back and raised his hands to take the hit, but the man just ran right through him as if he didn't exist, which in a sense, he probably didn't.

Once again, Harry felt that sharp disorienting tug on his lifeline and a moment later a transformed Anubis wolf charged out of the undergrowth. It was over seven feet tall with the body of a man and the head of a jackal, like the two pillars on the alkali flats. Its body was as black and shiny as polished basalt. The fur around its head stood out in a thick ruff as stiff as porcupine quills. It wore a bright red harness that consisted of two tank-top like straps that went over its shoulders and merged into one wide strip that went down between its legs and up its back. A wide black belt was cinched around its waist with some kind of weapon hanging from it in a long black scabbard tied down on its thigh.

Harry wondered momentarily if this was one of the Anubis wolves he had been trailing that had now taken on its jackal form. If so, then maybe that poor, frightened human was one of the kas, the rags of dead-soul stuff, they had been carrying back with them, but how did this poor human get a solid body while Harry remained a ghost? Could it be because Harry's body was still alive in another dimension with a lifeline back to it?

He had no time for answers, no time to even step aside before the jackal-headed Anubis crashed right through him. Unlike the human though, the Anubis staggered momentarily and shook its shaggy head in confusion. Then it sighted the fleeing human and whipped out its weapon in a lightning fast, gunfighter draw. The "gun" resembled a spun glass ankh, one of those ancient Egyptian crosses that had a round handle instead of the bar above the cross piece. The Anubis wolf held it by the handle and fired without even sighting.

A cone of blue-white light shot from the end of the ankh and struck the fleeing man high in the back. He screamed in agony and froze in mid-step as the energy beam peeled the skin from his back in a cloud of sparkling molecules that were sucked up the beam and into the ankh.

Like a human vacuum cleaner, Harry thought in horror, as he watched the beam peel the body from the bone in seconds. Then the skeleton crumbled into sparkles of dust that were also instantly vacuumed away. The beam cut off, leaving only a faint wisp of smoke and a burnt circle of vegetation where the man had stood. There was no sign of his ka.

The Anubis slowly turned and stared at the spot where Harry stood. It squinted and tilted its head from side to side as if trying to find just the right angle to see what was hiding there. Harry decided it was time to leave. He turned and started to run down the dirt tail. He imagined Anubis all around him, flitting wraithlike through the lavender fog that hissed and sizzled with the bright blue sutures of their beam weapons.

Just then, he felt another rush of vertigo and a sudden tug on his umbilical, this time more powerful and painful than before. The Anubis howled triumphantly and lifted its weapon just as Harry was snatched backwards with a powerful yank from his umbilical. He felt as if he was on the end of a recoiling bungee cord that had been stretched to its elastic limit. The world of the Anubis wolves vanished in the blink of an eye.

Harry felt the instant his umbilical snapped. One moment, he was being pulled back to his body; the next, he was like a balloon with its string cut, tumbling toward the white light of death, the resurrection trail, and the wolves that were probably waiting to tear his ka apart.

He had a momentary vision of Diana's face crushed with sorrow and defeat, and he screamed in denial.

42

Insomniac Ghosts

Roger couldn't sleep. That was nothing new. He hadn't been able to sleep for the last six months. He went into the bathroom, turned on the light, and looked at himself in the mirror. He didn't like what he saw, the hanging jowls, the broken blood vessels in his nose, the hint of gray in the ginger stubble on his cheeks. Harry was right. He looked like shit and the black eye the son of a bitch laid on him didn't help. How could he have let it go this far? He needed a drink or maybe something a lot stronger, but he was afraid if he started he wouldn't stop and this night would end like so many others with him passed out on the floor.

"No, you're just going to have to go through this cold turkey," he muttered at the image in the mirror. He thought of Susan. He tried to push it away, but the demons of guilt and pain kept coming back, tearing at his guts with their sharp, little teeth.

God, he needed a drink! He sank onto the toilet stool, closed his eyes, and buried his face in his hands. Closing his eyes only made things worse. Susan waited for him behind his closed eyes, Susan with her tortured, battered face, Susan screaming, "Help me! Please help me!"

"No-o-o!" he screamed and jumped up and came face to face with himself in the mirror. "No-o-o!" he screamed again and slammed his fist into his mirror image. The mirror shattered, and the sharp burst of pain from his bleeding fist brought him to his senses. He pulled a large splinter of glass out of his lacerated fist and dropped it on the tile floor. He watched the blood dripping onto the rose petal tiles. "Oh, Susan, I'm sorry," he said, his voice flat and hollow.

Me and Harry, he thought as he got out some bandages and

antiseptic and began dressing the wound. You can sure pick them, Susan. Me and Harry, we both led you down the garden path to perdition, didn't we?

He understood Harry now. They were as close as blood brothers. They both shared the betrayal of love and the agony of guilt. Their lives were so intertwined, their fates so scarily similar that he almost wondered if maybe there wasn't some kind of Old Testament god of vengeance and retribution pulling the strings behind the scenes.

He finished bandaging his hand and looked up and caught a glimpse of a blood-shot eye staring back at him from a long splinter of mirror that still remained in place. He turned away. "It's going to be a long night," he thought and shut off the light.

He was alone, the house as quiet as a tomb and filled with ghosts. He walked down to the gym and turned on the overhead lights. The skeletal chrome and plast-steel bars and rings and weights of the exercise machines gleamed with the cold comfort of an operating theater; or maybe a high tech torture chamber, he thought.

On nights like this, he would come down here, avoiding all those damned machines, and head straight for the heavy punching bag and the speed bag he kept in a little room at the back. On nights like this, he'd tear into them with a ferocity fueled by hate and despair until, at last, he hung against the bag drenched in sweat, exhausted, and gasping for breath. And sometimes after an hour or two down here beating up his rage, sometimes, if he was lucky and it was a good night, he might even be able to fall asleep without waking up screaming.

Tonight though, he didn't even have this way out. His bloody bandaged fist split open as soon as he began, and the bag was soon slick with blood and he had to stop. He wrapped a towel around his fist and leaned back against the wall. Slowly, he slid down to the floor, pulled his knees up against his chest, and stared out at the gym he hated so much.

It/she wanted it, not him. He watched her working out down here for hours, the unholy thing that possessed her driving her to exhaustion. They wanted to ride only strong, healthy animals.

He closed his eyes and thought about the party. He knew there was no use fighting it any longer. It always came to this point late at night when he could no longer put it off, when exhaustion and despair wore away his defenses until, at last, he just gave up. He always thought that maybe he would be able to sleep afterwards if he just got it out of his system, but it never seemed to work out that way.

It was the party, that goddamn party! Why did he have to go to that goddamn party? Why did he have to drag Susan along? A bitter smile cut his face like a razor. How many times had Harry probably asked himself the same thing?

Susan hated that crowd. She couldn't understand what Roger saw in those rich, powerful, greedy men and their beautiful, predatory, amoral women, the cream of society, the movers and shakers. What did Harry call them, "The not-so-beautiful people"? Roger wondered if Harry ever suspected how right he was. Scratch away the varnish of money and power, take away the makeup and clothes, and you were left with a pack of wild, ugly scavengers who devoured people and things in their insatiable hunger for more and more.

They were the perfect devotees of black ice addiction. No desire was too gross to satisfy, no perversion too obscene, no drug too dangerous. Hell, you hardly noticed any difference from before they were possessed and after, Roger thought.

So why the fuck did you have to go to their goddamn parties, he asked himself, just as he had asked himself a thousand times before. Who the hell were you trying to impress? You were already top of the heap, the king of the castle, you had it all. You didn't need to impress anyone.

He knew the answer even though he didn't like it. He'd been born dirt poor and brought up to resent it. He'd had his face pushed in it, made to feel worthless, never quite good enough. After his parents were killed, he grew up fast, like a feral animal, alone, despised, and feared.

Nothing much changed when he got to New Hollywood, where he ruthlessly clawed his way up from the bottom, wheeling and dealing, always on the outside looking in, always looked down upon and despised by those "not-so-beautiful people" who held the real reins of power. Then, when he finally saw his chance, he took it and when he became richer and more powerful than any of them, when he finally became king of the castle and didn't need to prove anything to anyone, it still wasn't enough.

He was like a man who had been starved all his life and couldn't stop eating. He needed constant proof that he really was someone. He needed those goddamn parties that he threw on his private island estate. He needed all the "not-so-beautiful people" scrabbling for invitations, and he needed an invitation to every major event, and it was never enough.

Sitting there under the harsh glare of the overhead lights, looking out at the gleaming chrome and steel skeletons, he realized for the first time that maybe he and "the not-so-beautiful people" were not so different after all. He was just as hungry, just as insatiable. No matter how much money or power or prestige he had, no matter how many parties he threw or how many of the rich and powerful patted him on the back and told him what a wonderful guy he was, it never seemed to be enough. It never filled the hole that years of poverty, slights, and scorn had left inside him.

The only thing he ever had that was clean and pure was his love of Susan and in the end, he betrayed even that to his insatiable hunger. He knew there was black ice at that party. He thought he knew how dangerous it was, how ruthlessly proselytizing black ice addicts could be, yet he took Susan there anyway.

Then he left her for a bit of backroom, back-slapping wheeling and dealing, left her unprotected, a lamb surrounded by a pack of wolves and when he came back, Susan was gone. Oh, her body was still there, unconscious on a settee, on a penthouse terrace overlooking the Emperor's fairytale castle. There was a half-empty glass on the table beside her.

Roger squeezed his eyes shut and banged his head back against the concrete wall again and again trying to drive away the image, trying to stop the inevitable scene from playing itself out in his mind.

He forced his eyes open and pushed himself to his feet with a heavy groan. He looked around, hating this place where the wolves had driven his wife, bending, twisting, and stretching her mercilessly on these mindless machines. The wolves had an almost neurotic need to drive their victims like racehorses, training and exercising them constantly.

How many times had he looked in and seen her here, running endless treadmill miles at her own reflection on the mirrored wall and when she/it saw him watching, it bared her teeth and gave a howl of triumph.

"Enough!" he screamed at the ghosts haunting this room. Why the hell had he come down here anyway? For peace? What a laugh.

He climbed back up the stairs. He wasn't going to get any sleep tonight. He could just as well accept that and try to get ready for the trip tomorrow. Diana wanted to leave early, but Jericho had convinced her to wait at least until noon to give Harry a chance.

Harry, he thought. At least he hadn't betrayed everyone, although it wasn't for want of trying. The wolves tried to get possession of Harry under his last resurrection. It looked like they almost succeeded. For a while he and Jericho were afraid they had. Even the wolves weren't sure. At least I managed to keep them away from him when he woke up, he thought.

Something about Harry scared them, and now Roger knew

what it was. According to Jericho, the wolves thought he might be a prophesied King of the Dead who was going to stomp the shit out of them. Roger had his doubts and so did Diana, but the wolves wanted to make sure. When the sons of bitches realized possession hadn't taken, they were furious. They forgot all about getting Harry to sign a new contract and wanted to shoot him up with black ice on the spot.

I had to do some fancy footwork to convince them otherwise, Roger thought. The stupid fucks weren't thinking straight. They weren't used to being crossed. "Masters of the Universe!" Roger snorted with contempt. They hadn't even thought about what would happen if Harry hadn't shown up for the media this morning.

It had been a hard resurrection thanks to the wolves, and he was already a day late. Rumors were spreading fast about all the people not coming back from resurrection, or coming back changed. It was getting harder and harder to keep the lid on. If Harry hadn't shown up at that press conference, it would have blown that lid right off. There would have been no possibility of containment.

When he finally got that through their thick "Masters of the Universe" skulls, they had reminded him again of what would happen if he didn't get Harry to sign a new contract that would give them another shot at him and keep the whole charade going a little longer.

And I did my best to oblige them, Roger thought bitterly, as he walked past the entrance to the living room and detoured over to the bar. "Screw it, I need a drink", he muttered. He needed more than one drink but with what he had in front of him tomorrow, one drink would have to do. He poured a tumbler of vodka and toasted his reflection in the mirror behind the bar. "Here's to you, Harry! Did you know I saved your ass? Did you know they probably spiked the water on your bedside table with black ice? Only you never touched it, did you?"

Roger's lips curled back in a feral grin. "Especially not after I dropped my cigarette butt in it. I bet that pissed off the wolves hiding behind those two-way mirrors, but hey, by then I had nothing to lose, did I?"

He tossed back his drink and said, "At least I made sure you got out of there in one piece. No matter what else you think of me, I did do that."

As he put his glass down, he looked past his reflection in the mirror to the reflected image of the living room. He closed his eyes and grabbed the edge of the bar hard enough to splinter wood. Ghosts, this whole fucking house was full of ghosts! Why did he have to come back here after last night and why the hell did he have to come back to this room? He looked down at the empty tumbler. Well, the answer to that last one was logical enough, a drunk's logic.

The room was just as they left it after they finished torturing Susan. They wanted to make sure he got the message. They had Susan trapped inside herself while they used her body and her social position to throw wild parties, orgies of unspeakable perversions, to lure other lambs to black ice addiction. And he accepted it. What else could he do? They had Susan and every once in a while they would bring her back just to remind him that she was still there and that if he played along, maybe, just maybe, he might get her back one day.

He looked at the overturned chair and the handcuffs that still dangled from one of the back slats. And sometimes, he thought, they would bring her back to teach him a lesson, like they did last night.

43

The Black Wolf Bash

There were four of them. They came home with Susan. At first, Roger was angry and irritated. They knew he was going to be home that night. One of the little concessions he had been able to wring out of the sons of bitches was that they would leave him alone when he was here. If they wanted his cooperation, they could at least spare him the sight of them pawing his wife's body in another one of their orgies. He had been wrong, though; they weren't there to throw another orgy, they were there to teach him a lesson.

He had been alone, drinking in the dark, when Susan walked in and turned on the lights. She leaned against the doorframe and looked at him with that mocking, provocative smile that the wolves had given her. She ran her fingers through her long blonde hair and licked her lips with a quick little flick of her tongue. "Roger Dodger," she cooed and gave him a slow, sultry smile full of perverse promise. God, how he hated them for what they had turned his wife into. She stumbled into the room trailing an expensive fur cape across the carpet. Her walk was unsteady as if she had been drinking too much. "Roger Dodger," she mocked again. She–they knew how much he hated it when she called him that.

She came over and took the drink out of his hand and tried to sit on his lap. She smelled of alcohol, cigarettes, and other men. He pushed her away angrily and was about to tell her to get the hell out when he noticed the four other men who had slipped into the room behind her. Four tuxedo-clad, black ice possessed addicts. They prowled around the room like curious animals, sniffing and snarling at each other; no longer necessary to keep up the pretense of humanness. Not in front of Susan, not in front of him. No, they were right at home.

"I brought some friends home for you to meet, and then we're all gonna party," Susan giggled as she ruffled his hair and laid a possessive arm around his shoulders.

"Now, be a good boy and say hello to, Rover, Lassie, Butch, and… Now what is your name?" she said, chewing on her fingertip with mock indecisiveness. "Oh yes, now I remember. Roger, meet, Wolfy!" She laughed triumphantly and the four, black ice possessed threw back their heads snapping and snarling and howling with laughter as they pranced around the room.

"I don't need this," Roger said and began to get up.

"Oh, but you do, Roger Dodger, honey," Susan said and pushed him back down with surprising force. "You really do." The four addicts circled around him, more than ever like a wolf pack, their lips pulled back in snarling smiles.

"Wolfy" broke from the pack and instead began circling around Susan. He was sleek and slim with slicked-down, oily, black hair, a pencil thin mustache, and the attitude of a hotwired, car bomb. He licked his lips and growled deep in his throat as he circled in towards Susan.

Roger suddenly realized he knew the guy, although the guy he knew usually didn't wear a tuxedo. It wasn't only that, though. The guy himself had changed physically. When Roger knew him, he was just a pale, skinny, pimple-faced wimp, a harmless, no-talent hustler. Well, he's not that anymore, Roger thought.

It was the wolves, of course. They liked their rides to be in top condition and that was one thing Anton Shane had never been. He was still thin but now it was wiry thin with whipcord muscles, clear skin, a healthy tan, and the attitude of the predator that rode him.

Without warning, Shane lashed out, grabbed Susan's arm, and dragged her roughly across the room.

"Oooh," she cooed. "Don't you just love strong, forceful men."

"Shut up, bitch," Shane snarled and slapped her hard across the face and threw her into a chair.

"That's enough, Shane!" Roger shouted and started to get up, but strong hands grabbed his shoulders and forced him back down. An arm wrapped around his neck and held him in a chokehold.

"No, Roger Dodger, it's not enough," Susan said, and put her hands behind her back as Shane took out a pair of handcuffs from his pocket. As soon as he cuffed her to the chair, Susan went limp. Her head fell forward until her chin rested on her breast. Her long blonde hair fell loosely around her face.

After a moment, she groaned and shook her head slowly. "Where am I?" she asked. "What's happening?" She slowly lifted her head.

"No!" Roger screamed and tried to pull free. "No, don't do this!"

Susan looked around confused and uncertain. "Where am I?" she muttered. "Roger?" she said when she caught sight of him. "Oh, Roger," she cried happily.

"Shut up, bitch!" Shane stepped around and hit her brutally in the face. The heavy signet ring on his finger tore a long, bloody gash across her cheekbone.

"No-o-o!" Roger screamed and tried to get free, but the chokehold tightened and dragged him back down coughing and gagging. "Susan," he whispered hoarsely. "Oh god, no!" They had brought Susan, the real Susan, his Susan, back once again, to torture and teach him a lesson.

He screamed in helpless, frustrated rage as they beat her unmercifully while she cried to him for help. At last they stopped. Susan's head hung limply, her body racked by sobs of pain and shame. They'd ripped away the front of her gown exposing her bruised breast.

"Please, Roger, make them stop," she moaned as Shane leaned

over and licked her breast and leered at Roger.

"Stop it!" Roger screamed. "What do you want from me? Just tell me! You don't have to do this. Just tell me!"

Shane sucked one of Susan's nipples into his mouth and bit down so hard she screamed and tried to twist away. He held on for a moment longer, watching Roger the whole time.

"Shane, you son of a bitch, I swear I'll kill you for this!" Roger rasped.

Shane smiled at him with dead eyes while he slowly caressed Susan's breast. Holding it in the palm of his hand, he said, "What did you say?" and squeezed until Susan moaned with pain.

"What do you want from me?" Roger said in defeat. "I'll do anything you want."

"That's better," Shane smiled and released Susan's breast and wiped his hand on his trousers as if he had just been handling something dirty.

"What we want is Harry Neuman."

"I don't understand," Roger said. "You got him. He came back possessed, didn't he?"

Shane looked at him and Roger felt the rage and frustration boiling behind those flat, dead eyes. "We're not sure," he said at last. "We missed him when he resurrected last time. Why was that? We never miss. We've found traces of him out there." Shane tossed his head as if to indicate someplace else.

Roger knew what he meant by "out there". It was where the black wolves came from. "Out there" was their hunting ground, where they captured and ate lost kas. What the hell was Harry doing "out there"? How did he get out there without dying? "There must be some mistake," he said and knew immediately the mistake was his.

"Wrong answer," Shane growled and casually backhanded Susan, splitting her lip. "We can smell him out there. How does he do it? What is he after? How did he get away from us?"

"I tell you I don't know!" Roger said as he watched a trickle of blood run down the side of Susan's mouth. "Please don't hurt her anymore. I'll do anything you want, but I can't tell you what I don't know!"

"If Harry gets away from us tonight…" Shane smiled and put his hand under Susan's chin and lifted her head. Susan opened her eyes and looked at Roger. "Please help me," she pleaded. "Please get me out of here."

Shane put a finger to his lips and shook Susan's head back and forth. "Sh-h-h-h, I'm talking."

Roger could see how Shane's finger dug into her jaw. "Now, as I was saying, if Harry does get away from us tonight… " Shane casually slid his hands around Susan's throat and began to squeeze. "… You make sure he signs another contract with us as soon as he wakes up." Susan fought for air; her eyes bulged with fear while her body flopped from side to side.

Roger struggled to get free, twisting and kicking and screaming obscenities.

"Do we understand each other?" Shane yelled and squeezed harder.

Roger gave up his struggle and bowed his head and sobbed, "Yes! Yes! Now stop!"

Shane nodded with a satisfied smile. "Good. I think we have a deal," he said and released Susan's throat.

Roger stared at the handcuffs dangling from the overturned chair. After they were through torturing Susan, they took her ka away again to wherever they take kas and a black wolf once again took possession of her body. Seeing that transformation was almost worse than watching the torture, Roger thought, and tossed back the rest of his vodka. He closed his eyes and concentrated on it burning down his throat, hoping that it would burn away the memories.

He wondered sometimes why they didn't take him too, but maybe they knew they didn't have to as long as they had Susan.

He wondered where she/it was tonight. No, he didn't want to think of that!

He threw away the empty glass, grabbed the vodka bottle, and stumbled across the room to the sliding glass doors leading out onto the terrace. "Off the lights," he said as he pushed open the doors. A cool breeze greeted him as the room went dark behind him.

The moon was up. It would be full in a few days. He wondered if he would be alive to see it. He wondered if it mattered anymore.

Tatters of clouds raced across the face of the moon. Rain coming, he thought as he walked across the flagstones to the edge of the pool. He watched the moon's reflection jump and break as the breeze stirred the water.

He thought of the cigarette butt floating in the glass of water beside Harry's bed and his lips curled in a feral smile. "I bet you didn't know they spiked your water with black ice, did you, Harry?" he asked. "I pulled your chestnuts out of the fire on that one, and I did it again when I ran interference so you could walk out of the building afterwards without getting whacked. I bet you didn't know that either." He waved the vodka bottle dismissively. "Doesn't matter... it's not much to be proud of anyway." His face split in a sudden derisive grin. "But these days I'll take whatever I can get!"

He looked down the dark slope of the hill, behind the pool, to where phosphorescent waves broke against the dark beach and the moon sparkled on the water. He loved this view. It was why he bought this island in the first place and built just here. In the distance he could see the glow of New Hollywood like a luminous haze on the horizon.

He raised the vodka bottle to the moon. "Here's to you, Harry, wherever you are," he said with tears in his eyes. "That's two you owe me."

44

The Day after the Night before

Roger woke up and groaned. He wondered where he was. Wherever it was, it hurt. His body was stiff and cold and... wet. In fact, he was soaked to the skin. He tried to open his eyes, but they were so gummed up the lids had trouble coming unstuck. When he finally blinked them open, he was rewarded by rays of bright morning sunlight that felt like someone driving red-hot ice picks through his eyeballs and pinning them onto the back of his skull.

"Oh, screw this," he moaned. As he moved his arm to cover his face, his hand hit an empty bottle and sent it spinning across the ground. Roger opened one eye. "Floor," he corrected and watched the bottle roll across the polished oak parquet floor and under a sofa. He carefully raised his head and looked around. He was lying in a puddle of rainwater, half in and half out of the open sliding doors to the terrace.

His mind started coughing and sputtering out thoughts like a rusty, old motor. He must have been trying to get in out of the rain when he passed out. The last thing he remembered was talking to Harry, trying to make him understand that he never meant to hurt or betray him. But Harry wasn't really there, and it didn't matter anyway.

He thought of Susan... "Oh shit!" he shouted, and sat up too fast. The world rocked and rolled and his head was filled with a thousand bright pieces of exploding shrapnel. He squinted at his watch and cursed. He ignored the pain in his head and the stiffness in his body and managed to get up. Then he stumbled back into the house with the wet, terrycloth robe slapping against his bare shanks. He had to meet Jericho and Diana in an hour and hadn't even begun to get ready.

He took a stim-tab, shaved and showered, took another stim-tab and began to feel half-way human again. He pulled on a thin body stocking of spider-spin armor and on top of that new khaki brown, whipcord trousers and matching shirt. Absently, he slipped on the elegant leather-tooled shoulder rig he always wore. It contained one of the newest R-pistols that weren't even on the market yet, a deadly little equalizer and status symbol all in one.

Diana had told him that where they were going they would not be able to take a grav-car, so he had better make sure he had hiking and camping gear and provisions for at least a week in case they had to rough it. He'd had a couple of outdoor types at Eternal Life pick up a pair of hiking boots and throw together a camping pack that he hoped would cover his needs. When he got home last night, he had dropped it in the front hall, planning to go through it later to make sure they hadn't missed anything, but a bad case of bad memories got in the way.

He snagged a light all-weather jacket from the closet and walked down to the front hall wondering why he came back here last night. There was nothing for him here but a world of pain. Maybe because this was where he and Susan had been happiest, he thought. This island, this house had been their dream. They planned and built it together. Maybe he returned to try to capture a tiny piece of the dream to take with him into the unknown. If that was the case, it was a dismal failure.

He stepped into his brand-new, heavy-duty hiking boots with the price tag still attached and shouldered the pack without even looking inside. Just then, his wrist phone beeped. He glanced at the display. A heavily encrypted number... Jericho. They'd agreed on this in case of an emergency. He tapped in the key and the display cleared and Jericho's face appeared. "I'm on my way," Roger lied.

"Change of plans," Jericho said. "My place," and cut off.

They were supposed to meet at Chueh's. The old Tong

Godfather was going to arrange for them to slip out of the city undetected. Roger wondered what had gone wrong and headed for the underground garage. On the way he stopped off in his private armory and picked up a pulse rifle and an automatic fléchette mini-gun. He figured if things were already going wrong, he might need all the help he could get.

After the fiasco at Eternal Life yesterday, the wolves had been totally pissed off at him. They blamed him for Harry's escape. They told him to kiss off any hope of seeing Susan again. They were taking her back to Las Vegas with them. Maybe, if she was lucky, they would let her be a pleasure slave in one of their temples.

When he learned that Diana was going to attempt to get into Las Vegas to rescue her sister, it was like an answer to his prayers... except Diana wasn't answering prayers. She took one look at his out-of-shape, overweight body and bloodshot eyes and said she didn't want him, didn't need him, and wouldn't take him. He begged, bribed, threatened, and demanded.

She said he was in no shape to follow her where she was going. At best he would slow her down, at worst he would get her killed. He told her she could leave him anytime he couldn't keep up. She said it might not only be a matter of keeping up. Where she was going, he might not be able to follow. It was as simple as that, whatever that meant.

In the end, Jericho interceded on his behalf, pointing out that two had a better chance than one and that if Harry didn't turn up, Roger was the only other candidate they had. Candidate for what was never explained, and he really didn't care as long as it got him to Las Vegas.

Then Jericho surprised him by saying that he, Roger, was someone Diana could count on to guard her back, and besides, he had a fleet of some of the fastest, best-armed grav-cars in the Empire. At least he wasn't lying about the last part, Roger thought, as he walked down the row of grav-cars in the garage.

He even had a couple of vintage ground cars with old internal combustion engines that had been lovingly restored.

He stopped before a small red roadster. It was the fastest, most maneuverable, and for its size the best armed grav-car he owned. It was spider-spin armored against most impact weapons and, like all his cars, had the finest military software upgrades money could buy. This one, though, had a few extras that might have raised eyebrows even in the Imperial Security Service.

The Tongs and the imperial police patrolled the seas around New Hollywood and kept them relatively free from pirates, Slavers, Seraphim, and other scum, but once you went beyond the boundaries of their protection, you were on your own. Before Roger met Susan, he frequently used the little roadster for illicit trips into the roadhouse fleshpots and gambling casinos in the criminal no man's land bordering the Sinks.

He could probably find most of what he was looking for in the brothels, casinos, and pleasure gardens of the District, but they couldn't give him what he really wanted. What he really wanted was the dangerous, forbidden thrill of once more walking on the wild side of his past, outside the laws and circumscribed boundaries of his life in New Hollywood. Out there, on the boundaries of the Sinks, anything could happen and usually did. He'd killed men out there, men who were trying to kill him for his flash car and pig skin wallet.

Out there, he could allow himself to be himself, to relive his hard scrabble life on the wild side before he came to New Hollywood. He had grown up dirt poor in one of the old Seraphim eastern provinces, back up in the hills, bordering the Quarantine. It was a hard, violent, precarious existence. He had killed his first man before he was twelve. It was a mutie, trying to rape his mother. By the time he was fourteen, he was on his own, his mother and father dead, their homestead burned to the ground. He'd tracked down the Jacker gang that did it and killed three more men.

After that, he fled westward with a price on his head and bounty hunters on his heels. He left their bones on his back-trail until, at last, no one followed him anymore, and he came to New Hollywood. He was sixteen years old, hard and feral and determined to claw out a place for himself at the top of all the wealth and glitter at the center of the Empire.

And when I finally got it, it was never enough, he thought. There was always a gnawing emptiness that couldn't be filled, that drove him back to the wild side roadhouses on the borders of the Sinks with their promise of bare knuckle violence and life on the edge.

Then he fell in love with Susan, another man's woman, and it changed his life. He rubbed his hand lovingly across the glossy, smooth front fender of the roadster. The little car was fast and deadly and had gotten him out of more than a few dangerous scrapes but since Susan, it had mostly gathered dust.

He climbed in and started it up. The hum of the oversize gravcoils was deep and even. He applied lift and slid smoothly out of the garage and out onto the lift pad. Before taking off, he reprogrammed the finish from bright red to automatic camouflage that would blend into any background.

Five miles from Jericho's island compound, he picked up a warning signal that he was entering restricted, private airspace. He identified himself and continued toward the island that was nothing but a long, overgrown ridge sticking out of the sea. Jericho's house was built into the side of the ridge in a classic twentieth century construction of wood and glass that seemed a natural part of the landscape.

The old man was waiting for him on the landing pad set in the middle of a large pond at the base of the ridge. A waterfall poured from the top of the ridge, past one of the house's large picture windows, and into the pond. Roger followed Jericho across an arched wooden bridge, onto a vine covered wooden deck and entered the house.

Roger knew that the house was only the tip of the iceberg and that buried beneath the ridge was one of the largest, best-equipped research facilities in the world. Very few people knew about it. Jericho kept a low profile and had sworn Roger to secrecy before he showed him. Roger always played his part perfectly, treating Jericho in public with the kind of offhand contempt that infuriated Harry. He wondered if Harry knew Jericho's secret. He doubted it. Even friends would be kept on a need to know basis as far as Jericho was concerned, and Harry definitely didn't need to know in Roger's opinion.

Jericho led him down a long corridor edged with a floor-to-ceiling, diamond glass window that looked out on the pond. They went up a spiral staircase of chrome and unfinished redwood planks and entered a spacious living room with another floor-to-ceiling diamond glass window. This one gave a magnificent view from the top of the ridge and out across the sea.

The room was furnished in mid-twentieth century American style; right down to one of only three Jackson Pollack's to survive the Crash. The painting hung above a black, low slung, leather sofa that faced the window. A coffee table of unfinished driftwood planks, resting on chrome mountings, stood before the sofa. There was a coffee service on the table and to one side Diana's open electronic notebook.

Roger noted its battered appearance. It looks like it's seen better days, he thought... lots of better days. It must have been over twenty years old. He wondered, in passing, what use she had for an antique like that.

He turned and looked at her. She stood with her back to him, staring out the window, a cup of coffee in her hand. She wore a pair of scuffed hiking boots, faded jeans, and a washed out, gray flannel shirt. The butt of what looked like an ancient Colt .45 Peacemaker stuck out of a worn leather holster strapped low on her hip. The walnut pistol grips were black with age. She turned.

The flannel shirt was open at the throat, and Roger noticed that she was wearing an insulated spider-spin body stocking underneath. He felt a little like a clothing store dummy in his factory pressed cords and the price tag still dangling from his new boots.

"You're late," she said, not criticizing but simply stating the fact. Then she seemed to see him for the first time. "You look terrible," she said.

"That's better than I feel," he said. He wondered what would happen to her cool composure if he told her that the reason he was late and looked so terrible was that he had gotten blind, stinking drunk last night and if it was up to him, he'd rather stay that way the rest of his life. Probably not a good idea, he decided.

"What did you do to your hand?" she asked.

"Accident," he said as he took a seat on the couch. Diana turned back and stared out the window. Jericho offered him coffee and then told him that Harry had gone missing in the Sinks. "He went there to meet Susan," he said.

"Son of a bitch!" Roger ran his fingers through his sparse ginger hair. "Why the hell did he have to do that?"

"From what I've been able to piece together," Jericho said, "I think he thought she was in some kind of trouble and asked for his help."

Roger thought of what the wolves had done to Susan the other night, how she must have looked to Harry, and how Harry had reacted to him. "He must have thought I beat her up," he said.

"Or maybe she told him you did," Jericho suggested.

"You didn't tell him?"

"That the wolves had taken her?" Jericho shook his head. "No, he didn't stick around long enough to hear."

"So the wolves got him too," Roger said.

"We don't know," Jericho said cautiously. "Chueh went down into the Sinks with a division of Tong soldiers to get him out and got into a fire-fight with Seraphim militias. The last I heard, it's turned into an all-out war down there. Apparently, the Seraphim have some kind of new weapon that can bring down grav-cars by stopping their engines. It sounds like the same thing the Norma-genes used to bring down that imperial search and rescue party in the Quarantine last year. According to Chueh's last report, his Tongs were taking a beating and were in retreat.

"We don't have much time," Jericho said, pacing restlessly back and forth. With his long thin legs, hunched shoulders, and undertaker suit, he reminded Roger of a big, black stork. "All hell's broken out in the city. It looks like an attempted coup. There's a lot of fighting around the Imperial Palace and even the Eternal Life building."

Roger nodded. "Yeah, there would be," he said and thought of all the wolf-possessed whom he had allowed to infiltrate the building in the last months. Even the coup didn't surprise him. He had met enough rich and powerful wolf-possessed to suspect something like this might happen.

"Chueh saw it coming," Jericho said. "Before he left the city last night, he sealed off all the entrances to the Silver Slipper and his garden. No one gets in or out. Then he dropped us off here, before heading into the Sinks. He left a squad of Valkyrie to guard the place...

"Valkyrie!" Roger said in surprise. "Since when are the Tongs in bed with the Church of the Goddess?"

Jericho shrugged. "War makes strange bedfellows," he said. "Anyway, the Church pulled their Valkyrie back when fighting broke out in the city."

"Wait a second," Roger said. "Has anybody bothered to check the monitor on Harry's ka?"

"Chueh had that covered," Jericho said. "He was hacked into Eternal life, tracking Harry through his ka. Just before the balloon went up in the city, the monitor on his ka went dead. He never resurrected."

"Dead," Roger repeated dully and closed his eyes. "Worse than dead. I've seen it happen more than once at Eternal Life. It means the wolves ate him! Susan told me they like to do that sometimes instead of taking possession. It's a kind of Masters of the Universe delicacy."

He shook his head in despair. "It's something you don't come back from. No rebirth in the light of the Goddess." He was surprised at how hard this hit him. "Harry and I were never close, but God damn it! No one deserves to die with their ka ripped into nothingness to feed a wolf!"

Jericho shot a concerned glance at Diana, standing ramrod straight with her back to them, staring out the window. "It doesn't necessarily have to mean that," he said without conviction.

"Yeah, right!" Roger spat and finished off his coffee and slammed the cup down hard enough to crack the delicate, pre-Crash, antique, bone china.

Jericho winced at the sight of the cracked coffee cup and then sighed resignedly. "The only positive thing to come out of all this is that no one seems to care about you two anymore. You should be able to get out of here without too much trouble."

"What about you, Mr. Morley?" Diana said with her back to him, still staring out the window. "Do you still have a monitor on your ka?"

"I went in and wiped the coding and removed the monitor yesterday like Jericho suggested," Roger said. "No one can trace me now."

"And you can die for real now," she said as if she was commenting on the weather.

"Yeah, that's right," Roger said uncomfortably. "What about you?"

"Me?" Diana said and turned and looked at him, her face cool and composed. "I've never had a monitor on my ka," she said and as she brushed back a stray lock of her jet, black hair, Roger noticed for the first time the ring on her finger, the black onyx ring of a Jaganmatri Valkyrie. "Well, I'll be damned!" he said.

"In all probability," Diana said and placed her cup on the coffee table. She picked up her notebook and snapped it shut. "It's time to go," she said decisively as if she was closing a business meeting. "Thank you for your hospitality, Doctor Jericho and for that information about the Nevada Quarantine." She shook his hand and turned towards the door. "I left my gear downstairs," she said over her shoulder to Roger as she walked out. "Are you coming?"

Roger eyed Jericho. "That is one cold, Valkyrie bitch," he said and irritably ripped the price tag off his new boots and threw it on the table beside her coffee cup. Then he noticed the cup was still full. She hadn't touched a drop.

Jericho noticed too. "Looks can be deceiving," he said.

On the way out, they picked up Diana's gear in the downstairs hall. Roger noticed that her pack was surprisingly compact with an old, brown, leather jacket folded on top. He also noticed the sawed-off shotgun in a battered leather shoulder scabbard leaning against the pack. The walnut butt had been cut down and sculpted into a stubby pistol grip that was scratched and worn and as black with age as the grips on the forty-five.

Before they took off, Jericho suggested they cut due east, keeping well away from the troubles in the Sinks before turning north. Roger thought this was a good idea. They might lose an hour or two in the beginning but they would make it up as soon as they got into the open waters of the Trench that ran all the way up to the Sacramento Palisades.

Then in a surprising sign of affection, Jericho leaned over and kissed Diana goodbye and wished her luck.

By late afternoon, they had left the Rift Archipelago behind and Roger had come to the conclusion that Diana was lousy company. Her mind seemed to be elsewhere and all his attempts at conversation petered out into brooding silence. He glanced over at her pale profile staring out the window and thought of the coffee untouched in her cup. For some reason, he thought of Harry.

"Here are the coordinates for where we're going," she said, breaking the silence for the first time in over an hour.

He'd asked for them before they left, but she told him to simply steer due north towards the Sacramento Palisades and the Northern Reaches. They were still over a hundred miles south of the Palisades and when he fed the new coordinates into the navigator he saw that where they were going was nowhere near them. In fact, they were going nowhere near the Northern Reaches or the Eastern Oregon Quarantine that he had been led to believe was their destination.

"Do you mind telling me what's going on?" he asked.

"I don't know what you mean," she answered without looking at him.

"Look, let's cut the horse shit!" he said. "We're in this together, remember? Back at Chueh's I got the impression we'd be heading for the Eastern Oregon Quarantine and a back door into Las Vegas. According to these coordinates, we're going to cut due east in a little while and then continue on that heading right up into someplace in the High Sierras."

"That's correct," she said.

"But that's in the middle of nowhere!"

She nodded. "That's just where we're going, the middle of nowhere."

45

Creatures from the Black Lagoon

He slammed back into his body like a Looney Tunes Wiley Coyote, riding a rocket sled into the face of a cliff. But old Wiley, spread-eagled and splattered against a cliff, couldn't possibly feel as bad as Harry, mashed back into a body screaming with pain and drowning in toxic shock.

On top of that, someone just tried to electrocute him. That's what cut his umbilical, he realized. He should be dead! Why wasn't he dead, he wondered, just before someone drove a rusty spike through his heart! Adrenaline rush kicked it up from zero to one hundred beats in two seconds flat. It jackhammered against his chest cavity with enough force to shake his whole body. What the hell was going on?

Now someone strapped the wrong side of a pincushion around his underarm and hundreds of small needles dug in. Who were these clowns? Were they trying to kill him all over again? He fought against the double trauma of being violently pulled back from the dead into his body and the rush of adrenaline shocking through his system.

He opened his mouth in a silent scream of protest, and they shoved a soft plastic tube down his throat and held his nostrils closed. He started choking on the hose as pure oxygen re-inflated his collapsed, burnt lungs. The initial pain was excruciating, and he struggled to spit out the tube as his body flopped around, raising thick clouds of silt from the seabed.

He managed to set up a pain block and began concentrating on slowing down his juggernauting heart and stabilizing his system. He realized someone thought he was dead or dying and had tried jump-starting his heart with electric shock and a needle full of adrenaline. They may have meant well, but if he didn't get his heart slowed down fast, he was afraid it was going to explode through his chest.

So intense was his concentration that he didn't even register the first tentative, feather-light touch of soft hands lifting him out of the muck of the sea bottom. Only when he was floating free and began to feel the pressure change as he was carried toward the surface, did he attempt to open his eyes. Miraculously, they had survived plasma burn, protected by the heavy diamond glass, night vision goggles that ripped off his head only after their plastic straps melted into his burning hair as he hit the water.

He rolled his eyes and squinted into the darkness, trying to make out the figures he could feel swimming around him. He caught a fleeting glimpse of a large shadowy figure, momentarily silhouetted against flashes of broken light, sheeting across the surface above. A large dolphin, maybe? Seconds later, large round, faintly luminous eyes swam into view, peering down at him. He could just make out a seal sleek, round head.

It reminded him of the creature he glimpsed when he popped the roof of the picket-runner. What was it? Something like a cross between a seal or a dolphin and a man? Once again, he remembered the childhood horror movies of genetic experiments gone wrong and terrible mutant monsters prowling the Sinks, but strangely these creatures hardly raised a ripple of concern.

In fact, nothing really bothered him. He was feeling pretty good. In fact, he was feeling better than good. In fact... he was drugged to the eyeballs! he realized. Then he remembered the "pincushion" still strapped to his arm. "Ah ha!" he thought. "Elementary, my dear Watson." He lifted his arm in a slow motion, underwater, way until he could see the red glow of the diagnostic readouts on the face of the little, emergency, field medivac unit strapped to his underarm.

All those little pincushion needles had been sampling his blood for the medivac to analyze. Then its little computer-chipped brain began filling him full of feel-good drugs and whatever else it thought he needed. Yeah, like a hypodermic full of adrenaline to the heart, he thought.

"Just take it easy partner," a voice whispered, and someone took his arm with the medivac strapped to it and gently lowered it to his side.

Harry thought that if he took it any easier he'd be too whacked out to even see straight. He started to giggle and choked again on the plastic tube down his throat.

"Better cut back ten cc's," another voice said, and Harry could feel someone tapping instructions into the medivac. As his mind began to clear, he realized that he hadn't really been hearing voices. Instead, words had been forming inside his head like someone was thinking them for him.

Gentle laughter. "That's right my friend. You catch on fast. I'm thinking it for you, like telepathy, nothing to it, and nothing to be afraid of. Just relax and enjoy the ride. You're with friends now." And a mental image of Chueh's old Chinese coin medallion formed in his mind just before they broke the surface.

Firm hands held him upright with his head just above the surface. A cold, wind-lashed rain stung his burnt face where new skin tissue was beginning to form. Despite the drugs and his own pain block, he still felt it.

On the other hand, he should be glad to feel anything at all, he told himself. All this emergency first aid had nearly killed him. In fact, it did kill him, he realized and remembered again his umbilical snapping and falling free into the white light of death. So how come he was still alive here, in his old body? For an instant, he caught a glimpse of an answer so horrendous that his mind sheared away and hit the "delete" button before it could register.

But something registered, and it started him retching. Then, he coughed up and spit out the tube in his mouth and gulped cool night air. His lung tissue was still regenerating, and it felt like breathing nails. He dove back inside himself, trying to recapture what he had registered, but it was like chasing a mirage and at last he gave up and instead did a quick reconnaissance of his physical status.

The medivac seemed to be getting it right for a change and things were stabilizing faster than he would have thought possible. On the other hand, despite this mysterious healing rush, the physical damage to his meat locker body was so extensive that he was going to need a lot more time powered down in his ka to complete the healing process and take care of the trauma of being so ham-handedly resuscitated by these clowns. Whoever they were, they probably meant well, but he would have been better off if they had just left him on the seabed for another day or two.

He opened his eyes and looked around. They had surfaced behind a little island of wreckage that was overgrown with pale magnolia blossoms. He could smell their sweet, heavy scent on the night air. He could also hear sounds of battle, but they were muted with distance and sometimes blown away by the wind and rain.

Sleek round heads bobbed around him in the water. Their faces were human and surprisingly childlike except for the round, luminous eyes, glowing like radium watch dials below a huge dolphin-like cranial bulge. But human, definitely human, he thought.

"Well, I'm glad we got that cleared up" the thought popped into his head, riding a caressing wave of friendly laughter as one of the creatures swam up to him. "You can call me, S-s-s-arge." He grinned, a wide cartoon grin that went from ear to ear and was full of sharp, needle like teeth. "Now, let's get the medic over here and see what the damage is."

While the medic took Harry's arm and began reading the diagnostics on the medivac, S-s-s-arge swam in close. He pushed his face up into Harry's, tilted his head from side to side, and examined him with his large radium watch dial eyes. Finally, he drew back and shook his head. "You look like you been through a meat grinder," he said.

"Always nice to get a professional opinion," Harry said.

S-s-s-arge ignored the sarcasm and bent down to confer with the medic. Then they both looked at Harry's head, examining the burns and gently prodding the wound in the back. Finally, the medic shook his head, shrugged, and swam away.

S-s-s-arge gave Harry another pointy toothed, jack-o-lantern grin and slapped him on the back. "Don't worry," he said. "In our professional opinion, you shouldn't even be alive, let alone conscious! Since you are, though, I guess we gotta keep you that way and get you out of here in one piece. First, we should take a look at the hornets' nest you stirred up."

He gestured at one of the bobbing heads, and the creature swam over to the little island and pulled himself out of the water. His pale arms were well formed and muscular but his hands were disproportionately wide and flat, the fingers spindle thin and spaced far apart with pale webs of membrane between. When he'd pulled himself halfway out of the water, he reached back and one of his companions handed him something that looked very much like Harry's lost rail-gun.

"You recognize it?" S-s-s-arge asked. "You should, it's yours. We thank you for your contribution to the war effort."

"Glad to oblige," Harry said absently as he watched the scout clamber up the island slope. Stubby, little legs that had the fat, chubby look of a baby's grew directly out of the side of his hips and ended in fleshy, muscular fins that scrabbled for purchase on the muddy slope. Harry noticed that the pale skin of his upper body gradually turned dark and shiny as it tapered down to a long sleek tail beneath the hips.

Distant lightning sheeted across the sky as the scout crawled beneath the magnolias. His long tail curled up out of the water and its tip fanned open into a broad-ribbed fin almost three feet wide and as gaudily colored as a butterfly's wing. The tail uncurled, and the fin slapped the water as the scout disappeared into the undergrowth.

"Why, you're mermaids," Harry whispered in amazement.

"I think in this case, mermen is more correct, don't you?" the laughing voice in his head commented dryly.

"But you're beautiful," Harry blurted out.

"You mean we're not monsters, is that it?"

"I didn't say that."

"But you meant it?"

"Yeah, I guess I did," Harry admitted. "In fact, you better believe I did. After all the horror films that have been made about this place and the genetic wars, I guess I expected you guys to look like a remake of 'The Creature from the Black Lagoon'."

Harry could hear the mermen's thought-voices whispering back and forth to each other, but he couldn't make out what they were saying. It was like listening at a closed door. "What's going on?" he asked.

"The scout reports the coast is clear," S-s-s-arge said. "The battle is still moving away from us."

The patrol swam out from behind the island, carrying Harry with them. "You're safe for the moment," S-s-s-arge added. "But when they find out you're not dead, they'll fight their way back here."

Harry looked down the long, back-alley waterway to where what was left of the apartment building was burning ferociously a couple of hundred yards away. He wondered momentarily what there was left to burn. Then he noticed that the little picket-runner had somehow survived and was still parked under the stairs. If they could get to it, he might have a chance of getting out of here.

"Don't even think about it," S-s-s-arge warned.

Harry looked at the merman treading water nearby. "Why

not?"

"Why do you think they left it there?" S-s-s-arge asked. "They were feeling generous maybe? Use your head! They booby trapped it. Then they burned overrides through the slaver circuits of your AI. So even if you discovered the bomb and disarmed it, they would still control the car."

"How do you know all that?"

"We watched them do it."

"Why didn't you stop them?"

"We're soldiers, not suicides. We were the only patrol in this quadrant when Master Chueh called my people and asked for help. He said he had a tracer on you that we could follow."

"The medallion, of course," Harry said, fingering the old coin that had miraculously survived and still hung around his neck.

S-s-sarge nodded. "We were supposed to keep an eye on you until Chueh got here, but all hell broke loose first."

"Where's Chueh now?"

S-s-s-arge pointed down the waterway to the distant flashes and occasional explosions where the battle was moving away from them.

"We have to leave now. Our orders are to get you out if we can. The Seraphim must know by now that you're still alive, and they will be back. For some reason, they want you pretty bad. This was a major operation."

"I was so careful," Harry said. "I scanned the whole area before coming in. I had top of the line detector..."

"They were dug in, shielded and waiting for you. Your detectors weren't going to pick up anything they didn't want picked up. Now, we don't have any more time. Let's get out of here. We've rigged a sling to tow you."

"Where?"

"Some place where you'll be safe, where master Chueh can find you, and where you can get proper medical attention."

"Whoa, stop," Harry said. "No more medical attention,

okay?" He reached down and began unstrapping the medivac.

"Hey, what are you doing?" S-s-s-arge swam up and grabbed his arm.

"Listen, you got to trust me on this," Harry said. "How do you think I survived so long under water before you guys got to me? You said yourself, I shouldn't be alive, right?"

The merman nodded reluctantly. "You were under water too long, and the extent of your injuries..." he shrugged. "We clipped on the electrodes to shock your heart into starting, but it was just a formality. No one expected anything to happen."

"Then you shot it up with adrenaline to really get it going and damn near killed me," Harry said. "You didn't mean to. You couldn't know I was still alive. I know this is going to sound crazy, but I can put myself into a state of suspended animation at will. My metabolic rate falls so low that it looks like I'm dead. In fact, my body is healing itself."

The merman kept a grip on Harry's arm and regarded him skeptically.

"You don't believe me?" Harry asked.

"I don't know what I believe," S-s-s-arge said. "I was the first one to find you, and I would have sworn that you were as dead as a doornail and had been for quite a while."

"You gotta trust me on this," Harry repeated.

"You know, the back of your head is caved in. There are probably bone splinters in your brain, and you still got third degree burns down the front of your body. I meant it when I said you shouldn't even be alive, let alone talking to me."

"Right now I'm making a big effort just to stay conscious. Look, in order to stay alive, I have to put myself back into suspended animation and when I do," he raised his arm with the medivac strapped it, "this will think I'm dying and begin doing all the wrong things."

Harry felt S-s-s-arge's grip on his arm loosen, but still the merman hesitated.

"Ask your medic what kind of chance there is of getting me out of here alive," Harry suggested.

S-s-s-age turned and looked at the medic who just rolled his eyes and shook his head doubtfully. The merman turned back. "How long?" he asked and released Harry's arm.

"Harry unstrapped the medivac. "I don't know, a day or two, maybe more."

"What!"

"I know what I'm doing." He held up the medivac. "Look, you can put this back on after I've gone into suspended animation. Put it on diagnostic only and at its finest setting. It should be able to pick up a vital sign now and again."

"And if it doesn't?"

"Then I'm probably dead and it wouldn't have helped me anyway."

"Wonderful," S-s-s-arge grunted resignedly. "When do you do it?"

"Now, on the count of three."

"The count of three," The merman nodded. "Good luck."

"One... Two... Three..."

46

Dodger Stadium

Harry woke up to the sound of children's laughter and the feel of warm sunlight. He heard the gentle lapping of water nearby and smelled the scent of flowers and rich plant life. Somewhere in the distance, a goat brayed. He opened his eyes to flickering sunlight. He squinted up at the palm trees, swaying gently overhead. Their feathered leaves cast sun-dappled shadows over him.

He dimly remembered a long trance-like period in his ka and a violent return to his body and then... nothing. He wondered where he was. He turned his head toward the sound of children's laughter and saw Doc dozing nearby in an antique, pre-Crash, aluminum lawn chair.

He had exchanged his usual undertaker blacks for a military-style, chameleon jumpsuit. Its camouflage graphics were turned off and it had a dull gray, metallic sheen. The sight of the old man touched Harry deeply. He knew he could depend on Jericho. Right from the beginning, through five years of craziness, the old man had always been there for him. Harry thought it was probably Jericho who had dressed him in the loose fitting shirt of unbleached linen and matching pajama-like trousers he now wore.

He looked past Jericho's sleeping form to an ancient, rusted guardrail set in a low, moss-covered concrete wall. A profusion of weeds, flowers, and bushes grew along the wall and he had to push himself up on his elbow to see over it. When he did, he discovered that he had been sleeping on an ancient nylon weave, aluminum-framed recliner from the same period (late twentieth century) and in the same style as Jericho's chair. There were collectors who would pay a fortune for such a matched set. Where the hell was he?

He looked over the guardrail to where the waters of a broad lagoon lapped against the concrete wall. Nearby, he could see a group of children playing in the water. Just then, one of them dove under, and Harry glimpsed a brightly colored tailfin flick the surface. Merman, he thought, or maybe, merkid. S-s-s-arge said he was taking him someplace safe. What safer place than the home of the mermen.

Harry looked across the lagoon to the opposite shore. He could see how it curved around and back towards him. He was on some kind of atoll, he thought. An artificial atoll, he amended as his eye followed the steep overgrown sides of the opposite shore up to where they ended in a jagged panorama of rusted girders sticking out of collapsed, sagging roofs. He turned around and looked up the slope behind him. Through the bushes and trees he caught glimpses of other broken-down, overgrown structures. He noticed how the steep sides seemed to go up in even steps. When he looked closely, he could just make out mottled, cracked concrete sticking out of a thick overlay of soil and vegetation.

"It was called Dodger Stadium," Doc's voice was full of quiet reverence.

Harry turned in surprise. "Hi, Doc, good to see you awake."

"It's good to see you alive, my boy," Jericho said with affectionate relief.

"What did you call this place?"

"Dodger Stadium," the old man repeated waving his arm in a slow, all-encompassing gesture. "Built just for the game of baseball back in the twentieth century. Over fifty thousand people gathered here to watch the Los Angeles Dodgers beat the New York Mets in nineteen eighty-eight. Can you imagine how they must have cheered?" he said reminiscently. "What it must have sounded like, fifty thousand baseball fans?" he shook his head sadly. "Gone, all gone and forgotten now." The old man turned and looked out over the lagoon but before he did, Harry thought he caught a glimpse of tears glistening in his eyes.

"The mermen found it nearly intact and fortified it," Jericho continued, his voice thick with emotion. "It was the perfect base for them. They tore down and blocked up the outfield pavilions over there." He pointed to an irregular, ragged stretch of the atoll wall at the far end of the lagoon. "They hauled old wrecks, cars, trucks, buses, whatever they could find, and piled them up." Doc shook his head. "It took them years. They brought in soil and plants and animals and turned the whole place into a garden. Probably the best fortified garden in the world. The only way in from ground level is through underwater passages. They've got missile launchers, laser canons, and rail-guns up there in the bleachers to handle aerial in-coming. Most of the mermen are gone now. Chueh's got his own soldiers guarding this place."

"What happened to the mermen?" Harry asked

"They're too valuable to keep penned up here. Chueh has them out on reconnaissance patrols."

"That's too bad," Harry said. "I kind of wanted to thank S-s-s-arge for trusting me and getting me back alive."

"Who was S-s-s-arge?" Doc asked too quietly.

Harry looked at him sharply. "He was the leader of that patrol that saved me. Why?"

"He didn't make it." Doc shook his head sadly. "The patrol was ambushed... twice."

"Oh shit!" Harry moaned. He thought of that pointy-toothed, jack-o-lantern grin and the laughing voice in his head, gone, all gone, just like Doc said.

"They were tracking you," Jericho said.

"Probably used the monitor on my ka," Harry said. "That means they've got someone working for them at Eternal Life, someone with a lot of authority to get the monitor access codes. Roger..."

Jericho shook his head. "The monitor on your ka went dead that night down in the Sinks. They couldn't track you with it." He leaned forward and regarded Harry gravely. "Son, it's about time you admit you got Roger all wrong," he said.

For once, Harry didn't argue. He thought of what Susan had become and all the lies she'd told him.

"You've got to understand," Jericho said gently. "Roger loves Susan very much. Maybe even as much as you… " Jericho hesitated, watching Harry closely, "… once did," he finished.

Harry felt as if he had been walking around with a bomb strapped to his heart and Doc had just cut the wires and disarmed it. "How did you know?" he asked.

"Know what?"

"Maybe even as much as you… once did," Harry repeated the words with a sense of wonder, as if they were some kind of magic formula.

"What? Oh that!" Doc growled impatiently. "You'd have to be blind, deaf, and brain-dead not to notice what was going on between you two back there at Chueh's."

"Diana… " Harry started.

"Later!" Doc cut in curtly. "First, it's important that you understand about Roger. He's a lot like you, a man capable of great love. Right now, he's wracked with pain and guilt because he blames himself for what happened to Susan. Does that sound familiar?"

"What did happen to her?" Harry asked.

"The world's a strange place sometimes," Jericho said. "When I was young, they used to say, "What goes around comes around". Roger took Susan to the wrong party, just like you once did."

"Son of a bitch!" Harry muttered.

Jericho nodded. "Roger always did like to run with a fast crowd, movers and shakers, the beautiful people, powerful, jaded, dangerous people. Even after he became king of the castle and had nothing more to prove and no one to else impress… " Jericho unhooked his wire-rimmed spectacles and knuckled his eyes like a tired child. "Anyway, to make a long story short," he said, replacing the spectacles, "they were at this party, and someone spiked Susan's drink with black ice."

"Oh no," Harry groaned. He closed his eyes and had an instant vision of Isis, with her painted face and little girl costume, fighting for possession of her soul.

"When she came out of it, she wasn't Susan anymore," Jericho said. "Something came back with her, possessed her, riding her like a horse, making her do and say things she would never do or say, terrible, perverse, evil things."

Harry thought of the recent rumors of wild orgies and unspeakable depravities coming out of Roger's island estate. "How long ago?" he asked numbly.

"Almost six months," Doc said.

"When did you find out?" Harry asked.

"Not until Roger came to me the night your resurrection went wrong. He was at the end of his rope. He'd tried everything to get Susan back. He even put her through medieval shock treatment and a secret resurrection to try to force the demon to release its hold." Doc shook his head. "They were acts of foolish desperation. He must have known that they'd already been tried and failed countless times. The trauma units in the sub-basements beneath Eternal life were filled to overflowing, many worse off than Susan, with their kas crippled and nothing left of their original personalities. They were the wolves' early failures, but with each failure they got better at possessing and controlling. With black ice their success rate went up exponentially.

"Maybe it would have been better for Roger if she'd been one of the failures, just a mindless, homicidal maniac," Jericho stopped and looked around the ruins of the once mighty Dodger Stadium. "Maybes and might-have-beens," he said quietly. "This place is full of maybes and might-have-beens."

For a while he sat staring out over the lagoon at nothing in particular. Finally, he turned to Harry. "Don't mind me," he said.

"I'm just getting too old, carrying around too many memories, too many maybes and might-have-beens." He ran his fingers through his always unruly shock of silver grey hair and said. "Now where was I?"

"Roger trying to get Susan back," Harry said, his voice as neutral as an actuary table.

"Yes, poor Roger," Jericho said. "He knows all about maybes and might-have-beens. After he tried everything he could to bring Susan back, one of the wolf-possessed came to him and promised that they would give her back if he just did them a few favors."

"A promise they never intended to keep, of course," Harry said scornfully.

"I think even Roger knew that," Jericho said, "but every once in a while, they brought his wife back just to show him that the real Susan, his Susan, was still there inside, alive and conscious and begging for help."

Harry remembered the brief, cruel glimpse the dying wolf showed him of Susan trapped, tortured, and begging to be set free. A low groan of despair escaped his lips.

Doc looked at him sharply. "What is it, Harry?"

"Nothing!" He closed his eyes and shook his head. "Just tell me what happened."

Jericho nodded reluctantly and said, "Each time they brought Susan back, Roger was reminded that his wife was still alive, trapped inside her demon-possessed body, and that only he could save her. What else could he do? What would you do? He gave them what they wanted."

"And what did they want?" Harry asked, his voice deceptively calm.

"Oh, they had quite a shopping list," Jericho said. "First, they wanted complete access to Eternal Life with wolf-possessed in key positions. Then they wanted Roger to use the full weight of his position as CEO to keep stone-walling, denying, lying, whatever it took, to keep the lid on the fact that the trauma wards beneath Eternal Life were filling up with wolf-possessed who had gone flat-out crazy, homicidal, and catatonic. Finally, when they were ready, they wanted him to empty the trauma wards, spilling these people out on the streets like an insane fifth column, creating fear and chaos and pulling in more souls either through murder or black ice.

"And if anyone made trouble before they were ready… you know, family members, friends, the media, talking too much, asking too many questions… then the black wolves took over. When that happened, these people either ended up dead or got slipped black ice. Either way, the result was the same. The black wolves moved into their bodies… but not always." Jericho hesitated.

"Not always?" Harry asked and felt something stir in his memory.

"Roger said there were times when a victim's ka never came back, and the body didn't resurrect. He assumed they just went into the white light of real death. Later, the wolf that possessed Susan told him the terrible truth, that, sometimes they didn't take possession of a ka but captured and ate it instead. Can you imagine a greater obscenity," Jericho's voice was raw with emotion. "To eat a ka and condemn that person to unbeing, to nothingness forever?"

Harry suddenly remembered the Susan-thing's tongue thrusting towards the soft palate at the back of his mouth and the insane hunger that drove it.

"Harry, are you alright?" Jericho asked. "You're looking kind of pale."

"It's nothing, Doc," Harry waved it away. "I assume Roger is no longer working for them," he said instead.

Jericho shook his head. "On the night you resurrected, when we all thought the wolves had taken possession of you too… Well, that was the last straw for Roger. He felt as if he'd betrayed everything and everyone who ever meant anything to him, and he came and told me everything."

"Just a minute, Doc," Harry said. "As far as I can see, I don't mean squat to Roger. Why would my getting possessed bring about such a sudden transformation?"

"Not so sudden," Jericho said and leaned back and stretched out his legs as the ancient lawn chair creaked dangerously. "Did you know he stayed by your bedside that first night and most of the next day after your resurrection went wrong?"

Harry stared at him with dumb incomprehension, and Jericho shook his head irritably. "You know, Harry," he said. "For a very smart guy, you can be incredibly stupid sometimes, especially about Roger. There's a common bond of guilt, love, and respect between you two that Roger always recognized even if you didn't."

"Susan," Harry said.

Jericho nodded. "Susan's a big part of it, of course, but it goes deeper than that. You two are very much alike not only in the choice of whom you love but how deeply you love and how far you'll go to protect what you love. And when you fail at that... " Jericho threw up his hands in a gesture of complete defeat. "Well, you know all about that."

Harry knew what Jericho was saying was true. In a sense he'd known it all along but pigheadedly refused to recognize it. Instead, he self-servingly blamed Roger for everything; for the resurrection torture that destroyed his marriage, for the unfor-givable betrayal of falling in love with Susan, and for stealing her from him. Now, he could finally admit that there was nothing to betray and nothing to steal because he had destroyed Susan's love long before Roger claimed it. As for the torture of those serial resurrections that destroyed his marriage and that he blamed Roger for... even here he had to admit, as he had admitted to Diana, that it was his own fault, a self-inflicted torture, a fruitless attempt to appease a guilty conscience.

A group of laughing mermaids suddenly broke the surface of the lagoon. They were towing nets filled with squirming fish. The children, playing nearby, yelled with delight and swam over to help pull the nets. As they swam for shore, the flick of their tailfins left a rainbow haze of droplets in their wake and the sound of their laughter and singing echoed through the vast ruins of the stadium. Harry watched them swim to a concrete ramp that led up into the bleachers.

Two men dressed much like Harry were waiting to take hold of the net and drag it up on land. There was a great deal of shouting and laughter and one of the young mermaids rose out of the water balanced on her tail fin and shook her ample breasts at the men to whoops of delight and playful teasing.

Harry smiled at this bright ray of normality in the midst of the darkness he felt gathering around him. He looked up at the bleachers and noticed other men working in the terraced fields while others manned gun emplacements high up on the ragged rim of the stadium. Holding back the darkness, he thought.

At last he asked, "What happened to Susan? Who beat her up?" He had a sick, sinking feeling because he already knew.

"The wolves, of course; they wanted you pretty badly and when you came back crazy like you did... " Jericho shook his head. "... Well, we all thought they had you. Even the wolves weren't sure what happened. We were all waiting for you to wake up and when you didn't after the first day, things got pretty tense."

"Tell me exactly what happened," Harry said in voice so matter-of-fact and without emotion that Jericho looked at him and hesitated. For a second, he felt as if he was standing on an open beach, the air crystalline, perfectly still, the world holding its breath, waiting for the hurricane that was surely coming. He wondered if Harry was aware of the scars that covered his body, like fine hairline cracks in old porcelain. Jericho didn't think so, not yet. And when he did, would he know what they meant? He felt a cold shiver of premonition, like the first, faint breeze of that approaching storm.

He shook it off with a resigned shrug. Isn't this what he'd been working towards all along? There would be no turning back now even if he wanted to. Instead, he said, "When you didn't wake up after twenty-four hours, Roger made sure that you were as secure as possible and then left you with me. He'd been under a lot of pressure the last few days and knew it was only going to get worse, no matter which way you woke up. He needed to get away from it all for a few hours and made the mistake of going home.

"The wolves were waiting for him with Susan. They were there to teach him a lesson. The wolf that possessed Susan released its grip and they brought her back to full consciousness. Then they tortured her in front of Roger. Afterwards, they told him what they wanted and that this was just a little sample of what would happen if he didn't do it."

"What did they want?" Harry asked.

Jericho eyed him, trying to gauge his mood and gave up. "They wanted you of course," he said. "For some reason, they weren't convinced they'd taken possession. If you woke up and weren't possessed, they wanted another crack at you. This time they'd make sure and use black ice if they had to.

"For the first time, Roger felt a glimmer of hope that you might have survived intact, and he began making plans. First, he had to convince the wolves that if you came back intact and they tried to give you black ice, it would be impossible to keep the lid on what was happening at Eternal Life.

"The reporters were already asking questions, he told them. You were usually out of rebirthing within twelve hours, and it was already way over that. If you didn't show up soon, they would begin taking a closer look at all those stories of demonic possession. It wouldn't take much to blow the lid right off. Then, no amount of damage control would help.

"You were all they had, all they ever had, to keep control of the situation. People trusted you. As long as you kept coming back whole and sane and assuring everyone that everything was okay, people were willing to accept it. But if you didn't come back soon or if you came back wolf-possessed crazy, Eternal Life and any plans the wolves had would be blown to hell.

"The wolves made a big show of accepting this, even setting conditions for what they wanted in exchange for not making a run at you if you came back whole."

"All that about signing a new contract or going on promotion tours," Harry said remembering Roger's halfhearted attempts to keep him tied to Eternal life."

"Nothing but misdirection," Jericho said. "They even made Roger suspect they'd slipped black ice into the drinking water on your bedside table."

"Son of a bitch!" Harry said, remembering Roger dropping his cigarette butt in the water so he wouldn't drink it.

Jericho nodded. "Nothing but misdirection. They already had other plans for you."

"Susan," Harry said.

Jericho nodded.

"So they decided to wait and get me someplace alone, where no one could see or interfere, and they used Susan to get me there," Harry said.

"They always have one of your clones ready at Eternal Life," Jericho said. "All they had to do was hook it up to the spin-generator."

Harry shook his head. "I think they had other plans for me," he said and told Jericho about the wolf dressed in Susan's body who tried to seduce him and then drive its obscene tongue up into his brain and suck out his mind and eat his ka.

"It was the ultimate solution to their King of the Dead problem," Harry said. "There would be no more messy uncertainties of resurrection because there would be nothing left to resurrect. It was neat, clean, and permanent, with no questions asked because everyone knew I was retired and would assume I took a long vacation somewhere and didn't want to be disturbed.

"They let me walk out of Eternal Life and didn't try to stop me because they were keeping an eye on me and knew I was heading for that side door and told Susan just where to wait." Harry closed his eyes and once again saw her battered face as she looked up at him with tears in her eyes. "I saw what they did to her, what they wanted me to see," he said without opening his eyes. "She told me Roger did it. I believed her. I had the feeling something was wrong, but I still believed her enough to go down into the Sinks."

He opened his eyes and looked up at Jericho. "Jesus, Doc, they were good. They knew all the right buttons to push, the guilt, the anger, the distrust of Roger, even the self-serving need to protect her against him; they got it all just right. Even that thing down in the Sinks dressed in Susan's body must have had complete access to her personality matrix and all her memories."

"Now you know the kind of pressure they were putting on Roger," Jericho said.

Harry looked away, out over the lagoon. "What happened to the real Susan?" he asked in that quiet, uninflected voice that was like the stillness before a storm.

Jericho eyed him warily. "Roger said they took her with them back to the Nevada Quarantine."

Harry sank back on the recliner and stared up at the sunlight flickering through the palm leaves overhead. He remembered Roger standing in the recovery room, cajoling, apologizing, threatening; doing everything he could to get him to sign another contract. Then finally, when he knew it was all in vain, turning to the two-way mirror and flicking his cigarette at it with the bravado of a man facing a firing squad and giving it the finger. Now that he knew who or what was probably sitting behind that mirror and what was at stake, he could better understand the hopeless courage and desperate defiance behind that gesture.

"I should have stayed at Chueh's and listened to him," he said half to himself. "If I hadn't been so pigheaded... " He stopped. Beating himself up wasn't going to change anything. "Where's Roger now?" he asked.

"He and Diana left for the Nevada Quarantine four days ago," Doc said.

47

The King of the Dead

"Four days! How long have I been here?" Harry asked.

"The mermen brought you in two days ago."

"And Diana left for Las Vegas four days ago?" Harry shook his head in disbelief. "Is everybody crazy? You told me the wolves moved the whole Nevada Quarantine out of our universe. How does she expect to get in? Even if she does, it's a suicide mission!"

He sat up and stared angrily at Jericho. "How could you let her go? You knew what she was getting into!" he said, turning his remorse and despair into an angry denunciation of the old man for letting her go and of himself for not staying to help her.

"There was no way I could stop her," Jericho said. "She's a Jaganmatri Valkyrie, Harry. They can usually take care of themselves. She waited for you though, despite everything. Even after the monitor on your ka flat-lined that night, she waited. But by morning, when there was no word, she and Roger figured there was no reason to wait any longer."

"But didn't Chueh tell you what happened?" Harry asked. "His people found me alive that night."

"Chueh was having his own problems," Doc pointed out. "Communications weren't that great. All hell was breaking out down in the Sinks. When he went in to get you out, the Seraphim and the wolves hit him hard."

Doc reached into a pocket and pulled out some kind of medallion on a silver chain. "His intelligence agents have been warning him for months about a new messiah uniting the Seraphim." He handed the medallion to Harry. It was the Seraphim double-bladed cross like the one he had seen down in the Sinks seven years ago. The only difference was the gun sight circle was replaced by a triangle with a growling wolf's head nailed to the center. Harry felt his hackles rise and a low, animal growl start deep in his throat as he stared at the medallion that combined the two worst nightmares of his life.

"Are you all right?" Doc asked.

"Yeah, copacetic," Harry said with a crooked, unconvincing grin. He nodded at the medallion. "I guess we know who their new messiah is."

"Yeah, it wasn't only New Hollywood types that got to try black ice," Doc said. "The Norma-genes and their Anubis wolf allies have been busy down in the Sinks. They made sure the Seraphim leadership got the first taste of paradise. After the wolves got control of the leadership, they spread the good news.

"They didn't need to take possession of the Seraphim rank and file. It was enough just to give them a taste of what the wolf temples offer, a night or two of paradise, running with their new god, raping, killing, fulfilling every bestial desire as the biggest meanest predators on the planet. After that there was no stopping them. The Slavers, the renegade Tongs, and all the rest of the sink rats got a taste too. Now, they're all true believers united under the wolf's head banner.

"Paradise was within reach and anyone who dies as a martyr to the new messiah gets their ka gathered up by the Anubis wolves and taken to their world to live forever, fulfilling every animal desire. They're told that they will be rulers of paradise with the kas of their slain enemies to serve them as slaves for all eternity."

"It sounds like they borrowed a page or two from the old Koran," Harry said.

"It's an even more effective witch's brew today than it was a thousand years ago," Jericho said. "The martyrs today have already had a taste of paradise to wet their appetites. It's turned a squabbling configuration of Seraphim, Slavers and Tong thugs into a fanatical army of martyrs.

"Unfortunately, Chueh's intelligence hadn't prepared him for anything of this magnitude, especially when the wolves showed up in their crystal warships and began turning his army to dust and shutting down the grav-units on his battlewagons. He lost so many soldiers that first night that he was forced to call in all his markers from the other Tong Godfathers.

"It didn't take much to convince them, though. The Tongs have had an uneasy truce with the Sinks for years. The deal was the Sinks keep out of New Hollywood and the Tongs keep out of the Sinks. Black ice has been straining that truce for months. Once the other Tong Godfathers realized what was really going on and what it would do to business, they put all their forces at Chueh's disposal. Nobody wanted religious fanatics running amok with something like black ice and the Anubis wolves pulling the strings. Even with the support of all the Tongs, Chueh had a full blown war on his hands, and it was getting nasty.

"The Seraphim holy warriors proved all but unstoppable. They came in waves and fought like berserkers and were unafraid of death because they had their living gods fighting beside them. These seven foot tall, black, wolf-headed deities rode in on crystal warships, unlike anything we'd ever seen, and they carried weapons that could shut down grav-units and bring down a fleet of battle-junks in seconds. On top of that, they've got blue death rays that strip a man to the bone in seconds. You can't hide from them; they penetrate solid walls and spider-spin armor. In less than twenty-four hours, Chueh and the Tongs lost over seventy percent of their troops and half their fleet to the Seraphim."

Harry had an instantaneous memory flashback. "I think I once saw a weapon like that strip a man to the bone," he said in surprise. "It was out on the astral plane."

"On the astral plane?" Jericho asked uncertainly.

"No, not exactly out on that astral plane," Harry shook his

head as if to shake the memory free. "I think I followed the wolves back to their home world, and I... "

"You what!" Jericho said. Then he raised his hand. "Stop, just a minute and go back and tell me exactly what happened," he said with barely repressed excitement.

Harry eyed him curiously. "What's the big deal?"

"The big deal is that no one knows where the Anubis wolves come from," Jericho said. "It's their most closely guarded secret. It's why Isis risked her life to steal a Pathfinder. It's... Just tell me what you saw," he said impatiently.

Harry felt like a poker player who had just been dealt four aces. "And Diana has the Pathfinder now?" Harry said.

"Yeah, so what?" Jericho said irritably.

"Is she going to use it to try to go there?"

"Go where?"

"The Anubis home world, of course."

Jericho looked at him in momentary confusion and shook his head. "No, why would she go there?"

"So where is she going with it?"

"I told you, Las Vegas to try to rescue her sister."

"And she needs the Pathfinder to get her there, is that it?" Harry asked.

"Ah!" Jericho nodded as he suddenly realized what the game was all about and nodded reluctant acceptance. "Yes, she's going to use the Pathfinder to try to get to Las Vegas," he admitted.

"And?" Harry prompted.

"And to do that she has to get to a place that her father found years ago," Jericho said reluctantly. "A kind of interface with all possible dimensions and worlds of the quantum field."

"Like one of those power points that shamans talk about, where the wall between worlds is thinned out?" Harry suggested.

"Exactly," Jericho said and Harry heard the relief in his voice and knew he was lying, but before he could do anything about it, his mind began opening up like an origami Pandora's box, releasing a host of repressed memories. They rushed up and swarmed around him, a multitude of accusing ghosts that would no longer be denied. An instant later, he came face to face with the King of the Dead. "No-o-o-o!" he screamed and buried his face in his hands. "What have I done!"

Jericho reached out instinctively. "What is it, Harry?" he asked and laid a comforting hand on his shoulder.

"Don't touch me!" Harry screamed. "Keep away!" His voice rose to a hurricane roar. It filled the stadium and shook the heavens. Birds rose from the surrounding trees, flapping and screeching in fear, and the distant laughing voices of the mermaids and their children fell into cowering silence.

Jericho stumbled back and fell into his chair. The storm he was expecting had finally come, and he was terrified at what it brought with it. No human voice could have made such a sound. It was like the cry of a crucified god.

Harry raised his head, his face a mask of ecstasy and despair. He seemed to look right through the old man, out past the distant walls of the stadium, and into a hidden place of terrible wonders; and his eyes burned with the cold, blue fire of that place. "So much power, so many chances to fail," he muttered to himself. "So many worlds to die."

All the hairline scars that covered his body began to glow like the coils on a toaster. His face became an eerie mask of glowing dendritic scars as if his blood was on fire. The fire went from cherry red to the intense blue-white of an exploding star. Harry opened his mouth to scream again and all the scars in his body split open in a blinding burst of energy.

Jericho squeezed his eyes shut and turned away until the flashbulb afterimages burned into his retinas disappeared. When he turned back to look, all the hairline scars had closed into a circuitry of softly glowing filaments, and Harry was surrounded by a shimmering blue-white aura. Like the halos around saints in ancient icons, Jericho thought. "Harry, can you hear me?" he asked, not daring to touch him again, not even daring to move. "Are you all right?" he asked fearfully.

Slowly, Harry turned. His eyes still burned with that cold blue fire. Instinctively, Jericho tried to look away, but it was too late. His eyes snagged on that fey light and instantly it blew his doors of perception wide open and unhinged his mind. He looked into an infinity of possible and impossible universes; of myriad worlds being born and dying, of space-time eternally folding in on itself through countless dimensions and, overlaying it all, were the branching lines of infinite probability that were also the branching lines of his own nervous system. "Too much! Too much!" he moaned as his old Darwinian monkey mind began chittering and screeching with terror, and all he wanted to do was curl up in a ball and bury his face in his crotch.

After an eternity that was no time at all, the vision passed, leaving Jericho dazed and shaken. He looked around the ruined stadium, across the lagoon and up at the sky, trying to fit the broken pieces of reality together again, to make the world make sense again. He looked everywhere except at Harry.

"Have you ever thought about how terrible it is to be a god?" Harry asked, and the pain and despair in his voice touched Jericho's guilty heart and drew his gaze back. The aura of power that surrounded Harry had disappeared, the hairline scars no longer glowed, and only a faint residue of fey light still flickered in his eyes, but he looked like he had aged fifty years.

Jericho avoided those eyes with guilty self-reproach. What's done is done, he thought, it can't be undone. He looked up past Harry to the collapsed, overgrown stadium bleachers and the blue sky filled with fat, white cumulus clouds like cotton candy.

"The mermen, who brought you in, treated you like some kind of holy, religious relic," he said at last. "They claimed you worked miracles. They swore that when the Seraphim ambushed them down in the Sinks and S-s-sarge was killed, you suddenly woke from the dead and stood on the water in a halo of light and called all the mermen to you. The Seraphim were shooting from everywhere and not a bullet, particle beam, or laser ray touched you or the mermen gathered around you."

Harry cocked his head and listened intently.

"They say you raised your arm and pointed at the Seraphim," Jericho said, "and your whole body cracked open and an expanding bubble of light poured out of the cracks and behind the light came an army of gods and demons, pushing the bubble before them and wherever they went, the earth and sea, the ruins of the city, the ships and the Seraphim were all wiped away as if they had never been.

"When there were no more Seraphim left, you called your army of gods and demons back into you, and you and your mermen were left on the floor of the seabed, in the center of a vast empty crater, surrounded by a bubble of light that sliced through the surrounding ruins and held back the waters. Then, you dropped your arm and the bubble collapsed and the sea rushed back into the crater. Later, the mermen found you floating as if dead on the water."

Jericho paused and looked at Harry. He sat perfectly still, his head cocked, his eyes hooded as if he was listening to something only he could hear.

Jericho shivered. "They took your body with them," he went on doggedly. "And the next day they were attacked again, this time by the crystal gunships and a battle cruisers of the Anubis wolves, and the same thing happened. You came back to life and not a ship or wolf survived.

"I've seen the aerial reconnaissance of both areas," Jericho said. "It looks like ground-zero, a perfect circle of destruction. Everything within a two hundred-yard radius has been scoured away and a six hundred foot deep water-filled crater is all that's left. There's no sign of the buildings, bodies, or ships that were there. It's as if they've all been erased."

He risked another glance at Harry. Except for the faint flicker of weirding light in his eyes, he could have been carved out of stone. "It's hard to imagine what could have done that, son," Jericho said gently, nudging Harry towards the truth.

Harry said nothing.

"The mermen say you were burned to death and buried in the bottom of the sea when they first found you. That you came to life, that they saw new skin growing out beneath third degree charred blisters. They say later the blisters sloughed off like an old snakeskin and even your hair grew back overnight."

Harry reached up and touched his face. It felt like it had always felt. He looked closely at the back of his hands. He could just make out a pattern of branching scar-like lines, so fine he might not have noticed if he hadn't been looking.

"Yeah." Jericho nodded. "Those scars are the real miracle. I've never seen anything quite like them," he lied. "But the back of your head is completely healed," he went on hurriedly, "not a scar in sight except for those, whatever they are, and no brain damage that we know of. The mermen say they watched the bone splinters being pushed out of your brain pan as the skull grew back and the wound healed. They say that the medivac monitor went nuts."

Jericho looked at Harry and tried to keep his guilt and remorse from showing. It was too late for guilt and remorse anyway, he told himself. Too late, too late, he repeated it like a mantra. "I think you've become what the Anubis wolves feared you would become," he said at last.

"The King of the Dead," Harry said tonelessly.

48

Eater of Universes

"I think I understand now why the Anubis wolves wanted you badly enough to start a war down in the Sinks," Jericho said and risked looking Harry in the eye. The weirding light was gone and a flush of youthful vigor was returning to his face. "But what exactly happened to you down there, Harry?"

"You should know. You told me the monitor on my ka flat-lined," Harry said. "I felt the umbilical connecting my body to my ka snap, and the standing waves of probability that had been my life began collapsing into the white light of death. They should have swept my ka along with them, only they didn't, because I turned away."

"Impossible!" Jericho said although he knew better and wondered if it wasn't time to tell Harry so. He rejected the thought almost at once. Too much was at stake, and even a little knowledge at the wrong time could tip the scales of probability he was so carefully trying to balance. "How did you do it, my boy?" he asked instead.

"I don't know," Harry said. "It was like the first time I learned to die. I don't know how I did it or how I learned to do it. I just did it, like jumping off a cliff and wanting to fly. Wanting is everything. If you want it enough, want it from the level of your ka, you can do anything, even change your destiny, even the destiny of your universe, but there's a price. There's always a price," he added darkly.

Jericho shifted uncomfortably but said nothing.

"I didn't know that then," Harry said. "Maybe if I had... " His lips twisted into a bitter smile of lost innocence. "Maybes and might-have-beens, huh, Doc?" he said and waved them away. "Anyway, I didn't know, and I really didn't have a choice. I was going to die. I'd done all I could, but the probabilities in that universe were all stacked against me.

"I should have died down there in the Sinks. I was fated to die there, but I knew that if I did, the wolves would be waiting for me with their final solution to the King of the Dead problem. They'd eat my ka. There would be no escaping them this time. There would be no rebirth in the light of the Goddess or in the spin-generators of Eternal Life. There would be nothing left of me, nothing forever."

He looked at Jericho, pleading for understanding. "You see, I really didn't have a choice," he said. He didn't tell Jericho the other reason for his choice, perhaps the most important reason. It was none of the old man's business that it was love for Diana that finally tipped the scale from nothingness to life.

"What did you expect to find out there?" Jericho asked.

"Life, the power to bend my destiny and change the direction of the universe, but I didn't realize that last thing was part of the deal. I should have though. I was trying to play god. The only problem with trying to play god is you're cursed to become one.

"You see, in order to perform this... miracle," Harry said spreading his arms wide to emphasize his healed body. "I destroyed a universe." He looked at Jericho and his eyes were like two black holes punched through his face.

Jericho closed his eyes and looked away. It had to be done, he told himself. It was the price that had to be paid to stop the Anubis wolves. Only it's not me paying the price, he told himself with bitter self-contempt. "Why don't you tell me what happened out there, son," he said gently and felt like the worst kind of hypocrite.

Harry didn't answer for a long time. He remained perfectly still, hardly breathing, his empty eyes staring blindly into the distance. At last, he drew a deep shuddering breath and said, "We're going to have to start like in the bible. In the beginning... there was only the nothingness of quantum space, like a vast sea of infinite potential where the standing waves of probability had not yet collapsed into the wave front of material reality," Harry stopped and looked at Jericho.

The old man nodded encouragement.

"We'll probably never know what first impulse set off the collapse of that wave front that in turn set off a chain reaction all over this quantum sea. I suspect that it was a touch of desire, the Goddess's desire, maybe even her loneliness," Harry said with a sad smile.

"That first touch of desire was like a rock thrown into a still pond. It set off the splash of the Big Bang with an infinite number of probability waves collapsing violently into reality. An infinite number of universes burst into existence, crashed into each other, and winked out again in those first nano-seconds of creation."

"You saw all this?" Jericho said in awestruck wonder.

Harry turned and looked at him and said nothing but the fey light was burning in his eyes again, and Jericho felt his mind start to unhinge and quickly looked away.

"Of those universes that survived, the majority were nonviable," Harry continued as if nothing had happened. "The natural laws that determined their existence were unable to support them for more than an instant before they burst like soap bubbles and returned to the quantum sea.

"Natural laws are like the concrete foundations and steel girder skeleton holding up a building. If your foundation is weak, maybe your concrete is too porous, or the steel girders are too thin or put together wrong, the whole building becomes unstable and collapses.

"Even though an infinite number of universes died in those first nano-seconds, there was always an infinite number waiting to be born out of the roiling waters of the quantum sea. Some universes survived the first minutes of the Big Bang, some the first hour, their coherence and stability dependent on how probability had collapsed into natural law.

"The effects of the Big Bang still ripple through the multiverse today. Some universes as old as our own, or even older, will suddenly wink out of existence due to inconsistencies in their natural laws that have gradually built up until the whole structure becomes unsustainable. Then, the universe loses stability, comes apart at the seams, and sinks back into the quantum sea.

"When I died and turned my back on the resurrection trail, I stepped out into the spirit realm on the shores of Samuel Kade's Shining Sea of Gods and Demons. I'm not sure why my ka chose this conceptual interpretation over any others. On the other hand, I never knew why Kade called it the 'Shining Sea of Gods and Demons' and never bothered to ask. I just assumed it was a metaphor, you know, colorful shaman language," he said and shook his head with a self-deprecating smile. "I should have known better."

"I'd stepped into the Shining Sea a couple of times with Kade, not very far, mind you, and not for very long but long enough to discover that it was a sea made of golden probability bubbles. This time, though, I went in way over my head, stepped off the continental shelf, so to speak, and I learned why Samuel Kade called it what he called it.

"As I sank into the infinite depths surrounded by these golden bubbles, they sang to me, and I realized that each one was a universe of worlds, and each universe was alive, singing with consciousness, and their songs were the songs of the gods and demons of the natural laws that created and sustained each universe."

"Gods and demons of natural law?" Jericho shook his head. "You lost me there, son."

"Yeah, I lost me there too," Harry said and laughed. There was nothing funny in that laugh. It was high and shrill like a dentist's drill hitting a nerve.

Jericho put a comforting hand on his arm. "Harry?"

"It's okay, Doc, just a mild case of indigestion," he said and started to laugh again and clamped down on it hard. "Just give me a minute," he said and sat silently, staring at the lagoon without really seeing it.

Finally, he turned and looked at Jericho. His features were calm and composed, his voice as steady and devoid of emotion as a science report. "Natural laws aren't the dead mechanical automatons that Newton made them out to be," he continued. "They're precipitates of consciousness expressed as gods and demons that create and sustain a living universe. They are, in fact, those gods and demons, good and bad, creation and destruction, two sides of the same coin, creating a constant dynamic interplay that sustains balance and drives change." He raised his hands palms up weighing them. "Like a scale," he said. "No creation without destruction, no destruction without creation... gods and demons, precipitates of consciousness. How could it be otherwise? As you, yourself, pointed out, the quantum field is a field of consciousness so everything that comes out of it has to be conscious including those laws or forces that structure reality."

It looks like there were some things Jake Lloyd didn't tell me, Jericho thought wryly.

"As I swam through that sea of universes, that multiverse, I could hear the golden songs of the laws that sustained them and each one was as different as the worlds that sang them. It's important to always keep in mind that these laws are expressions of consciousness, that they are in fact deities and demons. Our primitive ancestors got it right. There are gods of thunder, of lightning, of the earth and the sky, but there's also a supreme God or Goddess ruling each world and universe."

Harry's face darkened, and his voice got low and hoarse, and Jericho thought of dank cellars and rotting bones and that old shiver of premonition was back again. "I don't want to believe that what I did, I did on purpose," Harry said, "because how could I know?

"But I went out there looking for a miracle that would reconnect my ka with my body, flushing it with so much raw probability that it would twist my destiny from death to life. What I didn't realize is that a universe is a closely woven pattern of consciousness and each person's life is part of that pattern. When you die, it's not a break in the pattern, it's part of it. It's your time to die. I went out on the quantum sea to find something powerful enough to twist my destiny, which in turn meant twisting the pattern of my universe."

"And you found it," Jericho said quietly, dreading what he was about to hear.

"Oh yeah, I found it, or rather it found me," Harry said. "I felt like a god, I was a god, walking through the infinite sea of the multiverse with the golden bubbles of universes singing to me as my ka brushed against them. I realize now I was like a hungry predator, stalking a herd, looking for the weakest in the flock.

"I keep telling myself I didn't know what I was doing, but I should have known, just as those old twentieth century scientists knew that, on the quantum level, what you want to happen, happens. Wishes have a way of getting fulfilled, only, as the old saying goes, you gotta be careful what you wish for.

"My ka was a probability wild card, no longer tied by an umbilical to the structured laws of our universe that would have prevented what happened from happening. Each time I brushed against a bubble, my ka sent unpatterned probability waves rippling through the space-time of that universe until, at last, it touched a universe so unstable it was balancing on the edge of dissolution.

"It was like a house of cards just waiting for a little touch of unpatterned probability to break the weak bonds holding it together. When that happened, in the instant before it crashed into unreality, I opened my ka and let it crash into me instead. I ate it! I became King of the Dead, Eater of Universes!"

He suddenly got up and stepped over to the rusted guardrail and leaned against it with his back to Jericho so the old man couldn't see his face. His voice became a flat objective monotone as if he was trying to distance himself from what he was saying. "I felt their lives flow into me, I think I heard them scream as all their patterned consciousness dissolved into unpatterned probability, flowing into me... filling me to overflowing... "

He leaned over the railing looking down into the water as if searching for something he'd lost.

"... Filling me with gods and demons," he said at last. "Those gods and demons, those precipitates of consciousness that had structured the laws of that universe, would not go down into dissolution. Instead, they remain inside me bound to my ka... like an undigested meal."

So we're finally there, Jericho thought and remembered Jake Lloyd lying ghostlike in his bed, his body glowing softly, fading into his ka and too weak and too attenuated to do anything except prophesy the coming of the Anubis and the death of humanity unless... "An abomination," he had whispered to Jericho, "another one like me... " and his face was transfixed with horror, "but not like me... The only thing that can save us, an abomination, cursed with gods and demons... A King of the Dead! You must find this abomination!" Then he grabbed Jericho's hand and told him what he had to do.

"I wanted life," Harry said, his voice hardly more than a whisper. "But in my universe, the universe I left, I was destined to die. In fact, I did die. In that universe I never walked out into the Shining Sea but instead went down into the white light of death.

"You've got to understand, this isn't the only universe in which the earth exists. There are countless alternate universes with alternate earths, alternate timeline bubbles, that have split off from the original like those bacteria that reproduce by simply splitting in two. In the beginning the two universes look identical, but gradually, the difference between them becomes more and more pronounced as they follow different timeline trajectories."

He remained hanging over the rusted railing, staring down at the water, saying nothing for such a long time that Jericho thought he was finished. Then suddenly he asked, "Do you know what creates a new timeline universe?"

Jericho thought he knew but decided it was best to let Harry talk it all out of his system.

"It's conscious desire, the wanting, that drives you to make a decision," Harry said. "But not all decisions have the power of consequence that can split a universe and create a new one. It doesn't matter, for instance, if you decide to take a cup of coffee or tea in the morning or walk or ride to work. Every decision like that, probably every decision you'll ever make has no effect on the larger scheme of things. They're like pebbles thrown in the ocean. They cause small ripples that gradually get ironed out in the vastness of the sea. On the other hand, some decisions, an almost infinitesimal number, are like a huge meteor strike, raising probability tsunamis that shift the balance of the universe to the extent that it births an alternate timeline."

"And that's what happened when you turned your back on the resurrection trail... and ate a universe," Jericho said despite himself.

Harry nodded. "And somewhere in that original universe that still exists, there's a Doctor Jericho mourning the real death of Harry Neuman."

"In that case, the universe you destroyed still exists," Jericho suggested, trying to soothe his own conscience as much as Harry's. "In a sense you haven't killed it at all."

Harry nodded. "That's also true," he said. "A multiverse of useful paradoxes to save our souls," he added bitterly.

From the far side of the lagoon that had once been the Dodger

Stadium outfield, Harry heard distant shouts and laughter. He looked up and saw a group of mermaids and their children playing some sort of game. They began swimming in a circle and singing and even though the tune was slurred by distance, childhood memory supplied the words. "London Bridge is falling down / falling down, falling down / London Bridge is falling down / my fair lady... "

"London Bridge is falling down," he murmured as he straightened up. Slowly, he turned, walked back, and looked down at Jericho. His face was composed. The fey light was gone from his eyes, the halo, nothing but morning sunshine. He let a bleak, sardonic smile play across his lips. "You see, I know all the excuses, Doc, but they don't change what I did or what I'm carrying inside me."

"Gods and demons," Jericho said and looked away.

"My own private army from hell," Harry said.

"It doesn't have to be that bad," Jericho said, grabbing at any straw to assuage his own burden of guilt. "If we could just... "

Harry stopped him. "It's okay Doc," he said. "No need for platitudes. You see, one of the things I've realized is that I can shut this shit off like I can shut off pain or shut off my life. Shutting off bad memories is kid's play by comparison. I just stick them back in a drawer in my mind, close it, and throw away the key. Just watch," he grinned his old crooked, cocky, Harry Neuman blockbuster grin, and Jericho almost believed him.

Harry spread his arms and twirled around as if he was showing off a new set of clothes. "See, I'm all back together again, no more cracks in the tea pot," he laughed and Jericho was reminded of what a great actor he had been.

Harry stopped suddenly as a distant flash of reflected sunlight caught his eye. He squinted, trying to make out what it was. A moment later, it hurdled the far stadium wall and dove straight at them.

49

Eidolons and Kill-ratios

At the last instant, the camouflage-colored grav-car swerved sharply, skidding sideways with its rocker panels digging deep into the water. The passenger side lifted free of the lagoon as the car tipped dangerously on its side. For a second Harry was afraid it would start tumbling. The grav-coils screamed as they fought to compensate and slowly pulled the car back down.

A wave, plowed up by the car, washed over the low concrete wall. Doc grinned and put his feet up on his chair to keep them dry. Warm water washed across Harry's bare feet as he splashed over to the rusted iron railing.

"Marta!" he yelled, not sure whether he was relieved that she was okay or angry with her for scaring him with this circus stunt. Then he noticed the two women sitting in the front seat of his convertible. The driver leaned out and brushed a strand of brassy blonde hair out of her face. "Hi, big boy," she winked. "How's it hanging?"

"Mae!" Harry shouted in surprise as he recognized the eidolon from Chueh's. "What're you doing here?"

"Just doing my civic duty, honey," she said as she fluffed her hair with her fingers. "Mister Chueh needs all the soldiers he can get. What do you think of my uniform?" she asked, suggestively smoothing the military style jumpsuit down over her ample bosom.

Unlike Jericho's jumpsuit, Mae's had been set to a hot-pink, paisley, camouflage pattern that the military had never programmed. Harry gave a low whistle of appreciation. "Mae, you give a whole new meaning to the war of the sexes."

He noticed the other passenger who was sitting up very straight, watching him out of the corner of her eye. She couldn't have been more than sixteen and looked like a young Audrey Hepburn with her clean elfin features, dark hair cut in a short pageboy, and large doe-like eyes. When she realized that Harry was watching her, she blushed and looked down at her hands folded primly in her lap.

Mae looked from one to the other. "I think you two have met before," she said, with the look of a magician about to pull a rhinoceros out of a top hat. "Harry Neuman," she paused and made a sweeping, theatrical gesture with her arm. "Meet Marta, your "Lady of the Road"!

"Marta, say "Hi" to Harry."

Harry's jaw dropped in astonishment.

Marta looked up at him and smiled shyly. "Hi, Harry. I hope you're okay. I missed you."

"Marta, is that really you?" Harry asked in astonishment.

Mae gave a deep, throaty laugh. "Honey, "really" is getting really kind of relative these days, don't you think."

"If you don't like it, Harry, I can change back," Marta suggested. She bit her lower lip and looked back down at her hands, folded into a tight ball in her lap.

"How… ? Back to what… ?" Harry felt his brains turning to mush. For a moment, he wasn't even sure who he was.

Mae rolled her china blue eyes heaven-wards and shook her head in exasperation. "You're not very bright, are you?" she said to Harry. Then she patted his hand in commiseration. "It's okay, sweetie. I like that in a man. Now, tell her how good she looks."

Harry pulled himself together and looked over at Marta, sitting stiff and straight, her face a pale profile of uncertainty and despair. "But you're… you're beautiful!" he said astonished by his own awkward discovery. "You're just like I always imagined you would be, only better."

Mae beamed at him and nodded encouragement.

Marta looked up doubtfully. "You're just saying that because Mae made you."

Harry straightened up. "Cross my heart," he said making the sign across his chest. "Marta, I've never lied to you. You're beautiful. You're everything I imagined you to be. It was just that you took me by surprise, kind of blew my mind, and it took a minute to put it back together again. Did Mae help you?"

Marta looked up and smiled. "Mae's my friend. Mr. Chueh introduced us. When I woke up and you weren't there, I got scared and Mr. Chueh asked Mae to help. I thought she was the most beautiful woman I'd ever seen. Then I discovered that she was an eidolon. Isn't that wonderful!" she said, bubbling with enthusiasm. "I didn't know we could do this, be this. I always wondered what it was like to be human, you know, like Pinocchio wanting to be a real boy. I guess this is the closest I can get."

Mae was right, real was getting really relative, Harry thought as he watched her. He could hardly believe how well her expressions and gestures seemed to mirror real feelings. He thought of the enormous computer power, the complex software feedbacks needed to accomplish this. On the other hand, Marta had been intensively studying humans all her short "life". She had probably seen every film that had ever survived and watched all the holo channels twenty-four hours a day. On top of that, she was a quick study, one of the most advanced, sophisticated AI's ever produced... and with no slaver circuits to hamper her development.

"I mean, don't get me wrong," Marta continued. "I always loved having the car for my body, flying through the air, going as fast as I could, with all my sensors open... "

"And don't forget all that sexy weaponry behind your bumpers, honey," Mae whispered in a theatrical aside.

Marta looked at her and smiled uncertainly. "Yeah, that too, I guess," she said.

Mae gave a loud, brassy laugh and patted Marta's cheek affectionately. "Honey, you'll do just fine," she said.

Marta let a slight blush of confused embarrassment color her cheeks. She cast a quick sideways glance at Harry and hurriedly continued, "Anyway, now I can be both, I'm in constant contact with my mainframe in the car and can move back and forth between it and my eidolon anytime I want. I can even be in both at the same time. But best of all, Mr. Chueh lets Mae and me go out on patrol with his eidolon squad."

"Eidolon squad?" Harry said and shot a questioning glance at Jericho. The old man kept his face expressionless.

"Yes, and Mr. Chueh says that Mae and I are the best scouts in the Sinks." Marta bubbled proudly, her previous embarrassment all but forgotten. "Isn't that great?"

"Yeah, that's just great," Harry said. His smile was getting a bit ragged around the edges.

"Mr. Chueh says we're the best scouts because no one ever sees us," she said.

Harry nodded with relief. "That's good," he said.

"And we have the highest kill ratio of any squad in the Sinks," she added.

Harry looked at Jericho. "Highest kill ratio?" he said. His voice had a dangerous edge. This time the old man refused to meet his gaze.

"Did I say something wrong?" Marta asked, somehow sensing the sudden tension, perhaps reading the edge to his voice.

Harry worked up a convincing facsimile of a smile. "No, not at all," he said. "It's just that I realize I haven't eaten for three days and I'm starving." The funny thing was that as soon as he said it, he realized he really was starving. "Do you think you and Mae could maybe scout up some food while Doc fills me in on what's been happening?" He gave Jericho a hard stare.

Mae looked from one to the other, sizing up the situation, her processors working overtime. She nodded imperceptibly, put on a happy-go-lucky grin and gave them both a snappy military salute. Then she turned to Marta. "What do you say, kid, ready to do some scouting?"

Marta beamed with hero worship. "Aye, aye, sir," she said with a snappy salute of her own, and they both laughed loudly as the grav-car spun around on its rear bumper and shot off across the lagoon leaving a rooster tail of spray in its wake and Janis Joplin batting out a raunchy rendition of "I Need a Man to Love".

Harry turned to Jericho. "Highest kill ratio?" he said.

'It was Chueh's call," Jericho said keeping his voice neutral.

"And who are you, Pontius Pilate, just washing your hands of the whole thing? Highest kill ratio, for Christ's sake!" he turned his back on Jericho and looked out over the lagoon at the receding grav-car.

"Chueh and I talked it over," Jericho said. "I didn't see he had any choice."

"AI's killing humans." Harry shook his head in disbelief. "Are you two crazy? If you scrap the failsafes that prevent AI's from killing or injuring human beings, you're opening the biggest can of worms since the Tribulations. If the Emperor finds out, he'll brain burn you both."

"The Emperor already knows. He gave his approval."

"He what!" Harry shouted in disbelief.

"You heard me and don't be such a hypocrite. You had Marta armed to the teeth and customized with the most advanced, and need I point out, illegal hunter killer military software that Chueh could get his hands on."

"But there's no way she could use her weaponry against a human being. She could lay out strategy, track down, and even target, but only I could pull the trigger." Harry stopped as a nasty thought occurred to him. He looked at Jericho. "Marta's failsafes are still intact, aren't they?"

"She was being sent into a combat situation without you or any other human to guide her. She's too valuable to risk losing," Jericho prevaricated.

"What am I missing here?" Harry asked. "Has the whole

world gone nuts in the last four days? Have you forgotten the hunter-killer war-bots the old U.S. government turned loose on its own people at the end of the Plague Wars? Those things have become part of modern demonology. Some of them are still hiding out in the Quarantine, powered down, just waiting for someone to get close enough to kill. Do you want to start that all over again?"

Jericho suddenly looked very old and worn. "Don't you think I know all this," he said as he took off his glasses and rubbed his eyes. He leaned back wearily and the webbing in the old aluminum chair creaked under his weight. "But to answer your question, yes, the world has gone nuts in the last four days."

50

The Enemy at the Gates

Jericho raised his hand and began ticking off disasters on his fingers. "The day after Chueh started fighting in the Sinks, three fleet admirals and a number of junior officers in the Imperial Navy rebelled against the Emperor. They took over a Rapacious-class battlewagon and a couple of heavy cruisers and attacked the Imperial Palace and Senate. Before they were brought down, they slagged both buildings, killed most of the senators, and wiped out the imperial court."

"Holy shit!" Harry said.

"Holy shit indeed," Jericho nodded agreement. "Luckily, the Emperor survived. At the time, he and his most trusted advisors were meeting secretly with the Tong Godfathers. The war in the Sinks was going badly. Chueh and the Tongs were in retreat and the Seraphim were threatening to march on New Hollywood when the two admirals attacked the Imperial Palace and Senate.

"We're certain now that they were agents of the black wolves, probably possessed by them. Black ice wasn't unknown in the fleet. The higher ranks moved in circles where it was most prevalent, and junior officers tend to ape the behavior of their superiors.

"The attack was a sign for other black wolf agents to run amok, and the trauma wards beneath Eternal life were emptied to create as much chaos and confusion in the city as possible. Within hours, there was open rioting and looting in the streets and other pockets of the imperial fleet were in open rebellion. An imperial council of "leading citizens" announced that the Emperor was dead and proclaimed his degenerate cousin Emperor instead.

"As soon as it became clear that the Emperor wasn't dead, the riots and looting were soon put down and the rebellion in the fleet crushed. The Emperor's cousin and his council fled into the Sinks or headed south into the Burn. Most were captured or killed. The ones who were taken alive all showed the signs of black ice possession.

"I think you and Chueh forced the wolves and their allies to attack before they were ready. Given another month for black ice rot to seep into the ranks of the fleet and undermine society, we wouldn't have stood a chance. As it is, we've probably lost the eastern provinces from the Appalachian coast to the Missip Sea."

Harry shook his head in disbelief. "That's impossible!"

"Impossible or not, the Seraphim Caliphate is back with a vengeance. In fact, it never really left. After New Hollywood defeated their army at Winding Rock in the Arizona gap, most of its leaders fled either north into the Quarantine or back east into the heart of the old Caliphate.

"When New Hollywood annexed the eastern provinces, most of the Seraphim true-believers that were left went underground, biding their time and stirring up as much trouble as possible. New Hollywood never wanted the empire it inherited from the Caliphate, and its relations with the eastern provinces have always been ambivalent at best. The question was, were we an occupying force in enemy territory, or were we all free citizens of the Empire? The fact that three quarters of the imperial fleet was still stationed east of the Missip Sea seemed to argue for the first."

Jericho gave a deep sigh of resignation. "Maybe I should correct that," he said. "Three quarters of the imperial fleet were stationed there until three days ago, when the Seraphim Caliphate rebelled, and a mounted army of Norma-genes and wolf warships swept down from the Northern Quarantine. Within twenty-four hours, the living gods brought down most of the imperial fleet east of the Missip with the same weapons they used against the Tongs in the Sinks.

"A second Seraphim Caliphate was established and declared a

new Jihad under the crossed blades and wolf's head triangle of the living gods. The remnants of the imperial forces that got away are making a stand on this side of the Missip Sea."

"Now wait a second, Doc," Harry said. "You've got Marta and the other eidolons, completely dependent on their mini-grav-units, fighting in the Sinks against weapons that can shut down the grav-units of an imperial battle cruiser. They haven't got a chance!"

Jericho gave Harry a tired smile. "It's one of the few rays of sunshine in an otherwise abysmal couple of days," he said. "For some reason, whatever was taking out our battle fleet wasn't touching the mini-units in the eidolons. As soon as we realized this, it didn't take long to work out that the wolves were interfering with the frequencies of the phizo-electric, crystal lattice that's locked inside the spinning Danzig coil.

"You see, all grav-units, except those inside of the eidolons, operate within the same optimal frequency range. When I built the first eidolons, I discovered that with the grav-units and quantum computers packed so tightly together I was getting graviton wormhole feedback distorting the AI personality matrix. I solved that problem by randomly shifting frequencies in the grav-units every millisecond. As an unexpected side effect, it made it impossible for the wolves to lock on and block these frequencies in the eidolons. All we had to do to stop them taking down our fleet was install a random frequency generator program in all our ships."

"And they haven't found a way around that?" Harry asked.

Jericho shook his head. "I don't think they're very smart. They've just been around a long time and learned a few tricks."

"It sounds like that particular trick nearly finished us off," Harry said.

"It brought the mighty Hollywood Empire to its knees in less than three days," Jericho agreed. If it hadn't been for all the citizen militias that came to the rescue in their armored grav-cars, banshees, and Dumbos, riding kamikaze suicide missions against the ranked Seraphim and the crystal ships of the wolves, we could never have held the gates of New Hollywood. Even so, the city took heavy bombardment and would have fallen in another day or two if the wolves hadn't retreated into the Nevada Quarantine."

"Retreated? Why?" Harry asked nonplussed. "It sounds like they were winning!"

"They were," Jericho nodded. "We couldn't understand it either until Chueh brought in a couple of wolf-possessed prisoners who were screaming about the King of the Dead destroying their battle fleet down in the Sinks." Jericho cocked a meaningful eyebrow at Harry. "Sound familiar?" he asked.

"Sounds like the cat's out of the bag," Harry said, his expression unreadable.

"That it is," Jericho said. "And the wolves are scared spitless. Their seers have been warning them for months about you, telling the High Priests that the invasion would fail and the Anubis race would be wiped out if they didn't find and kill you first. And that's just what they were trying to do down in the Sinks when they ran into Chueh and his Tongs and it escalated into a full blown war.

"The wolves weren't ready, but now that the genie was out of the bottle, they figured they could still kill you and win the war at the same time. They didn't know what they were dealing with," he said, glancing at Harry. "Nobody did."

Harry shifted uncomfortably but said nothing.

Jericho pushed his glasses up on his forehead and rubbed his eyes wearily. "Even after you wiped out the Seraphim that ambushed you and the mermen the first time, the wolves believed they could still find and kill you. They were after all invincible, they had the blessing of their mad god, and they had never been defeated. This time they would make sure you didn't get away and they sent a fleet of crystal ships after you."

"Wait a second, Doc," Harry interrupted. "How did they find me? You said the monitor on my ka flat-lined and didn't come back."

"That's true."

"So, they couldn't track me with that," Harry said.

Jericho shook his head. "When you died... and did whatever you did, the monitor lost you and never got you back. We're certain of that."

"But still they found me twice," Harry said.

"Yeah, and we're not sure how they did it," Jericho said. "It's possible that they may have planted a tracker on your body, maybe under your skin, while you were fighting with them in that room in the Sinks."

Not fighting, Harry thought and remembered falling into the arms of the wolf thing wearing Susan's body and the long drawn-out kiss that turned into an assault on his ka. Had there been a telltale pinprick when a tracker was planted under his skin? At that point he wasn't noticing much of anything except the collapse of passion into blind terror as Susan's tongue drove into the back of his throat. They could have planted a dozen trackers and he wouldn't have noticed.

Harry looked questioningly at Jericho. "But why bother?" he said. "They already had me where they wanted me."

Jericho shook his head. "Harry, I don't know. All I can say is you were a wildcard. They weren't sure what they were dealing with. Maybe it was just backup insurance." Jericho shrugged. "I really don't know.

"What I do know is that after the second attack on you, the mermen stripped away all your clothes. They'd been reluctant to do it before because a lot of it was char burned and melted into your flesh. When they first found you and tried to peel off the night goggles that were half melted into your skin, they almost pulled away half your face and had to stop, but they were desperate now. They couldn't risk bringing you back here and letting the wolves and Seraphim discover their home base.

"This time, when they began to peel off your clothes, they discovered that your burnt skin was dry and loose and slipped off your body like an old snake skin. Underneath they found fresh new skin as soft and unblemished as a baby's. After that, they were never attacked again."

Jericho shrugged. "But of course, by then the wolves had run for the Nevada Quarantine, leaving their Seraphim allies to fight on alone, and they weren't giving up. As far as the Seraphim were concerned, the Empire was on its knees and they still had a chance to bring it down if only... "

Harry suddenly got to his feet and shaded his eyes with his hand, staring into the distance. "I think our scouts are coming back," he said, moments before a grav-car jumped the outfield wall and hurtled across the lagoon, accelerating all the way. He shook his head in disbelief. "AI hot-rodder's! What is the world coming to?"

Jericho pushed his glasses down from his forehead and stiffened into immobility as his gaze fastened on something only he could see, playing out on the lenses. "I think we've got trouble," he muttered.

51

Bad News

The grav-car braked at the last possible moment, the hum of its grav-unit rising to a tortured, high-frequency screech. Harry winced at the sound and what it was doing to the fine-tuning of the coils. This better be good, he thought, as the car swerved and came to a stop inches from the concrete. Once again a low wave broke over the wall and washed around his bare feet.

He splashed over to the guardrail and looked down. Neither Marta nor Mae were smiling. "Mr. Chueh wants to talk to you," Mae said.

Harry glanced over at Jericho who had returned from the data-sphere and was regarding him somberly.

Chueh's holographic image materialized on the hood of the car. A lacquered black screen carved in an ancient Chinese tradition of dragons and lotuses floated behind him. Marta shifted the image through the guardrail so that it stood beside Harry.

The Tong Godfather looked worn and tired. The camouflage pattern of his military jumpsuit was scorched and stained. One shoulder was ripped open. Harry wondered what could have done that to spider-spin fabric armor.

"Master Chueh." He gave a deep bow of respect. "It is an honor to see you again."

Chueh returned his bow. "The honor is mine," he said. "You are like a cat with nine lives... uh... Excuse me." The sound went off and he bent over talking to someone off screen. A moment later, the sound came back. "Please forgive the interruption. These are difficult times."

"I want to thank you for rescuing me from the Sinks," Harry said.

"Not me, thank the mermen," Chueh said. "Honor their dead."

Harry gave a bow of acquiescence.

Chueh glanced over at Jericho, and the old man gave a slight nod. "I'm afraid I have bad news," Chueh said, turning back to Harry. "We've found the wreckage of Roger's grav-car. One of my scouts came across it in the foothills of the High Sierras, northeast of the Rift Archipelago."

The lacquered screen behind Chueh vanished, replaced by an aerial view of a rugged mountainous landscape dotted with sparse forest cover. Higher up the forest thickened into dense rainforest, but just here an old rockslide exposed the bare spine of a steep, rocky ridge. The cameras zoomed in on the ridge and hovered over the wreckage of a once sleek, custom-built roadster.

It looks like it came down hard and fast, Harry thought, and felt curdling fear. The front end of the car was caved in and the tough, spider-spin armored, carbon fiber hood was splintered and curled back to the diamond glass windscreen. Chueh had apparently cut off the sound of the pilot's commentary so as not to distract them from drawing their own conclusions, he thought, but the silence was eerie. The car lay tipped on its side and wedged between two enormous boulders about half way down the ridge. The boulders were scorched and split by what looked like particle-beam fire from heavy pulse rifles. As far as Harry could see, there was no sign of any bodies in or around the car. He suppressed a sigh of relief. Too early to know yet, he told himself.

The image pulled back and slid down the ridge to where the crushed, burnt-out remains of a stripped-down Seraphim battle wagon lay twisted and half buried in the rockslide debris of the lower slope. Badly burnt bodies of Seraphim warriors who had been caught in the explosion and tossed out of the smashed gunboat lay scattered around the wreck. Four survivors, carrying pulse rifles, lay further up slope, apparently cut down in a fire fight by particle beam fire from the downed roadster.

It looks like someone survived the crash long enough to take those four out, Harry thought, riding a new wave of hope.

About thirty yards from the foot of the ridge, not far from a rushing river, lay the scattered remnants of what once might have been another battlewagon. They were spread out around the edge of a large crater gouged into fused bedrock. It looked like a grav-unit gone critical, Harry thought. The wreckage was so finely shredded that it looked like burnt paper scraps from an exploded diagram of some complex mechanical device, which in a sense it was.

"Roger borrowed an idea or two from you, Harry," Chueh said. "It looks like he took out one of the battlewagons and when its coils blew, he rode the explosion up while the second battlewagon took the brunt of the explosion and was smashed into the face of the ridge and then lost control "

Harry looked over at Jericho. "You're sure they took Roger's car when they left for the Quarantine?" he asked.

Jericho nodded. "That's it," he said.

"There are no bodies," Harry pointed out. "They could have gotten away. Didn't the scout land and try to find some sign of them?"

"Watch," Chueh said.

The sound suddenly cut in on the image. "I'm going up for a closer look," the pilot said as the image swung away from the wrecked Seraphim vehicles and climbed the slope. Roger's car grew nearer until the scout hovered directly above it, and Harry saw a long smear of blood on the inside of the wind screen.

"Blood spoor... driver's side windscreen... no sign of survivors. I'm initiating standard aerial search pattern," the scout's laconic voice cut in as he began to spiral up the ridge, widening his circle as he went. Just as he cleared the top of the ridge, the picture jumped wildly as an explosion rocked the scout.

"I'm taking fire! Repeat! I'm under attack! Seraphim battlewagons..." the pilot screamed as he tried to swerve away and was hit again, and then the ridge seemed to hurtle towards him. "Mayday, mayday! I'm going down! Repeat am going... " The pilot's voice cut off in a blinding flash of blue light and the screen went blank.

Harry turned to Chueh. "How long ago did this happen?" he asked.

"It came in on direct feed to my headquarters less than an hour ago," Chueh said.

"Right," Harry looked down at Marta. "It looks like we've got some scouting to do in the foothills of the High Sierras."

Marta looked at Chueh.

The Tong Godfather gave an almost imperceptible shake of his head.

"Before you go off half-cocked," Jericho cut in. "There are a couple things you might want to consider."

"Like what?" Harry asked irritably.

"Like how did the Seraphim find them in the first place? No one saw them leave New Hollywood. I'm sure of that. They covered their tracks and played it safe. They didn't drive directly north through the infected waters bordering the Sinks. Instead, they stuck to the commercial traffic lanes around the island and then ran north up the Dire Straits until they hit the Trench. If anyone was following them, Roger would have picked them up long before then."

"They must have used the monitor on Roger's ka to track him," Harry said impatiently.

Jericho shook his head. "Roger pulled the monitor on his ka the day before he left. After that, there was no way they could track him."

Harry thought of the blood smear across the windscreen of the downed roadster. "So if he died out there, he died for real," he said and was surprised by the stab of grief and deep sense of loss he felt.

"I'm afraid so," Jericho said. "But everyone's in the same boat now. The wolves took control of the Eternal Life building early on in the rebellion and held onto it until two days ago when imperial death commandos fought their way in and shut down all the monitors."

"So nobody resurrects anymore?" Harry said.

"You die now, you go into the arms of the Goddess," Jericho said.

"If the wolves don't get you first," Harry said.

"Russian roulette," Jericho said.

Harry closed his eyes and once again saw the blood smear across the windscreen of Roger's car. "Yeah, Russian roulette," he said.

He shook the image away and looked at Chueh. "I still can't see how they could have caught Roger even if they were tracking him. It doesn't make sense. His car was almost as fast as Marta. Those battlewagons couldn't even get close enough to attack him on the open sea, let alone drive him into the coastal foothills."

"They didn't force him there," Chueh said. "That's the direction he was headed."

Harry nodded absently. "It still doesn't explain how they caught up with him. Roger's car would run rings around anything the Seraphim threw at him."

"Maybe he didn't get a chance to run rings around them," Chueh suggested. "Maybe the wolves used their weapon to cut off his grav-units and bring him down. Back then, we still didn't know how to counter it."

The holo view of the downed grav-car reappeared. "Notice, there are no signs of blast damage. It looks like the car just crashed."

"But there's no sign of any wolves down there either," Harry protested.

"You haven't been looking close enough, Harry," Chueh reprimanded. The holo came to life, and once again they followed the doomed scout as he spiraled up over the ridge and was attacked. They heard his cries for help as his ship plummeted towards the ridge and that final flash of blue light before everything went blank.

Chueh spooled back and the image froze on that flash of blue light. "That's a flash from a wolf god-weapon," he said.

"Of course! How could I have missed it?" Harry said as his mind did an instant replay, standing on an alien world beneath an impossible orange sky, watching an Anubis wolf shoot a man in the back with a weapon that stripped the flesh from his body and turned bones to dust in a flash of blue light.

Chueh looked at him in surprise. "You recognize it?" he said. "Then you know that only the Anubis wolves carry them. No mere mortal is allowed to touch a god-weapon."

Harry didn't know but let it pass. "So there must have been at least one Anubis wolf down there... That means... that's why... " Harry stopped as his mind followed this line of thought to its logical conclusion. Sometimes, logic sucked, he thought in despair.

"It ain't necessarily so," Chueh said.

"What?"

"What you're thinking. It ain't necessarily so."

"So now you're a fucking mind reader on top of being the bearer of glad tidings!" Harry said bitterly.

"Careful, Harry," Chueh's voice was velvet over steel.

Jericho came up behind Harry and put a hand on his shoulder. "We're all on the same side, son."

Harry drew a deep breath and let it out slowly. It didn't help. It didn't change the fact that the reason there were no bodies in Roger's car was probably because the Anubis god-weapon had sucked them away. But that wasn't Chueh's fault, and, as Doc said, they were all on the same side.

He turned to Chueh and bowed deeply. "I am truly sorry. I let my feelings betray me into disrespecting you. Please accept my deepest apologies. It won't... "

"Enough, Holly! Enough!" Chueh said in his sing song China man voice. "You leally got to learn to keep it short... And lighten up!" He grinned. For a second, the Cheshire cat hung in the air between them, grinning from ear to ear. Chueh sending a holographic postcard, Harry thought, and couldn't help grinning back.

"Now, you've got to ask yourself, why are the Seraphim and the wolves there now?" Chueh said, dropping the China man act and instead sounding like a school master pointing out the obvious.

"My experts confirm that the car was attacked on the same day Roger and Diana left."

"How can they be so sure?" Harry asked.

"By the condition of the Seraphim bodies and the fact that vultures and other scavengers have clearly been at them for some time," Chueh said.

"The absence of scavengers should have warned the scout that something was wrong as soon as he saw the bodies," Jericho said.

"The perfect twenty-twenty vision of hindsight," Harry said. "The poor bastard probably didn't even think of it. I doubt if I would have."

"Which is why you don't go off half-cocked before you know what you're getting into," Chueh said.

Harry bowed acquiescence. What else could he do?

"Something else to think about," Jericho said. "The Seraphim are real particular about burying their dead and collecting their weapons. They wouldn't just leave them out there for scavengers."

"So the Seraphim just got there but didn't have time to collect their dead before the scout arrived," Harry said. "And if they'd been careful enough to land behind that ridge, they could have avoided detection."

Chueh began whistling "It Ain't Necessarily So".

"What now?" Harry asked, irritably.

Chueh just smiled his inscrutable oriental smile. "Even if the Seraphim are particular about burying their dead, they're still in the middle of a war," he pointed out. "They're not going to send a couple of gunboats to hell and gone just to bury a few dead brothers and remember, the wolves retreated into the Nevada Quarantine. They're not sending out warriors just to guard a burial detail."

Harry finally got it. "Survivors!" he shouted and felt an instant lift of hope. "They're looking for survivors!"

"Give that boy a cigar!" Jericho said.

52

Wheels within Wheels

Harry turned to Chueh. "You think they're alive?"

Chueh gave a palms up gesture. "It's possible. The Seraphim and wolves went to some trouble to try to get those two. If they got away, they might go through a lot more trouble to get them back."

"Or hunt them down and kill them," Harry said.

"That too," Chueh said.

"But why did they wait three days to send reinforcements?" Harry wondered.

"The wolves retreated into the Nevada Quarantine, and the Seraphim are still fighting a war. Things are pretty chaotic. They could easily have forgotten a couple of fugitives and the gunboats that went after them," Jericho suggested.

"The wolves didn't forget," Chueh said.

Then he turned to Harry. "Do you think you're ready to go now?" he asked.

Harry was impatient to be off, but something in the way Chueh asked made him hesitant.

"Where will you start?" Chueh prodded.

"I'll start at the wreck and... "

"And fight off Seraphim gunboats and wolves while you try to pick up a trail that might not even be there?" Chueh said scornfully.

"Perhaps it would help if you knew where they were going," he said and looked pointedly at Jericho. "You haven't told him yet have you?" he said.

Jericho shrugged it off. "There was no time."

"Perhaps you should find the time," Chueh suggested quietly. It was the kind of Tong Godfather suggestion that, if you didn't follow it, implied concrete shoes and a one-way trip to the bottom of the Trench.

The two old men stared each other down, their faces set, their bodies full of motionless tension. Like high noon at the OK Corral, Harry thought.

Jericho smiled thinly and suddenly the two old men burst out laughing. Harry looked from one to the other and wondered what he had just missed.

Chueh saw his look of confusion and smiled. "Old friends, old games," he said.

Then he bowed apologetically to the two eidolons and Jericho and said. "Please excuse us for a moment, but Harry and I have some unfinished business to discuss." Then his holographic image floated down the concrete path bordering the lake and stopped beside the low containment wall.

Harry arched a quizzical eyebrow at Jericho, but the old man just shrugged.

As soon as Harry joined Chueh, a privacy shield closed around them cutting off all sound from outside. Harry bowed. "I am at your service, Master Chueh." He'd decided to play it humble until he knew where this was going.

Chueh waved aside the humble act and got down to business. "I have a favor to ask of you," he said.

"A favor," Harry asked nonplussed. Then he remembered his manners and bowed respectfully. "Of course, Master Chueh."

"When you leave, I want you to take Mae along with you. She and Marta make a great team."

"Yeah, I heard," Harry said, careful to keep his voice as neutral as possible.

Chueh nodded. "But more important, they've become friends, with all that that implies. It's something we've never seen happen before with AI's. They communicate electronically, mind to mind, like telepathy; exchanging information, customizing each other's programs, modifying and improving their personality constructs to bring them more and more in line with a human ideal. In some ways, I think they've already gone beyond human."

"Doc says they're the best scouts in the Sinks," Harry said trying for studied casualness to hide his misgivings.

Not casual enough though. Chueh threw him a sharp, penetrating glance, hardly more than a flick of the eye, but it was enough to let Harry know that he knew. Then he gave him a benign grandfatherly smile and nodded. "Yes, they're not only the best in the Sinks. I think they may be the best team in the world. They have been exchanging military programs and constantly customizing and upgrading them based on what they experience. They've become so good that we're even thinking of using their upgrades in our newest troops."

"Very impressive," Harry said discreetly.

"Yes, aren't they?" Chueh purred. "And that's why you should take them with you, Harry. They're the best I have, and where you're going, you're going to need the best. Besides." He grinned. "They're both crazy about you."

"You're too kind, Master Chueh," Harry said. "But I couldn't possibly… "

"Please take them with my blessing," Chueh said with a humble bow.

The offer may have been couched as a humble request but Harry knew better. This was a Tong Godfather making an offer he couldn't refuse. "I would be honored to have them both along," he said, and just to let Chueh know that he knew the score, he added. "I thank you most humbly for your generosity and selfless concern for my safety."

Chueh stared at him for an expressionless moment, and Harry thought maybe he had spread the irony a little too thick. Then the old man burst out laughing and shook his head. "Harry, Harry, Harry, you're a constant source of amazement.

"One of these days you must tell me what happened to you in

the Sinks," Chueh said. "My mermen are building altars to you down there and burning candles. The stories are getting out of hand. They're talking about you like the Second Coming."

"We both know that's a gross exaggeration," Harry said.

"Do we?" Chueh said, and Harry wasn't sure whether he was serious or not. Then, the old man laughed and tried to slap him on the back, but his holographic hand went right through Harry's body. "You see, another miracle!" Chueh said, and they both laughed a little too loudly and too long.

Then the privacy bubble collapsed, and Chueh's holographic image floated back to where Jericho stood, leaning over the guardrail, talking to the two eidolons in the car.

Harry remained standing there alone, wondering what the old man was up to. He thought about the offer he couldn't refuse. "They're the best I have," Chueh said and by best he meant best killing machines.

I don't want to open that drawer, Harry told himself, but it was too late. It was already open. In his mind's eye he saw Marta wearing a white pinafore and the innocent doe-eyed eidolon form that suited her so well. "We have the highest kill ratio of any squad in the Sinks," she said and smiled, and her white pinafore was splashed with blood and the bodies were piled up all around her.

Harry closed his eyes and shook his head in futile denial. An uncontrollable rage of hatred boiled up inside him, and he grabbed the rusted guardrail with both hands as if he wanted to rip it out of the moldy concrete wall. When all this was over, he would kill both Chueh and Jericho for what they had done, he promised himself. There were few things he valued anymore, and they had stolen and debased one of the most precious. He'd left a happy, innocent, loving child in their care, and they turned her into a killing machine. "We have the highest kill ratio of any squad in the Sinks... "

He wanted to reach deep inside himself and seek the calm

serenity of his ka, but even that was denied him now, he thought bitterly.

Well, at least one good thing had come out of all this shit, he thought. He'd discovered he was almost as good at shutting off bad memories as he was at shutting off his life. He hadn't been lying to Doc about being able to do this, maybe just shading the truth a little, because those memories were still there, like the gods and demons haunting his ka, waiting to jump out at him, like mad, serial killer, jack-in-the-boxes, as soon as something or someone pushed the wrong button.

It wasn't a perfect solution but at the moment he didn't have anything else, he thought, as he stuffed the bloody image of Marta back in the drawer of his memory, slammed it shut, and turned the key. Then he composed his features into a casual smile and turned and walked back to the others.

53

Nano Trees and the Price of Godhead

Chueh was saying his goodbye to Marta and Mae, "Always a pleasure to see you ladies," he said with an affectionate smile. "And you too, Doc," he added mockingly.

"And you should get yourself a pair of shoes," he said turning back to Harry, "and some decent clothes."

Harry bowed. "Yes, Master Chueh."

"Take care of yourself, Harry," Chueh said and disappeared in a holographic blip.

After Chueh left, Doc sent Marta and Mae off to find clothes and shoes and whatever else he thought Harry would need. This included a backpack well stocked with essential camping gear and military ration concentrates to last him a week. He said that Diana took camping gear and made sure that Roger did the same, explaining that where they were going they might have to rough it for a while.

Before they left, Marta handed over a large carton filled with sandwiches, fruit, and bottled beer. "Where did they get all this stuff?" Harry laughed in surprise as he unwrapped a tuna salad sandwich.

"Just girl scouts doing their duty," Doc grinned as he reached for a bottle of beer.

They ate and drank in silence. Harry sat on the concrete wall with his feet dangling in the warm water. He was ravenous and the simple sandwiches and beer tasted better than anything he had ever eaten. Before he realized it, the box was empty, and he leaned back with a discreet belch of contentment. He realized that he had eaten everything and left nothing for Jericho and started to apologize.

"Don't worry about it," the old man said with a dismissive

wave of his beer bottle, "wasn't hungry anyway. Besides where you're going, you're probably going to need all the energy you can stock up on."

"And where exactly is that?" Harry asked a little too casually as he watched the sunlight break into diamond sparkles on the water.

"Somewhere back in the High Sierras," Jericho answered just as casually.

Just two old friends passing the time of day, Harry thought caustically. If it wasn't for Marta... he shoved that drawer closed before the mad jack-in-the-box inside could get out. Maybe he wasn't as good at this forgetting as he thought.

"Jake Lloyd spent a lot of time camping and hiking in those mountains, and he took the two girls with him," Jericho continued. "It wasn't just for the fun of it either. They were trying to track down an old Indian legend that talked about a doorway to the gods hidden somewhere in the High Sierras.

"It was supposed to be a sacred place of power known only to shamans and warrior initiates. It was where they went when they went on a vision quest, a place where the world tree grew into the realms of gods and demons. It was said that if a man was strong enough and pure enough and had enough personal power, he could climb that tree and walk out on one of its branches that disappeared into the sky where the wall between worlds was so thin that he might walk right through into the spirit realm."

"Whoa, back up a minute!" Harry said. "Are you saying they could walk out into the quantum sea or onto the astral plane in their own bodies? They could actually walk between worlds?"

Jericho nodded. "That's the story," he said. "But with the coming of the white man and the destruction of tribal culture, a lot of this knowledge got distorted, lost, or purposely buried. The location of the world tree was one of them. It became nothing but an interesting anthropological myth, and only a small group of shaman initiates knew otherwise and passed that knowledge down from generation to generation.

"There's another darker side to this story," Jericho said. "For centuries before the coming of the white man, the Indians were guarding the entrance to the valley where the world tree grew. They weren't trying to stop anyone going in. They were there to stop something coming out.

"The tree is old, maybe twenty thousand years old, probably a lot older, and it's dying. It's been dying slowly for the last thousand years. When it was young and healthy, men walked out onto those branches and back and forth between worlds but nothing followed them back. The tree saw to that, but I don't know enough about it to tell you how it worked." Jericho shrugged. "Some kind of filter, a one-way door against things not human entering our world. Whatever it was, it began breaking down as the tree began dying, and after a while things began walking out, things that didn't belong on this earth.

"In the eighteen hundreds a large area of the High Sierras became the center of wild stories of hunters and trappers seeing monsters in the mountains, of mining communities wiped out by demons or mule trains disappearing in the high passes without a trace. One trapper even claimed that he found smoking footprints burned into the bedrock where a demon passed.

"Jake said he found these prints and also the bones of some huge animal, bigger than a sperm whale, beached thousands of feet above sea level, in a box canyon surrounded by vertical cliffs.

"In the twentieth century hikers reported seeing strange lights in those mountains and meetings with half human creatures that fled at their approach. At the time the lights were called UFO's and the creatures aliens.

"Jake was convinced there was something up there, and that all the wild stories and sightings were somehow connected to those original Indian legends of a world tree and perhaps a doorway to the gods. He spent the last fifteen years of his life looking for it, and he took his two girls with him as soon as they were old enough to ride a horse."

"A horse? Why didn't he take a grav-car, or at least banshees?"

Jericho smiled. "Jake was old-fashioned. Besides, he liked horses. Every year as soon as the snows cleared in the spring, he and his two daughters would saddle up and tramp those mountains searching for his obsession."

"And they found it," Harry said.

"Yeah, they found it."

"And that's where Diana was headed?" Harry said.

Jericho nodded.

Harry suddenly remembered something. "Isis talked about the wolves growing a Nano Tree to bring in their army. Is there a connection to this world tree?"

Jericho nodded. "They're the same thing. Nano trees are what they call themselves."

"What they call themselves?" Harry asked.

Jericho gave a non-committal shrug.

Harry let it go. He had bigger fish to fry. "So why didn't the wolves just use the tree Jake Lloyd found and move in on us long ago?"

"They don't know it exists," Jericho said. "It's an ancient, well-kept secret."

"They could have stumbled on it like one of those things that burned their footprints into the mountains," Harry suggested.

"The chance that a branch of the world tree might brush against a wolf world or one of their quantum, crystal ships is infinitesimal," Jericho said. "Even if a branch did brush one of their worlds, the chance that anyone would notice, well... " He just shook his head.

"But they found us," Harry pointed out.

"Rielly Laughing Wolf and the Danzig spin-generator," Jericho said. "An unfortunate combination."

"What's that supposed to mean?"

"The recordings Isis made on the Vampire contained more information than Diana chose to play for you. The wolves have been looking for us for millennia. When Danzig turned on his first spin-generator and it interfaced with the quantum field and began pulling in zero-point energy, it set up the equivalent of ripples in that infinite quantum non-space. When we began using more and more Danzig generators to power everything from toasters to cars, that disturbance increased. In the larger scheme of things, those ripples were still infinitesimal, but the wolves were already looking for us."

"Why?"

Jericho waved the question away. "They had an old score to settle, but that's another story, and we don't have time for other stories just now. Suffice to say they were looking for us, and when Rielly accidently opened that window for them, they were ready."

"And now that they've got a world tree of their own planted on earth, their whole army and all their ships can just sail in on the branches, is that it?"

"That's about the size of it."

"Do you know where the original tree is?" Harry asked.

Jericho nodded reluctantly. "There's something else you should know," he said. "You gotta be real careful near that tree, or even near the secret valley where it stands. The Indians called it a vision place. Shamans and warriors went there to test themselves against the visions coming off that tree and the monsters that might be lurking there. Most times those monsters lurked in the visions, waiting only for a touch of consciousness to bring them to life. You can be killed for real by one of your own hallucinations if you're not careful."

"Is that what happened to Jake Lloyd?" Harry asked.

"In a way," Jericho said hesitantly.

"I read he died in a camping accident in the mountains. Slipped and fell into a river swollen with spring runoff," Harry prodded. "They never did find his body."

"You can't believe everything you read," Jericho said.

Harry waited for more, but for the moment Jericho wasn't giving any more.

A group of mermaids and their children emerged from the dense foliage overhanging the far side of the lagoon. Harry stood leaning against the iron railing watching them absently. One of the children caught sight of him and shouted and waved, but his mother quickly pulled his hand down. When Harry waved back, they all began giggling and talking animatedly among themselves as they cautiously swam closer but still kept their distance.

"There's something else you should know about Jake's girls," Jericho said with an odd, awkward hesitancy. "I'm not sure how to say this... "

Just then, the boy who had waved at Harry broke free of his mother and began swimming towards him. His mother put a hand to her mouth and screamed at him in terror, and the other mermaids cried out to him. The boy ignored them and swam up to Harry. At the last moment, his courage faltered and he stopped and looked up at Harry in wide-eyed wonder.

Hesitantly, he reached out with his long webbed fingers and touched Harry's bare foot.

His mother screamed in panic and swam frantically toward him. The boy ignored her and asked in a clear bell like voice, "Is... is it true... " he stammered. "Is it true that you are the One."

Harry looked over at Jericho for help, but the old man gave him a palms-up "the ball's in your court" shrug.

Harry turned back to the boy. "One what?" he asked.

"You know, the Messiah! Is it really true you're a god?" he blurted out just as his mother swam up and grabbed him folding her arms around him protectively.

She looked up at Harry with large, frightened eyes. "I'm sorry, Lord," she said. "Please forgive him for disturbing you. He doesn't know any better."

Harry glanced over at Jericho who was watching him closely. The old man sat so still he could have been cast in the same concrete as the stadium.

Harry smiled reassuringly at the mother. "He didn't disturb me," he said as gently as he could. "I enjoyed talking to him. He's a very beautiful and brave boy."

The mother's face underwent a transformation of joy. She smiled S-s-s-arge's sharp toothed, jack-o-lantern smile, and her eyes were filled with adoration. "Lord," she said, holding the boy up. "Would you... could you... " she hesitated as if shocked at her own audacity. "Would you give him your blessing?" she blurted out.

Harry was in way over his head and needed a lifeline. He looked over at Jericho who up to this point had been no help at all. The old man nodded. "Give him your blessing, Harry," he said.

And how do you do that? Harry wondered. Then, he just reached down and laid his hand on the boy's head and ruffled his fine silken hair.

"Thank you, Lord," the mermaid said and rose out of the water and bowed before him. There were tears in her eyes as she turned and followed her son back to the others. They gathered around the boy and his mother; touching them, glancing over at Harry, and talking excitedly. One of the mermaids broke into song and soon the others followed in a beautiful choral of reverent thanksgiving.

"What's going on? Harry asked.

"You're a god, Harry," Jericho joked. "Gods have to put up with stuff like this. By the way, you handled it well," he said as he watched the mermaids bow their heads reverently in their direction and then disappear one by one into the depths of the lagoon.

Afterwards, Harry stared at the empty lagoon, ruffled only by a gentle breeze. "Doc, this has gotten way out of hand," he said.

"It's part of the price you pay for godhead." Jericho grinned. "Did you know the mermen are building altars to you all over the Sinks," he said, and this time he wasn't grinning.

54

A Divine Stamp of Approval

Shortly afterwards, Marta returned with thermo-weave, spider-spin underclothes, jeans, a forest green wool shirt, a military style field jacket, and a pair of solid hiking boots.

"What, no camouflage weave jumpsuits?" Harry asked in surprise.

"Diana told Roger to keep it simple and keep electronics to a minimum," Jericho said. "She had a feeling that where they were going, they might not work so well."

There were backpacks stowed in the trunk and, after Harry got dressed, he went through them to see if there was anything he might want to add or jettison. Meanwhile, Jericho got into the grav-car with Marta and they began calling up data on the car's holo-screen.

Harry found that, as usual, Marta had thought of everything, right down to a modern replica of his old Los Angeles Dodgers baseball cap and a replacement for the pistol he lost in the Sinks. She knew he favored slug throwers and had found a compact military side arm, a miniature R-gun about the size and shape of his lost Glock, except it had a revolver like cylindrical power pack located above the trigger. Its barrel was woven with super conducting nano coils capable of throwing a small slug at speeds that converted it into a massive shock wave of destruction. The magazine in the butt contained two hundred stainless steel rounds no bigger than B-B's.

Harry eyed the power pack and thought about keeping electronics to a minimum. In a sense the power pack wasn't really electronics. It was more like a clockwork generator. When you spun the cylinder, it wound up a simple spring mechanism inside. When you pulled the trigger, it released the spring and generated the trickle of current necessary to fire up the nano coils and throw projectiles at subluminal speeds. Fully wound, it generated enough current to fire all two hundred rounds in the magazine, and Marta had included three extra magazines in case he wanted to start a major war. It was as rugged and self-contained as any weapon could be and Harry decided to chance it. Besides, he had a couple more traditional weapons buried in Marta's trunk if he needed them and if they were still there.

He strapped on the R-gun's shoulder holster and finished stowing the gear in the trunk, after first making sure his backup armory was still there. Then, he went to see what Doc and Marta were up to.

They sat in the front seat of the car, scrolling through a map display on the monitor while Mae lounged in the back. She had changed her jumpsuit into a yellow, polka dot bikini and conjured up a large straw hat and a pair of pink, heart-shaped, Lolita style sunglasses. She lay sprawled across the back seat, resting her head in the crook of one arm and with one long shapely leg dangling over the side of the convertible. "Surf City" was playing on the car's sound system.

Harry leaned in against the side of the car and gave a low wolf-whistle of appreciation. "You can fold out my Playboy any time," he said with an exaggerated leer and wondered if she would catch the obscure twentieth-century reference.

Mae regarded him from behind her hot pink sunglasses. Then, with studied languor, she reached up and pulled the glasses down her nose and looked at him over the top of the rims. "Be careful, honey," she cooed. "I bang like a bunny."

Jericho, watching this by-play, burst out in a loud guffaw. "Mae, you're a constant source of lewdity, nudity, and profanity. I'm beginning to wonder if we can entrust this innocent, impressionable young lady," he nodded at Marta who was giggling behind her palm, "to such a femme fatale Jezebel."

Mae gave him a long, cool appraisal over the rim of her

glasses. Then she pushed them back up her nose and leaned back. "Whoever said that wisdom comes with age didn't count on Alzheimer's," she cooed.

Harry grinned at Jericho. "You can't win," he said.

"Win? Who's talking about winning?" Jericho said. "I'd just like to break even sometimes."

Mae ignored them both and was now engrossed in a glossy woman's magazine that had appeared in her hands. It looked like a brand-new, twentieth century edition of Vogue that she had downloaded.

"What I don't understand is how so much stuff like that," Jericho hooked a thumb at the magazine, "survived the Crash while useful stuff like, for example, a decent geological survey map of the Sierras disappeared completely."

"Pop culture," Mae said glancing up from her magazine. "There was just so much more of it to survive."

"Yeah," Jericho said. "It's just that I don't think that the latest nineteen sixty-four fashion edition of Vogue will help us here."

"It can't hurt," Mae said. "Marta, honey, why don't you crawl back here with me and we'll let the boys talk."

"Problems?" Harry asked, glancing down at the map display.

"What else is new?" Jericho said and leaned back in the driver's seat. "Did you notice the river at the foot of that ridge where they found Roger's car?"

Harry nodded.

"Diana was going to follow that river all the way back up into the High Sierras," Jericho said. "It's the quickest and easiest way to get where she was going. The problem is you can't follow her that way without running into Seraphim gunboats and their trackers, so I'm trying to get you in the back way. The trouble is, I've never tried to go in the back way. I always followed that river up to where I wanted to be.

"Unfortunately, all the old US Geological Survey maps got lost or destroyed in the Crash. Probably wouldn't have helped anyway. Things got kind of changed around in the Crash, and New Hollywood hasn't had the resources or inclination to re-map the High Sierras. Quarantine patrols have mapped some of the high passes," he pointed to the map display on the monitor, "but the rest is terra-incognita. Hell, I doubt if anyone, except Jake and his girls, have been up there in the last four hundred years."

"People down here have had other concerns, like survival and getting civilization started again," Harry pointed out.

"Yeah, don't I know it," Jericho said wearily. "Anyway, after Jake found the nano tree," he continued, "he built a cabin a few miles outside of the secret valley where it grew. I haven't been up there for years, but I tried to give Marta a description of the area and altitude, especially the surrounding mountain peaks.

"I did some exploring while I was up there, took a banshee and followed the river about twenty miles up to its source. There's a big lake up there surrounded by mountains and fed by natural springs and melt runoff. The river drops out of that lake for about five hundred feet through some spectacular, stepped waterfalls. It's especially impressive in the springtime when it's swollen with melt water. Once you find that, it shouldn't be too hard to follow the river back down. There are some side branches that might be tricky, though."

"The problem will be finding the lake in the first place," Harry said.

"It shouldn't be too difficult," Jericho said. "I took some pictures up there. I had my eidolon download them into Marta's data bank. There's one peak up there, a landmark. I called it Mount Fuck You. You'll recognize it when you see it.

"One more thing," Jericho said. "Jake's cabin and the entrance to the secret valley are both hidden back in the woods. You can't see them from the river, but you'll know you're there when you come to a flat rock shelf that sticks halfway out into the river. You can't miss it. It's as white as alabaster and covered with ripple patterns of fused glass. That's where your search begins. Diana and Roger will be somewhere downriver of that point."

"It shouldn't be too difficult if they stick to the river," Harry said.

"Which they won't," Jericho said. "It's rough country, cliffs, waterfalls, avalanches. Diana knows those mountains like the back of her hand. She'll cut across country, take the fastest route whenever she can. It'll make following her difficult for the Seraphim."

"Make finding her difficult for me too," Harry said.

"That's why you got Mae and Marta with you. They really are the best scouts we've got. If anyone can find them, they can."

Harry grunted noncommittally and kept the drawer tightly closed.

"You got trouble with that?" Jericho asked.

Harry glanced at Mae and Marta sitting in the back of the convertible with their heads together whispering and giggling over the latest nineteen sixty-four issue of Vogue just like two normal young woman... practicing being human, he thought and shook his head. "No, I've got no problem with that," he lied.

"Good," Jericho said, eying him skeptically. "Now, let's get back to business. It's close to seventy miles from where Roger's car crashed to Jake's cabin."

"Seventy miles?" Harry said. "They've had almost four days. They could be there by now."

Jericho shook his head doubtfully. "That's seventy miles straight line distance. Up there, there are no straight lines. It's all up and down and around cliffs, waterfalls, rock slides, and tributaries swollen by the monsoon rains. That seventy miles as the crow flies could easily turn into twice that or more. And remember one of them is probably wounded. We don't know how seriously, but it's bound to slow them down."

"And now they've got a couple of Seraphim battlewagons on their trail," Harry said. "I think it's about time we saddled up and lent a hand."

He turned to Marta. "What do you say, Captain? Do you think we can handle that?"

"A piece of cake, sir," Marta grinned, and snapped off a jaunty salute.

"And Harry, if you don't find them or they don't make it," Jericho said. "Find the Nano Tree and use it yourself."

"For what?"

"To do as much damage to the wolves as possible. Maybe to bring back Isis and Susan. Maybe do a little miracle or two."

"I don't do that anymore."

"You may have to," Jericho said and climbed out of the car. "Why don't we take a little walk," he said and took Harry's arm.

"I've got to get going," Harry said and shook his arm free. "I've wasted enough time already,"

Jericho pushed aside a heavy banana frond and started up the steep overgrown slope of stadium stairs. "It's important Harry," he said over his shoulder. "It's something you want to know."

Harry watched him go and after a moment gave up and followed. The stubborn old goat could be infuriating sometimes.

The air was heavy with the smell of orange blossom as they climbed towards the broken bleachers. About half way up, Jericho found a little clearing and sat down on a fallen tree trunk. "Not as young as I used to be," he said with a heavy sigh.

Harry remained standing, his patience wearing thin. "What's so important that you had to drag me up here to tell me?"

"Private stuff, just between you, me, and Jake Lloyd," Jericho said. He paused, staring absently out over the overgrown stadium and across the lagoon. "Those twins of his are more special than you can imagine," he said at last. "We can't let the wolves get both of them."

"Then, why didn't you stop Diana before she left?"

Jericho snorted derisively. "I've already told you why," he said. "I tried to talk her out of it or at least to wait a day or two but," Jericho gave a resigned shrug. "Jake raised a couple of tough, stubborn, self-reliant women." He paused. "Remember Diana told you how she and Isis got their names?" he asked.

The sudden change of subject took Harry by surprise. "What's that got to do with anything?" he asked.

"Do you remember?" Jericho said.

"Yeah, I remember," Harry said. "It was something about the Goddess naming them in a dream."

"Diana is a careful lady," Jericho said. "Plays her cards real close."

"What's that supposed to mean?" Harry asked and sat down beside him.

"I was there when the twins were born," Jericho said. "I know all about that dream. Dreams are funny things. Science has been trying to explain them for centuries. Most prehistoric people believed, in one form or another, that dreams were messengers of the gods. Jake Lloyd believed it too. He'd seen enough strange shit in his life to give him a healthy respect for the gods, or let's just say, the Goddess.

"Shamans and mystics of all sorts always made a distinction between little dreams and big dreams. The little dreams are your common garden variety, everyday dreams that dredge up the day's events and slap them together with wish-fulfillment, memories, fears, neuroses, and maybe a dose or two of mythology thrown in.

"Your big dreams, on the other hand, are the ones where the gods talk straight at you, loud and clear. You know when you've had a big dream. There's no doubt about it.

"Jake's dream was one of the big ones, a real whopper. What Diana told you is true, as far as it goes. It just didn't go anywhere near far enough." Jericho paused to gather his thoughts. Despite his impatience, Harry let the silence draw out. He knew better than to interrupt the old man's train of thought.

"Jake didn't have that dream the night the girls were born. He had it before he even met their mother," Jericho said.

"Why didn't Diana just say that instead of lying?"

"She wasn't lying," Jericho said. "She doesn't know. Jake never told her."

"Why not?"

"Jake's reasons."

"Like what?"

Jericho shook his head. Harry wasn't sure if it was because he didn't know or wouldn't say.

"So why are you telling me this now?" Harry asked.

Jericho scratched his head thoughtfully. "Damned if I know," he said. "Jake's dream is important. I guess I figured you should know as much about it as possible since you were in it."

"What!" Harry spluttered in surprise.

"The Goddess is a two-faced bitch," Jericho continued at last. "She can be Gaea, the loving earth mother or Kali, the eater of the dead, the destroyer of worlds. When she comes to you in a dream or vision, she always takes on the appropriate guise.

"When she came to Jake, she came first as the great earth mother, the White Goddess of antiquity, holding Jake's girls one in each hand, Isis in the right, Diana in the left, the right hand of sunlit rationality and science, the left hand of moon-lit intuition and occult knowledge. She held them as if her hands were scales and weighed them, up and down, until the scales balanced.

"Then she spoke to each of them in turn, "To you I give the name, Isis. You will run with Anubis and open the way to the land of the dead, and there your heart will break on the stones. To you I give the name, Diana. You will hunt Anubis and drive him into the land of the dead and there your heart will break on the stones."

"Then she began to change. Two extra arms grew from her body, her stomach distended and fangs grew from her mouth. She wore a necklace of human skulls and her face took on the wrathful aspect of Kali, the destroyer. She still held the girls in two of her hands while the others held bloody knives and sickles.

"When the transformation was complete, she stood upon the back of a great chimera of a beast like nothing Jake had ever seen before, like nothing in this world anyway. He said it had a pelt of soft scales the color of dead fingernails, a body as thin and graceful as a greyhound's and as sinuous and half as long as a snake's with a tail like a serrated knife. Its four powerful legs were like piston-driven pile drivers, made for speed and crushing impact. It had sabre claws that gleamed like stainless steel and a black carapace head like an insect, with multifaceted eyes that glowed like an atomic pile and ripping mandibles around a beak-like mouth.

"Sounds like someone I know," Harry said quietly.

"Not a friend, I hope?"

Harry shook his head. "Met him on the Resurrection Trail, only he was wearing the body of a wolf. Just before he disappeared in the spin-generator's event horizon, he shape-changed into his real body. It was like Jake described it."

"Doesn't surprise me," Jericho said. "It's the same, age-old enemy. In his dream, Jake said it lay with its claws dug into the globe. Then Kali began dancing on its back, while the two baby girls danced in the palms of her hands. The girls were covered with blood and mimicking Kali's every move. The dance grew wilder and more violent, Kali spun, jumped and stomped on the back of the alien, who kept changing shape beneath her feet, trying to escape, but there was no escape from Kali.

"Jake said the thing howled and snapped and growled the whole time in some kind of language. As bloody bone splinters broke through its flesh, the Anubis screamed out all the dark secrets of its life and death, and Jake understood them all. He said they filled him with such horror and disgust that they almost drove him mad.

"Kali continued to dance, crushing the wolf underfoot, grinding its bones to splinters until the blood spurted from its ears and nostrils and flowed out of its mouth. She danced until the scales were crushed flat and the blood reached her ankles.

"Then she stopped and reached out to hand the two girls to Jake. They were each covered in blood and wore the carapace head of the monster. "Take them," she said. "And guard them well. They are the mothers of a dark destiny. They will sire gods and demons and bring forth a world of terrible beauty."

"Jesus!" Harry said.

Jericho nodded. "The dream didn't finish there," he said. "After she gave the twins to Jake, two more figures appeared in her hands. On the one hand stood a pillar of smoke in the shape of a man and on the other a black mirror cut in the shape of an angel.

"Kali held out the pillar of smoke to Jake and said, "This is the King of the Dead, my champion, my eater of universes. Where he walks, the Angel of Death is never far behind." And she held the mirrored angel up beside the pillar of smoke and said, "I give them to your daughters. They will be allies to the end, and in the end their hearts will betray them."

"Who is this Angel of Death?" Harry asked.

"Haven't a clue," Jericho said.

Harry eyed him skeptically but let it pass. "The Goddess called the King of the Dead, her, eater of universes," he said, "I guess that puts her divine stamp of approval on things, makes me her very own champion."

He closed his eyes and shook his head. "Screw this!" he said angrily and stood up and began pacing back and forth. "I never asked for this! I don't want it. I'm no hero, no Goddess's champion. I'm an actor! I'm not even that anymore. Look at me, Doc! I'm an alcoholic has-been. Nine months ago you were still picking me out of the gutter and cleaning off the puke. Now, I'm supposed to be some kind of hero, the Goddess's champion, her very own, "eater of universes"! What kind of hero eats universes?"

Jericho said nothing.

COSMIC
EGG
BOOKS

If you prefer to spend your nights with Vampires and
Werewolves rather than the mundane then we publish the books
for you. If your preference is for Dragons and Faeries or Angels
and Demons – we should be your first stop. Perhaps your
perfect partner has artificial skin or comes from another planet –
step right this way. Our curiosity shop contains treasures you
will enjoy unearthing. If your passion is Fantasy (including
magical realism and spiritual fantasy), Horror or Science Fiction
(including Steampunk), Cosmic Egg books will
feed your hunger.

Harry sat back down. He hung his head and dry washed his face with his hands. "Do you know what they say happens to heroes chosen by the gods?" he asked.

Jericho shook his head.

Harry looked up sideways and flashed his famous, block-buster hero, lopsided grin. "Buggered every time," he said.

The End
Of Book One of the King of the Dead Trilogy